ECSTASY

ECSTASY

EDITED BY

JANE LITTE

HEAT | NEW YORK

THE BERKLEY PUBLISHING GROUP
Published by the Penguin Group
Penguin Group (USA) Inc.
375 Hudson Street, New York, New York 10014, USA
Penguin Group (Canada), 90 Eglinton Avenue East, Suite 700, Toronto, Ontario M4P 2Y3, Canada
(a division of Pearson Penguin Canada Inc.)
Penguin Books Ltd., 80 Strand, London WC2R 0RL, England
Penguin Group Ireland, 25 St. Stephen's Green, Dublin 2, Ireland (a division of Penguin Books Ltd.)
Penguin Group (Australia), 250 Camberwell Road, Camberwell, Victoria 3124, Australia
(a division of Pearson Australia Group Pty. Ltd.)
Penguin Books India Pvt. Ltd., 11 Community Centre, Panchsheel Park, New Delhi—110 017, India
Penguin Group (NZ), 67 Apollo Drive, Rosedale, Auckland 0632, New Zealand
(a division of Pearson New Zealand Ltd.)
Penguin Books (South Africa) (Pty.) Ltd., 24 Sturdee Avenue, Rosebank, Johannesburg 2196,
South Africa

Penguin Books Ltd., Registered Offices: 80 Strand, London WC2R 0RL, England

This book is an original publication of The Berkley Publishing Group.

PRINTING HISTORY
Heat trade paperback edition / December 2011

Library of Congress Cataloging-in-Publication Data

Agony/ecstasy / edited by Jane Litte.
    p. cm.
ISBN 978-0-425-24345-9 (trade pbk.)
1. Erotic stories, American.   2. American fiction—21st century.   I. Litte, Jane.
PS648.E7A38 2011
813'.60803538—dc23

                                                            2011033894

PRINTED IN THE UNITED STATES OF AMERICA

10 9 8 7 6 5 4 3 2 1

CONTENTS

Transformed BY ANNE CALHOUN   *1*

Rescue Me BY MELJEAN BROOK   *21*

The Wooden Pony BY SHOSHANNA EVERS   *51*

Kiss of Life BY LILY DANIELS   *69*

Silverhouse BY SARABETH SCOTT   *89*

Bruised Ego BY CHRISTINE D'ABO   *107*

On My Skin BY DL GALACE   *127*

Just Say Yes BY HELENKAY DIMON   *147*

Into the Red BY CAMERON BELLE   *171*

Overtaken BY SARA THORN   *191*

About the Editor   *209*

TRANSFORMED

ANNE CALHOUN

The first rule of combat was to gain and maintain tactical advantage, preferably covertly. On the surface, Cole had orchestrated a seduction: a bed stripped to the bottom sheet, pillows mounded at the headboard, the floor lamp in the corner casting soft shadows on the maple bureau. He'd maneuvered Marin Bryant into his apartment, into his bed, and under him.

The perfect opening position.

Stretched out beside her, he let his gaze sweep her from head to the toes of her bare feet. She wore white jeans and a white cashmere V-neck sweater, and her black lashes, opaque sea green eyes, and full mouth were startling bursts of color in her pale face.

She seemed as cool and untouchable as moonlight.

His next move was to rest his hand on her taut abdomen. Immediately she countered, laying her hand on top of his and looking right into his eyes. "What do you have in mind for me tonight, Cole?"

His heart leaped against his rib cage. Only at the very end of the last of their nine previous encounters had his gaze met hers, so for him the effect was as stunning as the first seconds of a firefight. Marin, however, submerged all emotion under her maddeningly tranquil surface. Controlled in speech, controlled in movement, controlled even at the moment he fucked her full-throttle into a gasping, shuddering orgasm.

Sometimes control was a prison.

He didn't answer her question, too absorbed in watching her, assessing the situation as the seconds passed, adjusting his response. Despite the casual question and her seemingly unruffled exterior, she was rushing the scene, something she hadn't done before. He focused on the rise and fall of her stomach under his hand. A little rapid, a little shallow.

Keep it slow. You know how effective that tactic is. "What do you think I want to do?"

"Restrain me," she said without inflection, a living, breathing statue carved from alabaster marble. "Black leather, not handcuffs. Then put me on my knees to suck your cock."

That amused him, the corners of his mouth lifting as he slipped his hand from under hers to brush her fine blond hair back from her face, exposing delicate bone structure and skin so luminous he could chart the stages of her arousal by the blood rising in her throat and cheeks. He stroked her cheek with his fingertips and watched the heat he knew burned inside deepen the pale pink to rose. With his index finger he traced the swell of her lower lip, then dipped inside to touch the tip of her tongue.

The temperature of the air between them shot up ten degrees. Her pulse, visible above the V of her sweater leaped at the base of her throat as her tongue darted out to taste him.

Such mixed messages. She was an enigma, a quest wrapped up in a five-foot-tall, slender woman.

He trailed one finger down to her skittering pulse. "That's a tempting offer, but I've got ten inches and a hundred pounds on you. I don't need to restrain you."

Not a hint of reaction in her face, but a leap of blood under his fingertip. Her gaze sharpened as she took in his body as if seeing it for the first time, noting shoulders and hips, lingering at his hands, which were big enough to hold both of her wrists. If he were so inclined.

"What do you need?" she asked.

Asking the question subtly changed the dynamics. She'd never asked before, so here they went, over the cliff, into thin air. "To touch you. However I want to. For as long as I want to."

A charged stillness followed, quiet enough to hear the ebb and flow of traffic on Fifth Avenue, ten stories below, and the rush of blood in his ears. Such a simple word, *touch*, encompassing so much. Their previous meetings, arranged by Lady Matilda's Introductions service at Marin's request, involved exploring the pleasure found in searing, unavoidable pain.

Wary for a number of reasons, he used only his first name but Marin came to their encounters shrouded in a character, Miss Banks. The experience was so all-consuming it took him three meetings to realize Banks was a pseudonym and another six to discover the fine seam in her defenses, curiosity.

Is this the only thing that turns you on?

Hardly.

She'd paused after that single word. Sometimes silences were as informative as words or tone. This one wasn't hesitant. Marin owned her sexuality without reservation; the possibility of more and varied sex with him didn't crack her.

What do you have in mind?

Find out.

For nine heated nights *touch* was limited to restraints of leather on wrists and ankles, to sweat-soaked cotton sheets and his belt on bare skin, to his cock in her cunt, to thrusting and grasping, the smack of flesh against flesh, to agonized gasps and groans. Suffering, erotic and real. Then simple curiosity undid Miss Banks and, for a split second, ignited Marin.

He wanted more than a split second. Getting it was the problem.

At his statement, she reacted much as he anticipated, breathing halted, muscles tensed and poised for flight. It took visible effort for her to inhale and say, "You need to touch me."

Need didn't cover it. "Yes."

"You touch me every time we're together."

"According to your rules," he countered. Rules she'd established to protect herself. He wouldn't dismantle her physical or emotional walls.

By all means, keep out the rest of the world, or at least the rest of the male population of the world. But not me.

Intensity sat familiarly on his face, but its tight grip on his heart felt unusual. Urgent. "Be daring, Marin. Find out what I have in mind."

Clearly this wasn't what she'd expected . . . but he put enough of a taunt into his tone that she wasn't calling a halt to it.

His next move was a feint. He lowered his mouth to hers. As expected, she turned her head ever so slightly, her gaze flickering between his mouth and his eyes to gauge his response.

He adapted, brushing his lips against the heated flesh of her cheek and using the rough scrape of his stubble in counterpoint to the occasional flick of his tongue. When she turned her head to the side with a sigh, he set his mouth to the hollow under her ear.

A tiny, secretive shudder rippled through her. It was amazing what a precision stealth assault could accomplish where air strikes and heavy ordinance failed. "Put your hands above your head and leave them there."

"That has nothing to do with touching me," she said without moving.

True, but it had everything to do with surrender. "Surely you understand the concept of setting a scene," he murmured into her hair.

She turned her head to meet his gaze. Again, that heart-stopping jolt. Then, defiance in every line of her body, her mouth set in a firm line, she lifted her hands over her head, palms up, fingers curled, the movement as elegant and impassive as a ballerina's. He sat up and straddled her hips, then trailed his fingers gently over the cashmere and down her sides in sweeping movements, stroking the fine material clinging to the lines of her body. The tension in her body eased ever so slightly with each pass of his hands. Her full lips parted as sensation lapped at her resistance.

Then he switched tactics, increasing the pressure of his touch, catching the cashmere between his fingers and using it to caress the skin of her arms, then her shoulders, then abdomen. Eyes heavy-lidded, she undulated, then stiffened up again, as if reminded of her determination to defy what he made her feel.

He avoided her breasts entirely until her nipples peaked under the material, then stroked only the gentle swell of the undersides. Nothing came between his hands and her skin except the sweater.

"No bra?"

"I'm barely an A cup. You know that," she said. The words held a hint of Miss Banks' green-apple-tart tone but were low, distant. Absorbed in what he made her feel, despite the set of her body.

So the lacy bras and garter belts were part of the costume she wore for their encounters. He filed away this detail of the real Marin. "I like you like this," he said. "Bare. Accessible."

Another soft, distracted sound, but she went silent when he used the backs of his curled fingers to pet the sides of her breasts. The first time he grazed her nipples she gasped and the second time she arched into his hands like a cat. He kept the material between his thumbs and forefingers as he pinched and rolled the swollen peaks.

She grew taut underneath him, her body quivering with resistance. Her eyes opened, closed, opened again, fighting to stay alert and distance herself from what she felt. Another firmer pinch and she let out a whimper, bit her lip, then curled her fingers into the sheet above her head. His cock strained at his zipper, but he ignored his need and focused on the subtle battle she waged inside. Protracted, gentle touch generated an entirely different kind of need in Marin. Hotter. Softer. Languid. Her lips were pink and swollen from her efforts to muffle the noises growing throatier as the minutes passed.

Watching her sink into desire and fight it every step of the way sent hot lust cracking down his spine. He focused his attention on her breasts and nipples and let sensation work against her trembling body until he couldn't stand the barrier between them and pushed at her sweater.

"Off," he commanded.

She'd followed orders frequently enough to automatically obey the tone, and let him pull her sweater over her head. He smoothed the tousled hair back from her face then deliberately bent to her nipples, patiently seeking the right combination of teeth and tongue to make her quiver with the effort of not reacting. She moaned when he abandoned the pink, swollen tips to press a line of kisses down the center of her body. With little effort he worked her jeans down and off. He kissed each hipbone, the taut skin of her abdomen, the bottom of her sternum, then shifted back to her side, leaned his head on his doubled arm and slid his fingers over her bare mound.

The soft folds between her legs were wet and swollen. He didn't gloat, just trailed her slick juices up to her clit and began to circle the taut nub, all the while taking in the way she struggled to lash down her increasingly undisciplined response. The abrupt, halting movements of her hips were completely unlike Miss Banks' smooth, fluid responses, and blood dotted her lower lip. She'd bitten it.

He bent down and tasted the hot copper tang of her blood. "Stop fighting me. Stop fighting yourself," he said. "Let this happen."

"I'm not . . . I can't," she said on a desperate sigh, but her hips lifted into his hand and her thighs tightened as she said it.

"It'll be good," he murmured. "You know it will."

But a part of him wanted her to hold out. He'd seen her come more times than he could count, fucked her as ruthlessly as he'd ever fucked a woman, but he'd never seen her battle the riptide of pleasure's onslaught and lose.

A few more strokes along her swelling clit and sweat broke out between her breasts and in the delicate crease of her thigh. Suddenly, as if the prolonged caresses snipped a taut-strung wire, the tension in her body shifted from resistance to red-hot need. She pulled up one leg, giving him a little more room to maneuver, then her other leg came up and dropped open against his hip. Primitive male possessiveness surged in his chest as the delicate scent of sweat and female arousal drifted into the air.

Cole clenched his jaw to keep from ripping open his jeans and plunging into her. Hard and fast would get him physical release, his and hers. He wanted more. He kept the pace and the pressure, watched the familiar blood flush bloom on her collarbone, spread up her throat, into her cheeks as she arched, then went rigid and succumbed. Her clit pulsed under his fingertip as she tried to stifle her moan of release. Then the tension eased from her body, leaving her slack-limbed on his bed. He lightened his touch, then stopped moving entirely, simply resting his hand on her mound.

On the surface, it was such a simple experience, surrendering to a relentlessly gentle touch, but already they were off the map, physically and emotionally. He kept his body relaxed, his breathing even and waited for the results of the skirmish.

Marin's muscles bunched and she scrambled to her knees at the foot of the bed. "We're done."

Success.

He grabbed for her, his fingers closing around her delicate wrist. "We're not done."

Ten inches taller and a hundred pounds heavier hung in the air. He kept his gaze level, watching fire and fear snap in her eyes, and tried to look like a badass motherfucker who'd use physical strength to his advantage.

A long moment passed before her gaze went semi-opaque again; her shoulders straightened and her arm slackened in his grip as she pulled her serenity around her like a mantle of snow. "What did you hope to prove with that?" she asked. "We both know you can make me come."

He cursed mentally, because he could work with Marin in flight or fight mode but not on emotional lockdown. "You don't think that was different than our entire history to date?"

It was, and they both knew it. She lifted her chin and shrugged, distancing herself.

Keep her curious. Guessing. He let her wrist drop. "The deal was I touch you however I wanted, for as long as I wanted, but if it's too much for you . . ."

The taunt hung in the air, along with *Find out*. Marin was too smart to manipulate but too adventurous to walk away from a mystery. "Why?" she asked obliquely.

"Undress me," he said, tying the answer to her compliance.

A long moment passed, then she knelt in front of him and began to unfasten the buttons on his shirt. He waited until she was focused on the task, then spoke.

"I saw you dance Thursday," he said.

Searching her real name on Google gave him a shock equivalent to the one he felt when Miss Banks walked into the room their first night together. Marin Bryant, aka Miss Banks, was a principal dancer at the peak of her career with a modern dance company, and in a heart-stopping moment of realization when he clicked through reviews in *Time Out New York*, the *Post*, and the *Times*, the puzzle pieces of who she was and what they were about clicked into place.

She paused in the act of tugging his shirttails free from his jeans. "Thursday night was the closing show of our season. Tickets were sold out nine months ago. How did you get a seat?"

"I'm now a Platinum Circle Patron of the Selma Galenti Company," he said.

She let out a short laugh as she glanced significantly around his Fifth Avenue apartment, then pulled his shirt free. "God only knows who the front office browbeat into giving up a seat to please a new major donor," she said, then slid both hands up his chest to his shoulders and pushed the fabric down his arms.

The shirt caught on his still-buttoned cuffs. The error made a blush flare in her cheeks, but he liked the unscripted feel of this, and at an extremely base level, he really liked the way she looked kneeling naked in front of him.

She recovered quickly, murmuring, "What did you think?" as she unfastened one cuff, then the other, playing the subservient role to the hilt.

He couldn't put what he thought into words. When the curtain opened and he saw Marin rise off the stage, using what seemed like an acre of iridescent silk in her skirt as a prop in a whirling, leaping piece titled Transfixed, his heart seized tight and punched his ribs. Then his brain shut down entirely.

"I don't know anything about dance," he admitted, "but you were spectacular to watch."

At his faint, inarticulate praise, she glanced up. Electric shock times ten, because the wildness and power and intensity of the dance flashed in her eyes before she locked it down. He went still.

There it was. Transformation. *That* was what she locked down, except when she was performing. *That* was what he'd seen flashing under Miss Banks's serene surface, the surface no amount of erotic pain could crack. *That* was what he wanted to feel flowing through him, over him, what pleasure had almost broken free a few minutes earlier.

Life itself, channeled through Marin.

She pulled off his shirt and tossed it toward the foot of the bed. "You're not supposed to 'know dance.' You *feel* dance. At its best, dance steals into your soul and transforms you."

"Then what I saw was dance at its very best," he said quietly.

She halted in the process of hooking her fingers in his belt and looked up at him, absorbing his words. "Thank you," she said, but she didn't stop removing his clothes. With deft fingers she got his belt open and jeans unzipped, but he didn't lift up so she could push off his jeans.

"What do you have in mind, Cole?"

Her trademark serenity was a thin veneer over the passion he felt straining to break free. He'd come too far to flinch now.

"Kiss me."

The wildness glinted bright and hot in her eyes then disappeared as she bent her head. He smoothed his palm along the side of her jaw, cupped it, stroked her cheek with his thumb. There was nothing more intimate than mouth-to-mouth contact, the shifting, sliding pressure of lips, the mingled breaths, the soft words and pleas tasted as much as heard.

She looked at him then, really looked at him. He had no idea what she saw. She was Marin Bryant and Miss Banks and a conduit for Terpsichore, the goddess of dance, but he was Colson Fleming IV and Fleming from prep school and Captain Fleming to his fellow Marines and then Fleming again when he joined Cooper Benson-hurst as a trader. He had no idea what she saw in his eyes, but he prayed it was something like *You can own me and I can own you if you just let down those goddamn walls.*

"I don't like being vulnerable," she said finally.

No fucking doubt. "You're vulnerable every time we meet," he said, encircling one wrist with his fingers.

"I'm not," she whispered.

He lifted that wrist to his mouth and pressed a kiss into the inside. "Ten inches taller and a hundred pounds heavier, remember?" he said, then grasped the other.

"You wouldn't hurt me," she said, but he was kissing that wrist as she said it, then nibbling at the tendons under the skin.

Her eyes were closed, her voice low and distracted as the words tumbled into the air. As they dissipated into the room she opened her eyes and looked at him, the battle between wants and fears playing out in every line of her body.

With her he could be wholly himself. He wanted to offer her the same freedom.

"I won't hurt you in any way," he said. "Trust me, Marin."

He knew what he was asking her to do. For someone who experienced life deeply and had the talent to translate it into an intense, physical art, wild emotion felt dangerous. Threatening. Marin used the discipline of dance and their meetings to channel her strongest, wildest emotions—lust, anger, desire, love, need—into all-encompassing, explosive release. She'd never kissed him, never let him kiss her, and he wanted her mouth on his more than he'd ever wanted anything else in his entire life. Not for himself, so he could "claim her," although no lie, he would do that.

He wanted this for her. He wanted to give her the complete freedom to experience and show everything, no fear, no boundaries, no restraints, no roles. Just him and Marin.

She had to want to do this. He could strategize and maneuver, make her come a dozen different ways and times, but he couldn't make a kiss meaningful unless she offered it to him.

When she lifted her eyes to his, it was his turn to freeze. Everything lashed deep down in her soul was glinting in her green eyes, turning them a stormy sea green. He braced himself, waiting for her to come to him. Then she rose just enough to bring her face level with his, tilted forward, and brushed her lips across his.

He'd asked for one kiss, and one kiss only, but she didn't pull away. Instead her breath eased from her in a shuddering little sigh that soothed the sparks popping under the skin of his mouth. Delicate and sure, she stroked her tongue along his lower lip, then paused, as if evaluating the taste of him.

Barely daring to breathe, he stayed silent and still. A moment later she gave him another kiss, this one with more pressure, her mouth open against his, then her tongue dipped into his mouth. The faintest trace of coppery blood dissipated with the kiss. The instant when her tongue stroked over his, when the floodgates opened and she let everything she felt flow through her, into him, the brilliant, nuclear heat of the sun shot through his veins.

He cupped the back of her head with one hand and wrapped his other arm around her waist, pulling her naked body to his. He'd never felt so alive, not under machine-gun fire, not under the daily stress on the trading floor, not in Lady Matilda's shadowy boudoir with Miss Banks. There was adrenaline, and there was Marin, mouth open under his, tongue to tongue, trading gasps.

More.

She might have said it, he might have imagined it, but they both felt it. Breathing hard, he backed off the bed and shoved his jeans down, then grabbed a condom from his nightstand. He sheathed himself by touch because he couldn't take his eyes off her, sitting back on her heels in the middle of his bed all pale skin and white blond hair, transformed into a white-hot column of flame.

He crawled back to the middle of the bed, pushed her on her back, and moved between her legs. Braced just above her, her nipples brushing his chest with each inhale, his cock nestled just inside her wet, swollen folds, he looked down into her stormy green eyes and said, "Kiss me. Don't stop until I'm inside you."

She gave a high-pitched groan, then gripped his nape with one hand and brought his mouth to hers. He felt his pulse pound as she kissed him like she couldn't get enough, licking and nipping at his lips and tongue. Sweat broke out on his back as he slid in, inch by excruciatingly hot, tight inch, until he was as deep inside her as he could get, hip to hip, chest to chest, and finally, his mouth on hers. Limitless energy unleashed, she writhed under him, but he withdrew as slowly as he'd slid in, paused for a deep, thorough kiss, then eased forward again.

Again. Again. Again and again and he was going to go out of his mind, because she was surely going out of hers. Trapped between his body and the mattress, she writhed under him, strong enough to make him work to hold her down as everything she felt animated her body. He held her down and fucked her slow and steady until that wild, restless energy coalesced into pure need. On his next deep, gliding stroke she lifted her hips to meet his, her sheath clamped around his cock, her mouth open under his. A high-pitched, shuddering noise he'd never heard her make slipped from her mouth. She shoved at his chest but he didn't move for her.

"God, Cole," she gasped against his mouth. "You're cruel!"

Given their history, the irony of that particular statement made him laugh. "You love it," he growled, political correctness and everything he'd learned about being a gentleman long gone.

He braced his elbows above her shoulders to keep her in position and put the full power of his hips into the next thrust. Her eyes slammed shut as she arched hard and cried out. *Christ*, it felt so good, hot and slick and so right to be inside Marin, naked and sweating and striving together.

"Look at me," he said, and paused until she did.

The open vulnerability in her eyes had his heart battering his breastbone and his throat locked too tight to breathe. He could see how hard it was for her to be vulnerable like this, like the conduit of human emotion she became on stage, exposed for everyone to see, for him to see. But she did it, let the emotion he sparked in her flare through her eyes as she clung to him, fingers digging into his shoulders. Each plunging thrust forced a gasp from her. The pink flush of sex was high in her cheekbones, in her exposed throat.

"Don't stop."

The words were almost inaudible, a soft pleading unlike anything he'd heard from her before. He didn't stop. He kept up his relentlessly steady pace, felt her fly apart under him. Slick contractions gripped his cock as he thrust through the spasms and absorbed her helpless cries with his skin. Balanced on the razor's edge of pleasure and pain, he hung there, chest heaving, sweat dripping to plunk on her collarbone as she eased back into the mattress. She opened her eyes, and the yearning in the green depths gripped his throat.

"Please come," she said again in that soft, female voice. "I want to feel that."

He slid in, back out, in again to the depths of her body, felt her legs curl around his calves as she trembled in response. She looked down between their bodies, watching him plunge into her. He fought to keep his eyes open as sensation pulled him into the rip current.

One hand gripped his hip; the other pressed at the small of his back. "Yes," she whispered. "Cole, yes. Let go."

That was all it took. Orgasm hit him like running full tilt into a brick wall. He buried his face in her hair, spasm after spasm wracking him, and felt the world go black around him.

Hearing returned first, Marin's quick breaths into his neck. Vision. His forearm, the white sheets, her sweat-dampened hair, her ear. He'd slumped over her. He lifted some of his weight back to his arms and tried to remember how to breathe. Once he had that mastered again he got up and went into the bathroom to remove the condom.

When he came back into the bedroom Marin was gone.

Her jeans and sweater still lay in a heap on the floor, but his shirt was missing. He pulled on his shorts and strode barefoot down the hall, past the dining room, the library, the home theater, the three other bedrooms, the eat-in kitchen, into the living room overlooking Fifth Avenue.

She hadn't bothered to turn on the lights, instead standing in a semi-darkness that made her white-blond hair glow like moonlight. Dressed in his shirt, she was looking out the floor-to-ceiling living room windows at the Central Park West skyline, rising in the distance over Central Park and the Metropolitan Museum of Art. The angle of the ambient light shadowed her profile. He stopped just behind her and laid both palms flat on the glass on either side of her head, almost but not quite touching her, restating his opening position but not taking liberties.

The whoosh and rush of a bus's air brakes reverberated below them. "I heard Wall Street bonuses were down," she said.

There was always money to be made if you worked your ass off, so he could have bought the apartment in any of the last several years, but he told her the truth. "I inherited it. My great-grandfather built the building. I grew up one floor down."

Revealing that little detail to a woman was usually like throwing chum in the water, but she tilted her head in curiosity, nothing more. She studied his reflection in the glass, then her oblique gaze shifted back to the small figures in the glass-enclosed Sackler Wing. "You gave this up for the Marine Corps barracks?"

The last time they met was the first time they'd talked in anything other than a formal, scripted way. She'd guessed he was NYPD or FBI, which surprised him until he learned she was a dancer. Marin studied movement like he studied markets and commodities. She'd probably read his history in his body while he was still enamored with Miss Banks.

He waited until she looked at him again, then nodded. "Six years. Two tours in Afghanistan."

"You are one surprise after another," she said, her focus shifting back to the skyline.

"And you were expecting a scene like all the others," he said.

Again, he waited for their eyes to meet. When they did, she nodded.

He thought about her silk and pearl-clad alter ego Miss Banks, about Marin Bryant, Principal Dancer, about the passionate, sexual, adventurous woman no less under his skin than when they'd begun. She wouldn't be easy, but he liked difficult things. "I got the feeling boring you would be the cardinal sin."

"You are many things, Cole, but you're not boring," she said.

At that something in him eased. The glass reflected her swollen mouth, flushed cheeks, the banked fire in her eyes. "I'm glad you're here," he said, a statement, like so many facets of their relationship, that could be taken many different ways.

"I'm glad to be here," she said. "But does being here mean the end of Miss Banks?"

He shrugged, striving for casual. "Only if you want her to end. I don't."

A provocative smile curved her lips. "You like her."

"I more than like her," he said. "So, Marin Bryant . . . is this the only thing that turns you on?"

She laughed, the sound real, from deep in her torso, and utterly delighted. Then she stepped back and relaxed against him. He braced himself to take her weight and gave in to impulse, wrapping an arm around her waist. The remnant of her laughter became a small, satisfied sound, almost a purr. Marin, tamed.

"Hardly," she said. "What do you have in mind next?"

Everything. He had *everything* in mind, but there was no rush. "Find out."

Want to know what happens when Miss
Banks comes out to play? Flip to "Transfixed"
in the Agony side of this volume . . .

After doing time at Fortune 500 companies on both coasts, **Anne Calhoun** found herself living in a flyover state. The glamour of cube farm jobs in HR and IT had worn off, so she gave up meetings to take Joseph Campbell's advice and follow her bliss: writing romance. Her first novel, *Liberating Lacey*, won the 2010 EPIC Award for Best Contemporary Erotic Romance. Her next release, *What She Needs*, was chosen by Smart Bitch Sarah for the Sizzling Book Club.

Anne lives in the Midwest with her husband, son, and a rescue dog named Kate. She holds a BA in English and History, and an MA in American Studies. Visit her website at annecalhoun.com.

RESCUE ME

Meljean Brook

8:35 P.M.

As soon as Jenny heard Brandon Shaw shut the door, leaving her alone in the cabin's one stifling room, she relaxed the muscles in her arms. The binding around her wrists didn't loosen.

Dammit. She'd read about that trick years ago, in a Nancy Drew or Trixie Belden mystery, and had clenched her muscles when Shaw tied her hands behind her back. But apparently it only worked for blond teenage sleuths escaping their ropes—not an ordinary brunette wrestling against a nylon cable tie.

All right, so she wouldn't be wriggling her hands free. But she had a little time before Shaw returned with his knives, before he sliced her up like he had those *other* ordinary brunettes.

The details of those murders crowded into her head, leaving just enough room for panic. Her breath shortened, sawing roughly through her lungs, filling her with the cloyingly festive fragrance coming from the two candles burning on the table. Big jars of spiced apple, the red wax melted halfway down the glass sides. It smelled like Christmas in here, Christmas in July—and Jenny wanted to believe this was all a joke, wanted to believe that middle-school science teacher Brandon Shaw was just pulling a fast one over on the mechanic he'd met two weeks ago when he'd brought his car into her shop for repairs. Hell, she'd even appreciated him for not making a joke about lube jobs, the one that most men thought was so damn funny. He'd seemed like a decent sort of guy, but Jenny couldn't think so now—and she couldn't hang on to the hope that this was all a twisted joke. She'd spent too many weekends in her brother's garage, helping him restore that old Thunderbird. More often than not, Tom's friend and partner on the Bend police force, Ian Grayson, joined them in the garage, bringing along a six-pack and substantial amounts of elbow grease. Eventually, the two detectives would begin discussing recent cases . . . and lately, the conversation had always turned toward the string of brunettes found along the Cascade Lakes byway. Beneath the Thunderbird's chassis, Jenny had overheard details that the police hadn't released to the press, details that a middle-school teacher couldn't have known—that the women had all been found in their underwear, with red satin ribbons fastened around their necks.

Jenny wore a similar ribbon now. Though it was tied loosely in a bow, the satin felt tighter than the bindings at her wrists and seemed to constrict with her every breath. When Shaw returned, he would strangle her with it.

When he returned . . . and she'd fixed the transmission of the piece-of-shit car that would bring him here. That motherfucker.

On a surge of anger, she yanked against the cable ties. Nylon bit into her wrists, but she yanked again. And again.

That wasn't working. Heart pounding, Jenny stopped yanking and simply pulled, straining against the ties, hoping that the cable tie would give or that the chair's back would crack. Neither did. Terror seeped through her anger and took over, though she'd been sure she'd already felt the worst of her fear when Shaw had stripped her down to her serviceable cotton bra and briefs, when he'd shoved her into his trunk and began the hour-long drive out of the city. By the time he'd dragged her into the darkened cabin and secured her to the old spindleback chair, she'd felt almost calm—but that calm was gone now, and she yanked again, because it didn't matter that her wrists bled or that the sides of the chair had tenderized her forearms. It didn't matter whether the chair broke or her bones did, because if she didn't get out *now* then she wouldn't *ever* get out.

But it hurt. Oh, *God,* how it hurt. Hot tears joined the sweat on her face, but her sobs were smothered by the gag Shaw had made from a pair of her stockings, wadding up one and shoving the ball of silk into her mouth, stretching its mate between her lips and tying it behind her head. She tried to scream and almost choked when the wad hit the back of her tongue. Her stomach heaved.

Oh, *hell no.*

Jenny stopped struggling and forced herself to breathe slowly through her nose, waiting until the bile in her throat receded. She was *not* going to drown in her own puke. Though that fate was better than what Brandon Shaw had in store for her, she was *not* going out this way, panicking her way to death. And she was *not* going to die in a dirty little cabin in the middle of fucking nowhere, choking on sobs and snot.

And she was definitely not dying in her granny panties.

The police would find her first. *Ian* would find her. He and her brother weren't on the team tasked to find the serial killer; if they had been, Tom wouldn't have taken time off for a vacation, and Jenny would have been eating dinner at her brother's house that night instead of being attacked by Brandon Shaw in her kitchen.

But Ian would check his voice mail, where she'd been leaving him a message about a delay in Tom's return flight—a message that had been cut off halfway through by her scream. And although her phone had skidded across the kitchen tile when Shaw had jumped her, she didn't think the call had been disconnected. Ian might have heard her shout Shaw's name.

How long before he checked his voice mail? Not too long. He never let it go for too long.

Ian just had to be faster than Shaw—who'd returned to the city,

he'd said, for something *special*. Jenny didn't want to know what
that meant. The important thing was: it would take Shaw an hour
to return home. Hopefully, Ian and the Bend police force would be
waiting for him.

Would Ian know to come here, though? Even if he caught Shaw,
would the murderer give up the location of this cabin? If not, it
wouldn't matter if Shaw returned or was arrested—either way, she
had to get out of this chair.

And she had to do it without panicking.

All right. She drew in another long, calming breath and took
stock of her situation. The hardwood chair was old, but sturdy. Shaw
had bent her arms around behind the chair's back and positioned
her like a cop handcuffing a suspect, threading the cable tie around
her wrists and between two of the vertical rods. She didn't think
those rods were going anywhere; their ends were securely
joined to the seat and embedded in the curved wood forming the
top of the chair's angled back. He'd fastened her ankles to the front
legs of the chair, too—but only using one cable tie to each chair leg.
Jenny tested the strength of those nylon ties, pushing against them
until the muscles in her thighs began to cramp.

No luck. So she needed another option. Namely, she needed to
alert someone who could get her out of this chair.

Holding her breath, she listened. The noises outside the cabin
were the familiar sounds of a summer night: crickets and frogs . . .
and in the distance, the sound of a big engine passing at high speed.
A logging truck or a semi. That meant a highway, though the cabin
probably wasn't visible from the road. Shaw hadn't been concerned
about leaving the two scented candles burning on the table, where
someone might wonder about and investigate the light. But this time
of year, these woods were always full of hikers and campers—if she
could make noise, perhaps someone would hear her.

She was bound by hardwood and strong plastic, but the stocking in her mouth was just thin silk. She'd run several pairs just by snagging a fingernail; surely her teeth could do better. She just had to grind. She just had to ignore the disgusting soppiness of the material wadded against her tongue, the pain at the corners of her mouth.

Or, no—not *ignore* the pain. She'd tried to pretend it didn't matter before, and had begun to panic. So she'd use the pain and discomfort instead, turn it into something she could manage. Something good, not terrifying.

Something like . . . *Ian*.

A crash at the door brought her head whipping around—and he was there, Ian, his gun drawn and his stance low. His dark eyes met hers from across the room, and he stared for a long moment, his gaze sweeping over her in that intense scrutiny she'd often seen him give her when he'd thought she hadn't been watching him in return.

"Are you all right?"

His voice was low and deep, and before she'd finished nodding, he strode across the cabin. God, she loved to see him move, loved his smooth, coiled strength. But she'd never loved his stride as much as when it brought him to her side, where he sank onto his heels and reached for the knotted silk at the back of her head. He didn't watch his fingers, but studied her face—and now that she was safe, now that he'd come, she felt exposed. Aware of her sweat and her bare skin, of her slow and heavy breaths.

Silk tugged at the corners of her mouth while his fingers worked the knot. "Did he hurt you?"

Jenny answered with a slight shake of her head. *Not yet*, she thought.

No. That thought didn't belong here. Only Ian did.

Gently, he pulled the knot apart and drew the silk from her lips. His big hand cupped her jaw, and he smiled—the same smile that had made her belly flop over and her pussy clench the first time she'd seen it, three years ago. The same smile that had made her believe Ian Grayson had a mouth she ought to be kissing.

His thumb caressed the raw corner of her lips, and his smile widened to a grin. "If not for this situation, Jenny, I'd say the position you're in is ripe with possibility."

No, he wouldn't say it. He was just trying to make her laugh, to make her feel better—because even if Ian wanted to make such a suggestion, he wouldn't actually say it, let alone follow through on it.

Not with his partner's sister.

Maybe he'd imagined her in this position, though: hands tied, legs spread. God knew that Jenny had pictured it so many times, but the scenario had been filled with a different sort of ache: a pain that was sweet and needy instead of sharp and frightening.

With effort, she moistened her tongue, found her voice. "Thank you for rescuing me."

"Jenny." His gaze held hers. His thumb ceased its soft caress at the corner of her mouth. "You want to thank me?"

Oh, she could see the dark need in his eyes, but his desire remained unspoken. *She* would speak it, then. She hadn't for so long—and Brandon Shaw had almost made it so that she never could. Jenny wouldn't risk not saying it now.

"Yes."

It was breathless, her answer, and hard to form, but Ian's response was everything that she'd wanted. His fingers moved back to her nape, tightened in her hair.

"*How* would you thank me?"

By giving him what she'd needed for three years. What she thought that *he* needed, too. It would start by burying her fingers in his short brown hair and dragging him down for a scorching, pussy-melting kiss, but her hands weren't free for that. Only her mouth was.

"Stand up," she said.

Without letting go of her hair, he rose in front of the chair. Anticipation and excitement locked the air in Jenny's throat, but he didn't need another instruction. His free hand moved to his belt. Off-duty, he wore a white T-shirt that stretched across his broad chest, and faded Levi's. Jenny strained forward as he popped the fly open. She needed to touch him, needed to get her hands free and *out of this chair*—

"Slow," he said roughly, and Jenny realized that she was already losing herself again. She closed her eyes, breathed deep.

God, he smelled good. As always, he wore the cologne she'd given him that first Christmas—an impersonal gift for her brother's new partner, who wasn't returning back East to visit his family over the holidays, and so he'd been invited to the little dinner Jenny and Tom always shared. That scent wasn't impersonal now, and Ian must have thought so, too. Three years later, he still wore the same cologne, though the small bottle Jenny had been able to afford must have run dry by now.

And he smelled a hell of a lot better than spiced apple candles.

"We'll get your hands free in a minute." With his palm cupping the back of her neck, he urged her to him. "But we'll put your mouth to work first. You ready?"

Oh, she was. His cock hung heavy and thick over his denim fly, not hard yet—but she'd change that. Hungry for him, Jenny didn't waste time, dipping her head and catching the wide tip in her open mouth.

His fingers clenched in her hair. He made a harsh sound, like a sharp breath drawn through clenched teeth.

"Oh, *fuck yes*. Suck me in. Take all of me."

Jenny didn't know if she could. Already, his shaft was stiffening between her lips. Flaccid, she might have been able to take all of him in, but not now. His growing erection forced her mouth open wide and stretched the raw corners of her mouth. But just as she thought she'd reached her limit, Ian groaned his pleasure—and suddenly she *needed* to take more, needed to hear that sound from him again. She rubbed her tongue around the thick, smooth head, stroking the hardened flesh, tasting the salt that was her sweat and his. And when he shuddered, when his head fell back and his hips rocked back, she followed and tried to draw him deeper.

"Christ, Jenny." His breath was ragged. "I imagined this. Only two fucking weeks ago, when I came over to Tom's for a beer and you fell asleep on the sofa next to me."

She knew he'd been imagining *something*. She'd woken to a darkened living room, with her head on his lap and his thick erection straining against the pants beneath her cheek. He'd been still, utterly still—not the silence of a man trying to be quiet, but the tension of a man holding himself back. Filled with her own tension, Jenny had waited with her eyes closed, pretending to be asleep. Finally, just when she'd been unable to bear the silence any longer, his fingers had brushed softly over her hair and he'd slid out from under her. She'd heard Tom's door close behind him a few seconds later.

She'd spent two weeks wishing that she'd opened her eyes and looked up into his face. Two weeks wishing that she'd unzipped him and taken his cock into her mouth. But she'd known that messing with his partner's sister was against Ian's personal code—and as much as she'd wanted him, Jenny hadn't wanted to be the reason he broke that code.

And so for three years now, she'd been pretending. Not just pretending to sleep, but pretending she and Ian were only friends. That he was just a guy who let her use his shower when her hot water heater went on the fritz. The guy whose oil she changed for free, but who repaid her with a movie and takeout from her favorite Thai place, and neither of them considered asking her brother to join them. She knew that Ian was the reason he and Tom often stopped for lunch by her shop, and when she asked him to bring her something healthy he always complied—and he never made a comment when she swiped one of his fries.

He simply smiled that pussy-clenching smile, watching her eat. Watching her lips, just as he did now, but this time he allowed the stark pleasure on his face to show as he slowly fucked her mouth. She couldn't take his rigid length, but she tried, ignoring the deep ache in her jaw and fighting her gag reflex when he hit the back of her throat, loving his groan and the soothing words that followed.

"You can do this, Jenny." His eyes closed as he thrust past her lips. "Just a little more. I'm almost there, baby. I'm coming undone."

Unraveled.

He hissed and suddenly stilled, his cock seeming to swell against her tongue. "Now give me the edge of your teeth."

She obeyed, and felt silk tearing, loosening at the corners of her mouth and behind her head. Ian was going now, but—

With a cough, she spat out the gag between her feet, where it landed with a wet plop. *Holy shit.* Jenny stared at in disbelief until the reality of her sudden freedom sank in, and she gave a wild laugh.

Not usually a spitter, this time she had a great excuse. And she wasn't usually a screamer, either—but for Brandon Shaw, she'd make an exception.

She tilted her head back, and shouted for help at the top of her lungs.

9:20 P.M.

Her throat was raw. No one had come. And now she wanted to scream and scream, not for help but just because *she didn't want to die here.*

"Pull it together, Jenny." The hoarse voice emerging from her throat sounded alien, but just hearing the words helped her remain calm. And though she usually wouldn't consider talking to herself a sign of mental health, the fact she was still talking at all was a damn good sign indeed. "It's time to come up with another plan."

Her gaze fell on the candle flames, flickering in the glass jars. There was no point trying to break the cable ties again—but maybe she could melt them. The table stood only three feet from her chair. He'd tied her ankles to the chair legs, but her feet rested flat on the floor. By rocking forward and balancing on her feet, she could shuffle toward the table. And if she could turn and back up to the candle, holding her hands over the flame, the nylon might melt.

She'd probably fry her wrists in the process, but better to serve up a small Jenny-BBQ than being filleted by Brandon Shaw.

That thought was all she needed to brace herself against the pain and throw her weight forward. For a brief, exhilarating instant, she balanced on her feet in a low squat. Then her balance began to shift, threatening to topple her over and smash her face into the edge of the table. Desperately, she pushed with her toes and jerked her body to the right. Tipped on two legs, the chair spun onto one, the back of its frame clipping the side of the table. Jenny balanced there on the diagonal, stunned, with the edge of the table next to her shoulder. Then, with a sudden rasp of wood against wood, the table skidded back a few inches.

Oh, fuck.

She curled her chin into her neck to protect the back of her head, but the impact still rammed through her chest. Ribs screaming, she stared up at the underside of the table. Spots danced before her eyes and a strange rolling noise filled her ears. She'd landed faceup, and the angle of the chair's back had protected her hands and elbows, but she suddenly didn't ever want to move again. She didn't want to breathe again. Not if it hurt this much.

Ian lay on his side next to her, elbow braced against the floor, his jaw propped on his fist. "At least you stuck the landing."

She'd just screwed her chance of ever seeing him again. He didn't have to rub it in. "Fuck you."

"Maybe later. It's difficult now, with your ass in that seat." His brows lifted, and he glanced up toward the table. "What do you think that noise is?"

The rolling sound—like a glass spinning around on its side. Her fall must have knocked at least one of the candle jars over. She had the sudden image of the candle rolling off and shattering, setting the cabin ablaze and roasting her alive, trussed up like a turkey on a chair. But she'd no sooner imagined her eyebrows burning off before the rolling stopped. The flame hadn't gone out; the light flickered wildly against the wall. So she could still try to get up there, and still try to melt the damn cable ties—and then she'd drag herself out of this cabin with the chair fastened to her ass, if she had to.

But, no—the chair fastened to her ass was where she'd gone wrong. She wouldn't get anywhere squatting, because her butt was centered too low and behind the support of her feet. But she *could* have shuffled forward if she'd been able to get her ass off the seat.

To do that, however, meant that she'd have to get her hands up higher, too. She pictured the back of the chair, the wooden rods. Spaced closely together near the seat, the distance between them widened as they rose toward the curved top. So the ties would tighten around her wrists as she forced her hands up.

So it was going to hurt like a son of a bitch.

"I'll keep you occupied."

Ian's voice pulled her from thoughts of the coming pain. His forefinger traced a circle around her navel. Jenny shivered, her abdominals tensing.

He leaned over and pressed a kiss to her belly before shooting her a grin. "Nice panties."

"It's laundry day." *Shaw had said all the other girls were dirty, too.*

"I don't care. Cotton briefs or lacy thongs—I'll take them off you when your ass is off this seat."

That was incentive enough to push. She couldn't shove her feet down and slip the cable ties off the bottom of the chair legs, but she could raise her feet and brace them against the wooden rung between the legs and force her body upward. Helped along by the chair's angled back and gravity, she'd already moved up a few inches.

The cable ties bit like razors into her wrists. Her hands weren't numb yet, but it would happen eventually. She needed to move faster than this.

"That's it, Jenny." Ian rewarded her with a lick along the inside of her thigh. "Work your ass up there. Give me some space to get my fingers and mouth between your legs, and to get yourself out of here."

Dirty fingers, she thought.

As if he heard her, Ian made a questioning sound, a hum with his lips against the hem of her panties.

"Everyone's been wondering why the killer chose those brunettes," she told him. "It's because we have dirty hands and dirty hair. Shaw doesn't approve."

"Brandon Shaw is an asshole. I like your dirty hands."

Jenny smiled, then jerked her head up when she felt a splash on the inside of her left knee, hot as a tear. She stared at the red drop sliding down her thigh. Blood? But blood didn't leave a hardened trail behind it. Then a second drop splashed onto the first, and she realized: It was candle wax. Candy red wax, melting in the tipped-over jar and dripping down the inside of her splayed thigh. The jar must have stopped rolling near the edge of the table—and as long as she lay down here, as long as it burned, the melting wax would drip.

The next drop fell, and trailed almost down to her panties before hardening. Ian looked up at her. "I can't say that I've imagined this kink."

No. She wouldn't know if he had. "I have, though."

"You'd like this?"

"I'd love it."

Holding her gaze, he lowered his head and traced the hardened trail with his tongue, and the heat of that caress moved over her skin, burning hotter than the wax. She gasped, her back arching, her hands pushing higher.

"So you like a little pain," he said softly. "Maybe that's why you haven't made a move on me these past three years. You like it rough, but you're afraid I wouldn't. You're afraid I'd think you were a dirty girl."

Jenny closed her eyes. "Yes."

"I *do* think you're a dirty girl. But unlike Shaw, I enjoy that." His fingers drifted down her thigh, almost to her center. He teased the elastic edge of her panties. "You've got to give me more room if you want me to fuck you with my fingers and tongue."

Gritting her teeth, she forced herself higher, lifting her butt off the seat. Ian cupped his fingers over her sex. Jenny moaned, rocking her hips toward him. The heavy heat of his hand seemed to burn through the cotton, and he rhythmically pressed the heel of his palm against her clit.

"That's right. Lift your ass up, and I'll slide these panties down. Higher, baby. Are you wet for me? I want you slippery when I eat your pussy. When I fuck you."

Oh, God, she wanted that. But she was aware that her wrists were slippery now, too. Bleeding. Not a lot. But, Jesus—

"It hurts." Tears slid from the corners of her eyes, itched down toward her ears.

"I know, baby. But you just need to lift up a little more. Have you ever wanted me to handcuff you?"

More times than she could count. Sometimes to a chair. But it had never hurt like this. Instead, he'd treated her to a sweet, slow fuck, making her writhe through each endless thrust, denying her release until she'd begged to his satisfaction.

"You know you've got to move up higher before I can fuck you like that." His thumbs hooked the waistband of her briefs, began to draw them down. "I'm going to kiss you here while you do it, though, and make you feel better."

God, and he did. Openmouthed, he lowered his head to her sex, his tongue delving through her slit, and kissed her like a man starving for her taste. And with his mouth on her, his fingers in her, the pain in her wrists didn't matter, the agony that drew tighter and tighter. When he sucked on her clit, every flick of his tongue pushed her higher, higher. Jenny moved with him, sobbing with the pain of it, but he made it good, *so* good.

And then she was there, as high as she could get, crying out in anguish and relief. For a few moments, she lay panting, before lifting her head and considering her position. Sweat soaked her bra and skin, hardened wax had pooled on the crotch of her panties, and red streaks splattered the inside of her thigh. She was still on her back, her legs still spread—but now she lay with her ass halfway up the back of the chair. Once on her feet, she could shuffle around without tipping over.

"On your feet, but bent over," Ian mused. "If I found you like that, I don't know if I could stop myself from bending you farther, making you take all of my cock. Begging for it. Would you want that?"

On her feet? "God, yes."

"This cabin is a crime scene. Our forensic technicians will go over every inch. They'll find my come, and yours. Everyone would know that I fucked you."

Her brother would know. Jenny didn't care if Tom did, and she didn't think Tom would give a crap, either. Only Ian had a problem with it.

"I'd take that chance," she told him. "Would you?"

"When you escape from here, you can find out."

She nodded. "I will."

No more pretending, no more wasted years. She *would* find out.

"You'd better," he said. "But first, how will you get up on your feet? You've got dirty hands, working with them for a living, but it doesn't mean you don't have a brain in your head. You're smart enough, Jenny. Smart enough to yell out his name, and smart enough to get yourself out of here if he doesn't tell me where you are. So how will you do it?"

"I'll roll over." Though she was on her back, she wasn't a turtle. "My face will be on the floor, but I'll be able to scoot along with my knees to that wall."

Only a few feet away. If she turned her head, only one of her cheeks would be scraped up. And after making her way to the side of the cabin, she could slowly inch her way up, using her head and her shoulder against the wall for leverage. Once she was up, once she was steady, she could shuffle around. She could get the hell out.

"And I'll find you," Ian said.

Maybe. If Shaw had been caught, and if he'd given the police the directions to his cabin. If not, Jenny didn't know if she could shuffle the distance to the highway; a rough dirt road through the woods wouldn't be easy to traverse, especially barefoot and tied to a chair. So she had to bring help here, somehow.

"My hands are too high now to hold over the flame." And she wouldn't lower them again and trade mobility for a slight chance of melting the cable ties. She looked to the cabin's windows—at the moth-eaten burlap curtains. "But I could back up to those, and I bet I could pull them down. They'd catch fire easily, burn this damn cabin up. Someone will see the fire and come."

"But will you be able to get out, Jenny?"

"Shaw didn't lock the door."

"But can you open it?"

If her hands weren't completely numb by then. She had to do this quickly. "I hope so."

His mouth tight, Ian shook his head. "Hope isn't good enough, Jenny."

That was true. Hope hadn't gotten her anywhere so far. Only sheer determination had.

"Then I'll damn well do it," she said.

10:25 P.M.

And she did, but she'd forgotten about the two stairs outside the front door. Despite the crackling heat from inside the cabin urging her to hurry, she shuffled carefully across the small porch, and edged as close to the first step as she could without going over. She considered the best way to drop, the best way to keep her balance when she landed—but when she finally shuffled over the edge, the chair's back legs hit the porch, and she tumbled down. The chair's wooden frame cracked then, but not enough to free her, and Jenny stared up at the bright stars, winded again. When the heat from the burning cabin began to prickle her skin, she didn't try to get up—there was nothing to leverage her face and shoulder against. She rolled, instead, thumping along the hard-packed earth, letting the Big Dipper take a good look at her granny panties. At a safe distance from the cabin, she stopped, coming to rest on her side. She shoved her hands back down toward the seat to restore circulation, and waited.

Someone would come to investigate the fire. The wide, earthen clearing around the cabin and the still night air would help prevent the fire from spreading to the trees, but no one would know that until they got here. And at this time of year, this close to federal forestlands, this close to a highway, the response to any blaze would be swift.

Shaw would realize that, too. And so even if he hadn't been caught, he might not risk returning when he saw the fire—knowing that very soon, others would be arriving, too.

Sooner than she thought. Bright headlights appeared at the end of the road. Shriveling fear crawled down her spine. What if she'd been mistaken, and Shaw *had* risked returning to the cabin? Still tied to the chair, she couldn't fight him.

Fuck that. Her mouth was free now. If it was Shaw, she was going to bite out his eyes and spit them down his throat.

Behind her back, her fingers curled into fists. She couldn't hear the engine over the crackling roar of the fire and the pounding of her heart, couldn't determine whether it was Shaw's sedan or some other vehicle approaching. She thought the headlamps were positioned too high for a sedan, more like an SUV, but from her angle on the ground, she couldn't be sure. And, God—he was coming fast. She should have thumped farther off the road.

But the driver must have caught sight of her. He skidded to a halt a few yards away from her, and though he switched to low beams, she still couldn't make out more than a silhouette until the driver's door flew open and the SUV's interior lights fell across his beautiful, beloved face.

"Jenny!"

He shouted her name as he ran toward her. Jenny watched him come, disbelieving. She'd imagined him here, but— "Ian?"

Her voice wasn't her own, far too hoarse. But his voice was rougher than usual, too—and she couldn't imagine he'd been screaming like she had.

Ian fell to his knees beside her, reaching out but stopping just short of touching her. His desperate gaze searched her face. "Oh,

Jenny—thank God. Tell me where you're hurt, first. I don't want to make it worse."

Everywhere. Nowhere. There wasn't anything that wouldn't heal.

"I'm okay," she told him, and repeated it when he didn't seem to hear her. "I'm okay, Ian."

He must have heard her that time, and believed her, because suddenly his mouth was on hers. A stunning kiss, hard and fast—and it hurt her bruised lips, but that didn't matter. He said her name against her mouth like a prayer before sitting back, reaching into his jeans pocket.

"All right, sweetheart. Let's get you out of this thing." Flames reflected dully in the blade of his pocket knife. His jaw tightened when he looked around the back of the chair and saw her wrists.

"I'm okay," she said again, then made herself a liar when he cut the cable tie. Her arms flopped forward, and she shrieked as pain shot through her stiff muscles. Ian caught her with a forearm beneath her shoulders when she would have fallen on her face, and he quickly cut through the ties at her ankles.

Pocketing the knife, he slipped his arm behind her knees and froze, his gaze fixed on her thighs. "Fuck that, Jenny, you're *not* okay."

"I'm not bleeding. He didn't . . ." She let that thought trail off. "It's candle wax. Smell it, if you don't believe me."

But she saw that he'd already realized that the texture appeared wrong. Still, his face didn't lose its harsh cast, or his voice the rough edge. "The ambulance wasn't far behind me, but I don't want you in this dirt. Will you let me carry you to my rig?"

"Please." Unable to raise her arms around his neck, she simply rested her cheek against his shoulder and said, "And when we get there, will you help me untie this goddamn ribbon he put on me?"

"I'll do more than that, sweetheart," he said grimly. "I'll hang him with it."

He lifted her against his chest, began striding toward his vehicle.

God, she'd thought she loved to *watch* him move? *Feeling* him move was so much better.

And she vowed this wouldn't be the last time she did.

2:45 A.M.

In the quiet moments between the exams and the questions, when the terror of learning about the trophies that Shaw had kept in his home became too strong, when the possibility of what could have happened if she hadn't been leaving Ian a message or if he hadn't discovered the GPS in Shaw's car threatened to overwhelm her, Jenny returned to one simple thought: Ian had kissed her.

It had been sweeter than any kiss she'd ever imagined.

A part of her knew that she might be reading too much into that kiss. It might have been the kiss of a close friend who'd suffered genuine fear—and then blessed relief. She might have imagined the possessive light in his eyes, just as she'd imagined everything in that cabin.

Just as she might have misinterpreted every look he'd given her in the past three years.

And wouldn't that be just like her? By letting herself believe that a secret longing existed between them, Jenny created an excuse to keep every other relationship purely physical. When it came to men, her body liked a rough ride, but her heart didn't. In that way, she'd always been something of a coward.

Well, she wouldn't be a coward anymore. Perhaps she *had* imagined everything, but if she hadn't let the threat of pain stop her in the cabin, she couldn't let the fear of being hurt stop her now.

Funny, though, how working up the courage to take that risk seemed so much harder than throwing her weight around or setting a cabin on fire. It wasn't until after the questions were over, her wrists bandaged, and she'd dressed in a pair of Ian's sweatpants and his oversize T-shirt that she could even *think* of throwing herself at him. Yet when he suggested that she stay at his house so that she wouldn't have to spend the night alone in a hotel, her answer came easily.

The neighborhood was quiet, his house only a few blocks from the one she rented, and where the crime scene techs were still processing her kitchen. She let him open the passenger door and guide her through his hot, darkened garage with his hand at the small of her back. His kitchen wasn't quite as stifling; a little window over the sink had been opened to let the day's heat escape. She blinked rapidly when he switched on the light, amazed as always at how clean he kept his home, every counter and appliance sparkling white.

Hopefully, he liked his women dirty.

"You'll take my bedroom," he said. "There's A/C in there. I'll camp out on the couch."

She hoped he wouldn't. "I can't sleep yet."

He nodded and turned toward the fridge. "A drink, then?"

That was what they usually did on hot nights like this: They took a beer out to his deck overlooking his backyard, and kicked their feet up. But that wasn't what she wanted now.

Bottle in hand, he glanced around. His gaze met hers, and she saw the stillness that swept through his body, his sudden tension.

She saw the quiet intensity of a man holding himself back.

His eyes closed. "When you look at me like that, Jenny . . ."

He didn't finish the sentence. She didn't tell him that he was looking at her the same way. She simply said, "It means that I don't want a drink."

He apparently did—or he was just slowing her down, considering her statement and making certain he didn't mistake her meaning. Twisting off the cap, he straightened and let the refrigerator close before leaning back against the door. His dark gaze never left hers as he took a long swallow. She watched the play of muscle in his throat, the way the light hit the sheen of perspiration on his tanned skin.

He lowered the bottle. She wondered if it cost him to maintain that even tone when he asked, "What is it that you want, then?"

She wanted to lick his neck. She wanted to drop to her knees, and discover whether he'd harden in her mouth, if he tasted as good as she'd imagined, if she could make him lose control.

But she needed to tell him that, first.

"I want what we've been dancing around for the past three years. I know that getting together with your partner's sister would create too many problems on the job, and so I haven't wiggled my ass in front of you, haven't teased you at all. It didn't seem fair to play with you like that, to make you choose between your partner and a woman."

Though Ian's expression hadn't changed, his fingers tightened on the neck of the bottle. She paused, her heart racing. But he didn't tell her she was wrong, that she'd imagined anything.

"You're right," he agreed softly. "You didn't play with me. You didn't give me any sign."

"Because your code made sense. If you and I got together—and then if we fucked it all up and I got hurt—something might change between Tom and you. There might be a sense of betrayal, a lack of trust. That's not something that should be standing between you and the guy who's supposed to have your back. The guy who might hold your life in his hands."

"Yeah. That's my code." Ian gave a half laugh, but it must have been a bitter one. As if to wash the taste away, he took another swig. "You've nailed down some great reasons to have one, Jenny. Not a bad code at all, is it?"

"No. But tonight, it was *my* life in your hands. And I need to know: how do you feel about that code now?"

"I feel like I wasted three fucking years."

Oh, thank God. Giddy relief pushed a laugh from her. She supposed that this was the point where she should jump him, take him down to the floor, and dirty him up. Instead she just stood grinning in the middle of his kitchen and thinking, *Thank God.*

Quietly, Ian set his beer aside and pushed away from the fridge. Three long strides brought him within arm's length, but he didn't come any closer. He looked down at her, his gaze hot. "But what you've been through tonight is exactly why I shouldn't touch you right now. It would be taking advantage."

And she wanted him even more for his restraint—it meant that he'd be able to restrain himself in other ways. That he'd be able to drive her crazy, until it was time to let himself go.

But he didn't need to restrain himself now.

She shook her head. "You're thinking that I'm shaken up, that I'm just looking for comfort—and I am. But I only want it from *you*, Ian. If any other Detective McHottie had rescued me from that cabin, I'd have chosen to sleep in a hotel room alone tonight."

His brows rose. "McHottie?"

"Very." *So* very.

Ian smiled and lowered his head. Anticipation started low in her belly, a tremor that moved through her in shivers, tightening the back of her neck, shaking her hands. But Ian's hands were steady. He cupped her jaw, and the condensation on his palm felt cool against her skin.

"I wouldn't have left you alone," he said softly, and his warm lips covered hers.

A sweet kiss—and a frustratingly chaste one. He didn't delve into her mouth the way she wanted to be taken, possessed. He simply held her close, as if absorbing the feel of her. Wonderful, but not enough. Jenny rose up on her toes, seeking more of his taste, a deeper connection. His right hand slid back, his fingers tangling in the hair at her nape, keeping her still—and that easily, he exerted his control. *Oh, yes.* He didn't have to fuck her mouth with his tongue, but just do *that.* Just tell her, with the squeeze of his hand and the firm direction of his lips, that she was his.

Excitement zinged through her blood, carried along by the pounding of her heart. Though she hadn't even tasted him yet, his kiss resonated within her, dominating her senses—the tinge of his cologne on the air that she breathed, the heat that radiated between them. Her arms ached when she clutched at his shoulders to pull him closer, but that pain was overwhelmed by the delight of exploring the dense muscle beneath the tips of her fingers, and she moaned low in her throat.

As if he'd been waiting for that sound, Ian angled his head and traced the seam of her lips with his tongue, easing her open for his slow possession. Pleasure sizzled across her nerves, and each soft lick into her mouth sparked an answering flame between her legs. Jenny pressed closer, desperate to burn hotter. Sweet Jesus, this man could kiss.

With soft pressure against her chin, he urged her lips open wider, sweeping his tongue deep into her mouth. Need speared through her, painfully strong. She whimpered and writhed against him, seeking some small relief in the friction of her nipples against his chest, in the pressure of his erection against her belly. Too many clothes separated them. She curled her fingers into his shoulders, frantic for more.

Abruptly, Ian broke away, cursing. She stared up at him, her mouth open and panting. *Oh, God.* He couldn't quit now.

"What?"

"I'm going too fast." He touched his thumb to the raw corner of her mouth. "I'll hurt you."

Oh. That was all?

"At least this time it'll be real." She smiled up at him when his brows drew together in confusion. "This is good for me, Ian. This is what I want. And it's true that *tomorrow* I'll probably ache so bad that I'll kill you for touching me. But these little cuts and bruises?"—she gestured to her face, the gauze around her wrist—"They just make me feel even more alive."

And alive was good at any time. But after the night she'd had, alive was very, *very* good.

Understanding softened his expression. "All right. But we'll go slow. We'll take it easy."

"No." At her denial, he looked up from the bruise on her jaw. She met his gaze, held it. "I don't want 'easy.' I want you to fuck me like you thought you'd never see me again."

His expression changed swiftly, as if an agonizing spasm moved through him, leaving his features stark and tortured. He *had* thought that, she realized in horror.

His hand tightened in her hair. "When I saw the cabin burning, Jenny, I thought . . . I thought that Shaw had already finished, and he'd tried to cover his tracks. I thought I was too late. Until I saw you next to the road, and I . . . *God.*"

His mouth crashed down on hers, demanding entry, taking possession—as if the memory had unleashed something within him, stolen his control. Jenny clung to his shoulders, her desperation just as fierce. She needed to have him now, *now.*

His hand fell to her hip. He steered her back into the wall, wedging his thighs between hers and angling in. His erection felt hot and thick behind his jeans, a burning pressure against her belly. He broke the kiss and lowered his mouth to her ear, his hands sliding to her ass.

His voice was harsh. "You make sure that you know what you're asking, Jenny, because I can't go back. This isn't friendly comfort, and it isn't just sex to me. And so once I have you like this, it's all or nothing."

She needed it all, too. "And if we fuck it up?"

"We won't." He bit her earlobe sharply, making her gasp. "We've spent the past three years proving we're compatible."

"So they weren't a waste after all."

"They were. Because I could have spent that time finding out whether the thought of my mouth on your pussy gets you wet."

Her knees weakened. She sagged into him, and felt his smile against her neck.

"Well, then. Let's find out."

His hand slipped inside the elastic waistband of her sweats. His callused palm gently scraped the soft, sensitive skin of her belly, his fingers seeking the heat below. They both groaned when he encountered her wet folds. He slid his middle finger through her heated slit, found her entrance.

Jenny waited breathlessly, quivering. Her body clenched when he pushed his finger deep, and she cried out. "Ian!"

"I'd have known by now whether you come harder on a slow fuck, or when I take you fast." His thumb sought her clit. "I'd know whether you whether you like your nipples sucked on or pinched."

Her back arched, as if offering the stiffened peaks up to him. "Both."

"Christ," he breathed. "You're soaking my fingers. You love it when I talk dirty like this?"

"Yes." She laughed her answer, then moaned, trying to make him move his hand faster. "So, so dirty."

"God, I love that." He withdrew his hand, ignoring her protest. He gripped her hips. "Push down your pants, Jenny."

She trembled, realizing he meant to fuck her here, now, without any other preliminaries. Her fingers flew to the waistband of the sweats. The soft cotton seemed to caress her skin as she pushed them over her hips and let them slide to her ankles. Pressed into the wall by his big body, she couldn't bend and take the pants all the way down. She kicked them off her feet and toward the middle of the kitchen—and though the sore muscles in her arms screamed at the movement, she pulled the T-shirt over her head.

The lust burning in Ian's eyes told her he appreciated that effort. After a long look that left her nipples aching to be touched and her skin flushed, his gaze returned to her face.

"Now undo mine," he ordered.

Beneath her fingers, the buttons of his fly gave way to his straining cock. Greedily, she reached in and stroked her hand down his hot, steely length, loving his reaction: the sudden rigidity in his heavy frame, the hiss of his indrawn breath.

As if he could only bear a few seconds of that exquisite torment, he pushed her hands away and cupped her ass in his palms. Then Ian was lifting her up with a rough, "Wrap your legs around me now."

Shuddering with anticipation, she complied. He shifted his hips, positioned her. The head of his cock burrowed through her slit, lodged against her slick entrance. Almost drowning with need, Jenny squirmed, trying to push him inside, but he held her in place. She tried to urge him on, rocking her hips, fisting her hands in his hair.

"Ian," she begged, but still he waited.

"I'm not going to take it easy," he warned her, as if she hadn't been the one who'd demanded a rough, hard ride. "Not now, when I'm thinking of how I almost lost you. Not now, when the only thing that matters is making you mine."

Making her his. And she did belong to him. Not because some psycho decided she did, but because she'd offered herself. Not taking. Giving. And Ian would give himself to her in return.

She wanted that more than anything. "Then do it."

His eyes narrowed. Watching her face, he leaned his weight into her. Her back pressed hard into the wall, offering solid support, but her soft body gave way to the pressure at her entrance—stinging as the thick head of his cock stretched her delicate flesh, then an unrelenting ache as he moved deeper. She tensed, clenching her teeth against a whimper. He didn't stop, thank God. His unyielding possession hurt, but it was real, and he was here, and even the pain felt so good.

His cock fully embedded within her, Ian tightened his fingers on her ass before sliding his hands down her thighs, lifting them around his waist at a higher angle. Jenny cried out as the movement shoved him deeper into her. He paused, and she writhed against him, seeking more.

He gave her that, too. Pounding into her with hard, fast strokes, he fucked her until she might scream from the pleasure of being stuffed too full, of feeling more alive than she could remember. Then he shifted her so that his driving shaft grazed over her erect clit in a maddening tease, and she did scream, because she didn't think she could take any more. Yet still he gave it to her, each relentless thrust threatening to break her, to throw her over the edge—and finally did, her pussy clamping around his cock, a release that was relief and agony. With another powerful stroke, Ian came with clenched teeth, his flesh throbbing deep and setting off another shock of small convulsions inside her.

With a groan, he collapsed against her. He turned as they slid to the floor and pulled her onto his lap, her body a limp tangle of sweaty limbs. He tilted his head back against the wall, his chest heaving.

He smoothed his hand down her back, a gesture both possessive and soothing. "Are you all right?"

She thought so. Her chest seemed too full, and she felt like laughing and crying with the sheer joy of being here, of being with him, but she wasn't sure which would come out if she opened her mouth. She simply nodded and buried her face against his throat.

After a moment, she managed, "Thank you for rescuing me tonight."

"From what I saw, Jenny, you did that yourself." He was silent for a long moment, and when he spoke again, his voice had roughened. "And I'll be thanking you for that the rest of my life."

The rest of her life. She smiled at that, then looked up when he shifted around, and laid her back on the cool tile. He grinned down at her, and bent his head to her breast.

"And I think I'll start thanking you for it now."

Meljean Brook lives in Oregon with her family. She is the author of the Guardian paranormal romance series, and the Iron Seas steampunk romance series. For contact information and a full booklist, please visit www .meljeanbrook.com.

THE WOODEN PONY

Shoshanna Evers

Natalie Durso looked at her watch discreetly and sipped her Diet Coke. She had been hoping that her blind date would already be at the bar when she showed up, so if he was a freak she could just slide out the door without ever meeting him—no harm, no foul.

But it looked like Eric Turner had the same idea. Hell, maybe he even already showed up, saw a pale, half-Asian woman wearing long sleeves in the middle of July sitting at the bar and skedaddled.

"Natalie?"

She turned in surprise at the deep voice and jumped off the bar stool. "Eric?"

He smiled and put his hand out. Wiping off the condensation from the glass on her black slacks, she smiled back and shook his large hand, reveling in the feel of it enveloping hers. *Wow, he was good looking.* No way she'd have walked out on this one. She had to crane her eyes up to get a good look at him since he had at least a foot on her, even in her high heels.

He helped her back onto the bar stool and took a seat next to her, nodding to the bartender. "Just plain orange juice."

Natalie looked down at the bar, suddenly embarrassed. What was she thinking, answering that personals ad online? This man knew more about her secrets than any of her past lovers, because he had asked, and she had answered. What she wanted that she wasn't getting.

Pain.

And he had said he was more than willing to provide that for her.

"Thanks for meeting me in public," she said. "It makes me feel safer."

"Of course," he said. "Me, too. I don't just hand out my home address to strangers—what if you were a psycho?" He laughed and accepted his drink from the bartender, slipping him a folded bill.

"I feel a little psycho," she admitted. "I can't believe all that stuff I said last night." They had instant messaged each other for more than two hours. He got her to admit things she'd been scared to tell even her therapist—not that she had a therapist anymore. Therapists don't do much good if you can't tell them the real problem.

"Well, it was one of the hottest chats I've had in a long time, which is why I'm here." Eric smiled at her. "I want you to feel safe with me. But I also want you to come back to my place."

Natalie took an unladylike gulp from her glass, finishing the last sip of soda, and let a half-melted ice cube slip into her mouth. "What will we do at your place? I don't think I'm ready to just jump into bed with you."

"I told you online that I don't have sex on the first date anyway, and I keep my word. But I'd like to whip you, just like we talked about."

She crunched the ice and shivered. Her pussy got wet at the thought, but could she actually handle a real whipping? None of her previous lovers had played with her the way she truly desired. They didn't want to hurt her.

But she needed to be hurt, and somehow Eric got that on a primal level. Even better, he got off on it. Giving her what she craved satisfied his desires as well. Win-win.

"What if I can't take it?" she asked, her voice dropping so the other people in the bar wouldn't overhear.

"We'll have a safe word. But I think you can take it. No one ever died from a little whipping delivered by an experienced dominant.

And besides," he said with a smile, "if you start squirming so much that it affects my aim I can always tie you in place and then continue with your punishment."

She started to push up her sleeves since it felt hot suddenly, but stopped herself just in time.

"What's on your wrist?" he asked, grabbing her hand. *Fuck.* He had seen them. "Roll up your sleeves," he ordered softly.

Something about his tone made her obey, even though they were in public and the last thing she wanted was for everyone in the bar to see her shame. Looking around quickly, she lifted her sleeves.

Dozens of angry red scars from years of self-cutting marred the otherwise flawless skin on the underside of her forearms.

"You're a cutter." He said it in such a way that she couldn't get a read on his tone. Was he angry? Disgusted? God forbid, did he pity her?

"*Was* a cutter. I quit."

"When?" He was still holding her arm, tracing her scars with his fingers.

"Almost six months ago. I can't take it anymore, not being able to cut myself is driving me insane. That's why I reached out to you. I need an outlet. I miss the pain . . . and I think someone like you could help me experience that in a more healthy manner." She sighed. "I can't explain it."

"Let's go," he said. "You have a date with my whip."

ERIC looked over at Natalie as he walked with her up the front steps to his house. She was even more beautiful than her picture online. He had been hesitant to try and find a woman on the Internet, but he couldn't argue with the results. Dozens of women had responded to his ad. Married women and women who refused to chat online with him before meeting were cut from the list. But Natalie . . . she was something else.

"This is really your house?" Natalie asked, looking around at the high ceilings and marble floors in the grand foyer.

"It is," he said. "But you haven't seen the best part. The basement."

Suddenly Natalie turned to him. "This is crazy. *I'm* crazy to just go into a complete stranger's home and let him take me into his basement. You'll probably end up killing me and everyone will say 'Well, it's no wonder, who goes into a stranger's house?'"

"You're welcome to leave," he said. "I'll call you a cab if you want me to." But he had a feeling that she didn't really want to leave. *Please stay*, he implored with his eyes. Her lips looked so soft and full, and he took her face in his hand, caressing her cheek. "If this is good-night, can I at least get a goodnight kiss?"

She kissed him then, full on the mouth, her lips pressed against his with a ferocity that gave him an instant erection. "Do you promise you won't kill me?" she whispered, her breath hot on his lips.

"I'll torture you a little but I won't kill you. No marks, that's my motto."

"Torture?" she breathed, her eyes wide. Giggling nervously, she traced her hand down his chest. "Okay, show me your basement. I'm going to take a wild guess that you've got a dungeon down there."

He grinned. Tonight was going to be fun. "If you consider a very comfortable adult playroom a dungeon, then yes, that's what I've got."

Natalie smiled back at him, some of the worry disappearing from her eyes. "What if I get freaked out?" she asked suddenly.

"The safe word is your full name. So if you ever want me to stop everything, just say—um, what *is* your full name?"

"Natalie Alexandra Durso."

"Okay then. So if you say that, then I know you're done. I won't be mad, I'll just call you a cab and we'll call it a night."

She nodded, taking an audible breath. "Got it."

"Follow me." He walked her through the kitchen, smiling to himself as she glanced at the granite countertops and stainless-steel fridge. Maybe she knew how to cook—but the gourmet kitchen was wasted on him. All he knew how to work was the microwave and the phone to call for reservations. The basement door off the kitchen opened to a steep flight of stairs.

She hesitated at the top of the stairs, one hand on the door frame. "You go first."

"Sure." He took the stairs two at a time, familiar with their depth. The basement had been a pet project of his for years now. He had the major work done by contractors—putting up the drywall and ceiling, laying down the poured concrete floor, which he then had waxed to a high shine. There were no windows, but the lighting was perfect. He could dim the lights as needed, but right now he kept them on at full brightness to put his date at ease.

After the major work was done, however, Eric had stepped in and created the perfect playground for his fantasies. There was a spanking bench and a futon—and man, those futon slats came in handy when ropes were involved, and an array of whips and paddles hung on hooks on the wall. Of course there were also numerous restraints and a bondage chair.

He had shelves along one wall that contained every sex toy imaginable, including his favorite, the Magic Wand. That intense vibrator was perfect for forced orgasms. A woman cuffed to his bondage chair with the vibrator tied against her clit was a beautiful sight indeed. Most of the toys had never been used, unfortunately. The ones that had been used were sterilized. His eyes rested on his latest acquisition— a piece of furniture that he was dying to try out. The Wooden Pony. He had just gotten it last week on special order from Canada.

"Wow," Natalie said as she looked around, taking it all in. "Impressive."

"When we are in the basement you don't speak unless I grant you permission," Eric said softly. "And you address me as Sir. Do you understand?"

Natalie's mouth dropped as if in surprise, but Eric didn't say a word. She needed to get with the program right away. If she wasn't up for his rules then she certainly wasn't up for a whipping.

She raised her eyebrows and looked up the stairs toward the exit for just a moment. Then she looked back at him. "Yes, Sir. I understand."

Good girl. She was going to be fun to initiate.

NATALIE stood before him, unsure what to do. She was about to ask where he wanted her, but then she remembered he hadn't given her permission to speak. This was going to be more challenging than she thought.

Finally, after what seemed like an eternity, Eric spoke. "It might make you feel more comfortable if you text one of your girlfriends to let her know you're here. You can give her my address for safety."

Yeah, like she'd want anyone she was acquainted with to know what she was up to. But just the fact that he suggested that made her feel more at ease. Pulling her cell out of her purse, she texted the info to her own phone quickly anyway. He could make his own assumptions as to whom she had sent the text.

"Now that you've had a chance to see the place," he said, "I'm going to dim the lights a bit for ambience." He slid a switch on the wall and the basement playroom was instantly plunged into a semi-darkness, with just a few lights highlighting various elements of the room.

Thank goodness. If she had to get intimate with him in the bright lights he had on before, she would have felt even more vulnerable and exposed. But the dark suited her just fine.

She didn't even realize she was looking down at the concrete floor—which was unlike any concrete floor she had ever seen, as it was so nice looking—until Eric lifted her chin, compelling her to look into his eyes.

"Are you okay?" he asked.

"Yes, Sir."

"Are you scared?"

Yes. "No, Sir."

"Then I want you to take off your clothes for me." He made no move to help her, so she put her purse down and started unbuttoning her blouse. At least he had already seen her scars, so there would be no surprise there. But he hadn't seen all of them.

Letting her blouse drop to the floor, she touched her belly selfconsciously. She could feel his eyes linger on the crisscross of healed cuts across her stomach, but he didn't say a word.

She unzipped the fly of her black slacks and shimmied them down her pale thighs. When she stepped out of her heels, she dropped a good three inches. Eric positively towered above her at six foot three. He held his hand out for support when she wobbled, unsteady on her feet as she stepped out of the pants and kicked them to the side.

"God, you're beautiful," he said, running his hand across the underside of her brassiere. "Take off the bra."

His commanding tone had her wet already, but the silence he had imposed on her made her feel acutely off balance. She was used to saying what she wanted to, when she wanted. Unhooking her bra, it fell to the floor next to her other clothes, leaving her in nothing but a thong.

"Leave the panties on," he said, "and go pick out your whip."

What? How could she possibly pick out the very implement that would be used on her? She looked at the wall of floggers, whips, and paddles, and raised her eyebrows.

"Have you ever been whipped before?" he asked.

"No, Sir. I wouldn't know what to pick."

"I'd recommend the second from the right. It hurts like a bitch but it doesn't raise any welts or cut the skin. I could punish you all night and you'd leave here without a mark on you," he said. "Bring it to me."

Nodding, Natalie walked across the room to the wall of implements. Second from the right. She carefully grasped what looked like a long, flexible leather riding crop and held it reverently in her hands. Could this crop be the outlet she craved—a way for her to stop cutting?

"Where do you want me, Sir?" she asked, then instantly bit her lip since she had spoken out of turn. Being silent was more difficult than she had anticipated.

Eric shook his head with a smile as he took the riding crop from her trembling hand. "Did I say you could speak?"

"No, Sir."

"Then I think you need a reminder of who's in charge. Bend over this and hold on."

She looked at the wide, padded leather-covered spanking bench he was pointing to and carefully laid herself over it. Her heartbeat raced in anticipation of the first lick, but instead of the riding crop across her back, she felt his hard hand spank her ass cheek.

It stung more than she expected from just a simple hand spank. This guy meant business.

More spanks covered her ass cheeks, sometimes alternating back and forth between the left and the right buttock, and sometimes smacking the exact same spot over and over until she squealed and gripped the handles on the spanking bench tightly.

"Now, Natalie," he murmured, running his fingers lightly over her scorched bottom, "you're nice and pink."

"I thought you wouldn't leave any marks," she said. *Oops*—she kept forgetting she didn't have permission to speak whenever she felt like it. "Sorry, Sir."

He smacked her ass again, hard, in response. "It'll fade. This is actually the best way to avoid leaving bruises and marks. A nice light warm-up spanking to get you all pretty and pink before I get serious with your punishment."

That was a warm up? What on earth was the "real thing" going to feel like?

"Don't move," he said softly, and she heard the sound of the riding crop whipping through the air before it made contact across the center of her ass cheek. She howled in surprise more than pain. "You're a drama queen, aren't you," he chuckled, bringing the crop down again, hitting the other cheek.

It hurt. *Damn,* it hurt. But she was still here, still hadn't disappeared off into subspace like when she truly lost herself in an endorphin rush of pain.

He whipped her again, the crop falling on a slightly different part of her bottom, feeling like it was cutting her skin, but she knew it couldn't be. Even though Eric Turner was a stranger, she trusted him to keep her safe. Something about him felt right. She gasped as the whipping picked up pace, not leaving her time to catch her breath or compose herself.

But she wouldn't even think about calling it quits. She needed more.

Suddenly, Eric stopped. "You've had enough."

"No!" she wailed. "Keep going . . . Sir."

"I decide when you've had enough. Not you." He lifted her up, her knees feeling weak and shaky, and pulled her toward his muscular chest. "This is the reason you're covered in cuts on your arms and belly," he chided. "Because you don't know your limits."

"Please, Sir," she whispered. He couldn't stop, not now.

"You're a pain slut, aren't you," he said, dropping his hand to her cunt, his thumb dipping under her thong, feeling her wetness there. She felt her face flush with embarrassment and she nodded, looking away.

"I think I have the perfect experience for you," he said.

She looked at him again, feeling that glimmer of hope once more. "I'll do anything you want, Sir."

He slapped her ass once, pressing her against his chest. "If that were true then you would respect me enough to obey my rules. You only speak when I give you permission. Do you understand? Speak."

"Yes, Sir."

"Have you ever ridden a wooden pony?"

"No, Sir," she said, her eyes wandering to the corner of the basement where he had gestured.

"Then I'd like to suggest we give this a try. I think it will be right up your alley."

Natalie opened her mouth to agree but quickly shut it, nodding instead.

The wooden pony, as Eric had called it, was basically just a two-by-four plank of wood, narrow side up, supported by adjustable wooden legs so it was about waist height.

"Take off your thong," he said, and she did. "You know, before you go for a ride on the pony, I think your clit should be nice and swollen, to really drive home the experience for you."

She smiled. That sounded like a good time.

"Sit in the chair," he said, guiding her by the arm to the bondage chair. She sat immediately, looking at the restraints on the chair with interest. "Now spread your legs."

Spreading her legs, she felt her nipples become erect as he kneeled at her feet to cuff each ankle to the chair, keeping them spread wide. Her hands were cuffed to the arms of the chair. She loved the feeling of being helpless, but what on earth could he do to her while she was sitting in a chair?

He walked out of her sight line and she twisted in her seat, trying to get a handle on where he had gone. Then he was back, holding a roll of duct tape and a large back massager with a cord. "My favorite, the Magic Wand," he said. "This thing can bring you to orgasm literally within seconds."

Plugging the Magic Wand into a surge protector, Eric positioned it between her legs, spreading her labia so that the little nub of her clit was exposed, pressed up against the massager head. He ripped a piece of duct tape off the roll with a loud tearing sound

Is that for my mouth? she wondered, but she didn't dare ask. Every minute he kept her from speaking plunged her deeper into a submissive mind-set, and she was enjoying it. It was nice to let go control and have the fantasies they chatted about online come to life.

Eric lay the duct tape down over the Magic Wand, securing it in place between her legs by taping it to the chair. Then he turned it on. Natalie gasped as the vibrations hit her clit and she gyrated in the seat, unable to move away from the sensation. Not that she wanted to, because it felt incredible. Where was the pain in this? She cried out as an orgasm wracked her body, the contractions nearly lifting her up off the seat as she curled forward.

You can turn it off now, she thought, but again she didn't speak. *I came.*

Surely he noticed that she climaxed, though, right? So why wasn't he doing anything . . . where did he go? She looked around the room frantically, the vibrator still going, the constant stimulation to her post-orgasmic pussy almost too much to bear. The sensations began to build and she inhaled sharply as she came yet again.

"Sir? Won't you turn it off?" she asked, her voice shaky, not knowing if he was even in the room anymore to hear her.

He came up behind her and whispered, his breath hot on her ear, "What did I say about speaking without permission?"

"I'm sorry, Sir," she said, unable to even think straight as the vibrations shot through her, making her climax again. Her muscles shook like she was having a mini-seizure and she gasped as the vibrator kept going.

"You just earned yourself a punishment," he said, coming around front and dropping between her legs. He flipped the switch, and it went from the low setting to the high setting. The buzzing was so intense that there was no way she could come from it, it simply caused her to focus all of her attention right on her swollen, over stimulated pussy. "Five minutes on high." He walked behind her chair again and she moaned, biting her lip to keep from begging him to let her free. She knew she could always say the safe word, but she wanted the experience he had promised her—she wanted to ride on the wooden pony.

A minute into it she started to sweat and wondered how much longer she had. Just when she thought she had reached her orgasm limit, another electrifyingly painful climax ripped through her body, leaving her gasping and panting for more.

"Please, fuck me," she begged, barely aware she had spoken the words.

"We're not going to fuck—not tonight," Eric murmured. She groaned in response, her head falling back against the chair as her legs shook from sensation overload. By the time five minutes was up, her clit had popped out of its hood and stuck out between her nether lips like a crude tongue.

He turned off the vibrator and smiled, touching her swollen clitoris before he uncuffed her from the bondage chair. "*Now* you're ready to ride the wooden pony. That is, if you're still up for some real pain. Are you?"

Natalie stood up, staring straight into his cool gray eyes. "Yes, Sir."

She wanted to ask what she should do, but Eric led her by the hand to the "pony."

"Hop on," he said. "Straddle it."

Raising one leg carefully, she positioned herself so she was standing over it, with the narrow plank between her legs about an inch below her pussy.

"Up on your tippy toes," he said, "so I can adjust this."

She rose up on her toes as he ratcheted up the height just a little, so that when she was on her toes the plank wasn't touching her labia.

"Drop down on your heels," he ordered.

The plank ground into her tender flesh, pressing against her pubic bone. "Oh," she said in recognition, before covering her mouth with her hand. So *that* was what the wooden pony was all about.

Then Eric ran his fingers along her labia, separating then, pulling her outer lips wide so that the board was pressed directly against her engorged clitoris. She moaned at the new sensation.

Without even meaning to, she went up on her toes, trying to relieve the intense pressure on her pussy. But her calf muscles soon began to tremble and tire, and she used the last bit of strength left in them to slowly lower herself back down onto the wooden pony.

Shifting her body, Natalie tried to find a slightly different area between her legs for her weight to rest on, but the pressure of her body resting all its weight on her clit had her in exquisite pain almost immediately.

She couldn't take it any longer. Rising up onto her tiptoes, she breathed a sigh of relief as the pain in her pussy went away, only to be replaced within moments by a cramp in her calf muscles.

"Fuck," she groaned, unable to even slowly lower herself. She slammed against the plank, screaming as it hit her clit with over one hundred pounds of her own body weight.

"Scream all you like, Natalie," Eric said. "The walls down here are soundproofed."

She rocked back and forth, trying to put her hands in front of her to hold up some of her body weight. The pain moved but was always there, just relocating to torture a slightly different area of her groin.

"You've only been riding the wooden pony for less than ten minutes," he laughed. "You can go much longer without causing any damage."

"No, Sir, please," she said, panic in her voice at the thought of him keeping her on there for a long time.

"If you want to see how much you can truly take, then you'll stay on the pony until I say you've had enough," he said, his voice quiet but firm. "But if you've changed your mind, then you're free to go. Just say the safe word."

She shook her head. Why did he have to give her a choice? She wanted her choice taken away. She wanted to be bound, told what to do, with no way of escaping it. Choosing her torture just didn't seem right to her. But now she was affirming, once again, that yes indeed she was a pain slut. She'd stay right here on this pony for the duration—because as much as she wanted to get off the ride in that moment, she knew she'd be masturbating to this experience for years to come.

"Hands on your head," he said, and with that order went any hope she had of keeping some of the pressure off her pussy by pushing up off her arms.

She cried out as the plank ground against her clit.

"Now we're going to make it interesting," he said, as he came up beside her. "Up on your toes."

She obeyed even as her calf muscles burned in protest, her eyes widening as she saw what he was up to. He raised the pony so that even on her toes the board pressed against her. Raising it just half an inch past that, her feet cleared the ground and the real torture began.

A sheen of sweat broke out across her upper lip as she breathed raggedly, the sensation more than she could handle.

"Breathe into the pain," Eric whispered, and she exhaled slowly, rocking carefully back and forth, her hands still on her head, tangled now in her thick black hair. The pain came in waves like an orgasm, flowing through her, and suddenly she was flying, floating through the atmosphere, the stars twinkling around her, glowing brightly as she glided effortlessly across the sky.

She threw her head back, lost in ecstasy, and then she felt Eric's arms around her, lifting her against his muscular chest, holding her to him, showering her lips with kisses.

He let her rest against him like that for a while before he softly murmured, "Are you with us again, Natalie?"

She smiled. "Yes, Sir."

He touched her pussy, spreading her with his fingers, inspecting her closely before turning her around and looking at her ass. "Looks good. No marks, just like I promised. Do you want me to put some ice on your pussy to make it feel better?"

She shook her head. The soreness was good. She'd like to hold on to it for a while at least, the way the effects of a glass of merlot stayed with her past the last sip of wine.

Taking her clothing off the concrete floor, he dressed her tenderly, as if she were a beloved doll. "Ready to go upstairs?"

"Yes, Sir." But she didn't want to leave his basement just yet. She wanted to stay there, chained to his wall, ready for him to do with her as he wished. But the real world called. She had office hours in the morning, and she was the doctor on call for the hospital next weekend.

"Thank you for a lovely evening, Eric," she whispered as he led her up the basement stairs.

Back in the grand foyer, he leaned down and kissed her. "Don't cut yourself anymore, Natalie," he said. "Call me instead."

"I will," she said. She meant it, too.

Multi-published erotic romance author **Shoshanna Evers** is published with Ellora's Cave, The Wild Rose Press, Cleis Press (*Best Bondage Erotica 2012*) and Berkley Heat (*Agony/Ecstasy*). When she's not writing hot romance, she's a syndicated advice columnist, a registered nurse, and a stay-at-home mom. She's the editor of *How to Write Hot*

Sex: Tips from Multi-Published Erotic Romance Authors, which includes essays from several of the authors in the *Agony/Ecstasy* anthology.

Visit Shoshanna Evers at www.shoshannaevers.com, on Twitter @ShoshannaEvers, and on Facebook.com/shoshanna.evers, *Sexily *Evers* After . . .*

KISS OF LIFE

LILY DANIELS

Theodora clutched at her nightdress with damp hands. White bridal silk decorated with lace insertion and embroidery. Above the square neckline her pulse hammered.

Her groom was sitting on the bed, quietly disrobing.

She must tell Hugh the truth; she ought to have done before now. But her father's heart was weak, and he had so wanted them to marry. What if Hugh decided on an annulment?

Her husband was sure to be angry. The damask-papered walls and coffered ceiling inched nearer. She'd been relieved by Hugh's sensitivity in suggesting they forgo a honeymoon trip. After the *Titanic*, the *Carpathia*'s rescue, and the voyage back home, she'd sworn never to board another ship. But she did not yet know Hugh well. How would he react when he learned what she'd done? Here, in the privacy of his Berkshire country manor, he could do anything—

"Come, Theodora."

Nude, Hugh reminded her of a sleek Arabian. He was as handsome as Martin; handsomer, if one preferred the dark, broadshouldered sort. His keen gray eyes sought hers as she neared him.

"Nervous?" He reached for her hands and pulled her closer. She tried not to stare at the erection that reared between them.

"There is something you must know," she said.

He quirked a dark brow.

"I'm not a virgin."

There, it was out. But he said nothing, and she could not read his expression.

"I know this must disappoint you, but it was only once and I no longer care for him."

"Are you pregnant?"

Her face heated. "No."

"Then I am not . . . entirely displeased."

"And you don't wish to know more?"

He looked away. "I know enough. I would prefer to spend our wedding night on other things."

Hugh must truly love her and trust her, to say that. Relief spiraled through her, heady, almost exciting. She wanted to throw her arms about him. "I shall be the best wife, I promise," she said.

"You may begin by opening your wedding gifts."

Two boxes lay on the bedside cupboard, wrapped and beribboned. Eagerly Theodora opened the smaller. It contained a glass bottle.

"Almond oil," Hugh said, and removed the stopper before setting the bottle back on the cupboard. When she gave him a puzzled look, he added, "Unwrap the other."

Thea did, and gasped. Inside the second box was a long piece of polished, pink marble shaped like a—a phallus.

"Do you like it?" Hugh's voice was soft, warm.

What could she say? She stifled a nervous giggle. What did one say to a man who gave his bride a phallus on their wedding night?

"I bought it with you in mind, Thea."

Her mouth went dry.

"Pick it up."

The veined stone was heavy and cool against her warm skin. Her heart skittered. Was it meant to go inside her?

"What an innocent you are. There is more than one sort of virginity, you know."

He withdrew the phallus from her hand. "Time enough for that later," he said, placing it back in its box and setting it aside.

He took hold of her and kissed her, a long, drugging kiss. When he lifted his head away, she drew it back down. More kissing, and then Hugh lowered his lips to her sensitive neck. She was in need of breath when he said, "Let's remove your nightdress."

As he undid each button he kissed and tasted her spine. Theodora felt dizzy by the time she was bare. Hugh licked her ear. "Come, straddle me," he whispered, and sat back on the bed. She complied.

"Did your lover teach you dirty words?"

She shook her head, feeling her cheeks burn.

"Touch my cock. Yes, that's it there."

His blood pulsed beneath the cock's silky, hot skin. He was rosy with it, ready, so ready to couple with her.

"Now, I'm going to taste your nipple." She shivered when he took it in his mouth. His hand slipped between her legs. "Ah, you're already wet here. That's good. Open your thighs further, love."

His fingers were hot, long. "This is your pussy," he said, sliding two inside her. "It's where my cock goes, or the phallus." He stroked away her fear of the phallus. "And here is your clitoris." She gasped as he touched it. Martin had never . . .

"Would you like me to lick your clitoris, Thea?"

The very idea was depraved. He licked her neck, and she went even damper around his fingers. "Yes," she whispered.

"Well, I won't. Not today. But thank you for asking."

The remark might have been meant to tease but it stung. Hugh inserted his fingers within her again and gently sucked a nipple so that the pain of her shame mingled with pleasure. Another finger circled her clitoris. "You're awfully wet, Thea." The pleasure built unbearably. "No, not yet," he said, and his fingers slipped out, leaving behind an empty ache.

"Now," he said, moving farther back on the bed and drawing her knees alongside him. "A man can fuck a woman this way." She took his meaning as he guided his cock inside her. It felt exquisite to be stretched and filled. She craved more, but how could he move in this position?

Hugh gave her a pointed look. *She* was meant to do the moving. Her whole body scalding, she began to raise and lower herself on his cock. It was . . . mortifying . . . and yet . . . so satisfying. She was trembling, on the verge of climax, when he said, "That's enough," and lifted her off him.

"But . . ." Her pussy tightened vainly on nothing. "You haven't spent."

He laughed. "Don't worry about me. I think you're almost ready. But, Thea, you must tell me if at any point you want me to stop."

Stop? She only wished him to continue!

"All right. Now, on your hands and knees. I promise I will not pull out before you come."

Anger and embarrassment, as much as desire, heated her skin now. But she craved his cock inside her, so she followed his bidding.

From the periphery of her vision, she glimpsed him taking the phallus. Her breath went shallow. On all fours she could not see Hugh without looking back—or worse, down at herself, which she refused to do.

He tongued the cheeks of her bum. "Did I say I wouldn't lick your clitoris? Pity." But he fingered it lightly. "Ah, you're pulsing with life, Thea."

Life. Even in the midst of passion, the word hurt. All those people dead, at the bottom of the North Atlantic, and she was alive. Yet strangely, the pain of that knowledge made her pleasure more acute. She felt the same need that had led her to Martin's bed, the need to affirm life.

Something cold, smooth, hard entered her. It was the phallus; it must be. Its girth and weight filled her, but they were not enough. "Hugh," she said, begging, she didn't know for what.

Oil dripped on her backside, and she was staggered to feel a finger probing her bum. Slowly he added a second finger, and then a third, while she struggled to comprehend her gladness. Relief or loss: she could not say which was stronger when the warmth of his fingers left her, but neither lasted, for then she felt his cock, not at the entrance of her pussy, but at that of her bum. Stunned, she hissed, but his left hand brushed her nipple, his right thrust the phallus, and she felt her body go supple with pleasure just as he entered that other opening. An imperative gripped her. She was desperate, desperate to be shagged in any way. *I will not pull out*, he had said, and she clung to that promise as she was doubly penetrated, doubly taken.

The strokes of the phallus gentled, taunting her.

"Do you know why I married you, Thea?"

"No," she said. That much was suddenly obvious.

His cock went still while he rocked the phallus slowly inside her. The fragrance of almond oil filled the air.

"I married you because Martin Wilkes was determined to do so. He wanted your money and I couldn't let him have it."

A finger circled her clitoris. But her distress cleared the haze of pleasure.

"Why?"

"Because my cousin Cyril died for you and Wilkes. He might have survived the *Titanic*, had he not promised you he'd find Wilkes and bring him to the boat deck."

Theodora had first met Hugh when she and her father had called on him to tell him how bravely Cyril had convinced her to get in the lifeboat. *I will find Martin and see him out alive, Lady Theodora.*

She'd been reunited with Martin aboard the *Carpathia*, but Cyril, who had given Martin his lifebelt, had been lost.

Had Cyril loved her?

"They were friends and business partners."

"Yes, but Cyril had soured on Wilkes," Hugh said, gently easing his cock in and out of her bum. "He wrote me of it, and of his feelings for you. 'Minutes ago, when *Titanic* arrived in Cherbourg, Lady Theodora's eyes lit. She robbed me of a heartbeat, I do believe.' In the end, his feelings for you robbed him of many more."

Pain stabbed her. She didn't love Hugh, though she had hoped to, and she had fallen out of love with Martin when she'd realized her father was right, that it was only her family's money he'd ever wanted. But to learn that Hugh too had only pretended to care for her, and that poor Cyril Darrow, drowned with over fifteen hundred others, truly had . . .

Hugh began to move faster inside her—inside her bum!—and pumped the phallus with his hand. Despite herself, despite the sorrow, his deception, everything, sensation brought her back to life. And it hurt, how it hurt, to feel the pleasure that encompassed her. "Come, Theodora," he said, and flicked her clitoris, so that she couldn't help but follow his command.

I was aware you were not a virgin, he'd said afterward. *When he was smashed Wilkes boasted that he'd fucked you, so it's just as well that you did not pretend.*

Throughout the railway journey she made to London the following morning without her husband's knowledge, those words lingered in her ears. She thought of them as she faced a brandy-soaked Martin, having barged past the servants into his smoking room.

"Lady Theo . . . dora," Martin said when she'd finally finished heaping invectives. "Are you . . . pleased with *Mr.* Carter?" He leered at her. "I hear your husband has no regard for the proper way to fuck a gentlewoman. Has he buggered you yet?"

The hand she lifted to slap him was caught from the side. "He means to insult me, not you."

Hugh. How long had he stood behind her? He must have entered the room silently. Odd, seeing him clothed, knowing now what lay beneath the worsted and cashmere. Her body heated in all the places where his hands, his mouth, his cock had been.

"I do adore my Rolls-Royce Silver Ghost," he said outside Martin's house. "Isn't she a beauty? She made it easy to catch up to you once I realized you were bound to vent your fury on Wilkes."

Now it was Hugh's face she itched to slap.

"It isn't worth it." His expression sobered. Had her wordless departure the day after their wedding weighed on his conscience? "Wilkes certainly is not. But if you want a taste of revenge, I can help."

"KEEP your voice low," Hugh said. "You can remove your veil now. They can't see us."

It was nighttime. Her husband had brought Theodora to a brothel. They stood facing a large window in a dim, furnished passageway.

"How is that possible?"

"It's a special mirror. So long as our corridor remains dark, and the rooms on the other side brightly lit, we can see them, but they see only their own reflections."

"You're certain?"

"I've been on the other side, love."

How easily he called her "love," when he did not love her. Despite the temptation to keep her veil, Theodora removed it. Better to amuse Hugh with the sight of her heated face than evince shyness.

On the glass's opposite side, a young man sat on a bed while a woman wearing a gentleman's lounge suit and bowler hat disrobed before him. She undulated as she unbuttoned her jacket. Waistcoat, bow tie, trousers, she discarded slowly, seductively. She smiled in Hugh and Theodora's direction as though she knew she'd an audience, and it pleased her. When she was clad only in her bowler, she arched her breasts toward the young man.

From a drawer in a bedside cupboard, she withdrew a phallus. Unlike the veined marble piece Hugh had gifted Thea, this one was fashioned of brown leather. The woman caressed the man's face with it, so that he flushed. Then, with a languid motion, she pointed the toes of her right foot and placed them between his thighs. Her knee thus lifted, she pushed the phallus into her exposed, pink pussy, and delicately moved it back and forth.

Liquid heat flooded Thea's own pussy. She was conscious of its emptiness, and she craved her own leather phallus with which to fill it. Dismayed at her longing, she turned to Hugh. His breathing had been audible in her ear, but his face was composed.

"Lovely as she is, she isn't what I brought you here to see."

They moved down the dim corridor and approached another window. In the room beyond, two men lay nude in a bed on their sides, each facing the other's cock. As Thea watched, one put his mouth to his fellow's organ, and the other, his face twisting, followed suit. It had never occurred to Theodora that such an act was possible, and yet, there was a strange, stark beauty to the men and to the service they performed for each other with such concentration. They seemed to have something she hadn't until this moment known to long for. The freedom each granted the other, their equality, and their complete acceptance of one another's passion brought an unexpected ache to her heart.

"Stimulating, but that isn't what I wanted to show you, either," Hugh said.

He had to pull her from the sight and guide her before a third window. "Ah, here he is." And Thea was shocked to see Martin. "I learned he was a customer here," Hugh whispered in her ear. Martin lay naked, blindfolded, and bound with scarves to the posts of his bed. "Blindness can sensitize one, and helplessness frees one of inhibitions," Hugh said. "Perhaps I'll show you."

Or perhaps, Thea thought, emboldened by all she had seen, *I will show you.* The notion of binding and blindfolding Hugh curled her toes and stiffened her nipples.

"Watch now," said Hugh. A woman sat on a chair alongside Martin's waist. She slipped a wide strip of leather with laces sewn to its ends around the base of Martin's cock, then laced it tightly, so that the organ appeared to engorge further. Next she applied ointment from a small jar to his cock, and Martin groaned helplessly. Finally she took his cock in her hand, and began to milk it. Martin's face reddened, and just as Thea thought he would spend his seed, the woman ceased her squeezing and lightly licked his cock.

"Please," Martin called out, but the woman ignored his supplications.

"Does this satisfy you?" Hugh breathed into her ear.

Only three months before, Martin had broken her heart. He'd taken the virginity she'd foolishly offered him, and then, when she'd tested him at her father's urging, telling him she would be disinherited if they married, he'd revealed he thought her worthless without her fortune. *I wish you luck in finding a man who would take you now,* he'd said. And Hugh had come along and offered for her, like a prince from a fairy tale, and her father had insisted she marry him.

Hugh and she had this much in common: both had longed for a pound of Martin's flesh. She could never get all Martin owed her, but for boasting to Hugh that he'd slept with her, this was a perfect retribution. Martin would be mortified if he knew she watched him bound and tormented by a prostitute; it was as much a violation of his privacy as the one he'd perpetrated on hers.

She turned to Hugh. Martin had hurt her, and Hugh had comprehended her need to balance the scales better than she had herself.

But Hugh had also brought her pain, had tormented her with plea-sure. How to balance the scales with *him*?

"No," she whispered back, "I'm not satisfied."

One last look at Martin, his cock now being lightly grazed by the woman's teeth, and she closed the mirrored window's curtains.

A mahogany settee stood against the corridor's other wall, and Theodora pushed Hugh's chest so that he stumbled back toward its plush beige seat. Then she was on him, skirt and petticoat lifted, garters unfastened from corset and corset hem raised, straddling him as she had on their wedding night. She unbuttoned his trousers and pulled his swollen cock from his underlinens. Taking the moist, hot flesh in her right hand, she milked it as she'd seen the prostitute do. With her left hand, she teased the soft spheres that dangled below. Hugh gasped and struggled to keep his groans low, lest someone overhear them, but she would not allow him the dignity of silence. Her milking strokes grew more determined. "God in heaven," Hugh said, unbuttoned the flap of her knickers, and pulled it forward and up. She nipped his ear, and lifted herself onto his engorged cock. "Christ," he swore while she rode him. She did not slow till pleasure made his face go slack.

THE Silver Ghost embraced the road. To Thea's left, trees blazing with autumn's fire appeared to rush backward, bestowing the occa-sional leaf on the occasional passerby. Only a few gray clouds drifted in an uncommonly blue sky. Ahead, the country lane stretched like a ribbon of possibilities.

It was a splendid day for riding in an open motorcar. Still, Thea was conscious of a churning at her center. She watched her husband's sure hands on the steering wheel.

Last night, after they'd returned from the brothel to his London house, he had not sought her bed. She had lain alone, tossing and turning for want of him, tears of frustration forming in her eyes.

Behind his driving goggles, Hugh's gray eyes now focused on the road back to his Berkshire manor. Why had he not come to her? She knew her fierceness at the brothel had aroused him. Had he deprived her to regain the upper hand?

"Tell me, Thea," he said, still looking ahead, "did you miss me last night? Was there an emptiness between your thighs? Did you touch yourself and think of me?"

The bastard. Let him stew while waiting for an answer.

"Lift your skirts," he added, not once glancing at her. "Unfasten your garters. I'll touch you now."

Shawls and rugs protected her from wind and dust; so did her hat and her veil. The road ahead was empty now, straight and flat enough that Hugh's left palm would not be at the gearbox often. It could handle her heated pussy instead, beneath the rug on her lap.

But she could also refuse. *You must tell me if at any point you want me to stop,* he'd said on their wedding night, but his hands, his tongue, his cock, and his diabolical phallus had taken her past the point of saying any such thing. Even when he'd struck out with his cruel words, the pain had not been enough to jolt her into crying *Stop.* She'd been too hot and confused, and she suspected he'd intended that.

"Come, Thea," he said now. "Let me satisfy you."

It was the hoarse edge in his voice, as much as the words, that burned her to her toes and sent her trembling hands beneath the rug. She lifted and unclipped and unbuttoned her clothes, until she felt the motorcar's leather seat kissing her moist flesh.

At first his long fingers brushed the valleys at the very top of her thighs, and his hand cupped her pubis. His touch was delicate, teasing, and it required all her will not to shift forward and press herself against it.

Slowly, slowly, he dipped a finger into her. She shifted back on her bottom to give him greater access, but he prolonged his penetration.

"Such a sweet, welcoming pussy," he said, still gazing ahead, damn him. "Always wet and ready for me." He slipped a second finger in and began massaging the walls of her pussy. By the time he removed his fingers, Thea's thighs were quaking. He brushed them with his left hand.

"Not yet, love," he told her. "It will be more potent if I draw it out."

She struggled to take deep breaths, teetering on the edge of climax. Desire was a painful, sharp sensation.

A distant carriage appeared in the lane opposite. Hugh trailed his fingers up again. One entered the opening of her bottom, while his thumb circled her clitoris, a hairsbreadth from touching it. Just as the Whitechapel cart approached them to the right, he gave her clitoris the contact that it burned for.

While Hugh nodded politely to the carriage-driving farmer, the climax rocked through her like an enormous tremor from beneath the earth. She had to bite her lip to keep from screaming, and pray the other man would not look past the windscreen and her veil.

She was still cresting on aftershocks when the carriage was long past and Hugh finally looked at her, smiling like a cat who had swallowed the cream and lapped up the butter. Then his eyes returned to the road.

"Look at me," she said.

He spared her another glance. "Would you like me to crash this motor?"

Yes, she thought as she restored her clothes to order. *That would be a sign of feeling.* "How did you know?" she asked instead.

"Know what?"

"That I . . . thought of you and touched myself last night."

He took a long moment to answer her. "Because," he said, "I thought of you then too, when I grasped and stroked my cock."

What a delicious admission. But she was still confounded by his having stayed away. Like a mountain climber unable to find another foothold, her mind swung to the night she tried never to think of. The bitter cold of the boat deck, the din of steam from the boilers roaring through pipes. And Cyril Darrow urging her to get in the lifeboat.

"Tell me about your cousin," she said. "If he is the reason that you married me then I deserve to understand."

For a moment she thought he would refuse. "It's difficult," he finally said. "To explain regarding Cyril I must begin with myself."

She waited.

"My mother was a lady," he said. "You must know of the scandal. In eighty-four, when she was just eighteen, she ran off with her father's footman. Jack Carter, my father, was that man. He found other work as a costermonger, but took a bad chill and died two years later.

"It's one thing for a lady to marry a wealthy man of common birth." He cast an ironic glance at Thea, who had done just that in marrying him. "But another to stoop to one's footman. My mother and I were left alone, hungry, struggling to survive. She pleaded with her relatives to take us in, but they refused. Finally Cyril's mother, a distant cousin to whom my mother had been close, implored her husband to shelter us. He was a haughty man, Cyril's father. He never let any of us forget his generosity.

"I know how ruddy sentimental it sounds, but Cyril's kindnesses were the few bright spots in my life. When he was about, he didn't allow his brothers, or . . . anyone else to abuse me."

"The servants," Thea said gently. "They must have resented you."

"Oh, yes. They hated deferring to their so-called betters, but to a footman's son?" He clenched his jaw. "There was resentment, and worse."

Thea's heart ached for Hugh, and yet . . . If he could confide this much, show her this sort of trust . . .

I could fall in love with this man.

She took his left hand, and slowly, it tightened about hers.

"After my mother died of consumption when I was five, Cyril was the only family left to me. He insisted that I be educated with him, and much later, lent me the first capital I invested. Of course, I reimbursed him in full, but even so, I owe him more than I could repay. He loved you passionately, you know. He wrote me that you had eyes only for Wilkes."

What an oblivious girl she had been—a sleeping princess waiting to be kissed to life, little realizing how much life could hurt. Infatuated enough with Martin that at his suggestion, she'd cajoled her aunt into a trip to New York, where Martin had business dealings, so that she could remain in his company. Thank God, Aunt Lucia had survived *Titanic*. Theodora hadn't lost a loved one.

Hugh had not been so fortunate.

"I'm sorry," she said.

He seemed not to hear. "I don't think Cyril would approve of all I've done to you."

"How do you mean?"

"I don't entirely begrudge Wilkes his desire to survive, but that he should have you and your fortune after he attempted to bilk Cyril of his— Oh, yes, Cyril learned Wilkes was skimming from their joint shipping venture. But he put off confronting Wilkes because Wilkes was his sole connection to you. I believe he was trying to find the courage to tell you of his love and of Wilkes' dealings, when that iceberg converged on your ship.

"In any case, since Cyril never had the opportunity to do so, I set out to foil Wilkes' plans myself. I told your father of the thieving, and suggested he tell you to pretend to Wilkes that you were being cut off from your fortune. But even after Wilkes broke off with you, I wasn't certain you would not reveal that it had been a lie. Wilkes boasted to me that you had slept with him, and I feared that might make you feel obliged to marry the sod. And so I courted both you

and your father. I sometimes use every means available to me. But
then, you know that intimately by now."

Why did those words arouse her? Because despite the pain he
had inflicted, she had been pleasured, too, by the punishment he'd
meted out?

As always, he seemed to sense the tenor of her thoughts. "Perhaps
I should have been gentler on our wedding night," he said. "But I
was angry, Thea. No, not because you were not a virgin. I'm hardly
one myself, now am I? But it seared me to know it had been Wilkes.
And if you thought your having taken a lover worth confessing, you
should have told me prior to the wedding vows."

What could she say to that? She would only look worse for defend-
ing herself, even with her father's ill health.

"What do you want from me, Hugh?"

A rueful laugh escaped him. "Beside the obvious? I want you to
acknowledge what *you* want. Christ, Thea, you've lived through
something fifteen hundred people did not survive. And Cyril died
so that you could. Throw caution to all four winds, grasp life about
the neck. Live with abandon. Not many people get a second chance."

BUT at the house, a message from her father's butler waited. "No,"
Theodora said when she rang him back and heard the news.

Hugh paled when she told him. "Let's hurry," he said. "I'll drive
you there."

This time there was no blunt conversation, no confident fingers
exploring her. Hugh's mouth was grimly closed, his strong hands
both on the steering wheel. The Silver Ghost rushed through the
afternoon at topmost speeds while Thea pleaded with God not to
take her father's life.

They reached her father's home at sunset. "A mild attack," the
physician said. "Your father's heart will recover with rest."

That night, Thea ached for Hugh. *Grasp life about the neck*. Easy to say, when one was not a woman. *Titanic* flashed through her mind: her bows and her bridge submerging as Thea watched from the lifeboat, then the lights from the portholes dying at once. It had seemed irrelevant, after that, to wait for marriage to be with the man she'd believed she loved. And so she'd gone to Martin's room, at a house party one night three months past.

She didn't trust her judgment. But sometimes, she thought now, one had to take a risk, even when one was afraid—or had begun to love a complicated man. She crossed the cold corridor between her room and the one her father's housekeeper had given Hugh, and knocked on her husband's door.

He opened it. "I was on my way to you," he said.

"Why?"

"Come inside," he said. And when she had, "Your father's heart was the reason you did not tell me sooner?"

"Yes," she whispered. "I'm terribly afraid to lose him."

"You've seen so much death. And I've refused to think of what that does. I've been such a rotter."

"Really, it hasn't been so bad." She blushed, and at that, a slight smile passed across his face, like moonlight peeking from beneath a cloud.

"Cyril always was nobler than most; that never was your fault. I would have seen that sooner if I hadn't been full of angry grief. And as for Wilkes—everyone makes mistakes. *I've* been a sodding bastard."

She put her hand on his lips, hushing him. "Hugh," she said. "Be with me."

"Always."

Their nightclothes seemed to divest themselves. Naked, she lay on her side, turned toward him. "I'm falling in love with you," he told her, and she shivered with joy. He seemed to know just what she wanted, for he lay beside her with his head near her thighs and said, "Lift your knee." Ah, he put his mouth to her, and did, with utmost gentleness, what he had said he would not do on their wedding night: he licked her clitoris.

Pleasure curled through Thea, irrepressible, undeniable, like a wave lapping the seashore, cresting higher and higher in the pull of the moon. She took Hugh's cock in her mouth, as she had seen the two men she'd envied do, and felt the same freedom, the same equality, the same complete acceptance.

Hugh's seed spurted in her mouth just as that wave broke over her, splintering into sparks of sensation so intense that they were nearly painful.

Pleasure and pain, she thought later as she lay in Hugh's arms. Pleasure and pain were how one knew one was alive.

"Mind you," he murmured, "I'd still like to fuck your delightful arse from time to time."

"Darling," she laughed. "I wouldn't have it any other way."

Lily Daniels was born in Israel and came to the United States with her family at the age of eleven. Two years later she read her first romance, thus embarking on a decades-long love affair with the genre. She is currently working on a novel-length historical romance, and contributes book reviews to Dear Author under the name Janine Ballard. You can find her online at dearauthor.com and lilydaniels.com.

SILVERHOUSE

SARABETH SCOTT

She was a symmetry of curves and arches. The curve of her neck echoed the curve of her hip. The bustle of her gown followed the same line as the lace at her neck. Her hair was up, intricately braided and immaculately confined around her head in a coronet the color of chestnuts. He knew her uncoiled hair would reach beyond the small of her back. So much weight to carry, wound around her head. There must be dozens of pins holding those coils in place.

He pushed her shoulders down until she sat, regal and proud, on the low stool in front of him. There was no padding, just smooth walnut beneath her. He wasn't gentle, but her graceful balance was not offset in the least. A small push was not enough to upset her.

He began to pull the pins from her hair. His hands were brisk, moving quickly, not so much that he pulled her hair painfully, but enough that her braid unwound and slid in a languid curl down her back. The scent of soap, of her perfume, of sugared candies and beeswax in the parlor, of holly and pine in the drawing room, drifted up from her hair. All the scents he associated with her, her location in his life, combined in one moment and he was torn between breathing deeply, and not breathing at all.

The fire beside them cast enough of a glow to warm them and the rug beneath them, but the rest of his chamber was hidden behind flickering shadows, no light penetrating the darkness. Only the gleam of tiny black polished boots reflected the fire from the far corner of the room.

Her hair shone gold and russet brown in the light. He reached down for the end of the braid and wound it around his hand, pulling back her head until she was pinned low against his abdomen. She would feel his cock like an extension of her corset, pressing her spine and neck in a straight line.

She pushed back against it, against him. He pulled harder on the braid coiled in his fist out of instinctive shock, but kept the tension after a moment's thought.

"You'll pay for that," he whispered.

She said nothing. The temptation in the press of her spine was agony—he'd never thought a woman's back would be so dangerous.

"What shall the response be, Clara? All those little insults today. You've returned my gift. You've caused me pain."

He punctuated his sentence with a press of his hips against her neck and another tug on her hair. He heard and felt her low gasp. "Have you not pushed me enough, Clara?"

She said nothing. She rolled her shoulders against his erection, and the soft pressure spread like fire through his cock, across his hips, and around his back like an embrace. The press of his body against that soft curve of her neck was arousing, and he pushed against her, making sure she felt the length and hardness.

Then a pin pierced the placket of his trousers and stung him.

He jerked away, and without the support, she nearly fell backward.

"Oh, my Lord, I am so sorry," she cried, reaching up with her hands that had been folded in her lap. Her fingers dove beneath the collar of her dress and removed a single straight pin from the lace that lined the edge.

"A pin? You stabbed me with a pin?" His voice was quiet and even, not even the slightest bit incredulous.

"No, sir." Clara kept her eyes downcast. "It is to keep my posture straight."

He believed her. "I don't believe you."

He lifted the length of braid still partly looped in his fist and saw the tiny red welts on her nape, the remnants of one ill-timed slouch or another.

"You punish yourself," he said. He leaned down and ran a fingertip, then his lips, over each tiny scratch. Then his teeth.

"Yes, sir," she replied.

"You have wounded me by wounding yourself. These pinpricks are unnecessary."

She nodded, barely moving as his lips moved over her skin.

His eyes narrowed as a thought occurred to him. "They are also far too small to adequately punish you."

He lifted his head from her neck and looked down at her for a moment. He released his grip on her hair and moved to stand in front of her. He undid his trousers with one hand and cupped her face with another. The placket of his trousers fell and he lifted his rigid cock forward toward her mouth.

"Come. You will soothe the pain."

Her lips parted on a gasp, and he slid his cock between them, guiding it into her mouth, feeding her. His engorged cock slid past her lips an inch at a time.

"That's right. Gently. Lick it." He kept one hand at the base of his cock and one hand on her cheek, his fingers, long and powerful, reaching toward the back of her neck, guiding her movements.

"Suckle it. Just like that." He didn't let her move her head while he fed her his cock. He used his hips to slide it against her tongue. He felt her moan against his balls as he slowly thrust toward her.

"Such pain you caused me. Suck my cock, deep into your mouth. Good girl."

He could barely keep from moaning aloud at the sight of her lips around his flesh. Her hands were fisted in her skirts, tight in her lap as she'd been instructed to keep them, and her fingers flexed as he fed her mouthful after sliding mouthful of his cock. He watched his flesh emerge shimmering and wet from between her lips as he slid forward and back, slowly pushing all the way into her, feeling her throat on the head of his cock, then pulling nearly all the way out.

Her lips pursed around the head, just at the flare of his crown, trying to hold him inside her. She looked up at him. He pulled himself from her mouth roughly, the edge of her teeth skirting the flesh at the head of his cock. She didn't look away from him, or reach for him with her hands. Clara paused with her mouth open, waiting for more of him.

"Better," he said. He tucked his cock away and rebuttoned his trousers and she followed his movements with an interested gaze, as if she were watching a play she'd never seen before. He knew she could see the ridge betraying his arousal, awkwardly defined against the fabric. He raised a brow at her when her eyes met his, and she lowered her gaze to the floor.

"Stand," he said. He did not offer his hand to assist her, yet she rose in graceful movement until she stood straight before him. Her lips were red. And moist.

"Unbutton your dress." Her hands flew to the line of buttons down the front of her gown, and in moments it lay in a crumpled heap on the floor.

"Remove your stockings." She perched on the edge of the stool, and slid the silk from her legs. The stockings landed in wanton curls atop her gown.

"Turn." He unlaced her corset using only the tips of his fingers so the sides of the tightly wrapped structure released themselves only a fraction at a time. He could see the flying pulse in her neck but her breathing remained calm and slow, deliberately confined and controlled. He wanted her to pant and gasp for him. Soon.

He unwound the strings holding her corset tight against her back, keeping the long laces coiled in his hand as he placed them on the bureau, ready for him should he need to relace her again later. While the stiff garment fell away to land on the floor, he looked at what it left behind, the creases of her shift in fierce, sharp points after being pressed beneath a corset for so many hours. He followed the red marks on the skin of her back with his gaze, then one finger.

"You had it laced more tightly than usual, didn't you?"

"Yes," she whispered.

"Again, unnecessary. And not enough."

He sat down on the stool, warm from her body and from the fire. "Kneel next to me. Face the bed. Now lie across my legs."

As she followed his orders, he watched the auburn firelight spread across the smooth curve of her back as she lay across him, her skin rippled with goose bumps from the cool air. Her long braid slid across her shoulder and fell to the floor, and he slowly gathered it back into one hand while he smoothed the fabric of her shift with the other, soothing her with long, firm strokes of his hand.

"You punish yourself for nothing, causing inadequate discomfort when what you crave is suitable recompense for your outlandish thoughts and inappropriate behavior. It is not enough what you do to yourself, is it?"

"No," she whispered, her voice nearly lost in the quiet.

"You know I am here, and yet you attempt to circumvent me. You are rude and invite my anger, and then try to punish yourself instead."

While he spoke, he continued to smooth the fabric of her shift upon her back, the fine, nearly translucent linen warming from the fire and from his hand. His hand stroked her neck, her back, down her spine, over her hips smoothing the linen over the curve of her bottom. His fingertips would linger a moment on the back of her thighs, then begin again at her neck and work its way down.

Despite his gentle stroking, she did not relax against him. He noticed her spine stayed as straight as ever, her posture even as she bent across his lap as refined as possible, though certainly no etiquette could have predicted her current circumstances and prescribed an appropriate response. Somehow, Clara found a measure of poise and elegance. It excited him.

"Do not move," he whispered.

Clara was a feast for his eyes, his hands, his thighs beneath her. He looked and stroked her until he noticed her posture begin to soften, her back begin to mold over him. He brought the end of her braid against her neck, painting her skin with the tips of her hair. With the other hand, he slowly lifted the edge of her shift so her backside was bared to him. She faced away from the fire, so the heat was strong and the light moved across her smooth skin, casting his hand in a dark, clawed shadow against her.

"Lift your head." He passed the end of her braid to his other hand, and swept the soft hairs across the top curves of her ass, dipping in to the valley between them. He did this again and again, moving with firmer strokes, and when the sharp points at the end of her braid touched her deep between the curves of her ass, she flinched. He dropped her braid.

The flat of his hand slapped her smooth round skin. The sound echoed as did the gasping moan that followed. He smacked her again, outlining in a whisper the slights against him.

"For greeting me rudely." A slap on one plump cheek.

"For smiling at everyone but me." Another.

"For lifting your nose at me, and don't think I didn't notice."

"Which time?" Her voice held a whisper of laughter.

"Both," he replied. Another slap fell across both cheeks, increasing the redness there.

He continued through each moment of the evening wherein she snubbed him, taunted him, rebuffed him, served him tiny portions of rudeness unseen by anyone but him. While to the room she was effortless perfection, to him she was a thorn, a gathering heat he couldn't soothe, increased with every tiny act of defiance. The space of four hours of dinner and evening entertainment was relived in moments, punctuated by slaps of flesh against flesh amid moaning gasps. Her backside was red and her legs began to spread open as he continued. When he spanked her for neglecting him after dessert, she tilted and lifted her hips and his hand froze.

"Wet for me, are you?" He reached down slowly. He touched the red skin of her backside, the heat between her cheeks, and slid his fingers farther to trail his fingers through her folds. "So open for me, so wet." He slid a finger into her and she moaned. He curved the finger inside her, stroking the inside of her through the abundant moisture. She moaned again, louder.

He spanked her again.

"Be silent."

He allowed her hips to remain tilted up, and moved his hand so that his next downward slap hit across her folds. He watched her bite her lips. Her back was a shuddering arch made of the gasps and moans kept locked in, and her arms were shaking as she held on to his leg.

He brought his fingers back to her wet, open folds and stroked her. She bit back a noise, trembling more with her silent restraint.

His fingers were drenched, dripping as he teased her, dipping into her moist and slippery heat then trailing up over her flesh, drawing curls and trails on her skin. He idly circled over her backside, across the backs of her thighs, then down to the tight pucker of her ass. She shook.

"I cannot tell you how it felt to see my gift returned to me. I go to my rooms to dress for dinner and find it here, taunting me from my bureau, when minutes before it had been safely with you. When did you put it in my room?"

She didn't answer. His hand was moving slowly from her pussy to her ass, sliding cool moisture and wicked heat over her flesh and leaving her trembling in his wake.

"Are you sorry?"

"No," she whispered.

He slapped his hand down onto her ass, right over the skin that glistened in the firelight. He spanked her again.

"Are you sorry?"

"No." He spanked her a second, then a third time, making sure to strike her against her tightly closed entrance, watching a shudder begin there and spread across her body. Her hips tilted upward, her knees no longer on the soft rug beneath them as she reached for his touch as much as she could. He rewarded her eagerness by sliding his fingertips down into the curls not reached by the firelight, stroking three fingers deep into her clenching heat. He saw her throat constrict as she struggled to stay silent.

"Will you do it again?"

"Yes," she replied.

With a growl, he removed his hand and pushed a finger deep into her ass. She bit his thigh, her fingers gripping his skin as she pressed her upper body downward and her hips up toward his fingers. He removed his finger, pulled his hand again through her moistened skin, then plunged two fingers back into her tightened hole.

She threw her head back, panting, her mouth open. Her eyes were closed, and her face was flushed. The only noises in the room were her low gasps and the slight wet sounds of his fingers pushing into her again and again. He watched her face, glancing at the impossible sight of his fingers sinking deep into her ass, her legs spread and her hips reaching for more.

"You are a very naughty girl," he whispered. She didn't make any sound or gesture of agreement nor argument.

"Clara," he said, continuing to pump his fingers in and out, slowly and deeply, feeling the clenching shudder of pleasure inside her. "I have my hand on your backside. My fingers are up your ass." She didn't make a sound in reply.

He slid his fingers out, slapped her trembling flesh, then plunged his fingers back into her.

"Only I know how naughty you are, what you crave," he whispered. She nodded. "No one suspects you, no one sees what you are, what you need. Only I know."

Keeping his fingers curved into her ass, he spread his bent legs wide so she was positioned across only one of his thighs.

"Unbutton my trousers," he said. "Take out my cock." She obeyed.

"Suck me again." She reached for the hard length jutting from his rumpled trousers, and latched on with her mouth, pulling him deep.

"Nice and wet. That's right, make me drip." He pumped his fingers into her ass, then removed them and spanked her. It made her mouth water.

She feasted on him, pulling the flesh of his cock into her mouth, sliding her tongue on the sides and beneath it. He felt her cup his balls through the fabric, and told her to release them from confinement. As she sucked him, painting him a glistening wet gold in the light from the fire, he continued to dip his fingers into her ass, speeding up when she did, slowing down with her movements as well. He wondered if she noticed she was controlling his movements. She grew more and more drenched the more she sucked him, the more he pumped her.

He asked her again, "Will you do it again, return my gifts to me?"

She lifted her head from his cock and licked her lips, swollen and wet. He nearly came.

"Yes," she said, and smiled knowingly.

With a roar, he stood, lifting her up and pushing her to the foot of the bed. He bent her body over the edge of the bed, ass in the air and legs hanging off the tall mattress, one hand pushing her shoulders down so her head was resting in the thick duvet. She was panting, shaking—and smiling.

He shed his trousers, his coat, and his waistcoat and drawers in moments, leaving his shirt on as he then stepped closer to her and pressed a hand against the reddened curve of her ass. She moaned as he massaged and molded her hips and backside with his hand.

"Only I know what a naughty girl you are. How rude, how daring, how badly behaved you can be." She nodded and tried to press back against his cock, but he held his body away from hers and she couldn't get enough leverage to move more than a few inches forward or back. Her legs didn't quite reach the floor, while his strong body, with years more experience and muscle than hers, was more than enough to keep her pinned to the bed with just one hand.

"You like to be rude to me, don't you?" She nodded. "You know I'll punish you perfectly." She nodded again.

"I may allow you to punish yourself, Clara."

He moved behind her, holding his cock, still dripping wet from her mouth, and slid his erection through the folds of her pussy, covering himself in the moisture that coated her. Then he stood back and pressed the tip of his cock against the tight opening to her ass, lifting the hand that held her down while stroking the tight puckered hole with the tip of his cock.

"Show me what a naughty girl you are, Clara."

She slid back onto him without hesitation.

If he had thought watching her mouth swallow his cock was impossible to bear, seeing her ass slowly, firmly, slide onto his cock nearly made him come in seconds. Her tight skin stretched and he watched the length of him disappear, deep into her ass as she mounted him.

When the red, tender flesh met the skin of his hips, she pressed back for a moment, her knees flexed, trying to find purchase with which to move away and back again. He was fully seated in her, and for a fraction of a second, he closed his eyes and let joyous amazement and wonder wash through him again.

Then he planted his legs firmly and pushed her against the bed, pinning her. She squirmed and moaned, but he held her hips firm in his hands. Her arms reached, her hands grabbing his wrists, tugging, trying to get him to move, to thrust, but he held her still, pinning her against the mattress with his cock deep in her ass.

"You want more?"

She nodded.

"You are shaking, you want more so badly," he said. He pulled one hand from her grasp, but before she could move her arm and allow herself to thrust back against him, he ran one fingertip over the stretched and taut skin that surrounded his cock. She turned her head and screamed into the duvet.

"I am in your ass so deep, Clara, up to my balls in your backside, and you want more?"

She nodded, her face turned into the coverlet, her body shaking and gasping as one finger traced a delicate line back and forth across the tiny ridge of straining flesh that held him inside her body.

"You like having my cock in your ass?"

She didn't answer except to fist the coverlet in her hands and twist.

He spanked her again, hard, this time low on her thigh near where his own pressed against her, then again higher, on her ass. She screamed.

"There is a cock up your ass. My cock." He flexed his muscles, making her feel the jutting movement inside her. She moaned and he slapped her flesh again.

"The next time you dance with me, you'll feel my cock. The next time you snub me, raise your nose, or even turn your back, you'll think of me. You'll remember me right here." He flexed again, knowing she felt the subtle thrust, knowing she wanted more.

She shook her head. He pushed deeper, angling his hips down-ward, knowing it would burn and sizzle through her. He was rewarded with a gasp and a low moan, and a deep tremble of her legs.

"Yet you are not answering me." He stepped back, nearly pulling free, and she scrambled to push back onto him as soon as she had room to do so. He held her hips down, his cock half into her, stretch-ing her as he moved with minute thrusts of his hips, in and out, a fraction of an inch. She cried out, nonsensical sounds as she tried to reach for him, to fill herself with him.

"Tell me, Clara. Tell me what you want."

"Please," she whispered. He looked at her, leaned forward to blow a gentle puff of hair onto her back. She flinched and stretched her arms up, trying to reach anything that would perhaps give her lever-age against his hands holding her still, to allow her to push herself back onto him.

Her lips opened but she didn't speak. He wondered when the agony of unfulfillment would kill him.

He caressed her gently, reaching around his cock, still half-buried inside her, sliding his fingers just barely through the folds of her pussy, now drenched and hot. "Please what?"

He reached a finger, then two, and slid them down toward her clit, swollen and now covered with moisture. "Say it, Clara. Tell me what you want."

She lifted her head and looked over her shoulder at him. In her beautiful, low clear voice, she replied, "Put your cock completely back in my ass and fuck me there. Fuck me until you scream, Christoph."

Her use of his name nearly brought him to his knees.

"Please, I want you, deep, hard, and fast. Now."

At that, he did fall to his knees. He pulled his cock out of her, and buried his face in her. Spreading her wide with his hands, he bit and sucked at her flesh, her folds, the deep, wet tunnel of her pussy, her clit, using his tongue and teeth. She moaned his name, urging him on, pressing back onto his face. Then he stood abruptly and plunged his cock deep into her ass.

Christoph lifted Clara's upper body upward with his arms until her back rested against his chest. Her knees were bent just over the edge of the bed and her body curved back against him, the pale smoothness of her skin meeting the dark coarseness of his chest hair. He gripped her hips to keep her still and watched her breasts bounce as he thrust deep into her.

"Yes, oh, yes, Christoph." Her pleas were strained and soft, as if she tried to keep herself from screaming.

"Say it, Clara."

"I like it. I want your cock in my ass," she whispered between moans. His thrusts deepened and the length of his cock tunneled into her in time with her gasps.

"No, not that," he said. He bit gently on her shoulder, then licked the spot where his teeth had met her flesh.

"Harder, Christoph," she said. He obliged. He slid one hand slowly over her hip, across the sensitive flesh of her pelvis, taut with the position he held her in.

"Say it, Clara." His fingers almost reached her clit, where he knew she was aching and hot. "Say it."

"I won't do it again," she said.

"Good."

He pressed a finger, then two, against her and slid upward, then down, in time with the deeper, faster thrusts. She screamed, and finally, finally came, the clenching rhythm of her orgasm an ecstasy he'd never experienced. Her body tightened on his cock, and she fell forward onto her hands, pulling her knees onto the bed and pumping herself back onto his cock faster and faster through her orgasm.

He threw his head back and yelled her name, filling her with his own hot release as he cried out, "Clara!"

His knees had folded beneath him, but before he hit the floor, he crawled onto the bed alongside Clara. She'd curled up on her side, with her hand on her chest. He pulled her into the circle of his arms and felt her heart and breath racing one another, matching his own. Their bodies were still, but inside they were flying at unnatural speeds. He didn't think his heart would ever slow down.

On the bureau next to the bed, the painted wood eyes and teeth of his gift gleamed. It stood at attention, stiff and somewhat fierce, ready to crack nutshells in its jaw and find its way to Clara. Two years prior, he had given it to her in front of everyone. Later, when she'd broken it accidentally, he'd seen her remorse as a living, growing thing burning her from the inside, the rage and sorrow barely contained in her perfect exterior as her parents scolded her mildly and dismissed her. He'd known.

She'd been too old and too young and he'd hated himself for the year afterward, but when she found her way to his rooms late that night, hair unbound, womanly curves barely concealed by her robe, looking for her broken gift, he'd known what she needed. He'd gently managed her attempt at seduction, explained her punishment, spanked her until she came, kissed her and held her through her tears of relief and whispered confessions that she'd thought something was wrong with her. He had whispered through the night that she was pure and perfect as she was. He knew her. He understood. There was nothing wrong with her.

She'd been truly his since then, more than merely his intended bride, though she'd been that since her birth.

The following year, he gave her the repaired wooden doll, again, in front of everyone, and watched the blush on her neck stain her pale skin for hours. It was then she began to taunt him, to break those slender rules of conduct secretly, quietly, beneath the notice of everyone. He was both proud and enraged by her courage.

But she didn't visit him that year. He'd had to seek her out, and

explain what she was to do to herself in detail until he relieved her
of her punishment an hour before he left. Her deep moan of relief at
his removing the slightly bent pin from her neckline and the other
scattered punishments he had devised had nearly brought him to
orgasm in his trousers.

This year, she challenged him again, this time taking the doll he
had placed in her room, and returning it to his within the same hour.
He still didn't know how she'd managed it.

When the sun rose, he would pack up her wooden soldier, returning it to its carrying case inside his lone traveling trunk. It would
stay there, safe and wrapped until next year, when he would return
with his gift, this time to marry Clara.

He reached onto the bedside table where he'd left her second present, the one she didn't know about. He lifted her hand from his chest,
her arm limp, and laced his fingers through hers. Her fingers were
pale, flawless and smooth, while his were roughened with years and
lined by use, but they fit and held perfectly. He opened his mouth.

"Yes, I will marry you," she whispered. His mouth shut with a
click. She laughed.

"How did you know I would ask?"

"I knew," she replied.

"You are mine. You have always been mine, promised to me."

"I know."

"Then how did you know I would ask?"

"You always like it better when it's my idea."

He smiled into the darkness that had snuck into the room as the
fire burnt itself down.

"Will you marry me, Christoph?"

"Yes. Yes, I will."

Sarabeth Scott is a published author who writes romance fiction that is sometimes silly, sometimes serious, but always sensual. She adores stories rich in emotional conflict and forbidden attraction. Sarabeth lives in the northeastern United States with far too many pets, a dangerous predilection for red wine and dark chocolate, and an ever-increasing collection of blank notebooks.

BRUISED EGO

CHRISTINE D'ABO

The house wasn't what Lee had been expecting. He slipped the business card into his jacket pocket after confirming yet again that the numbers were the same. Jamming his helmet under his arm, he swung his leg over his BMW and cast a quick look around the neighborhood.

Rick had told him not to worry about a thing when he'd pressed the damp and crinkled card into his hand after the fight. But it was all the things his business partner *hadn't* said that still pissed Lee off.

He didn't need help, despite what Rick thought.

He *certainly* didn't need to see a therapist.

Lee had used the boxing ring as his stress reliever of choice for years. The lumps and bruises he bore beneath his shirt and tie helped calm him, gave him the presence of mind to do what he needed to keep his company on top.

So what if things had spiraled out of control recently. Lee's nightly rounds in the ring hurt no one but himself, and what he did in the privacy of his home afterward was his own business.

"Do this for me." Rick had squeezed Lee's shoulder. His thumb biting into the sore spot where Stu had landed a right cross. "I know Diana and I'm certain she can help you find what you've been looking for. It's better than letting yourself get beat to a pulp out there."

When Lee's cock had twitched to life as a rush of pain slid down his arm, he knew he couldn't handle this on his own any longer. It was wrong what he did alone in the dark after a fight with his fist on his cock and a hand pressing against his bruises.

He was wrong.

The card had disappeared quickly into Lee's pocket without further comment.

Now the crisp fall air chilled the sweat at his temples and along the back of his neck. His breath rose in a swirling cloud, to trail behind him as he strode across the concrete walkway to a worn and pitted backdoor.

Lee hesitated with one glove off and his hand balled into a fist at his side. Shifting his weight, the pulled muscle in his shoulder sent a pleasant ache down his lower back. He waited for the endorphin rush to work its magic on his brain. The fog of lust was better than the blush of embarrassment he endured every time he bumped into a bruise or jammed a finger. The best defense, in Lee's opinion, was denial.

Fuck it.

He cringed at the force with which he knocked on the door. This woman hadn't done anything to him. Hell, she didn't even know who he was if her unimpressed tone on the phone was anything to go by.

Before Lee had a chance to knock a second time he heard the sound of approaching footsteps. Straightening, he waited for the snap of what sounded like several locks being unlatched, and then the door was pulled open.

Diana wasn't quite what he'd expected.

Deep auburn hair crowned her head, pulled up into something that at one time must have resembled a bun. Several strands had escaped to hang loose around her pale face. A tight T-shirt pulled across her breasts, showing off hard nipples unencumbered by a bra.

Diana cocked an eyebrow at him as she braced her hand on her hip and gave him a good once-over.

"You're late." Her voice was deep for such a petite woman.

Lee shrugged. "I was held up."

Dina snorted. "You're also a terrible liar. Come in. Put your helmet on the table and your boots by the door."

Lee's gaze landed on the sway of her denim-encased hips as she walked through the small kitchen, tossing the tea towel she'd been holding into the sink before crossing into the living room.

His helmet and gloves took up most of her tabletop. He kicked off his boots and shrugged off his leather jacket, feeling nearly naked without its comforting weight. But wasn't that what therapy was about?

"I was expecting an office. Or a home office at least," he called out. The floor was cold on his socked feet after being trapped in the hot boots. "Would it be better if we do this someplace else?"

"Not unless you're an exhibitionist."

Her soft laugh brought a smile to his lips. Diana had taken a spot in the middle of her comfortable-looking couch. The cushions seemed to rise up and cup her shapely ass. She wasn't the type of woman he'd normally be attracted to, but there was something about the way she held herself that he found appealing. Another twitch from his cock and Lee knew he'd have to be careful or else his therapy would take on a whole different angle.

"So, you're Rick's friend?"

"Business partner, actually. Thanks for agreeing to see me on such short notice." Looking around the room, he realized all the other chairs were covered with books and clothing. "Do you mind if I sit next to you here?"

"No."

"No problem. Any particular place—?"

"No, you don't have my permission to sit."

Lee snapped his head back around and stared at Diana. "What?"

Diana caught a piece of her hair and coiled it around her finger. "Did Rick explain who I am or what I do . . . specifically?"

"He said . . ." Lee frowned, suddenly wishing he hadn't left the business card in his jacket. "He told me you could help. I just assumed you were some sort of therapist."

"Not exactly."

The muscles in her forearms danced beneath her skin as she continued to twirl her hair. Lee couldn't help but wonder what those long fingers and strong hands would feel like pressing against the deep purple bruises on his chest and sides.

Grinding his teeth, he quickly counted down from ten in his head. "I think there has been some sort of mistake. I won't take up any more of your time."

He only got halfway to the kitchen when he heard her chuckle. "Well, you're clearly not a submissive."

That stopped him short. "What the fuck, lady?"

"I guess Rick is right to a certain degree. What I do could be considered therapy for some people, though I doubt you'll get many psychologists advertising my skill set."

Turning back, Lee took another step toward her. "You said submissive."

It was her turn to shrug. "I'm a professional dom."

Lee couldn't help but blink, looking at the woman closer than he had before. The person he saw lazing on the cushions didn't match the mental image of what he thought a dominatrix would be. No leather or chains. No tattoos or piercings—that he could see. Her well-worn jeans, soft cotton T-shirt, and fuzzy blue socks held the promise of comfort, not pain.

Diana's lips curled up into a small smile. "I'm off duty."

What the hell had Rick gotten him into? "So you hurt people and they pay you?"

"Yes."

"Do you fuck them?"

The crude question didn't seem to faze her. "I'm not a prostitute. What I do isn't about sex. The people who come here are looking for my help. For some it's to be tied up and hurt. For others it's to have their control taken away so they don't have to think. A sexual release isn't always the goal."

When she'd finished speaking, Lee found himself step closer once more. He stopped when he reached his original position, only a foot away from the couch.

Licking his suddenly dry lips, he forced himself to look into her eyes. "What *is* the goal?"

"I could tell you," she said, tucking the strand of hair she'd been teasing behind her ear. "However, it will make more sense if I show you."

Lee's heartbeat pounded in the hollow of his throat as the blood rushed through his body. "How?"

Diana shifted forward until she leaned with her elbows on her knees. "Take off your shirt. Drop it to the floor."

This was it. Diana had given him a choice and it was up to him to take the next step. There was nothing stopping him from walking out the door, getting back on his bike, and going out to a bar to pick a fight. Hell, he had some pretty choice bruising from last night. He could go home and get himself off at least twice before the exhaustion kicked in to drag him off to oblivion.

But if he stayed, there was a chance he could learn how to fix this *need* he had. There must be a way to make it better. *Anything* to get rid of this burning desire to hurt.

Lee's gaze locked on Diana as he grabbed the hem of his T-shirt and pulled it off. He needed to know if she could see the twisted darkness bleeding through the bruises coloring his skin.

When she didn't react for several long minutes, he began to feel uncomfortable. Exposed. It took effort not to fold his arms across his chest, to hide the evidence of last night's fight. He knew exactly what he looked like. Lee had gotten up before the alarm this morning and stood in the harsh light of the bathroom, pressing one fist into the largest of the bruises and jerking off while he watched in the mirror.

Twisted, sick, wrong.

"Beautiful," she said in a hushed voice.

Lee couldn't find his voice. She got to her feet and walked over to him. Having her so close, he realized the top of her head barely reached his chin. Not that she needed height to scrape her nails across the black and purple mark on his shoulder.

She didn't press, but her light caress sent a powerful shiver through his body. Diana continued her examination of him, mapping every blemish on the canvas of his skin with her gentle fingertips.

"Rick said you're a boxer? You do that for fun?"

"Yes."

"Do you win?"

"Sometimes."

"Do you lose on purpose?"

"Never."

"How about letting your opponent land a blow or two? Ever drop your guard a little?"

Lee shifted his weight from one foot to the other. "No."

The word had barely left his lips when she pressed the heel of her hand against a sensitive patch over his kidney. Lee moaned. His cock jerked in response to the unexpected assault. Gasping, he twisted around and glared at her. Diana didn't shrink away, instead lifting her eyebrow again.

"I said you were a terrible liar."

"How can you tell?"

She pressed once more against the spot and rose onto her toes until her mouth brushed his ear. "That wasn't a moan of pain."

Long fingers raked his stomach, pulling at the light dusting of hair trailing below his waistband. Sucking in a deep breath, Lee held it and watched Diana pull his belt open, leaving the ends to dangle at his waist.

"I thought you said this wasn't about sex?" Fuck, he sounded desperate even to his own ears.

"Not for me. Clearly it is for you. Before I can help you, I need to see exactly how far this goes, learn what it is you need, or think you need, from me."

Before she was done with her little speech, Diana had finished working open his pants. Somehow he stopped himself from jerking back when she pressed the tips of her nails down and gently clawed the tip of his cock.

"It arouses you. But is it the pain that's the turn on, or something else? I think we should find out."

Lee closed his eyes and tried to calm the storm raging inside him. "If you do discover what it is, can you make it go away? Make me stop wanting this?"

Diana paused in her exploration of his half-clothed body. He felt the cool touch of her fingers on his chin and opened his eyes to look down at her.

"Why do you want to stop?"

Lee stepped away, stumbling over his feet in an attempt to put as much space between them as possible. He didn't stop until the wall was at his back, and then he turned, leaning against the door frame. He pressed his forehead hard against the wood molding, willing the sudden panic to go away.

"Lee?"

He waved his hand, hoping Diana would understand. He needed

space. Just for a minute. Why would she think he wanted this? It was sick and twisted, miles away from normal. He *needed* normal and routine and control if he was going to survive. Rick and everyone else at the company needed his head in the game if they were going to get through the next nine months and avoid the takeover threat.

"Lee, come here." The steel in her voice made it clear that she expected him to follow the command unconditionally. Unlike before, he was under no compulsion to comply.

"You were right about one thing. I'm not a submissive." He rolled his head, peeking out from under the arm he had braced high. "I give too many commands to follow someone else's."

Diana frowned before nodding. "How about following a friendly suggestion then? Come back over here and get down on your knees. I'll just look and we can talk if that's what you want."

"I thought you said you weren't a therapist?"

"I do a pretty solid impersonation." She re-tucked her hair behind her ear and bit her bottom lip. "Please."

He couldn't help it. Between the bizarreness of the situation he found himself in and the uncertain pleading of the dominatrix, Lee started to laugh. The muscles in his stomach tightened and tears pooled in the corners of his eyes. "Christ, I'm losing it."

The sound of a clock ticking somewhere in the room helped him focus and regain a hold on his fragile control. Only when he knew he wasn't about to bolt, did he straighten and chose to return to his spot in the room. *Like a moth to a flame.* Without any further prompting from the tiny woman, he dropped to his knees and sat back on his heels.

"See, that wasn't so bad. Now, I want you to tell me what it is you do at your company." Diana set her hand lightly on his shoulder, the one with the worst bruise.

Lee found it suddenly difficult to breathe. It was an effort not to push up and into her hold. He wanted the bright sparks of pain worming through his tender muscles, and knew the pleasure her touch would bring.

"I'm the co-CEO. I look after our product innovation and engineering teams." Invisible hands squeezed his chest as the rising tension threatened to overwhelm him.

"How long have you been doing this? Being in charge?"

"Ten years."

"How long have you boxed?"

A slight pressure now as she pressed her thumb firmly against his skin. It wasn't much, but it helped him focus. "Rick introduced me to it three years ago. I go four or five times a week when I'm able."

"Tell me about it. What is it about boxing that you like?"

Lee curled his fingers into his palms, nails biting into the skin. He didn't know if he was trying to hold himself back from speaking the truth, or if he was angry that this woman had so easily pulled these thoughts from him.

"At first it was only for the exercise. I got an adrenaline high every time I stepped out into the ring and I got hooked fast. It didn't matter if I won or not. I got off on doing something physical rather than sitting behind my desk all day. I only needed to focus on the other guy and his weaknesses."

"I bet you got laid a lot." Diana moved her free hand, running her nails through his hair. "Bet you went out and fucked some fight groupie the first chance you had. Maybe even in the locker room or out in an alley. You had her screaming your name, came in her cunt, and walked away without another look. Didn't you?"

Memories of moaning and sweating, teeth nipping at soft breasts and the slide of his cock into wet pussies . . . he was rock hard in an instant. "Yes."

"When did it stop being enough, Lee?"

He groaned at the sound of his name coming from her in a husky whisper. It was the first time since the madness had begun that she'd said it. Needing to hear her say it again, he didn't hold back the impulse and pushed himself up into her touch. Instead of the feeling of increased pressure, Lee gasped when Diana took a step away.

"I asked you a question. I didn't give you permission to move and certainly didn't tell you to get your rocks off."

"Sorry," he whispered.

The slap to the back of his head was hard enough to send his chin jerking toward his chest. Everything stopped in that moment—the thoughts swirling in his brain, the tension in his chest, his pounding heart.

Lee let everything go.

Another gentle brush of her fingers along the top of his shoulder. "Answer the question."

"We've had some problems with the company. One of our major competitors is threatening us with a hostile takeover. It started about two years ago and we've been fighting them off ever since. The boxing was still there, but the sex . . . changed."

"How?"

A rush of embarrassment heated his face. His hands trembled. "I can't."

"I asked you how."

Lee shook his head. "I *can't.*"

"I'm not the one who thinks he has a problem." Diana sighed. "You can't expect me to help you when you're not willing to help yourself."

"It's just . . . wrong. I'm fucked up and broken and you can't understand what I'm going through. I should just get the hell out of here and forget everything."

He didn't move and Diana did nothing to stop him from following through on his threat. She shifted closer to him, dropping to her knees, close but not touching.

"You think it's wrong to get aroused when you feel pain?"

Lee snapped his head up to stare at her. "Isn't it? What the hell does that make me, some kind of masochist?"

"Not at all. It makes you a man who has lived on the edge for so long it's dulled your senses. When the rush from the perfect deal has become the norm and the pressure from your job is so intense you think your head will explode and your heart will pound its way through your chest, things get mixed up inside you."

Without warning, Diana pressed her fingers to his stomach and the vibrant purple mark that distorted the skin, while leaning in and licking a path up his neck. Lee's cock pulsed in his underwear, straining to poke through.

Diana eased up on his stomach. Her fingers drew concentric circles over the patch as she nipped at his earlobe. "When did you first realize about the pleasure you got from this?"

Lee could almost smell the stale locker room air as the memory of that night came to mind. "She was a groupie. I'd seen her around after the fights plenty of times, but she never approached me. I was pretty beat up after that particular match and it seemed to get her fired up."

Diana moved her hand up his chest to pinch his left nipple. "Bet the little slut was waiting for you when you got back to the locker room."

With his eyes closed, Lee tipped his head back and let the feelings of pleasure and pain mix together. For once he didn't try and fight his reactions, a sense of relief at Diana's unspoken permission to simply enjoy allowing him to relax.

"Lee, answer me."

"Yes, she was." He licked his lips. "She had on a short skirt and didn't bother with the panties. Any other night I would have fucked her and gotten us both off in ten minutes, but it had been a crap day. I lost the match, I hurt, and I'd been dealing with shit at work."

Without warning, Diana moved her hand down his body and thrust her fingers into his underwear. She squeezed his cock and used her other hand to press against one of the smaller bruises on his back. "So you weren't interested in sex?"

His chuckle morphed into another low groan. "I'm *always* interested in sex, but I just couldn't get off."

"I want you to pull your pants down," she said against the side of his neck. "I want to see your cock."

Thankfully, she helped work the fabric over his hip, pushing them halfway down his thighs. The air was cool on his overheated shaft and balls, but the relief of being free from the cloth prison was worth the chill.

"Look at you," Diana whispered as she ran a nail up from his balls to the tip of his cock. "What did the girl do when you couldn't get off? Bet she was pissed."

The curses still rang in his ears. "She punched me. I think she might have kicked me, too. I didn't even try to stop her. When she pushed me into the lockers and stormed out I just stood there and watched her go."

His cock twitched and Lee heard Diana's breath catch. "That's not everything."

"I didn't follow her because when she'd pushed me, I landed with my bruised back against one of the locker handles. I just about came when the pain raced through me."

Diana pulled away from him. Lee opened his eyes, trying to ignore the sudden disappointment at the loss of her touch, but was shocked at what he saw. Her breath came in uneven heaves, lifting her taut nipples, teasing him from beneath her shirt.

When she realized what he was looking at, she smirked. Very little color remained as her hazel irises were blown wide with lust. A light flush covered the pale skin neck and crept up toward her cheeks. At least she wasn't completely unaffected by him.

Diana licked her lip and nodded her head toward the floor. "Lie down on your back. Now."

"I thought you said this wasn't about sex?" Still, he moved quickly to follow her command.

"I thought you said you weren't submissive?"

Lee smiled as she adjusted her jeans, popping the button open and sliding the zipper down. "I'm open to negotiations."

"Good, so am I." Diana toed off the fuzzy blue socks. She dropped down and straddled his hips, trapping his cock between her T-shirt and his stomach. "Your back was against the locker and the bitch had left. What did you do next?"

Bracing her hands on his shoulders, she pressed her full weight against him, driving his upper body into the cold floor. Pain flooded him as the bruises on his back were simultaneously compressed. Lee cried out, bucked his hips and wished he was slamming into her body.

"Lee!"

"I grabbed my dick. *Fuck*. I grabbed it and I jerked off. I almost fucking blacked out when I came."

He thrust up, relishing the friction of cotton and her body against him. When he reached for her jeans, trying to pull them off her, Diana slid back. "No."

"Dammit."

"Not about sex," she reminded him.

"Like hell it isn't."

Lifting her hips from his body, Diana leaned forward and nipped once more at his earlobe. "It *isn't*. This is about needing to feel *alive*. You're drowning in shit on a daily basis. Your brain isn't listening to what your body has been trying to tell you, so it's *making* you pay attention."

"I'm broken."

"You're not. But things have gotten rewired on you and you don't like the new rules. You need to listen and accept it."

Lee grabbed Diana by the shoulders and yanked her close so he could see her face. Physically he was stronger than she was, but emotionally he saw that the woman was a rock. "How do you know all this?"

"My business is to understand pleasure. In all its forms. You think you're the only person to ever feel these things? Have you never watched a porn movie? Heard of a BDSM club? The only barriers are the ones that exist in your own head."

Lee swallowed, ignoring the way his pulse increased. "I don't want to be controlled like that."

"So it's not about control for you. It isn't for everyone. But you need to accept these changes in yourself before your world implodes." She reached out and cupped his cheek.

Lee leaned into her touch. "It sounds like you're speaking from experience."

"Let me show you how good it can be. If you just go with this, I promise you won't regret it."

God, he didn't want this. Yet, even as the denial crossed his mind, Lee knew he wouldn't say no. "Do it."

Diana lowered her hips once more so that the soft seam of her jeans was pressed low against his cock. The pressure was exquisite, but not enough to push him over the edge. Either because of her vast experience, or the look on his face, Diana seemed to know exactly what he needed.

Lowering her mouth to one of the smaller bruises on his chest, she sucked the skin hard, lathing it with her tongue at the same time as she ground her hips down. Lee pressed his palms flat on the floor and arched his back up, trying to increase the pressure. Pain spidered from that single point to fill Lee's chest with heat. His balls tightened. His cock strained to be free of the vice-like pressure, even as Lee realized he wouldn't last much longer.

Reaching up, he grabbed her hips and squeezed her small body.

Diana didn't let up on his chest, even as he forced her hips down hard once more. Together they used her denim-clad pussy to grind against his shaft, both moaning at the increased pressure exactly where they both needed it to be.

He wanted more. Though awkward, he shifted her forward so her clit would bump against the head of his shaft. Lee knew he hit the right spot when she moaned low in her throat.

Diana pulled her mouth away, to replace it with her thumb. "Fuck, yeah. You're so close now, aren't you? You're so hard against my cunt. I bet you feel the pressure building in your balls, like you're going to fly out of your skin."

Tears escaped Lee's eyes and rolled down the side of his face to pool behind his ears. "So close."

"I'm here to hold you down. Let it go, Lee."

He cried out once more as she leaned her weight against his shoulder and snapped her hips forward. Pain blossomed, grew, and changed into a blinding pleasure that set fire to ever cell in his body.

The damn broke and his orgasm exploded out of him. Grabbing her shoulders, he squeezed her hard as pulse after pulse of come coated the skin between their bodies and clung to the cotton of her shirt. Lee leaned up and bit down on her shoulder, sobbing from the overwhelming pleasure his body could barely process.

Diana continued to grind down, her moans increasing as he tightened his grip on her body. Lee had enough presence of mind left to realize what was happening. He curled his fingers making sure to dig his fingernails hard into the fleshy part of her biceps. Increasing the pressure of his bite, he continued to thrust up so she could rub off against him.

"Fuck, *yes*." She squeezed her eyes, threw back her head, and moaned loud and low. When she went limp in his hands, he eased her down and she lay across his chest.

They didn't speak for several minutes. For the first time in days, Lee's mind felt calm and his body relaxed. Even the aches and pains from the fight had receded into the background and he was more firmly settled in the here and now.

Reaching up, he caught a lock of her hair and wound it around his finger. "So. Not about sex?"

Her body shook as she chuckled. "Not normally."

"You seemed to enjoy that. At the end."

Diana lifted up and placed her chin on his chest. "Let's say I understand your dilemma."

"You get off on pain? I thought doms were more about dishing it out than taking it."

She shrugged. "I'm off duty."

Lee gave her hair a gentle tug. "Now what? Do I pay you?"

Diana bit just above his nipple. "I think it might be for the best if I don't see you as a client."

"Why the hell not?" He lifted up, bracing his weight on his forearms. "I thought you said you could help me?"

Diana waited a heartbeat before sliding off him to lay by his side. "I can."

"Then why not take me on as a client?"

She kept her gaze focused on a point somewhere on the ceiling. "How about we try going for coffee instead."

"Coffee?" *What the hell?*

"You said it yourself, you're not a sub. But I think you might be an interesting person to get to know."

"So what? Like a date? I just met you."

"Coffee." She smiled softly. "It's just coffee."

Lee took a deep breath and when he let it go he realized the sense of peace that had settled on him seemed rooted. Somehow in less than an hour this woman had ripped him apart, fortified the bits, and pieced him back together.

"I'm not a freak." The words were both confirming and reassuring. "Nope."

Reaching over, he cupped her cheek and turned her head to look at him. His thumb found her plump bottom lip and he gently tugged. "Coffee sounds good."

ON MY SKIN

DL GALACE

Marnie had always wanted a tattoo.

An orchid on her shoulder blade, maybe an *orobus* on the small of her back. She saw it on a brown-skinned girl at the beach last week while she was having lunch with her sister. Suzie had said it looked slutty, but Marnie thought it was beautiful. When she was in high school, she used to doodle designs on her notebook and show them to her friends, bragging that she was just saving up the money then she was so going to do it. But she never did. Not in college, not while she was married to Eric . . .

And now, here she was, standing in front of a tattoo parlor on a night as cold as a meat locker, wearing a pair of sweats she hadn't taken off in three days and a bottle of Wild Turkey wrapped up in a brown paper bag in her hand. The lamppost above her head fizzled. A homeless man wearing a Mitt Romney for President T-shirt under three to four layers of coats nodded at her and pushed his shopping cart across the street. She looked at the bottle of Wild Turkey, then switched her attention to the neon lights on the storefront window that said DRAGON TATTOO.

There was a tall dark-haired man inside mopping the floors, seemingly concentrated on this one task as though some deity had ordered him to do it. She couldn't see his face very well because a lock of his black hair had fallen over one eye. He was wearing a black tank top, which showed off his lean, corded arms, and a black pair of pants. Soon enough she found herself raptly watching his movements, sure-footed and precise, the muscles in his arms flexing as he pushed the mop around. He paused as though he could sense her gaze on him and slowly looked up.

Marnie gasped and ducked behind the lamppost. Behind her, a car carrying a bunch of drunken revelers whizzed by. One of them threw an almost empty can of beer at her and its contents spilled down her sweatshirt. She yelled at them as they sped away and was called a slut for her trouble. Even in the fading yellowish light of the lamp she could see that she had a splotch the shape of Canada on her abdomen.

What was she doing here anyway? She could be at home now, getting piss-drunk and watching *Seinfeld* reruns on TV. She hugged her paper bag of Wild Turkey to her chest and turned to leave. She froze as she heard soft tinkling bells letting her know that the door of the tattoo shop had been opened.

"Hello," he said. "Can I help you with something?"

She stashed the paper bag in the front pouch of her hoodie, brushed her hair out of her face with her hands, scrubbed the area around her mouth with her sleeve to make sure there was no drool, and turned to look at him.

He was gorgeous. His skin was the color of honey and his eyes—almond-shaped and deep-seated in a solemn face—were the color of night. His mouth, second only to his eyes, was his most striking feature. The lower lip was full, almost pouty, but the upper lip was thinner, had a curve to it that she could imagine tracing with the tip of her finger.

And here she was, in her old faded hoodie from college and dirty, unwashed sweats, staring at him like a starstruck fool, her mouth flapping open and close like she was a trout out of water.

His brows knotted together, forming a crease on his forehead, and the corner of his lips tilted up slightly. "Listen, it's cold out there.

Do you want to come in for tea? If you have nowhere to spend the night tonight, there's a shelter five blocks from here. I can drive you there after I close up here. I know the night manager."

Her initial outrage lasted only a moment and made way for shame. When was the last time she had truly taken care of herself? Ever since the divorce was finalized, she had been wallowing in her studio apartment, drinking herself till she passed out, and stuffing herself with Chinese takeout. She hadn't shampooed her hair in days and there was a pimple the size of Manhattan on her chin. On top of that, she now smelled like cheap beer. Why wouldn't he think she was homeless?

"Oh, I'm not . . ." she started to say. "I mean, I have an apartment."

"I apologize." He bowed his head briefly. When he lifted his gaze again, a small smile curved his lips. "Would you like to come in, anyway? It's cold out there."

He couldn't be possibly hitting on her . . . could he? No way. But there was something in his eyes that she liked—something warm and good. It would be nice to chat and hang out with someone other than the liquor store clerk or the Chinese restaurant order-taker for a while. "I should get going," she heard herself say. "I have food waiting for me at home."

"You can warm it up later." He pointed to the storefront window, which displayed a dizzying array of tattoos, both large and small. "You like tattoos?"

"Oh, yes." She tried for a smile, but it had been so long since she had done it that she didn't quite succeed. "I've always wanted one, but I'm not very good with needles."

"A little pain can be good for you," he said. "There is beautiful sincerity in it. Something pure and honest. You can't mistake it for anything else. It doesn't lie."

"Umm . . ." How the hell do you respond to that? She saw a documentary on HBO one night about people who got off on pain—

masochists who derived pleasure-pain specifically from tattoo needles. She shivered. "I'm not really a big fan of pain. I've had enough of it to last a lifetime. I'm . . . I'm gonna go."

His eyes glittered with amusement. He crossed his arms over his chest and leaned against the doorway. "Just look through our designs. Something might catch your eye."

She stared pointedly at his tightly muscled, ink-free arms. Most tattoo artists she had seen in real life or on TV were usually covered in tattoos. "I'm gonna go home," she said firmly. "Enjoy your evening."

"You need change," he said just as she was about to turn away. "A shock to your system, to get the blood flowing again."

She narrowed her eyes at him. "What?"

"Embrace the pain of the needle. It's real . . . tangible. You can take it in, breathe through it, turn it into something exquisite. It's a good pain . . . you can ride the adrenaline buzz and handle more pain than you can ever imagine."

She gawked.

He smiled. "Don't you want to feel something new? Something other than the emotional pain you seem to be carrying on your shoulders?"

And then the spell was broken. For a moment, she couldn't breathe. She couldn't even blink. She opened her mouth to respond, only to close it again because she couldn't even formulate a coherent response. Finally, she was able to take a deep, steadying breath. "How dare you. You don't know a damn thing about me. You've never even seen me before today."

He raised an eyebrow. "Haven't I?"

"What are you talking about?"

He shrugged. "I'm just saying I've seen you around. You walk past my shop all the time."

And he had noticed her? She did have to walk past the parlor each time she went to the liquor store. She wondered what he thought whenever he saw her carrying a brown paper bag that was obviously hiding a liquor bottle. "Whatever, dude. I'm going home."

"You keep saying that and yet you're still here." He held out his hand. "Come."

Despite her annoyance with him, she found herself reaching for his hand. She snapped out of it in time and slapped his hand away. "I'm not going anywhere with you."

His smile dimmed a bit, but stayed in place. "Then I'm sorry to have bothered you. Have a good night."

He pushed away from the doorway and turned away, giving Marnie an eyeful of his back as he walked away. From what she could see that was not covered by the tank top he wore, his back was entirely covered in tattoos. Peeking from his left shoulder blade were the burning yellow eyes of a dragon. The colors—blue, black, green, red, and yellow—looked so vivid and bright on his skin that when he reached for the mop again, his muscles flexed, making it look like the dragon had jumped.

"Hey, wait," she muttered, but he didn't look up. She reached for the paper bag in the front pocket of her hoodie, pushed down the bag to reveal the top of the bottle, and broke the seal with one hard twist of the cap. "Christ."

With a sigh, she lifted the mouth of the bottle to her lips, tilted it at an angle, and swallowed a healthy gulp. She fought the cough as the bourbon threatened to burn through her throat and esophagus. She had never drank straight out of the bottle before. This was a new low for her. She pulled on the bottle two more times, thumped her chest with her fist, and reached for the door handle. The little bell tinkled as she opened the door, but Mr. Back Tattoo did not turn around.

The girl sitting at the front counter—her black hair tied back into pigtails and her eyelids heavy with glittery blue eyeshadow—raised her head to look at her, smirked, then returned to painting her nails.

She looked like the slutty-goth version of a Catholic schoolgirl. And if there was one thing Marnie knew, it was how to be the perfect Catholic schoolgirl.

"I'll take that cup of tea, after all."

Mr. Back Tattoo spoke rapid-fire of what sounded like Cantonese to the girl. The girl rolled her eyes, slid the strap of her messenger bag over her head, and slammed past Mr. Back Tattoo on her way out.

"My baby sister Mei," he said. "She's a bit headstrong, I'm afraid."

"Trust me, I know. I'm a high school guidance counselor." She bit off a curse. "Was."

He glanced at the bottle she was still holding in her hand. Chagrined, she immediately capped the bottle and stashed it in the front pouch of her hoodie.

"I was let go," she blurted out. "Not because I was drinking or anything. I was going through some personal stuff . . ." She bit her lip. Why was she telling him any of these things?

Her eyes became blurry with tears. She tried to blink them back, but soon they were running down her cheeks and she was wiping them with the sleeve of her sweatshirt. If Mr. Back Tattoo noticed the tears, he gave no indication.

"Here." He pressed a warm San Diego Chargers mug into her hands. "That's chamomile. It'll soothe you. Let me just lock up so we can get started."

She could only stare at his back as he walked to the door. "You're doing my tattoo after hours? Is that normal?"

"Of course not." He grinned and turned the locks. "I close up every night at nine o'clock on the dot so I can be home in time to put my mother to bed. Tonight I assigned the task to my sister."

Marnie shifted uneasily and brought the mug up to her lips but did not drink. She blew on the hot surface as she surveyed the reception area. It was well-lit, clean, and looked more like the waiting room of a dental office than a tattoo parlor. There were eight large portraits of nude, artistically posed women Asian women on the white walls, each of them covered with strategically placed tattoos. Each frame had its own light source, a spotlight to enhance the contract of color against the olive brown skin of each woman. They all looked high fashion and professionally done. Meanwhile, the proprietor thought she was a homeless person. It was not the first time in the last fifteen minutes that she felt shame.

"Nice pictures," she mumbled, nodding at the far wall. She placed the mug on the counter and pulled at the drawstring that secured her hood. "Maybe we should do this some other time. I mean, I haven't showered today"—which pained her to admit,—"and I'm sure you wouldn't want to work on a dirty . . . um . . . canvas."

"I have a shower in the back."

"Oh." She swallowed hard. "Convenient."

He was leaning against the locked door with his arms folded over his chest, watching her. He was standing so still he could have been a statue. She willed him to blink. He did not.

"All right," she said after a moment. "Let me take a shower so we can get started."

"I'll get you a towel."

She nodded and he pushed away from the door. She found herself breathless as he approached her and her pulse thrummed like a tuning fork in her throat. He moved with a feline grace she had never seen in anyone before. She bit her lip. When he lifted a hand toward her face, she flinched.

"It's all right," he said, pushing her hood off her head. "You have nothing to be afraid of. I won't hurt you."

But he would, she *knew* it. She forced herself to remain still as he swept her hair out of her face. His nearness was making her light-headed. She was sure she didn't smell so great and fervently hoped he wouldn't say a thing about it. He, on the other hand, smelled clean and woodsy and male like . . . Irish Spring or something.

He took her hand and led her down a narrow hallway toward the back of the store. Though she was dimly aware of the way her hand was engulfed in his, Marnie was able to observe a few more pieces of the art hanging on the walls. If they were his work, he was brilliant. She didn't know much about art—Eric was the art buff—but she was sure these were gallery-quality. It was obvious he really cared about his work. She also appreciated how everything looked so clean and sterile. It went a long way to assure her that she could get a quality tattoo here without having to worry about getting an infection and dying of sepsis.

He pointed to a door on the left, which was adjacent to another door that had the familiar neon-green EXIT sign having over it. It was, however, secured with a heavy-duty padlock.

"That has to be violating some fire code or something," she muttered.

"Crackheads," he said. "We had a break-in last month. You can never been too careful these days." He handed her a towel.

Marnie couldn't help but bring the towel to her nose. It was soft, neatly folded, and smelled like Tide. Her eyes began to burn with tears again and she held the towel against her face until she could get herself in control.

"You go on in," he said. "I'll be out here, setting everything up."

"Okay."

The bathroom was a small cube, maybe eight feet by eight feet. There was a toilet, a sink with a mirror above it, and a shower stall with glass doors and walls. There were no windows. The light above her head was a soft yellow, suffusing everything with an amber glow. She pulled the bottle of Wild Turkey out of her pouch and placed it on the counter. While she removed her clothes, she avoided looking at the mirror. She dropped her dirty clothes on the floor and entered the shower stall. The initial blast of cool water on her face and head made her yelp, but did a good job waking up her senses. As the water gradually warmed, she washed her hair and soaped her body, taking care to work up a lather before scrubbing her face. She liked the smell of his soap.

She stepped out of the bathroom a few minutes later wearing a bathrobe that was hanging from a hook on the back of the door. It was a little big, but she wrapped the sash around her waist twice and tied it tightly in the front. She wrapped up her hair in a towel and stashed her dirty clothes in a plastic bag, which she found under the sink. Now that she was clean, she just couldn't stand the idea of putting them back on right now. She glanced wistfully at the bottle of Wild Turkey on the counter, but left it there.

When she entered the session room, which reminded her of a doctor's exam room, he was washing his hands at the sink. She looked around and found that he had set up everything they would need on a little tray next to a chair that looked like a dentist chair, but shorter and not as wide. On the tray, there were little bottles of various colors, sterile pouches containing tubes and needles, latex gloves, a spray bottle, a jar of what looked like petroleum jelly, and several tiny cups about the size of a thimble. She gulped and felt light-headed with panic. She took a step back and stumbled into a black leather stool, which caused her to fall on her ass.

He was at her side within seconds, pulling her up. "Are you all right?"

"Yeah." Her face was hot and beet-red, she was sure, with mortification. She didn't realize how much taller and just . . . *bigger* he was than her. He had to be a few inches over six feet. Large men made her nervous. She cleared her throat. "I'm all good. What's next? Jeez, I don't even know your name." She tried for a chuckle and hoped it didn't sound hysterical.

"Hey, you're shaking. It's all right." He put his hands on her shoulders and gave them a squeeze. "My name is Michael." He reached for a binder on a shelf behind him and gave it to her. "Do you want to look through this while I finish setting up? Everything in this book is my sister Mei's design. She's very talented."

She opened the binder and tried to ignore him as he cleaned and prepared an instrument that looked like the unholy child of a glue gun and a tiny jackhammer. Each page contained a drawing of various flowers, all colorful and intricate in their own way. There were images of roses, daisies, orchids, and while they were all pretty, nothing really grabbed her attention. It wasn't until she came upon a picture of a lily that she stopped and stared. With a shaking hand, she touched the plastic sleeve that held the drawing and traced each petal with her finger. The entire image was about six inches and maybe five inches wide from petal to petal. The leaves and stem were black, as well as the pistil and the pollen, but the petals were starkly white, outlined with black. It was breathtakingly beautiful in its simplicity . . . something she could proudly wear on her skin.

"You've found something?" he asked a moment later.

Without a word, she handed him the binder, pointing to the page that had the image she wanted. He tilted her chin up with his knuckle and searched her face. "It's a fine choice. Why this one?"

"It's . . ." She shrugged. How could she put it into words? "It called to me."

He nodded. "I'll prepare the stencil. Have a seat. I'll be right back. Do you know where you want it?"

She bit her lip. A tattoo wasn't really something somebody should get on impulse. She thought about asking him to place it on the side of her body, along her torso, but she didn't have a bra or anything to cover up with and just the idea of him hunkered over her naked body made her dizzy. The leg or the arm weren't the best places for it, either. She wanted to be able to cover it up just in case she had to go to a job interview or something. The thigh was too close to . . . *no.* It would have to be on her back. If she wore a backless or a low-back dress, the tattoo would be stunning. Of course, she would have to lose ten to fifteen pounds first . . .

"I'd like it on my right shoulder blade."

He met her eyes and nodded. "All right, I'll need you to straddle the chair, turn your head to the side, and lay your cheek on the back cushion. You'll need to lower the robe so your entire upper back is exposed. I'll be back with the stencil."

Marnie took off the towel from her head, hung it on the back of a chair, and shook her wet hair. She searched the immediate area for something she could use to put up her hair and found a pencil, which she used to secure her bun.

Taking a deep breath, she approached the dentist chair, placed her legs on either side of it, and exhaled slowly as she lowered herself onto the chair. The leather felt weird on her bare parts, so she pulled up the hem of the robe from the back, slid it between her legs, and sat back down. It took her a bit to undo the knot on the belt of the robe because her hands were shaking so badly, but she managed it, sliding off the robe from her shoulders until the terrycloth was gathered around her elbows. She looked down at her bare breasts and covered them up before leaning forward to lay her cheek on the leather, wrapping her arms loosely around the back cushion. She forced herself to concentrate on how the leather felt against her skin as she began to breathe deeply: inhaling, holding it for three beats, then exhaling until all the air out was out of her lungs. Inhale, exhale. If there was one thing she got out of the obscenely expensive therapy sessions that she took after Eric filed for divorce, it was how to breathe properly.

"Don't move," Michael said. "You're perfect just like that."

She froze. She couldn't help it. She had never felt so vulnerable in her life. He could do just about anything to her now and she wouldn't be able to do a damn thing about it. She glanced over her shoulder and watched as he pushed the black leather stool up to where she was. When he sat and placed one gloved hand between her shoulder blades, she closed her eyes and released the breath she didn't realize she'd been holding.

"Are you all right?"

"Yes." She heard a ripping sound and the sharp smell of ethyl alcohol wafted to her nose.

"I just need to clean the area little bit. I'm sure you did a good job in the shower, but it's important that the skin is disinfected. This will feel a little cold."

She gasped as he began to wipe the area with the alcohol pad. She willed herself to relax, to let go and trust that this man knew what he was doing, but with him being so close to her, his thighs wide open and almost cradling the lower part of her body, she felt as taut and tight as a guitar string.

"I'm going to apply the stencil now. I'm going to spray a little bit of water . . ." He touched the side of her torso. "I need you to relax, my lily. This part won't hurt a bit."

She could feel the heat of his body against her back. It radiated from him in waves, caressing her skin like ghostly fingers. She was tempted to lean against him and curl into him like a cat seeking affection. It took all of her control to resist against it. She might be feeling this way about him, but to him, she was just another paying customer. She glanced down and stared at his knee. If she wanted to, she could reach down and brush it with her fingertips. He was that close.

She hissed as cold water misted over her overheated skin and craned her neck over her shoulder as he pressed what felt like wax paper against her back, which he smoothed over her skin with the help of something that looked like a tiny paint roller. She couldn't see much past the long, nimble fingers covered in latex and once again, she was afraid. She was really putting an awful lot of trust in this man. No one knew where she was. And she was all alone with him.

"All right." He peeled off the transfer paper. "I have the stencil laid out on your skin. Would you like to see what it looks like before I begin the line-work? I can take you to a mirror."

She swallowed. If she got up from this chair now, she knew there was no way she was going to return. It was already taking up all of the courage in her reserve to stay exactly where she was. "You're the professional. I can always sue you if you give me a wonky tattoo. My sister is a lawyer."

"Good to know." He patted her back. "Now here's the important part. I want you to listen carefully."

She bit her lip. "I'm all ears."

"No matter what, don't hold your breath. You can pass out that way. I want you to breathe evenly through your nose, a steady inhale and exhale. The first minute or so is the hardest part. I won't lie to you, you will be in agony. It's not going to be a pricking pain; it'll be a slicing, burning pain. But you must keep breathing."

"Umm . . ." She gritted her teeth. "Dude, you suck at pep talks."

"It's not meant to be one. It'll hurt. The sooner you accept the pain, the sooner you'll be able to embrace it. You can cry out, if you want to, but it's important that you stay still. Line-work is crucial to holding the tattoo together." He applied jelly to her shoulder blade and began to rub the area. "Most people are bothered by the sound of the tattoo gun, which is a loud buzzing noise. I can put on music, if you wish."

"No." She reached down and gripped his knee. "Don't leave me."

"Don't worry, my lily. I'm not going anywhere. I'm staying right here."

God, his voice sounded so good; deep and velvet-smooth. Maybe if she concentrated on it, she'd be able to coast through the pain. It was like aural chocolate. She still couldn't believe she was going to go through with this. She had to be drunk. No, that wasn't true. She had never been more sober. She had never been as alert, as aware of her surroundings than she was at this moment. "I'm ready."

But a second later, she wasn't. The moment he turned on the tattoo gun, the buzzing noise he described instantly began to tear into her calm.

"Wait!" she gasped. "Wait!"

The tattoo gun was switched off. "It's all right, sweetheart. It's all right."

Marnie slumped face-first against the back cushion of the dentist chair, defeated. She was such an idiot. Why did she think she could do this? She had never been brave a day in her life. She thought she was ready, that she could finally jump into something scary and exciting for once in her life, but that was a lie. She couldn't go through with this. She should just put on her clothes and slink back home with her bottle of Wild Turkey.

"My lily . . ."

"Marnie," she muttered into the cushion. "My name is Marnie."

"We don't have to do this, Marnie. I can see you're not ready. I pushed you into it. I apologize."

She wrapped her arms tightly around the back cushion and sighed. He didn't push her into anything. The truth was, she was just sick and tired of the way her life had been going for the past few months and jumped onto the first opportunity for change. The change wasn't necessarily Michael; it was the urge to do something . . . different. The tattoo was going to serve as a beacon of her new life.

And then he began to stroke her back, gently at first, and then gradually with more pressure. Marnie could only surrender to his ministrations as he began to knead the flesh surrounding her spine with his fingers, pressing into the muscle with his thumbs while the rest of his hands massaged the sides of her torso. She gasped as he grazed the underside of her breasts. She held her breath, anticipating his touch on the aching mounds, but it never came. Instead his hands descended along her spine again, kneading and stroking, until he reached where the robe pooled around her waist.

"Marnie," he breathed against the nape of her neck.

She shivered as he captured her earlobe between his teeth and softly bit down. He was hovering over her now, his arms braced on the seat. She arched against him, craving to feel his body against hers. He was so warm and he felt so good. "Just do it, Michael. I'm ready."

"Are you sure?" His voice sounded harsh and strained.

"Yes," she whispered, undulating her hips against the apex of his thighs. She could feel his erection against the small of back, could feel it throbbing with need. For her.

The buzzing noise of the tattoo gun broke through the stillness of the room. Marnie pressed herself against the back cushion, her hardened nipples grazing the leather, which had been warmed by her body heat. It was the anticipation, really, the expectation of pain. Her body's involuntary response was to brace for the pain, to tense up. She should not be fighting against it. If she surrendered to it, if she embraced it like Michael said, if she just gave in, she could become something else . . . a canvas for Michael's art. She could be beautiful, just like the women in those portraits. For the moment, that was better than anything she could think of. And it was enough.

"That's it, Marnie, keep breathing just like that."

He touched the tip of the tattoo gun to her skin and Marnie hissed. The pain was not . . . was she thought it would be. It felt incomplete. It was not a deep, penetrating, stabbing pain. It was more like a searing, scratching, digging pain. Like a sharp fingernail worrying over an itch, over and over, only about a thousand times more intense. And it was hot. Not sexy-hot, but temperature-hot. And it didn't stop. She did not realize she was biting down on her lip until she tasted blood in her mouth.

"Marnie, you're tensing up again. Breathe, sweetheart, breathe."

He laid one palm against the middle of her back and pressed her harder into the cushion, restricting any hope of movement of Marnie's part, as his other hand continued to move over her skin with the tattoo gun. She forced herself to concentrate on the rhythm of her own breathing: inhale three beats, exhale two beats. She breathed in and out through her nose, filling up her lungs with air until her chest could expand no more, then slowly releasing it, imagining her lungs flattening like pancakes as she did so. After a while, the incessant buzzing noise of the tattoo gun began to fade into the background until all she could hear was her own breathing and the heavy, steady throbbing of her own jugular.

And then it began: a tingling sensation at the base of her skull, spreading slowly but steadily all over her skull. Goose bumps sprouted all over her body and beads of sweat formed on her forehead and above her upper lip. She could feel herself melting deeper into the cushion, her bones liquefying and her flesh humming with the sensation so pleasurable it was painful . . . so painful it was pleasurable? She was drunk and floating and boneless. And God, she *needed* to touch him. She reached down and grasped Michael's knee, her fingers digging deep, closing and opening over his kneecap. She caressed all of him that was within reach, which was a couple of above his knee and halfway down his calf. She stroked and groped and squeezed.

The buzzing stopped.

"Marnie," he groaned as though he himself were in pain. "You have to stop that, baby. Just a little bit more. We're almost done here." He leaned over her, bent his head, and sucked her flesh into his mouth, laving the area with his tongue. "There's time enough for that soon."

Marnie dropped her hand to her side and Michael returned to his seat. The buzzing started again and it didn't take long for Marnie to return to her breathing. She licked her lips as she felt Michael's restraining hand slide down her spine, stroke her hip, and follow the line of her body all the way down to her bare thigh. With his calloused palm, he caressed her, sliding it up to the area where her thigh met her pelvis under the robe. And remained there. Maddeningly still. But Marnie could not move, could not adjust her body to accommodate his questing fingers, not if she wanted a perfect tattoo. A canvas did not squirm and wriggle. She reached for his hand and moved it to her knee. And held it there.

"All right," he said after what seemed like an eternity. "All done."

Marnie couldn't believe it. She had survived. She chanced a glance over her shoulder and Michael was there smiling at her as he applied the bandage to her shoulder. Their eyes met. She winked at him. An unfamiliar sound escaped her lips. A laugh. She hadn't laughed in months. She felt giddy and drunk with joy. She felt . . . fabulous. She was still giggling as Michael guided her out of the dentist chair and laughed even harder when she realized she could not stand on her own. Her legs had turned to jelly. She would have slid to the ground if Michael hadn't picked her up and swung her into his arms.

"Where are we going?" she asked airily, looping her arms around his neck.

"Not far."

He set her down on the counter, spread the robe open, and appraised her body with a knowing smile. Chuckling, he placed his hands on her thighs and stepped in between them. "You are amazing."

"I know," Marnie said. "I'm ready for my prize."

She helped him unbutton and unzip his pants with the eagerness of a child on Christmas morning, pushing them to the floor with her foot. Cupping his face between her hands, she slid her mouth over his and kissed him until they were both breathless.

"Congratulations, Marnie." Then he gripped her hips and thrust deep into her.

DL Galace enjoys long-distance running and yoga, considers herself a voracious reader, and indulges herself once in a while with a huge, overflowing serving of Carne Asada Fries from Sombrero's and a six-pack of Tsingtao. She loves watching reruns of *The X-Files* whenever she can find it and lives in hope that a super-good *X-Files* feature film will be released someday when Mulder and Scully can finally get married outside of fanfic. She lives in San Diego, CA. Visit her blog at www.dionnegalace.com/wordpress.

JUST SAY YES

HelenKay Dimon

One

Her back slammed against the door. Firm hands slid up to cradle her head as his mouth crossed over hers. Again and again, the slant of his lips and sweep of his tongue burned through her.

She craved this. Day after day, sitting in boring conference rooms and never-ending staff meetings, watching him explain and negotiate, she wanted him.

At home, or in any safe place where she could close her eyes and steal a moment, she imagined the broad slope of his shoulders and the pleasures promised by those lean fingers. At the office she lived for the peppery ginger scent that tickled her senses during those dangerous times when she got close enough to smell him.

Colin Banks. Brown hair bordering on black, soft gray eyes, and a voice so deep it vibrated down to her toes with every syllable. He was completely off-limits. And he was seconds away from being inside her.

"God, yes." He whispered his plea against her lips when her fingers found the flat stomach under his shirt.

Heavy breathing mixed with the rustle of clothing and shuffling of feet. One hand reached down to catch her thigh and pull it high on his hip. The seductive dance inched her slim skirt straight into danger territory.

Ignoring common sense and every rule she'd ever set for her life, she dove in. She grabbed for his suit jacket. Clawing and pushing, she worked the material down his arms, letting him leave her only long enough to shrug it to the carpet.

Then he was back. Warm air blew across her bare skin the second before his mouth closed over the vein thumping hard at the base of her neck.

The pressure of his lips, the sucking and coaxing, sent a rush of blood to her head. She slid her fingers beneath the collar of his dress shirt and lifted his face. No more than a shimmer of air passed between them before her mouth found his again, making her wonder how she went eight months without kissing him long and deep.

The heat and unexpected growl vibrating in his throat fed the need growing inside her. Hands moved over her silk shirt, cupping her breasts before shifting to her hips. As he bunched her skirt at her waist, his leg eased between hers.

A rush of cool air hit her exposed thighs. Fingertips skimmed the lacy tops of her stockings before brushing against the damp crotch of her panties. Back and forth he rubbed until her insides tingled and ached.

Her head fell back against the door as he tugged the tiny scrap of material down her legs to pool on top of her high heels. She kicked them off.

"Colin . . . now."

He mumbled under his breath, blocking out the steady hum of the overhead lights and the slight buzz of excitement filling her brain. The faint sounds of the off-duty office faded into a beating sensation of heat and desire.

The quiet darkness shattered as he dipped a finger deep inside her. "You're soaking wet."

The words rumbled against her ear as her fingers eased the belt from his pants. "Please tell me you have a condom."

"Suit pocket." Before she could question the convenience, he explained. "Been planning for weeks."

A flash of reason seared across her brain. "Colin?"

"Later." He whispered the word against her lips.

"Maybe we should—"

"No more talk." His palms cupped her ass, lifting both her legs to wrap around his lean waist.

Her body was open to him. Vulnerable and ready. Balancing her between the panel at her back and his body at the front, he shifted one hand and pressed two fingers deep inside before sliding out then plunging them back in again.

He repeated the sensual massage until her hips flexed in time with his hand. Tension crackled across her nerve endings, snapping her muscles tight and forcing her ankles in a clench against his back. She wanted to squirm and shift until the grinding inside her subsided, but it kept growing and pulsing.

The screech of his zipper broke through the room. She wanted to reach down and help him with the condom, but her mind kept misfiring and her control slipped out of her grasp.

When she heard the package tear and felt the tip of his cock press against her, her palms smacked against the door for leverage. Back and forth he rubbed, making her wetter with each deepening stroke.

Before she could drag a gulp of air through her dry throat he was inside her. One long, steady push and he filled her. With a reverent whisper of her name, part groan and part plea, he moved. In and out, faster with each successive stroke, the long-suppressed need for him roared to life.

Heat pounded her. The act of possession and being possessed thrilled her. When he touched his finger against her clit, the simple pressure broke the coiling inside her. Her body bucked and her hips slammed against his. Sharp breaths rushed out of her in pants as she came.

When his shoulders trembled and palms clasped her flesh, she knew the orgasm had overtaken him. His heartbeat thundered against her as his body pulled tight. With a rough grunt, his shoulders grew stiff one last time then with a whoosh of air relaxed. He balanced his full weight against her as his body shook from the force of his release.

She tried to absorb his heat, to drag his body even closer against hers as the harsh breaths pumped through his chest. In the quiet minutes after, she ran her hands through his soft hair and over the firm muscles even his shirt couldn't hide, enjoying the chance to touch him without any repercussions.

Exhausted, both her resistance and bones melted, she cuddled him as his body returned from flaming to normal. She doubted she could stand or even think.

He lifted his head, those gray eyes sparkling with mischief. "Nice."

"Very." She waited for embarrassment and regret to hit her but they never did. Still, she had to be reasonable. Smart. At the very least, engage in a little self-protection. "We should—"

"Try the desk next."

"What?"

His lips turned up in a smile, one that promised hours of mind-numbing sex. "You didn't think we were done, did you?"

"I don't even have the brain cells to spell my name."

He trailed the backs of his fingers down her cheek. "Give me a few minutes and you won't even know it."

Two

~~~~~~~~◈~~~~~~~~

THREE DAYS LATER . . .

"Even with the delay we shouldn't have any trouble meeting the deadline."

Colin tried to concentrate on her verbal replay of the conference call but his mind refused to stay focused on work. He couldn't take one more second of her practiced detachment. "You're actually going to sit there and pretend it never happened."

Her explanation stopped in mid-sentence as her shoulders froze. Even her pen skidded to a stop on the yellow legal pad in front of her. "Excuse me?"

It was just after two on a Friday. The lights were on. They were dressed in matching blue suits. The shades were up. The floor of the real estate development company buzzed with activity. And Allie Garner acted as if he hadn't stripped her naked and come inside her three times earlier that week in that very room.

"You. Me. This office." He sat across the desk from her and thought about being more descriptive. He would have if he'd bothered to lock the door.

Anyone could walk in. There were twenty cubicles lined up outside the corner office. The fact the door was closed would cause enough of a buzz. Almost as much as Allie's early morning snap over a malfunctioning copier.

She usually stayed cool under pressure. Having struggled her way up from secretary to vice president, she appreciated how hard the staff worked. It was one of the things he admired about her. She didn't blow up or pull rank. Until today.

She pressed her palms into the arms of her big leather desk chair. "Now isn't the time to discuss—"

"Allie."

"I'm trying to tell you—"

Screw appropriate. "I took you up against the door. Again on the carpet."

"That's enough. I am your boss." As if being her assistant wasn't enough of a clue, she adjusted the nameplate on the edge of her desk.

He shoved the engraved plate to the side and balanced his elbows on the now-open space. Not the most respectful move but this discussion didn't have anything to do with the job or her position of power. "I'm not talking about work and you know it."

"This topic is off-limits."

"I'm done ignoring it."

She exhaled a ragged breath. "Tuesday was a mistake."

"Not by my calculation."

"I was out of line."

Which he took as code for *I didn't follow the rules*. He knew all about the corporate policy prohibiting management from dating within the company. Allie actually made him email the section of the employee handbook to the entire staff the day before.

She missed the simple fact he was a grown man. If he wanted a woman, he went for it. And he wanted Allie. Had from the day he met her. He saw those long legs under her trim black skirt and almost blew his interview. Then he got to know her and he was really a goner. Wavy brown hair, eyes that hovered that sexy line between green and blue, and a body that crushed his control to dust. They'd had eight months of foreplay and one night of sex. He vowed to adjust that imbalance.

He had to get around her paralyzing worries first. "You think I'm going to report you or get you fired."

"I take full responsibility for what happened." She stared at the desk, at her computer monitor—everywhere but at him.

"I remember being a pretty active participant."

"I was in charge."

"No, you weren't." If she were the one in charge of their attraction, he'd still be dreaming about what she looked like naked instead of recalling the image from memory.

She was looking at him now. The flat-lipped frown might scare someone else. Not him. He knew the passionate woman underneath the big work title. She'd always been a fair boss but panic gripped her now. Her body trembled with it.

"We work as a team, with you negotiating the contracts I secure, but I'm still your boss."

"You said that already."

She cleared her throat. "It was unfair of me put you in that position."

She wouldn't stop fighting him. Energy bubbled right under the surface. He could sense it and was desperate to harness it, but she stifled her needs in favor of long hours at her desk. He'd hoped their after-hours playtime would help her appreciate the sexy woman he saw, but that wasn't happening.

If he backed off now, she'd retreat just like she did every time he tried to knock down that professional barrier she erected between them. "You think I don't see the way you look at me in meetings? How I sometimes catch you glancing at me during presentations instead of listening to the speakers?"

The last of the rosy pink leeched from her face as she reached for the phone. "I should call Human Resources."

He folded his hand over hers before she could hit a button. "Since you're about to completely piss me off, let's get one thing straight. I'm not going to tell anyone. I'm not going to file a complaint."

"You have every right."

"You're still not hearing me. I pushed you against that door and tore off your panties because I wanted to do it. No one forced me."

She frowned. "What do you expect me to say?"

"That you're not sorry."

"I can't."

He squeezed her hand and then let go, trying to ignore the kick behind her words. "Allie, you're killing me here."

"You work—"

"For you. Yeah, I get that." He reached into his suit pocket and dropped a small envelope on her desk blotter. "Here."

"What's this?"

"The key to my condo."

"Why are you giving it to me?"

He thought she could have looked less appalled by the gesture. "Be there at seven and plan to stay the weekend. If you don't show, I'll hunt you down."

"Colin, no."

"I'd give you until eight but you'll over-think this."

She shoved her chair back as if the key would jump in her hand if she got too close. "You've lost your mind."

"And don't bother packing a bag. You're not going to need any clothes."

She frowned at him. "What are you talking about?"

"You naked for days. You'll be lucky to go five minutes without me inside you all weekend."

Three

She didn't give him a second to say anything. Hours later he opened his front door and she shoved him out of the way to step inside. Didn't even let her gaze sweep over the room before turning on him. "I didn't appreciate the caveman act in my office this afternoon."

He locked the door then leaned against it. "I think you did or you wouldn't be here."

She was going to do this. Just let the moment take her, enjoy the feel of him without worrying about the consequences later back at the office. But she still had to be smart. She couldn't let the sexy faded jeans and slim gray T-shirt he wore or the hint of stubble on his chin take her to a place she'd regret.

She glanced around but barely saw the sectional sofa on one side of her and the big-screen television mounted on the wall on the other. "We need to set some ground rules."

"No."

Her carefully crafted speech fell apart in her brain. "What do you mean, no?"

"This isn't about work or who we are or even that damned employee handbook you've been waving around. It's about two people naked and knocked speechless with need."

"The handbook is there to protect you."

He snorted. "I'm a big boy. I can handle myself."

"No kidding."

"And you aren't the boss tonight." He pushed off the door and came toward her nice and slow. "I am."

He didn't so much walk toward her as he stalked. Circling her until she felt cornered and out of breath while standing in the middle of the open family room. "You."

"Yes." He brushed his thumb across her bottom lip. "Your body is mine. Your thoughts, your desires."

Their bodies didn't touch anywhere else, but the soft contact from the pad of one finger was enough to send every nerve inside her jumping to awareness. She knew what he could do with those hands, that tongue, how he could bring her to orgasm in a wild frenzy and then soothe her only to start again.

His hand dropped to his side. "Take off your shirt."

"What?"

"Now, Allie."

Her brain balked but her fingers went to the pearly white buttons. One by one she slipped the material apart and exposed inches of bare skin. "I suppose you think I'm one of those women who just needs a good fuck to loosen her up."

"I happen to know you had a good one earlier this week." His gaze dipped to the top of her lacy pink bra. "And, no. You're not cold or stiff."

"Is this about your ego?"

His gray eyes lasered in on her. "Your shirt is still on. I want it off."

She thought about refusing but knew she wouldn't. Need danced through her belly as every inch of her flesh flamed to life. With the buttons open, she let the silk slip to the floor behind her. The coolness of the room couldn't extinguish the burn racing through her.

He didn't move. "Now the bra."

She ached for him to strip her, skim his fingers over her, kiss her. Fast or slow, it didn't matter. She craved the sensation of having every last barrier torn from her. Of seeing him lose control as he gave his body over to her. She wanted him to feel as helpless and trembling as she did.

She ran her fingertips across the tops of her breasts. "Can you help me?"

"The bra then the pants."

With a slice of regret she unsnapped her bra and caught it in her hands in front of her. "There."

"Let it fall. I want to see you. All of you." He reached out his hand and she dropped the undergarment into it. "I missed this part on Tuesday. I plan to savor every inch of you now, just as I do every night in my fantasies."

His words washed away the unease rumbling in her chest. "Do I get to savor you?"

He nodded in the direction of her waist. "The pants and panties."

She tamped down all her insecurities about the soft curve of her stomach and fleshy tops of her thighs, all those dark voices in her head that told her to eat less and actually use her gym membership for once. But despite her obvious flaws, she could see the growing bulge in his pants. She remembered the way he sucked on her nipples as she lay on her office floor. He wanted her. With every problem and every obstacle, he still wanted her.

Without another thought, she lowered the zipper and let her pants slide over her skin. The matching pink panties she picked with him in mind that morning followed. Kicking off her shoes, she stood before him naked and shaking. She could barely control the mix of want and anticipation pulsing inside her.

He watched, his gaze roaming as a clock somewhere behind her ticked loud enough to echo in her head. She was just about to break the quiet, to beg if she had to, when she saw it. A fine tremor moved through his hands. The stiffness in his shoulders hid the truth but he felt it, too. The realization gave her confidence. He was thirty and heart stoppingly handsome with his firm jaw and wide eyes. A man everyone liked. She was four years older and a mass of insecurities and concerns she tried to hide behind her office door.

But he didn't seem to care. That fact washed through her and wiped away everything else.

"I'm going to take you on the floor, so every time I walk in the front door I'll remember you sprawled naked with me all over you." He dropped to his knees in front of her. "Later we'll move to the bed. I've dreamed about what you'd look like lying on my sheets."

"You planned this."

"Every night for months." His fingers skimmed up her inner thighs, spreading her stance as he moved between her legs at her feet.

When his mouth settled on her, her mind went blank. His tongue flicked over her as his hands held her steady. She could feel her body grow wet, see it on his lips when he pulled back to slip two fingers inside her.

Her knees turned to liquid. "I can't—"

"You can." He mumbled the words against her clit. The vibration mixed with the heated air from his words.

His fingers pumped into her as he licked. The tempo increased until her lower body bucked and her feet stretched while her heels left the floor. The orgasm swept over her in a rush. Primed by his words and coaxed by his hands and mouth, she couldn't hold on to the slim thread of control that kept her from falling over the edge. Her palms pressed against the side of his head and her body ground against his lips.

Before she could catch her breath, he pulled her down on the floor with him. Her muscles trembled and her hands shook while she slipped her fingers through his hair. His mouth met hers in a shattering kiss that stole the rest of her strength. His exotic scent wrapped around her as she tasted her body on his lips.

He pulled back, his gaze searching her face. "Are you ready?"

"I don't think I can move."

"Oh, you're going to move. You'll want to. Need to."

His warmth disappeared as he slipped away from her to lay on the floor. With his arms folded behind his head, he waited. His erection pulled tight against his jeans and his eyes turned the perfect gray-blue.

"Undress me."

The husky tone called to her to undo his belt and roll down the zipper. The staccato clicks echoed through the room. Denim rustled as she peeled the jeans down his legs and off. The sneakers, the boxer briefs, she stripped him of them all. She didn't want anything separating his body from hers.

He reached down and guided her legs until she straddled his upper thighs. His erection brushed against her, not entering but pressing against her sensitive folds.

"The condom is in the pocket of my jeans."

She didn't talk. Couldn't. Excitement filled her. She needed to satisfy the winding sensation inside her before she could manage anything else. To get there fast, she grabbed for the leg of his pants and dragged them across the floor to her.

All that moving around pressed her tighter against him. His sharp intake of breath mirrored hers, making her work faster. In two seconds she had the package open and the condom fitted over his length.

"Ride me."

The rough words whipped through her. She was on top, but he was in control. "Yes."

"Hard." His fingers clenched against her outer thighs as he spoke.

With her hands balanced on his chest, she raised her body. She fit him against her and slid down slow and easy. The sensation stopped her breath but he didn't allow her time to adjust.

He rubbed his thumb across her clit. "Move, Allie."

She did. Without a signal from her brain, her senses took over.

Up and down, increasing in speed with each plunge and retreat. She let the pressure build, let her hands explore his toned shoulders. Let the raw desire take over until her body was slick with sweat and her mind was clear of anything but pure pleasure.

"Damn, baby." His upper body lifted off the floor.

She shoved him back down. Her rhythm never faltered. She followed her instincts and kept her pace until her body begged for more and a low moan escaped his lips.

His hips pumped faster, meeting her with equal pressure every time she slid back down. With one final push, she settled over him, holding him deep and letting him explode beneath her. His arms fell to the sides as the muscles in his neck pulled tight.

Seeing him surrender his control touched off her orgasm. Her mouth dropped open as her body splintered. Her last thought was that his body belonged to her.

AN hour later they lay diagonal across the bed with the sheets crumpled beneath them.

He traced her breast with the tip of his finger. "What happens now?"

The gentle touch set off a fluttering deep in her stomach. "I don't see that anything has changed."

He leaned up on his elbow and stared down at her with a face blank of emotion. "How can you say that?"

It would have been easier if he yelled or cursed. Instead, he continued to caress her breast until her nipple pulled hard and her legs shifted to make room for his hips between them. "You're thinking more sex."

"Definitely." He leaned over to kiss the puckered skin around her nipple. He sucked then flicked his tongue against the hard bud.

She forced her hips to stay flat against the mattress. "What's the plan here, Colin? We're going to concentrate on work all week and then have sex all weekend?"

"Works for me."

"I can't separate my life like that." She struggled up to balance her upper body on her elbows.

He finally pulled back. "You mean you won't try."

"I could lose everything."

"You still don't get it." He sat up, sliding his hand down her body to lay flat on her stomach.

"Tell me."

The skin pulled tight across his cheeks as his mouth went flat. "I'm thinking you'll have to figure it out on your own."

Four

~~~~~~~~~~~~~~~

The message came at ten minutes after ten on Monday morning. Allie sat at her desk, replaying every minute of the weekend in her head. The memory of Colin's touch warmed her. The stunned look on his face when she made her hasty exit still haunted her. The call from her boss demanding a meeting about Colin in a half hour made her dizzy with rage.

Colin betrayed her. She turned him down and he walked into Mr. Friedman's office this morning and turned her in. She'd expected his anger and disappointment, but Colin had convinced her he wouldn't go after her out of spite. Wouldn't target her job while he ripped her confidence to shreds.

The more she thought about it, the harder the anger shook her. The least he could do was be a man and admit it to her face. If he was going to ruin her, smash her business reputation to pieces and make her out to be some sort of whore, he would not be able to hide while he did it.

She knew she should call her attorney and stay away from Colin unless there was a witness present . . . *Fuck that.*

She blew out of her office, not even bothering to hide her fury or slide into the office next to hers without attracting attention. If he wanted to make a scene, she would give him one.

She pushed open his half-closed door and then slammed it

behind her. Trapped in the eight-by-eight space, it was all she could do to keep from reaching for the nearest object and lobbing it at his head.

She settled for walking right up to the edge of his desk and staring him down. "You lied to me."

He didn't even flinch. Just glanced up from his computer screen and kept typing on the keyboard. "About what?"

"You told me you could separate the office from what happened between us outside of work."

The clicking of the keys stopped. "I was wrong."

The comment sent her fury flaring in every direction. "You admit it?"

He sat back in his chair. "Before I say yes, why don't you tell me what has you pissed off and stomping around."

"You talked to Friedman this morning."

"Yes."

The simple word sliced through her. Ripped through her insides and plunged straight into her heart.

"You told him we had sex." When Colin didn't bother to deny it, the rage boiling inside her spilled over. "You know, I almost bought your act. When you begged me to stay last night, I nearly caved."

"But you figured out I only wanted sex."

If he threw her on the floor and punched her, kicked her right in the gut, it would have hurt less than the flat tone of disinterest in his voice. "Yes."

He stood up. "So, you decided I'd turn around and tell everyone how good you were in the sack. That I bagged the boss."

"It's not bad enough you endanger my career. You have to—"

"Shut up." He said the words as he stepped around the edge of his desk to stand next to her. He grabbed her elbow before she could race out of the office. "You don't know what the hell you're talking about."

"Why don't you enlighten me?"

"I quit." He shook her but it didn't restart her brain.

The world whirred down to a stop. The edges blurred and words jumbled in her head. She saw him and the sharp tension drawing across his jaw. None of it made sense.

"What are you talking about?"

"I accepted a position with another company for one reason. You. And stop shaking your head. I realized I had two choices. If we're not going to keep seeing each other, I can't be in an office with you every day." His fierce grip eased on her arm but he didn't let go. "So close, knowing how good we are together, and forced to play the role of platonic subordinate? Not fucking going to happen."

Her breath hiccupped inside her chest. "You're not making any sense."

"But if we're going to figure out what's going on between us, and I hope to hell that's the choice we're picking here, then I still have to leave because you're never going to ignore that damn employee handbook and let yourself go."

She still couldn't put the words he was saying together and have them make sense. "So, Friedman . . . "

"Doesn't know a damn thing about us."

Colin pulled her closer until her world consisted only of him. His voice. His scent. His blue eyes begging with intense need.

She balanced her hands against his chest, both wanting to stop the flow of words and urge him to keep talking. "This is your career. Your life."

"You're still not getting it."

"Then explain."

"The work is part of my life and leaving here is not exactly a sacrifice. This is the third offer I've gotten since I started working for you."

"But you have a future here."

"Damn it, woman. Stop talking about work and listen to what I'm saying to you." His palms traveled up her arms to rest on her shoulders. One thumb traced a lazy pattern over the base of her neck. The other hand slipped into her hair. "The decision is now yours. I offered to work out two-weeks notice but Friedman told me to clean out my desk and get out. He also shut down my computer password, so all I can access is my calendar. I'm sure security will be here any minute to escort me out."

"He can't . . ." Her fury on Colin's behalf died hard. "Well, he actually can."

"This company has a real hard-on for rules." For the first time since their play last night, he smiled. "And as of a few hours from now I am officially not a handbook violation."

"We need to talk about this."

"You know where to find me. You still have the condo key."

This couldn't happen. It was too fast, too risky. She believed in thinking things through and making plans. "You don't change the entire course of your life for one night of sex."

That fast his hands dropped from her body. "You refuse to see what's right in front of you."

"One of us has to be reasonable and put the last few days in perspective. We've slept together That's it."

"If that's the way you really feel, throw the fucking key away."

"You're making this into some sort of test and I don't like it."

He walked back to his side of the desk. "No test. If you want me, all you have to do is say yes."

HE'D pushed her too hard. Colin realized the mistake the second after he dismissed Allie from his office. He was a dumbass. A total fucking dumbass.

After eight months of carefully biding his time while she dated that idiot accountant Bill from down the street then dumped him, and all that time planning her seduction, Colin knew he'd rushed the end and blown it.

He didn't care about the job because he had the safety of another one. But the idea of not seeing her every day, not hearing those heels click as she walked down the hall or feeling the kick of anticipation as he waited for her to hover by his door and say good morning, left him feeling restless and frustrated.

Hell, she left the office right after their confrontation and without even saying good-bye. He'd half hoped to see her car parked in his condo guest spot as he pulled in. Even the empty concrete mocked him.

"Damn." He fumbled with his keys. Balancing a box in one hand and a briefcase in the other made getting into his place tough.

He managed to open the door and use his elbow to shove it shut behind him. The scent of crushed roses filled his head. Damn, he could still smell her. It wasn't bad enough her image lingered in his head, now her presence haunted his place.

"You're late."

He dropped the box. Something shattered in the crash against the hardwood, but he ignored it. He was too busy taking in the beautiful woman in front of him. The long robe fell open to the shadowed valley between her breasts and the slit highlighted her lean legs to her upper thigh. The same sweet skin he had tasted and touched for hours.

He said the first words that popped into his muddled brain. "I like you in pink."

"I thought you liked me naked." She twisted the belt between her fingers as she walked barefoot through the gap dividing them. "Aren't you going to ask me why I'm here?"

Desperate to get this right, he nudged his ego to the side. "I want you to be here because you couldn't stand the idea of being away from me."

She untied the belt and let the material slide open to expose miles of rosy skin. "I'm standing in your house because I realized I don't want to be anywhere else."

The words he'd wanted to hear. "What about the job?"

"You of all people should know this isn't about work. This is personal." She slid her fingers under the edges of the robe and dropped it to the floor.

He knew what it took for her to take this step, to risk being hurt and rejected. To put her needs as a woman before her responsibilities as a boss.

"I know you like being in charge, but I'm thinking I'll take the lead tonight." Her fingers danced across her nipple before brushing down her stomach. "Yes?"

"Definitely."

Her hand stopped just inches above the reaching the place he longed to touch. "I'm going to need you take your pants off."

He stripped them down before she finished the sentence. Standing there bare from the waist down and still wearing his shirt and tie should have been strange, but it felt so right.

She pressed her body against his. Wrapping her arms around his neck, she slid skin against skin, leaving no question about what she wanted.

"We're going to need a condom." Her heated kisses followed along his jawline before traveling down his neck. "And a bed."

"I have both." What he didn't have was a prayer against this Allie. He'd sensed the sensual creature hiding under those proper suits but the reality was much more potent.

"I have nothing but time."

But he had to be sure he didn't push her into this. "No doubts?"

"No." She loosened his tie. "No regrets?"

"None."

She dragged his hand to her breast, letting him cup and caress her. "Then you better get to pleasuring me."

"You'll be amazed at what a hard worker I am."

Her ankle slid up his calf. "I'm pretty demanding."

"I can handle it." His other hand snaked down to her ass. The smooth skin had his hips flexing.

"You have all night to show me."

He rubbed his erection against her, loving the way she cuddled and held him. "I plan on taking a lot longer than that."

"Good."

From anyone else the word would have been meaningless. From Allie he felt the vow, the promise of commitment. "And I happen to have off tomorrow."

"I have a feeling I'm going to need to call in sick."

Relief poured through him. "You never take a sick day."

"I'm thinking you're worth it."

"I promise I will be."

Her mouth hovered over his. "Stop talking and show me."

National bestselling and award-winning author **HelenKay Dimon** is a former divorce attorney who is thrilled to write romance full time. Two of her novels have been designated as "Red-Hot Reads" by *Cosmopolitan* magazine and excerpted in its issues. Her books have been featured at numerous venues, including *E! Online* and *The Chicago Tribune*, and have been published by Doubleday Book Club and Rhapsody Book Club and translated into a dozen languages. Other than her readers, the best thing about her job is the commute—which consists of going from one side of the house to the other. You can visit HelenKay at her website, www.helenkaydimon.com.

INTO THE RED

CAMERON BELLE

Shortly after lunch, the suits came and escorted Carlson from the premises. Scuttlebutt is he was slipping enhancements to the contestants, something about a gambling addiction and that alone would have been enough. Since the Network takes "fairness" and "integrity" seriously, we're not allowed to bet on anything, let alone the Tournament. The drugs just make it sexy, which makes for coverage and with the first elimination sweeps around the corner, they would want him gone before a scandal brewed. So gone he was.

Which leaves them down one exam tech for the night.

So far, I've only ever worked in the rehab wing of the aftercare center, but I do have certification, a spotless record, and—thanks to my birth—financial resources that make bribes and debts a nonissue. That may be why they chose me, or maybe it was luck of the spin. I hope so. One of the points of my having a career is to earn advancement through my own merit, and I'd like to hope that's how I got this opportunity. But I'm not naive.

It's thankless grunt work, screening the early-season rabble, but it's still a game-night task at the megarena itself, one on one with active contestants. It's a foot in the door that an intern of my seniority shouldn't expect for another season at least. So yeah, chances are some admin type realized who I was and saw Carlson's slot as a chance to curry my family's favor. That doesn't mean I can't prove myself equal to the task.

They pull me from PT with last year's second runner up, and on the van ride over, I struggle to recall the last time I saw a full game, some time before med school for sure. My last stadium visit is easier to pinpoint; it fell the weekend before my fifteenth birthday. While I'll admit it's what drove me toward medicine, I try not to unpack the crystal-clear memory too often. Mostly, I succeed.

After a security screening, I find myself in a long tunnel many levels below the thundering floor of the megarena. A story or so above my head, the motion-activated lighting flares up, then drops back into darkness as a quartet of armed and armored guards hustles me along. Our steps echo off the vaulted ceiling and tremors of bass pulse down from the pre-competition music, so loud that if I pressed a palm to the cool, concrete walls, I'd feel it.

The lead guard stops abruptly and smacks the companel beside an entrance. He states my code, his code, the date and, after leaning in for a retscan, the word, "Authorize." The door whispers open and dim blue overheads flick to halogen white.

Only the lead follows me in. "You know the routine," he says, and I nod. "Good. Show me your wrist, boy."

I manage not to bristle. I may be lean, with a face that has many patients asking where the real doctor is, but this man's got five years on me at most. He hasn't worked nearly hard enough to earn my visible disdain. I flex my wrist, holding it up impatiently.

He extracts a wristband from a vest pocket and after strapping it on more snugly than necessary, he taps his compad. The wristband beeps and a green light starts flashing in time with my pulse. "You're all set. Panic button's here." He taps the left side. "Something happens and you can't reach it, no worries. If it goes into the red, it drops him long enough to give you a chance."

"I told you I know the routine. You can go now. I have men to see."

"Just the one," he says with a knowing smirk.

I ignore his tone, fetch my compad from my bag, and as the door closes, I pull up the chart to familiarize myself with the essentials. I flip past the contestant's bio—don't care. "Personality" is B-roll to charm the viewers. All I want to know is what's been done to his body. The answer, I discover as I scan, is "not much." He's a rookie with just three games behind him and nothing worse than a broken nose and the usual cuts and bruises.

The rehab patients I'm used to dealing with are all incapacitated with injury. They're also game players who've mellowed with experience and for the troublemakers, we've got drugs. I've got none of that here, just a powerful, lucid, barely trained prisoner and an opportunity I probably didn't earn. One I'm not entirely prepared for.

I roll up my sleeves to just above my elbows and anticipation stirs in my gut. In response, my wristband blinks faster, green taking on a yellowish hue. Deep breath in on a slow count of three then out through pursed lips. Twice more and the blinking slows, shifting back to emerald. Good. I will do this, I resolve. I will handle whatever walks through that door without calling for the guards.

Long before they arrive, I hear the heavy clomp of boots, the rise and fall of one man's voice. Then the door opens and he's shoved in. "Been a pleasure," he barks, then he spits a fat wad of saliva in one of their faces.

Instead of wiping it away, the guard taps a button on his chest, and the competitor's muscles go rigid. He yelps involuntarily then does a half-lunge at the guard, the kind of fake out that's over before it starts. Instead of flinching, the guard jabs the button and holds it. And holds it. And smiles.

The competitor's hands fly to his metal collar. He struggles to stay on his feet, but the longer the guard presses, the further he curls in on himself, thickly muscled thighs trembling. I rush forward and wrap both arms around his chest, keeping him from hitting the unforgiving metal floor. "Enough!" I snap.

The guard twists the button and the competitor goes limp. I strain to ease him to the ground. I'm not weak, but at 218 pounds, it's an awkward task. "You're welcome," the guard says as the door closes.

"Terrific," I say as I kneel. That probably just cost me any chance of cooperation, and if I don't get my pulse under control by the time he snaps out of the stun, I'll be the one setting off his collar. I roll him onto his back, supporting his freshly shaved head so it doesn't bang on the floor. The collar on his tan, short-sleeved shirt looks irreparably stretched, like he's been dragged by it. A fresh cut on his mouth leaks blood, the red smearing just past the pink of his full lower lip.

I'm about to rise and retreat to a smarter distance when I'm stopped by an iron grip right above my wristband. The blinking light is lemon, which means right now the collar is inducing moderately painful sensations all over his body. "Easy," he says in a strained whisper. "Easy now. There's a good boy," he croons as if to a skittish animal.

With my free hand I dig a thumb into a pressure point on his arm and wrench myself free, then I rise and put a few steps between us. My wrist aches and his finger marks fade slowly from my skin. I resist the urge to rub at them. "You baited him. Don't bait me, and I'll make this as painless as possible."

He sits up and rolls his head until his neck cracks. Then his eyes widen as he slowly looks me over. "*Not* a boy, but new, yes? My name's Tom, by the way." He extends his hand, and it's not clear whether he's looking for a handshake or help up.

I'm not nearly green enough to offer either, but I do note the rust of healed scrapes on his knuckles. I select a pair of transparent sanitary gloves and tug them on, unrolling them to just below my elbows, and since he's still on the floor, I tell him to please sit on the exam table.

After a smooth kip-up, he stalks toward me, circling me and the table once. He stops beside me, leans a hip against the edge of the table, then slides a couple fingers up under his collar, scratching. "Love how they leave us in here alone with you lot. You haven't even got a gun. It's like they don't care what happens to you."

"That collar works fine," I say.

Slowly, deliberately, he reaches out and lays a hand on my throat. It's rough and hot, heavy even though he doesn't squeeze. His tone isn't menacing so much as curious. "I could snap your neck, you know. You'd be dead before the collar dropped me."

"And lose your chance at freedom? You don't look particularly stupid."

He holds on for another half a minute, his blue-green eyes locked on mine. Tanning lamps have lent his cage-kept body a healthy glow. His nose, which his chart says has been broken at least once, is as straight as a well-carved marble statue. The Network's hand has done its part making him close-up ready, but it's his mouth that really wants my attention, full, round, natural lips whose softness looks out of place on such a hard body. He presses a thumb to my carotid. "You don't look all that brave, but your heart tells me you're not scared."

"Sit on the table, please."

With a reluctant sigh, he lets me go. "How 'bout you tell me your name first."

"This isn't a negotiation."

"You look like a Fredrick."

"I can get you declared unfit for the tournament. If you want to wait until next season, please, stay where you are."

He cocks his head to the side, looking for all the world like a curious dog. "I think I like you, Fredrick. I think I like you very much." He hops up onto the table and drops his jaw, lifting his tongue to the roof of his mouth.

I tug my glove taut and check under his tongue for hidden blades. With two fingers, I explore the slippery heat of his cheeks, then all along his gumline. As I withdraw, he bites gently and wraps his lips around my knuckles. My heart rate jumps and the tendons of his neck show the exact moment his collar responds. After swallowing a groan, he sucks.

I yank my hand away and continue my exam, logging his vitals and ignoring his smirk. Absolutely ignoring the way he follows me with his eyes and licks his lips every time I touch him. I just focus on crossing items off a mental checklist. For the most part, this exam is just a bureaucratic paper trail, proof he hasn't snuck contraband onto the megarena floor and that no one's graced him with any synthetic boosts.

On my command, he inhales, exhales, then in a husky voice, he says, "I believe you like me too, Fredrick."

I pull an autosyringe from the rack and without preamble, I jab it straight in his thigh. Silently, I count to five as it pulls, turning the cylinder from clear to dark, swirling red. When it's full, I pop the sample in the right slot and set the scanner to work. "My name's not Fredrick," I tell him. "It's Brendan."

He's smiling sweetly as he rubs his leg. "Brendan. Even better. Have you got a girlfriend, Brendan?"

"No."

"A boyfriend, then?" His jaw clenches, then he touches his collar. "There's a yes. Or maybe a regretful no."

"Or maybe it's none of your business. Please drop your shorts." I flip open a tube of lubricant and coat my right-hand fingers, then I look at his sculpted trapezius muscles, the door, my own slick fingers rubbing together. Anywhere but his playful grin.

"How could I refuse you?" He slides to the floor and draws himself up to his full height, only a couple inches taller than me. It's the breadth of him that's striking, especially when he tugs off his shirt. After he pushes down his shorts and steps out of them, he clasps his hands behind his back and stands before me, shoulders squared, naked save for the tattoos scattered all over his skin.

And, of course, the collar. It's the same dull semi-gloss silver as my wristband, the width of three fingers and the thickness of one. I tear my attention away from it and tell him, "Bend over the table."

He doesn't move a muscle.

"I don't enjoy this part any more than you do, so let's just be done with it."

He pouts. "It's not that I mind having you in me, but you didn't say please."

"Seriously?"

"It's common courtesy," he says, rubbing at his mouth. "Nothing you owe a man like me, sure, but—"

I hold up a hand and he snaps his mouth shut. *I* want to be done with this, so I give in and say, "Please."

He turns, smiling like he's genuinely surprised.

"Thank you," I tell him as he puts his thick, ink-wrapped forearms on the cold steel table. Violet stripes mar the back of one thigh, day-old bruises that cosmetics will mask before he's on camera. Experimentally, I press on one with a few of my unlubed fingers.

He chokes back a noise.

"Sorry. Do you want an analgesic? I could—"

He shakes his head. "Least of my troubles. You just caught me off guard. Go ahead," he says, planting his feet a little farther apart.

For the first time, I wonder what he did to put himself here. Nearly all competitors are criminals of one sort or another, most violent, but every year a crazy few sign over their lives for a shot at the purse. Some of the ink on his skin is jagged and hand scrawled, obviously the work of some prison amateur. But some isn't, and the multi-colored feathers that curl over his left shoulder blade are profession-ally intricate. Along the edge is a line of what looks like Latin. I trace it with my thumb. "What's this say?"

"That's a second date sort of question, don't you think?"

Sympathy stabs at my chest and I yield to it. "Look. If you're smuggling anything, tell me now and get it out. Otherwise, I'm obligated to report what I find."

His buttocks clench and he looks over his shoulder at me, frowning. "What, exactly, do I get out of owing you one?"

"Nothing. I mean, you wouldn't," I say, feeling stupid for offering. I wipe slick from the back of my middle finger over his hole, then twist the tip against it. He tightens completely and I lift an eyebrow at him. "If you'd relax—"

"If you'd fucking get on with it," he snaps, facing forward. "You're hardly popping my cherry."

"Fine," I say, giving up all pretense of gentleness. I'm too slippery, insistent, and one twisting thrust later, my slim finger pushes into him, the clamp of his entrance slowly squeezing down the length until it's choking the second knuckle. He is nothing but smooth and hot and empty inside and I pause for several seconds. I lay a hand on the small of his back and, low-voiced, I tell him, "Exhale all the way and relax for me." When I hear the air rushing out of him, I murmur, "Good." Tension shifts in all the muscles of his back and then, incrementally, the tightness around my finger eases.

As I withdraw, he gasps and his scrotum tightens. When I look up and away, I spot the flush creeping down the back of his neck. He drops his head to his hands and whispers, "You know, I wish I were hiding something. I'd owe you."

I have nothing to say to that because it summons thoughts of repayment. Specific thoughts directly related to his current position. Thoughts that dry my mouth and draw my attention to my own flesh. I try, but I can't help myself; I harden as my two fingers slide in with unexpected ease. Carefully, I feel around, hitting a particular and unavoidable spot.

He takes a ragged breath. "I'd like owing you."

My face heats, as much from guilt as arousal, and when he abruptly clamps around me, I notice the blinking on my wrist.

I realize I'm pushing into goldenrod territory and my face grows hotter. I ease out of him and turn away, stripping my gloves and dropping them in the trash. After counting to ten, I turn back, composed, and inform him, "The blood scan takes a few minutes."

He pulls his shorts back on and eases up on the table. While I busy myself updating his chart, he crosses his ankles and swings them, watching me. Before long, he says, "You'd never make it in the arena."

I don't bother looking up. "Obviously."

"Not with your hair. Too easy for a man to get his hands on."

I glance at him, and of course my bangs have chosen that moment to fall in front of my eyes. My dark brown hair is wavy, long enough to tuck behind my ears and earn me more of my father's disappointment, but it's nothing noteworthy. "Yeah. That's what's holding me back."

"C'mon. I bet you're a scrappy one."

"I'd never make it *to* the arena." I'd never break the sorts of laws that would put me in that position. And if I did, I'd like to imagine I'd be smart enough not to get caught.

"Never's an awfully big word," he says. "You've never been in the wrong place at the wrong time?"

"This is where you tell me you're innocent, right?"

"Hardly." He grins broadly, then winces and licks at his split lower lip.

"I can fix that if you'd like," I say.

"I would." He's compliant as I clean him, only hissing once as I paint a thin line of dermaglue over the cut.

"You shouldn't start with them before the game," I tell him. "You should save your energy."

He presses his lips together a few times, licks at the sealed cut, then nods his approval. "Your concern touches me deep in my heart. Tell me something. You ever think maybe the guards started with me?"

"Did they?"

"And that maybe," he says, voice taking on an edge, "I know best what I need to get ready for the floor."

"Pissing off the men with the sticks? That's what you need? That's the best you can do?"

He narrows his eyes and studies me. Then, with the lightning-fast reflexes that have kept him alive this long, he's on his feet, gripping the back of my neck, and swinging me around 'til the table digs into my back. "I've got a couple other methods," he grinds out past clenched teeth. "But I like this one. Go ahead. Push the panic button."

"You're smarter than this," I say calmly, even though my heart pounds against my ribcage. Deep breath, slow exhale, and again as I try to bring myself down. But he's right *there*, a wall of hard flesh just a hand's breadth away, head dropping 'til it rests ear-to-ear beside mine. His hot breath gusts against my neck and one of us, I'm not sure who, moans.

He closes the last few inches and as he presses his body against mine, he must feel my cock stirring to life. As seconds pass, one heartbeat at a time, I know I should feel humiliated. I should feel scared. Instead, I feel more alive than I have in a long while. This time, I know that it's me who moans.

He relaxes his hold, then swallows hard and carefully rakes his fingers through my curls before grabbing the table on either side of my hips. "Go on, Brendan. Do it."

I clear my throat. "You need to step back now. You need—" I startle as his mouth opens against my neck, just above my shirt collar. Heat sinks from my cheeks to my chest and then lower, prickling its way through me 'til it pools between my legs. "I'm not going to help you get yourself hurt."

His lips barely brush my jaw, then they're moving against my ear, hot and soft. "But isn't that your job?"

"Step back, *please*."

He looks me in the eye, and whatever he sees there makes him frown thoughtfully and lean back.

I run a hand through my hair, and as it drops, he catches my wrist in a light grip, easy enough to break if I tried. Instead I just watch as he undoes the wristband's strap and slides it two notches looser. He refastens it so it's secure, but no longer biting into me, then he brings my inner wrist to his mouth and kisses the faint pink dent in the skin. "Getting smacked around," he explains, uncurling my fingers and kissing the tips. "It gets me in the right frame of mind. The pain helps me focus. God, your hands are soft." He kisses my palm.

"Hey!" I snap, jerking my hand away, then I grab his chin and force him to look at me. I'm ready to tell him to quit this, then I see it. He's terrified and this is how he hides it. I want something reassuring to tell him, but I'm at a sudden loss for words.

"No, it's all right," he says, shrugging out of my grasp. "I'll just start with them on the way to the floor."

"Whatever," I say, stepping out from between him and the table and rolling my sleeves back down. "Just don't involve me in your masochistic games."

"I don't like the pain," he says slowly, as if to a half-wit. "I use the pain. If I weren't here—"

"But you are, so whatever you're about to say is pointless."

"But I am," he says ruefully, "and you're right. Doesn't change the fact that you're too scared to play with me."

"Nice try."

His expression darkens. "Oh, and far too smart to fall for such ham-fisted manipulation, right? Too *good* to enjoy hurting me. So noble, you'd never enjoy something so base as the Tournament. Yet here you are, with your fine shoes. Here not by need but by some twisted choice, rubbing shoulders with brutes like me. Patching us up when we break and shoving us back in the grinder. Not a chance you're a sadist."

"Are you finished?"

"Hurt me," he demands, lunging into my space. "Just hurt me and I'll owe you."

"You've got nothing I want."

"Liar. Another place, another time, and you'd be on your knees by now, wouldn't you? I'd be down your throat. I'd be licking my taste out of your mouth and fingering your ass until you fell the fuck apart." His breath catches, then one of his thumbs is pressing to my mouth and tugging it open as he leans in, first-date slow.

He's close enough for me to taste his breath when I step back and hold up a hand. "*But* we are here, and in a few minutes, you'll be on the floor. So just sit down and wait for them to collect you."

"You could be my very last kiss." He tucks a lock of hair behind my ear and smiles, but something in his eyes makes me want to cut myself. For a moment I'm stupid enough to ponder the impossible, another life where I bring him home to scandalize my parents. I imagine the things I could do to his mouth. I realize I'm staring at it when the corners curl up and he says, "Oh, I'd love to see the inside of your head right now."

Fate smiles on me and the scanner chooses that moment to chime. I step back, and when he follows, I press a palm to his chest. "Shut up and sit down," I say. Then I turn away and busy myself with the scanner. Screens of charts scroll by, declaring him clean. I pretend my hands aren't shaking.

Of course he's silent. Of course I've got no warning before his warm hands settle heavily on my shoulders. I manage not to jump, barely, as the solid bulk of his body presses flush against my back, but when he shifts his hips, nestling his erection against my ass, I drop my stylus. He covers both my hands with his, lacing his fingers through mine, and then he rubs his face against the back of my head, breath gusting hot and fast on my scalp. "You didn't say please," he murmurs.

I drop my chin to my chest and try to summon the sense to push the panic button.

"You could be my last everything." He kisses the back of my neck. "Wouldn't that be horrifically romantic?"

My chest tightens. "No."

"Say please, Brendan," he whispers, releasing the hand without the wristband. I could reach for it. I could stop this. I should want to. He sets a hand on my hip and squeezes. "Say please," he says as he carefully untucks my shirt from my trousers, then he's spreading his big, hot hand, skin to skin, over my belly. "Say, 'Please stop.'"

I cover his hand with my own and breathe, "No." Then, trembling, blood racing through my veins, I summon the courage to push his hand down between my legs. I don't recognize my own voice when I say, "Please."

He grunts like he's been gut-punched and I reach for my wristband. I've got it half undone when he seizes my hand and slams it down on the counter. Then he's fumbling with my fly. I try to help him, but he growls, "Quit," and mouths the nape of my neck until my knees weaken.

Just as I begin to sink, his free arm wraps around me, supporting me and as he shoves down my trousers, I scramble to grip the edge of the counter. When he finally closes his hand around my dick, I drop my head back to his shoulder and thrust forward, desperate for friction. "Go *on*," I beg. I reach up and back for his face, turning my head; his mouth finds my cheek, my jaw, then my lips, capturing a hysterical laugh as he drags his thumb over the slick head of my cock.

Another shudder passes through his frame and then finally, finally, he begins to stroke. I arch my back, grinding against his erection and he ruts forward, mouth falling open, sloppy and hot against my chin. I moan when he releases me, but then he's shoving down his shorts and my briefs and the hot, bare length of his cock against the cleft of my ass all but undoes me.

"I need, I need, oh God." I close my hand over his, squeezing tighter, stroking faster. "I need—"

"I know." His cock slips along the sweat between my cheeks, shallow thrusts in time with our hands, nudging me over and over into his fist. "Next time."

When the tip of his dick catches on my hole, the thought jolts through me—*No. Now.* I go up on my toes, trying to lean forward, but his arm's an immovable bar across my chest. I shift and press back and feel the exact moment he realizes what I'm going for. He shudders against me, going still except for the rise and fall of his chest against my back. I squirm just enough and finally the hot, slick head of his cock pops in.

It's blunt and rock hard and fat enough to hurt, just sitting there, stretching an ache into me. He spits and a second later, it's rolling down my tailbone and he's smearing it around the circumference of stretched skin. I whine—humiliatingly high and sharp—and then he pushes, sinking just a little deeper.

The sharp, hot pain steals my breath for a few seconds and I brace for more, but he goes still again. The burn melts into a heavy, aching need to be filled all the way up and I reach blindly for the supply drawer, saying, "I need you slick and I need you moving and I—oh God." I clamp my fingers around my shaft, fighting the inevitable. "Fucking lube."

"Too late," he chokes out as he slips from me. A heartbeat later, he pitches forward, pinning me down on the table as he shoots, hot and sloppy, all over my back. He's heavy and I'd worry about breathing if I gave a fuck about anything but my own climax barreling down on me. He fumbles for my cock and seizes it, tugging and urging me, "C'mon, almost, that's right. Give it."

I thrust against his fist once, twice, then he drags his dick through the wet mess and I do fall the fuck apart, spilling into his hand and clutching at the counter as I white out and make some throat-ripping noise I can't hear over the rush of blood in my ears. I can't catch my breath or feel my fingers, but somehow, when the world comes back to me, I'm still standing, barely, semen cooling as it rolls down my thighs. Suddenly, my back is exposed to air. And my watch is blinking red.

I look over my shoulder and see him on the floor, eyes rolled back, body jerking. I drop to the floor beside him and the skin on my knees tears. I barely register it as I get a hand under his skull and cradle him until the seizure passes. After what feels like an eternity, he finally goes limp. Limp but breathing, thank God.

I fall backward onto my ass, panting hard. The trickle of blood from my knees catches my eye and some automatic part of my brain hauls me to my feet, locates some bandages to slap on, then grabs my trousers and mechanically pulls them back up. It takes four tries to button them, because I watch him the whole time. Him and the crimson stains next to him on the floor.

A glance at the clock tells me I've got minutes, at most, before the guards return, so I grab some towels and get to my knees beside him, ignoring their screams of protest and the way my shirt clings wetly to my back. I mop up his stomach and hand and then lower my forehead to his and breathe, willing him to wake up. "Please." I grab his sticky hand and squeeze.

He gasps and I sit up to watch as his eyes flutter open. They meet mine, go wide, and then he just throws his head back and laughs. He keeps laughing as I sit back and wipe my hands on my trousers. By the time I get to my feet, it's subsided to a chuckle and he's propped himself up on his elbows. "Look at you."

"Get dressed. They'll be back any minute."

He groans at me, but tugs his shorts up and eases himself to his feet. As he fetches his shirt from beside the exam table, he says, "I would murder for a fucking smoke."

I'm still trembling and he thinks this is a joke. I spit out, "Yeah? That what you're in for?"

His smile disappears, replaced by something cold and hard. He says in a flat voice, "No, darling. I killed for love."

The hairs on the back of my neck prickle up.

"Your shoes," he says after a few moments.

"Yeah, right." I wedge my feet back into them, then run my fingers through my hair a few times. "I'm not," I start, then I pause, searching for how to put what I feel into words. "I don't—"

He holds up a hand. "You don't do this, you're not like that, this never happened. That about cover it?"

"No, that's not it. This happened."

"Then what?"

After a moment's hesitation, I know what to say and it comes out in a rush, "Tonight's a melee round. You'll want to get to higher ground early."

His lips compress into a suspicious frown. "How the hell do you know that?"

"It's been promoted all week. 'First real bloodbath of the season.'"

The echo of boots in the tunnel reaches us and he asks, "What do I owe you for the tip?"

"Stay alive."

He narrows his eyes at me. "And?"

Something unfamiliar and horribly warm twists in my gut. Softly, I say, "Ask me next time."

Then the door's sliding open and he's spinning on his heel. "Gentlemen," he shouts, spreading his arms wide. "Let us get this dog and pony show on the road."

I remove my wristband and toss it to one of the guards, nodding as he catches it. "He's good."

"Wrong. I am *fantastic*." I can't help but hear the false edge of his bravado and it rips at the ache in my chest.

As soon as the door shuts behind them, I force myself to finish his exam report. I use a few alcohol wipes to clean myself more thoroughly. Then, advising myself against it the whole time, I go somewhere I haven't gone in years.

MOTHER is the only one in the box tonight. "Sweetheart. What in the world are you doing here? Is something wrong? Did someone—"

I kiss her cheek. "Everything's fine." Onscreen, the opening titles flash. The sound's muted, but the theme music vibrates up from the floor below. I sink down beside her on the plush couch and watch as the camera pans slowly over the contestants, pausing on each long enough to bring up their names. When a popular veteran appears, the arena rattles with tens of thousands of stomping feet. I lean forward, watching intently. The second to last is Tom, and unlike the rest, he looks directly into the camera. Then he winks.

My heart skips a beat. Below us, the crowd goes wild. Beside me, Mother says, "He is a cheeky one. What do you hear about him, Brendan? The one I was sponsoring left last week."

The one she was sponsoring bled out last week. She complained about it for three days. I ask, "Isn't last year's runner up more your style?"

She glances back at the screen where they're taking their positions. "He is awfully attractive."

I frown.

"Oh, hush. I know, you signed all those papers and you won't even give your own mother a tiny hint because you're such a good boy. I raised you too well."

There's an edge to her teasing, but affection as well, and I know she won't push. Truth is, a patron of Mother's stature would boost Tom's chances, but it would also paint a target on his back. Worse, I'd have to recuse myself from contact with him for the rest of the season. It would be the smart choice. The safe one. But as they leap off the blocks, I spot him. He's tearing recklessly across the open floor, straight toward the stairs to the upper levels.

I picture myself down on the sidelines during finals, part of his acute care team, waiting for the quarter to end. Even if he survives that long, it's a slim chance at best that I'd get that assignment. Unless, of course, I pull some strings. And first, pull Mother off Tom's scent. "Sure he's handsome," I tell her, "but did you see last week's point leader? Now, you did not hear this from me, all right?"

> **Cameron Belle** has been writing slightly twisted love stories since the turn of the century. After imprinting young on such romantic classics as *Terminator, Fight Club*, and *Universal Soldier*, she earned a journalism BA before realizing that what she really wanted to do was lie for a living. She currently lives in NYC, where she does her best to break hearts and put them back together again by the final chapter. Learn more at CameronBelle.com.

OVERTAKEN

SARA THORN

Liz had never seen John fight.

She watched him now, a silent shadow in the shouting crowd around the ring. The old gym was packed, everyone pressed tight against one another, except maybe in the back rows where they stood on wooden benches. The loudest were the kids in the front, the ones John trained. She could hear them clearly from where she hid in the middle of the fifth row, their voices on the cusp of changing.

"Get him, Coach!"

"Come on! Move those feet!"

Did he use to tell them the same? she wondered. She'd never seen him train them, either.

There were a lot of things she'd never seen of John Watts.

It was dark back here, the only light coming from the low windows at ground level, but glaring spotlights lit the ring where John fought, his bare chest gleaming with sweat, his gloved hands raised to protect his face. When he scored a hit, the sound could be heard even above the crowd.

Her pussy clenched at that sound.

She hadn't expected that; it wasn't why she'd come.

The gong rang and the two men withdrew to their corners. One of the kids handed him a towel, and he wiped off his face. Next came a transparent water bottle. She watched his Adam's apple as he tilted his head to drink.

"Last round!" someone called.

John gave the bottle back, scanning the crowd. His eyes halted on her. Could he see her, from up there? She couldn't tell, and as the gong rang again he turned to his opponent.

It had been three months since last they met, three months since she'd last touched the muscled back sweating up there under the light. He had ended it, but she didn't know why. Not the truth of it anyway.

Her throat closed; she regretted it now, holding anything back from him. She'd thought she could just let the intimacy grow slowly between them, but . . . Well, no matter. Tonight, she was going to make sure there'd be nowhere to hide.

For either of them.

JOHN was alone under the row of showerheads, the cold water washing over him. The white tiles shone in the fluorescent light, his blue towel the only one on the metal hooks by the doorway. If he closed his eyes, he could still see Liz's face out there in the crowd, watching him. Drinking him in.

He turned the heat down further, shivering as the freezing water slid over his scalp and down his back. He wasn't ready to see her, not yet.

But she'd be waiting.

He turned off the shower and padded across the wet tiles into the dressing room, wiping off his hair. The wooden benches stretched out, empty. He opened his locker and pulled on his jeans and T-shirt, stepping into his tennis shoes. *Dammit*, why hadn't she stayed away? He'd given her every fucking cliché in the book.

He stuffed his gloves into the bag with his wet towel and hefted it over his shoulder as he headed for the door. Taking a deep breath, he pushed it open.

She stood in the corridor just outside, leaning against the brick wall, hands shoved into the pockets of her tight navy blue jeans. Her short hair curled over her ears, only the tips sticking out.

Liz.

"Good fight," she said, smiling. "I should have come sooner."

He didn't reply; they both knew who hadn't wanted her to come.

At the end of the corridor, the crowd roared; someone had scored a good hit. A couple strolled by, carrying sodas in red and white paper cups.

"Why are you here, Liz?"

"I came to see you."

He couldn't resist. "To see me fight you mean."

She frowned; she didn't understand his point.

"I saw you, out there," he said. "Does it always turn you on to see men pummel each other?"

Faint color rose in her cheeks. "It's not the violence," she said, attempting a grin. "It's the dress."

He didn't smile back. "No, it's not."

Another match had finished, and a stream of spectators came through, heading for the refreshments. They passed between him and Liz, a blur of colors. Her eyes didn't leave his.

"In here," he said at last, and turned down the corridor for the utility closet. The keys jangled as he fished them from his bag and unlocked the dented metal door. The dark green paint was peeling; they really ought to do something about it. He ducked inside and pulled the string hanging from the single lightbulb in the ceiling, inadvertently sending it swinging.

Liz followed more cautiously, eyeing the stained metal bucket in the corner, a mop haphazardly thrust inside. The back wall was covered with crude shelves, filled with paper boxes, sponges, plastic bags, and a couple of flashlights.

The door slammed closed behind them, shutting out the noise.

She turned to him, hands shoved back into her pockets. He watched her T-shirt rise and fall with her breathing, the shape of her breasts clearly visible beneath. She was close enough that he could smell her flowery perfume. His groin tightened, remembering the scent of it on her skin.

"Is that why you left me?" she said.

He blinked. "What?"

"Because you thought . . . Because watching you up there . . . Because it turns me on."

He blanched. "No."

"But it is because of the sex," she pressed.

God. "There's no point in talking about this, Liz. It's over."

She ignored him. "Why did you run away? Every time you touched me, afterward . . . What were you afraid of?"

"I wasn't."

"What, big men like you can't be afraid?"

He had been afraid, of blowing it.

And he had.

But that wasn't why he'd left.

She was looking at him with her fierce amber eyes.

He couldn't lie to her; he couldn't answer her. "What do you want?" he said harshly.

"I've missed you." She hesitated, visibly bracing herself, pulling her hands from her pockets and squaring her shoulders. "I love you."

He closed his eyes, chest constricting. "What do you want?" he repeated, his voice low this time.

"I want another chance. I want to fix what went wrong." She faltered, glanced at him, then looked away.

He raised his hand to touch her cheek and let his thumb stroke across her lips until they softened, quivered.

Finally, she said, "Have you ever been . . . rough with a woman?"

He froze. "Rough?"

Her blush deepened and she stiffened, preparing to jerk free.

His grip tightened on her chin. "Do you want me to be rough with you?" he said.

She didn't move, eyes stubbornly averted.

"To hurt you, perhaps?"

He saw her waver, shifting from foot to foot, poised between fleeing and truth.

Her eyelashes rose, her determined eyes fixing on him. "I never told you what I hungered for. I never asked for it. But . . . I'm asking now. I'd like you to do whatever you want. To me."

He searched her eyes for a moment, then he dropped his hand. "No, you don't."

His voice sounded flat; she flinched, but persisted. "I *do*."

"No," he repeated. "You want me to do whatever it is *you* desire."

She was chewing her lower lip now, the color darkening under her teeth. "Try me."

But he shook his head, took a step back. "I'm not a fucking mind reader."

"What do *you* want then?" she challenged, halting him in his tracks. "You never told me, either."

His cock hardened; he couldn't have what he longed for.

She came after him, placing a hand on his chest. His heartbeat thundered in his ears—did she feel it? She looked so earnest, asking him for truths he wished he could burn from his bones.

"I'm not going to take a whip to you," he said at last, the half-admission making his voice hoarse. "I couldn't."

She put a hand on his arm, squeezing lightly, as if trying to soothe him. "You don't have to."

He shot her a sardonic smile, turning his face toward her, breathing in her scent.

She leaned in, her soft hair brushing his cheek, the smell of her rose-scented shampoo enveloping him. "You don't have to tell me what you want," she said against his ear, a mere whisper. "Just do it. Here, now."

His hand went to her back, trailing up the arch of her spine. He should say no, but instead he found himself cradling her neck as she rested her face against his shoulder. His cock throbbed painfully. He let his hand climb further, into the mass of her hair. Gently, he fisted his hand and pulled her head back, searching her face. Her lips were parted now, moist.

Outside, the sounds of the crowd could still be heard, chanting. Footsteps passed their closed door continuously, and occasional words drifted through.

". . . a match like this . . ."

". . . you think . . . ?"

"Kneel," he whispered.

Her eyes didn't leave his as she complied, legs folding beneath her. Her hands rose to his thighs as she settled onto her knees, steadying herself. He felt the warmth of her fingers through his jeans, the slight press of her fingertips.

His free hand drifted to his fly; each button gave way with a distinct little zing. He unbuckled his belt.

Her eyes left him, fastening on the white cotton of his boxers, following his every move as his hand closed on his cock, drawing it out. Her hot breath wafted against the exposed head, a drop of pre-come glistening on top.

"Open your mouth," he said, his voice gravelly, sounding like someone else's.

Her eyes lifted to his face and for a moment she strained forward, her hair pulling against the hand in her hair. She parted her lips, wider.

He shifted his stance, kept her still as he rubbed the tip of his cock against her tongue. It fluttered against the underside of his glans, then went still.

"How far can you take a man?" he said, but he knew the answer. Not very far.

Her tongue throbbed against him. She couldn't answer without letting go of him; she gazed up at him, silent.

"What if I wanted to go deeper?" He eased his hips forward, and her mouth closed around his shaft. "What if I wanted to go all the way?"

He didn't move, his eyes fixed on her face. She was watching him, eyes shining in the light from the single exposed lightbulb overhead.

"You'd gag," he clarified, pressing slightly on the back of her head. He didn't hold her hard enough that she couldn't pull away if she wanted to. But she hadn't moved. Not yet. She was waiting, waiting for him to tighten his grip, to tilt his hips, to follow through on his threat and bury himself in her throat.

He didn't; he couldn't.

"Your turn," he said softly.

She stiffened, her fingertips digging into his thighs for a moment. Her gaze lowered; she pushed forward. One inch, another. The tip of his cock nudged the back of her throat. One more inch; her throat convulsed around him and he shuddered at the exquisite feeling. She pulled back, leaving a string of saliva on his skin. Her eyes sought his—pleading?

His hand tightened in her hair; he stopped himself from forcing her head down. "You asked what I wanted," he said hoarsely. "I want to fuck your mouth. Like it was your pussy."

She shuddered.

"Does that turn you on?"

In answer, her eyes closed, the breath from her nose sounding loud in the small room. She moved forward again. This time she didn't stop, pressing on when her throat convulsed around him, until her nose brushed against his pubic hair. His nostrils flared, watching her, her slight form kneeling between his legs, his cock buried in her mouth.

He held her head still as he slid back out, until only the head was sheltered in her mouth. Her tongue flickered up, teasing the hole at the tip. This time, he flexed his hips forward. "Look at me," he said, sliding inexorably deeper.

Her eyes fluttered open, glazed. Her breathing was ragged now, beating against his skin in time with his pulse.

He pushed himself down to the hilt. She made a strangled sound and one hand left his thigh. He held still as she yanked open her jeans and shoved her hand inside.

He widened his stance, slid out, in again. Her cheeks were bright red now, and she made little moaning noises that vibrated through his cock. Her throat convulsed around him, squeezed him, and he thrust instinctively deeper. Her eyes were shining, drinking him in. She blinked; a tear trailed down her cheek.

He let go of her so fast, she pitched forward, landing on her hands. His cock throbbed mercilessly and he squeezed it, hard. "Fuck."

SHE blinked at the green linoleum, her right hand slick against the dirty floor. John had one hand over his eyes, his lips taut with some emotion. He was squeezing his cock so hard his knuckles whitened, inches from her face.

"Why did you stop?" she said. She'd been so close . . .

He lowered the hand from his eyes. His face was shuttered now, unreadable. Slowly, he let go of his cock and began to button up his jeans. There was a slight trembling to his fingers as he forced each metal button through its hole.

He was going to leave her here, like this.

She felt her cheeks flame and wiped her hand on her jeans, scrambling to her feet, her legs clumsy from kneeling and aborted pleasure.

He was watching her, hazel eyes flat. "Are you all right?"

How could he ask her that, when he'd just rejected her in the most primal way a man could reject a woman?

She lifted her chin, felt her erect nipples brush against her T-shirt. "You should've done what you promised." Her voice quavered, but only a little. Perhaps he wouldn't notice.

His eyes darkened. "And what did I promise?" His voice was silky now, dangerous.

For the first time, she regretted coming here. "You didn't do what you wanted."

"Didn't I?"

"No."

He tilted his head, his face still hard. As if he were angry with her. As if it were *her* fault.

"No," he agreed at last. "I didn't do what I wanted."

She frowned. Three times, she'd been in his bed. Every time, afterward, he'd been withdrawn. That last time, he'd sat silently at the edge of her bed, his elbows on his knees, staring out the dark window with only the moon to light his features. He was so beautiful, it had made her ache to look at him. She knew she shouldn't have touched him, but she couldn't resist. Her hand had drifted through the darkness, settling lightly on his shoulder. He hadn't leaped up and stormed out, but he might as well have. It had amounted to the same thing, even if his touch had been soft as he removed her hand. Even if he'd bent to kiss her before pulling on his clothes and leaving her. She hadn't known it would be for good; or maybe she had.

She didn't want to watch him walk out of her life again.

His eyes hadn't left her, even if she'd been silent too long. "I'm sorry," he said abruptly. "It's not you, I—"

"Stop!" She couldn't bear to hear his excuses. "Why didn't you do what you really wanted?" she said instead, needing an answer. "Are you so sure I wouldn't have liked it?"

He looked away, as if the plastic brush and old shovel in the corner held a sudden interest. "No," he said softly. "I'm not sure."

"And this . . ." Her trembling hand encompassed the closet. "What you did . . . Is that what you thought I wanted?"

For a moment, she hoped he would say no, so she wouldn't have to face him knowing, and still rejecting her.

His eyes returned to her face. "I didn't dislike it."

She felt the color rise again to her face and discovered it was she who couldn't look at him. "Then why did you stop? You made me feel . . ." *Uncertain, inadequate, rejected.*

"You cried."

Had she? "I didn't mean to."

He accepted this news in silence, but his expression was not quite so stony now. Tension coiled through his body; she could see it in his stiff back, in the muscles cording on his neck. This time she recognized the feeling stark on his face—she had seen it in her own.

He didn't want to be alone.

The thought gave her courage. "Have you never asked for what you really need?"

"No." He hesitated, then his lips curved. "I've taken it."

"What do you mean?"

"Liz, don't ask any more, okay? Leave it."

But she couldn't back down now. "Have you taken . . . by force?"

"Is there another way?"

She took a step closer. His nostrils flared. "What are you telling me?"

He looked at her a long, interminable moment. "I wasn't one of those smart kids you grew up with," he said at last. "I did bad things." He grimaced. "I did fucking unforgivable things. I was a damned lowlife."

She licked her lips. "You . . . You raped someone?"

His eyes snared hers again. "No, I've not raped. But I've beaten people up. I've felt their noses crunch under my fist. I've had people beg me to stop, Liz. But I didn't." He took a deep breath, let it out again. "I've put all that shit behind me. I *can't* force you."

She stared at him, the T-shirt stretching over his tense muscles, the jeans not quite hiding the bulge in his crotch. "But you want to."

"No!"

She searched his eyes. "You're lying."

For a moment, he looked so helpless, her heart squeezed in her chest.

"You want to hurt me," she said, her pussy clenching at the words.

His words were flat, final. "I can't."

Her clit had started to throb again, a hollow echoing through her body. "I'll stop you if you go too far."

He laughed bitterly at this. "How?"

"Trust me," she said. "Like I trust you."

HIS breathing was coming hard and fast. She didn't know what she was asking for.

She took another step closer; her fingers closed on his belt buckle.

His hand shot out, grasping her wrist.

Her eyes rose to his. "Trust me," she repeated.

She wanted to save him, he realized. She wanted to heal him.

But he couldn't be healed, not in this. "It's too late."

"Why?"

He floundered for a moment, his grip involuntarily tightening on her wrist. "I'm too old."

She ignored this blatant lie and took another step closer. She was so near now, he could feel the heat all along his front. His cock seemed to strain toward her crotch.

She lifted her free hand, traced it down his cheek, over his chin, the stubble rasping against her fingers. "Trust me," she repeated again, leaning in toward him, lips rising toward his own.

He stood frozen, unable to move. "Don't," he begged.

But she didn't stop, and he couldn't stop her, didn't want to stop her.

Her lips brushed against his, soft and moist. His left hand went to her back, clutching her to him. Her tongue teased along his lower lip. With a groan, he tilted his head and pushed into her mouth. His hands went to her ass and he ground his cock against her soft belly.

She pulled back, gasping for breath as she stared up at him, her eyes dark with arousal.

How could he not give her what she wanted?

What *he'd* wanted, every time he'd touched her; the desire he'd reined in, that had made their lovemaking something that shriveled his soul instead of freeing it. He had touched her, forcing himself to stay aloof when all he'd wanted was to feel her, like she felt him. Lose himself in her, like she lost herself in him. Her sweaty body, sliding along his. Her moans. Her pussy, clenching around his cock. Her body, arching as she gave him everything—her pleasure, her pain.

It had killed him to make love to her while remaining aloof; it was why he'd left her, when everything in him had told him to stay. And God, he wanted her back.

"Do you want me on my knees again?" she said, voice breathless.

"No." He swallowed. "Turn around."

She took a step back, another, unbuttoning her jeans as she went. The blue denim slid down her pale thighs. She worked one high-heeled sandal through, then the other, the red plastic shining. The heels scraped against the floor. She turned, bending over, placing her hands on the shelf covering the back wall.

He stared at her ass. She wore pink cotton panties, the triangle in the back barely covering her cheeks. Between her legs they were askew, showing him a glimpse of dark, curly hair.

She bent her head, her long fringe falling forward, swaying before her face.

He forced his feet to move, stepping over her discarded jeans. His fingers caught the line of her panties, tracing the soft skin beneath. He tugged them down, transfixed by the plump lips they revealed, barely aware that she bent to remove the slip of cloth.

He put a finger on her slit. A drop of white moisture beaded on his fingertip.

She shuddered, and widened her stance in invitation. "Please," she whispered.

He put both his hands on her ass, leaving them there, immobile. "Shall I fuck you?" he said, squeezing. "Or hurt you?"

She didn't hesitate. "Both."

He rubbed a thumb across her skin, feeling the tiny bumps, the taut muscle beneath. He lifted his hand. For a moment he stood there, gazing at her pale skin, the puckered hole, the swollen, waiting lips. He didn't make a conscious choice to move, but his hand descended, connected with her flesh, the sharp sound resounding through her body—and his. She jerked; his testicles tightened.

He lifted his hand. There was a red mark where his fingers had hit. The skin on his palm tingled. Did hers? "How does it feel?" he rasped.

Her breath hitched. "It . . . prickles."

He shifted a bit to his side, stroking the fading pink spot.

This time, he watched the hand fall, watched her jerk again at the impact, watched the force of the hit spread across her skin. He did it again, her left cheek, her right. Harder, until his palm became hot. Until she gasped at each hit.

"Fuck me," she said, panting. "Please, I . . ."

Her cheeks were bright pink, warm. Like his palm. "What do you feel now?" he demanded.

"Burning," she managed. "Good. Like . . . Like I can really feel it. Myself. Feel my ass."

He closed his eyes, pressed his tingling palm against his crotch. Wanting her. Needing her.

But it wasn't enough.

Not yet.

His hands went to his belt. He released the metal clasp, slid the leather through the loops.

Her head lifted, looking over her shoulder. Her hair stuck to her face; her cheeks were flushed the color of her ass. She watched the belt slide free, lips parted. "Are you going to beat me, John?"

God help him, there was only one answer. "Yes."

SHE let her head fall back, fingers digging into the wooden plank serving as a shelf. Her pussy pulsed, so slick and sensitive every little movement made her want to moan. Her slit seemed to gape, clenching futilely on nothing. She wanted to beg him, again, to fuck her, but she didn't.

She wanted this more.

She closed her eyes, trembling, waiting. Imagining she could smell the leather. She sensed him shift behind her, but didn't hear the belt slice the air. It landed on her ass with a sharp snap; she heard the sound ricochet through the room an instant before the pain hit—a sharp, knife-like pain, thrusting her forward toward the shelf.

She grunted, muscles tensing as the pain turned into warmth, a wave of it rushing from her ass, through her legs, to her clit.

She was still glowing with the warmth when he hit her again. She cried out, the shelf before her shifting, the boxes rattling. Her hips lifted, legs widening. Her clit throbbed.

"God," John said behind her, his voice a rasp, raw, broken.

She turned her head to look at him. The belt was clenched in his right hand, his chest rising and falling rapidly. His gaze met hers; he raised the belt.

She watched it fall this time, watched it cut through the air. She recoiled before it hit, unable to stop herself. It hit anyway, a band of fire across her buttocks. Her throat closed up, the cry strangled. The warmth in her limbs smarted.

She registered the dull thump of something falling to the ground, then his hands were on her tender ass, his cock at her slit. He thrust in to the hilt. She cried out, hips bucking. His hand fisted in her hair, wrenching her head back as his cock pounded her womb, his hips hitting her bruised behind. The grip in her hair pulled at her scalp, tiny pinpricks of pain. She burned. Inside, outside. Her body tensed, every muscle humming as she arched. Her breath caught. The sound of flesh hitting flesh filled the closet.

The wave broke; pleasure roared through her. She screamed, hips lifting, neck arching. Her pussy contracted and her scream turned into choked little moans.

He let go of her hair abruptly, both hands fastening on her hips as he plunged faster into her. She felt the moment he stiffened all the way to her core, couldn't stop a breathless grunt as he cried out hoarsely, jerking against her, inside her.

HE leaned forward, resting his forehead against her shoulder, tasting the salt on her skin. His arms closed around her and he felt her slowing heartbeat. "You okay?" he managed.

"I think . . . I need to sit down."

He felt his lips quirk. "Are you sure your ass is up to it?"

She glanced at him, smiling. "No."

He realized her legs were trembling—he felt none too steady himself—and gathered her up in his arms, sinking down onto the floor. His jeans were still bunched around his ankles, but he managed not to fall on his face somehow.

"Do you think anyone heard us?" she murmured, nestling against his chest, oblivious to his drenched T-shirt as she shifted to find a comfortable position.

He stroked a hand over her hair, pulling stray strands from her face. "Who cares?"

She smiled. "It was good."

He let out a breath, feeling pleasantly relaxed, rubbing his thumb over her flushed cheek. He didn't know what to feel about what he'd done—what they'd done—quite yet. But he hadn't been alone; neither, he thought, had she.

He bent to kiss her lightly across the lips. "Come home with me," he said.

She did.

Sara Thorn lives way up in the cold north, where she's warmed by her husband, hot chocolate and erotic romance. She loves writing because "it's like reading, only better." By day she's a computer engineer, which means she spends two thirds of her waking time with her keyboard, be it typing in code or novels. Other than reading a lot, she likes to fiddle with computer games, music, drawing, knitting or anything that keeps her hands busy. Visit her website at www.sara-thorn.com.

ABOUT THE EDITOR

Jane Litte is a blogger, a reader, and now a collector of stories. *Agony/Ecstasy* is a collection of very steamy stories that explore the twin concepts of pain and pleasure. These stories represent fresh new voices in erotica and erotic romance, exploring the interiors of the bedroom and the mind.

Readers can learn more about Jane and her love of books at Dear Author, a website devoted to discovering good books, or they can send her an e-mail at jane@jdearauthor.com. Follow her on twitter, @jane_l, to let her know what you thought of the selection of shorts. She is always looking for feedback and recommendations for other readers.

AGONY

AGONY

EDITED BY
Jane Litte

HEAT | NEW YORK

THE BERKLEY PUBLISHING GROUP
Published by the Penguin Group
Penguin Group (USA) Inc.
375 Hudson Street, New York, New York 10014, USA
Penguin Group (Canada), 90 Eglinton Avenue East, Suite 700, Toronto, Ontario M4P 2Y3, Canada
(a division of Pearson Penguin Canada Inc.)
Penguin Books Ltd., 80 Strand, London WC2R 0RL, England
Penguin Group Ireland, 25 St. Stephen's Green, Dublin 2, Ireland (a division of Penguin Books Ltd.)
Penguin Group (Australia), 250 Camberwell Road, Camberwell, Victoria 3124, Australia
(a division of Pearson Australia Group Pty. Ltd.)
Penguin Books India Pvt. Ltd., 11 Community Centre, Panchsheel Park, New Delhi—110 017, India
Penguin Group (NZ), 67 Apollo Drive, Rosedale, Auckland 0632, New Zealand
(a division of Pearson New Zealand Ltd.)
Penguin Books (South Africa) (Pty.) Ltd., 24 Sturdee Avenue, Rosebank, Johannesburg 2196,
South Africa

Penguin Books Ltd., Registered Offices: 80 Strand, London WC2R 0RL, England

This book is an original publication of The Berkley Publishing Group.

Copyright © 2011 by Dear Author Media Network, LLC.
Please see page 225 for a complete listing of copyright information.
Cover photo by Shutterstock 313904765 (male) and 50494849 / Olga Ekaterincheva (female).
Text design by Kristin del Rosario.

PRINTING HISTORY
Heat trade paperback edition / December 2011

Library of Congress Cataloging-in-Publication Data

Agony/ecstasy / edited by Jane Litte.
    p. cm.
    ISBN 978-0-425-24345-9 (trade pbk.)
    1. Erotic stories, American.   2. American fiction—21st century.   I. Litte, Jane.
    PS648.E7A38 2011
    813'.60803538—dc23

                                                                    2011033894

PRINTED IN THE UNITED STATES OF AMERICA

10 9 8 7 6 5 4 3 2 1

CONTENTS

Transfixed BY ANNE CALHOUN   *1*

The Sybil BY JEAN JOHNSON   *21*

Caged BY J.K. COI   *41*

Each Step Sublime BY BETTIE SHARPE   *61*

Safeword BY DELPHINE DRYDEN   *83*

Stitch and Bitch BY A.L. SIMONDS   *103*

Bachelorette Party BY JESSICA CLARE   *125*

Wicked Wedding Night BY MARGARET ROWE   *145*

Shameless BY EDIE HARRIS   *167*

Taken BY REBECCA LANGE   *187*

Wetwire BY SUNNY MORAINE   *205*

About the Editor   *223*

TRANSFIXED

ANNE CALHOUN

Cole waits for me as I've ordered: on his knees, fingers laced behind his head, in the dark. I walk into the still air of the studio apartment, close the door, twist the dead bolts, the sounds sharp and final. With a flick of the switch next to the door, several table and floor lamps situated around the apartment come on. As I set my purse on the marble-topped table by the door, I treat myself to a long, thorough look at him.

Even kneeling he's large. His bowed head comes to my rib cage, and while his fingers in their woven position are relaxed against his closely cropped reddish-brown hair, as the seconds tick past I see his shoulders tense ever so subtly under his black motorcycle racing jacket. Threat is implicit in his size and strength, but for me his power is tightly leashed.

Standing close enough to hear his deliberately even breathing, I study him for a moment. In the past he's waited in a businessman's armor—suit, tie, wingtips—so this insight into his leisure activities intrigues me. He smells of fall wind and sweat, with a hint of oil underneath, as if he'd worked on his bike before he rode it.

Slowly, methodically, I remove my gloves and my coat. The pace is intended to get Cole into a certain frame of mind, to move him from nervous anticipation to inexorable submission. Until I am finished with him tonight, we move at my speed. At my command.

More important, removing my trench coat reveals the antithesis of dominatrix gear. Tonight I am the idealized version of a 1950s house-wife in a light green watered silk dress, sleeveless, full-skirted, and belted around my waist. I'm quite petite, with chin-length white-blonde hair, pale skin, and green eyes.

Standing slightly to one side, I lay my palm against his laced fingers, and he tenses again. His breath eases from his broad chest as he makes himself relax. I may look like an ethereal fairy, but Cole knows exactly how deceiving appearances are.

This is the ninth time I've met Cole. We are both clients of Lady Matilda, an expat Brit who will, for a rather considerable fee, arrange meetings between like-minded individuals. I heard about Lady Matilda from a friend who found a Cantonese conversation partner. I wanted a man who wanted me to whip him. Lady Matilda didn't bat an eyelash.

Three weeks later, Cole waited for me for the first time. I don't know what he does to afford Lady Matilda's fee. I don't know his last name. He knows neither my real first or last name or my phone number or job. When he wants to meet me, he calls Lady Matilda; she calls me, and I choose a date and time. I don't know if he lives in the city or comes here on business. I know he's not married because I refuse to play with a man who is, and Lady Matilda does a background check run by a very expensive security firm. I know he's completely self-assured, and hot as hell.

I know he fears this as badly as he wants it. But there is so much we don't know about each other.

I step behind him, my heels clicking against the parquet floor. Lingering behind him makes him uncomfortable, so I remain there for a few more moments, examining his ass in his faded jeans, the worn soles and scuffed leather of the black motorcycle boots encas-ing his feet. He can't be comfortable kneeling in those boots. He will be even less comfortable when I make him undress.

I complete the circle, noting the dark stubble on his jaw, the way he keeps his gaze forward and down. He will not meet my eyes. He will address me as Miss Banks. He will follow my every command. At the end of the night he will say "Thank you, Miss Banks" before he goes. At some level, that will be the most gratifying part of the evening.

I seat myself on the damask-covered bench at the foot of the room's sole piece of furniture, a king-sized four-post bed, and spread my skirt to either side. Although his eyes are trained on the floor in front of him he gathers details with his peripheral vision. A muscle in his jaw jumps before he controls it. I smile. Something about the delicate nature of this dress, the fabric, the color, makes this so much harder for him. I admire how he faces what makes him tremble.

"Stand up, please," I say. *Please* is a necessary part of this game, as is *thank you*. The niceties emphasize that I am making requests he is free to decline but chooses to obey. He's not my slave. I'm not his mistress. I'm something worse. I'm what he fears, yet can't resist.

Hands still behind his head, he rises easily to his feet. A T-shirt clings snugly to his torso; memory fills in the details of his biceps and triceps under the leather biker jacket while I contemplate the lean length of his abdomen, the brown leather belt through the loops of his jeans, the thick shaft of his cock straining against his zipper. He's tall, heavily muscled, and outweighs me by at least one hundred pounds, which makes him a delight to handle.

I leave him in that position while I pour myself a glass of chilled water from the pitcher in the kitchen, then I seat myself in front of him and look him over again, from his face, carefully neutral, to the tips of his boots.

"You look well, Cole."

"Thank you, Miss Banks."

I insist on Miss, not Ms. There is nothing politically correct about what we do in this room. Ms. implies a measure of equality. We're not equals, and while I think we're about the same age, Miss makes me seem younger than I am, another facet of this that gives Cole pause.

"The jacket, please, Cole."

"Yes, Miss Banks," he says as he lets it slip from his shoulders, lays it neatly on the bench beside me, and resumes position. I request his shirt, then his boots, and each time he returns to the indubitably submissive position with his hands behind his head.

I eye his now-bare torso, muscles nicely delineated under the tanned skin, and feel my pulse pick up. His is already visible at the base of his strong throat, and we've barely begun.

"Your belt, please," I say.

Even after nine encounters there's the slightest hesitation, then his long fingers go to the buckle, jerk back the tongue to release the prong from the eyelet, and slip the leather through the loops. He leans to place the belt on the growing pile of clothes to my left, but I stop him with a quick, palm-up beckoning gesture.

"Hand it to me, please."

He does, offering it, the warm leather across both of his open palms. I take it. He resumes waiting, and now a dark flush creeps up his chest and into his face.

"You forgot," I say idly.

"Yes, Miss Banks," he says, but I can hear the hint of strain under his even tone. "Forgive me, Miss Banks."

This is where it gets difficult. Any man can strip for a woman. Admitting his error and begging pardon is another thing entirely. I lay the length of leather across my lap and stroke it like I would a cat, savoring the warm, supple material, the darker places where the leather rubbed against belt loops or the buckle. Wide and

brown, worn black in lots of subtly interesting spots, this is Cole's own belt.

I'm going to strap him to the bed and lash him with it.

"The rest, please, Cole," I say, without giving him absolution.

In seconds he is naked before me, his cock straining away from his body. Cole's red-blooded American male brain has been conditioned to tell him he's supposed to be the dominant one. Cole's animal body, however, gets very, very aroused when we play this game, when I dress in the most delicately feminine clothing I can find and whip him until he's clenching his teeth against the groans. In a delicious turnabout of roles, tonight I will make him shudder and sweat as *he* services *me*. Tonight I will use him with no regard for his comfort or pleasure, and he will thank me for the privilege before he leaves.

The thought sends a rush of hot pleasure coursing down my spine, trickling in rivulets to every nerve ending until my body feels like licking, flickering flame.

I stand, walk around him again, moving slowly, the click of heel-to-sole audibly reminding us both of our positions. The tanned skin of his back lightens abruptly at his hips. When I'm finished with him he'll be a dark, vibrant red from the backs of his thighs to his waist.

"Shall we begin, Cole?"

"Yes, Miss Banks." The words are firm, but low. I don't envy him the struggle he feels inside, and I don't pity him, either. That's not my role tonight. Tonight I'm implacable, diamond hard, so that the only way out is through the shame of succumbing to his fears.

I point to the bed. "Facedown, please."

He stretches out, arms and legs wide, positioning his wrists and ankles near the leather restraints attached to the bed frame. Lord, he's *big*. In a rustle of silk I kneel beside him and begin at his feet,

buckling the brown leather first around one ankle, then the other. There's a bit of give in the chain joining cuff and post, but not much. When I'm finished with his wrists, I seat myself on the bed, the silk whispering as I do.

"Are you comfortable, Cole?" I ask as I trail my index finger from the nape of his neck to the base of his spine. Shivers chase each other over his skin and his hands close into fists, then open again.

"Yes, Miss Banks."

I brace one hand on his shoulder and slip my finger under the wrist cuff closest to me. His pulse thumps along, elevated, strong. He's not lying. At this moment he's very comfortable, body fully supported, arms and legs secured in such a way that he can't grip anything. This position leaves the mind with nothing to fixate on except the searing, unavoidable pain. Other postures can quickly grow uncomfortable. I prefer Cole suffers no distractions from the agony.

Tonight *I* am distracted. With each increasingly captivating encounter, Cole slips a little deeper under my skin. He is unlike any other man I've played with, and despite the facade of anonymity we've maintained, I need to know more.

I flatten my hand at the base of his spine. "Why do you do this, Cole?"

"To please you, Miss Banks."

He gives me the ritualistic response, but he stiffens as he speaks. I don't doubt the authenticity of his answer, but there is something underneath. A deeper truth. But diving deeper into Cole requires offering more than I'm willing to give.

I get to my feet. He waits. He can only lie there as I pick up his belt, fit the buckle end in my palm, and take up position beside him.

To test how much movement I have in my fitted dress, I give him a few warm-up strokes. I start with the taut curve of his buttocks,

the sweet spot, the lighter lashes driving his hips forward, mimicking the motion of plunging into a hot, wet body underneath him. He shudders, turns his face away from me, into his shoulder.

A tremor rolls through me. The sound, his big body completely under my control, the involuntary movement of his hips all meld into a dark, hard pulse in my core. Wetness surges between my legs.

Without warning, I begin in earnest, the first truly hard, truly uncompromising stroke in perfect rhythm with the others across the tops of his thighs, and from then on, I don't let up. I keep a slow, steady pattern of lashes, moving up and down the only truly tender curve in his otherwise hard-planed body, watching, always watching as he first winces and endures, then subtly tenses and fights what I'm doing to him.

This is a fight he cannot win. It is as inevitable as it is exquisite, that pain will course along his nerve endings as the blood rushes through the layers of his skin, the sensitive underside of his cock stroking against the fine cotton sheets as he begins to writhe, almost imperceptibly, under the lashes. The belt lands with a sharp, loud clap; his muscles tense then release as his breath huffs from him in increasingly audible grunts.

I'm strong, but Cole's stronger. The battle between what his mind resists and his body demands does half my work for me. More important, I'm slow, cruelly slow when I strap Cole to the bed and whip him. If I went at him hard and loud and fast, I'd wear myself out. Instead I give him time to feel the leather mark his skin, feel the blood rush into the welt, feel the nerve endings begin to itch and sizzle as the inevitable sweat rises from his pores, and then I hit him again. Over . . . and over. There are no clocks in this room, only the light of the setting sun he can't see because he's closed his eyes and hidden his face from me. There is no way to mark the passing of time.

There is only torment, mental and physical, the rustle of my silk dress, my even breathing, and the charged moment when our breathing merges before the brown leather cracks against his ass again. This time he cries out, low and agonized. A less experienced woman might mistake this for the surrender she seeks. I know it's just the beginning. With the next stroke he shudders violently. Then comes a moment that sends a rush of sheer erotic arousal from my pussy to the edge of my skin: all the tension in Cole's body alchemizes into white-hot surrender. The image is exquisite, his masculine body a conduit for searing, liquid desire. I continue, and now with each clap of leather against skin his groans, soft and helpless, rise into the silent air.

There is a fine line between erotic torture and torture. I am careful to stop when I see that line, not when my four-inch heels are toeing it. I halt, breathing hard, shifting my shoulders so the sweat-soaked silk teases my nipples. For a long moment he doesn't move, then the cessation of rhythm seeps into his brain and he turns his head to look at me. His eyes are two brilliant hazel pools in his flushed, afflicted face.

"Ten more for forgetting to hand me your belt," I say.

Something—gratitude, fear, dread, longing—cracks through him. This display of emotion makes the desire hardening my nipples stream along my spine, into my brain. "Yes, Miss Banks."

This time, because the strokes are pure punishment, not for his pain and my pleasure, he counts. When I'm finished I drop the belt with a clatter and undo his restraints in reverse order, ankles then wrists.

"Kneel up."

Slow and beautifully awkward, he pushes back, knees spread wide. He sits back on his heels. I hand him a condom. Still in a daze he puts it on, then clasps his hands behind his head. Sweat streams

down his body, has soaked the sheets, the scent indescribably erotic as I climb onto the mattress, shoes and all. Eight hundred dollars of watered silk ruined, but I don't give a damn. I lie back on my elbows, bend my knees, and spread my legs. My skirt drops to my hips, exposing the silk stockings and garter belt that frame my bare, flushed pussy.

With any other woman, in any other situation, this pose would mark the moment of my surrender. Tonight it's simply the next phase in Cole's.

"Fuck me," I order.

In an instant he's on me, over me, his erect cock pushing unerringly into my slick folds. When that granite-hard shaft strokes into me, forcing its way over nerve endings stimulated to the point of torment, when his hips slam hard against my pelvis I cry out, the sound sharp and shockingly helpless in the air of this private, silent room. He growls and knocks me flat on my back, bearing down on me with his full weight as he does it again, again. I palm his red, welted ass and grip hard. He gasps against the pain, but doesn't break rhythm.

The discipline required to take what I give him sends a sharp electric current searing through me. I explode. All the pent-up tension releases in wave after wave of obliterating pleasure that wracks my body. I strain under the sheer mass of Cole, pinning me to the mattress so I can disappear into the void.

When I slip back into the rasp of wet silk against my back and the intimacy of his hips between mine, tremors are rippling through Cole from shoulders to knees. He's hard inside me, hard against me. The right word from me will call his orgasm from his cock and end this.

"Sit back," I command, omitting the *please*, making my voice as crisp as I can given the satisfied purr humming in my throat.

One second stretches into two and the red-blooded American male in Cole looks down at me, his carved torso streaked with sweat, his mouth somehow both full and hard, the line of his jaw taut. He could easily ignore my command and spend into my body. Instead he pushes back, wincing as his cock withdraws from my cunt.

"On your knees on the floor, please," I say as I get up. My dress falls back into place as I walk into the kitchen to pour another glass of water.

He's in position when I turn around, sitting back on his heels, erect cock gleaming, hands behind his head. The manacles left no marks, and I marvel at his strength, his discipline. I offer him his glass, as I sip from my own.

"Thank you, Miss Banks."

While he drinks, I seat myself on the bed, legs crossed, the skirt slipping with my movements, one heel dangling from my toe. "More?"

He sets the glass on the floor at arm's length. "No thank you, Miss Banks."

I nod and study the flush, hot and strong on his throat and cheeks, his face completely vulnerable yet utterly male, absolutely transfixed with sexual need. I dominate Cole, true enough, but through his surrender, he owns me. In my lonely bed I dream of these encounters. I spin little fantasies about us, about him, who he is outside of this room. Finding a man caught up in the typical alpha male chest-beating is simple. A man who can control his own impulses, explore the furthest edges of his masculinity, and fuck like a dream ensnared me. But for tonight only, he's mine to do with as I please. There is never any promise of another night.

We are not finished. I hook my heels in the sideboards of the bed, knees spread wide. Then I edge up my skirt, slowly drawing it up to the crease where my hips meet my thighs, exposing the silk stockings and pale cream garter belt holding them on. As I lift my skirt, the

scent of arousal and fucking rises into the air between us. I slide my fingers around the back of his skull and bring his mouth to my cunt.

He begins with the soft opening to my vagina, hardening his tongue to first circle, then gently probe. Until instructed otherwise, he will either fold his arms behind his back or leave his hands on his thighs and use only his mouth. With one hand braced behind me for balance, I knot my fingers in his sweat-dampened hair and succumb to the pleasure coursing through my veins. Cole is pure, undiluted male kneeling between my legs, tongue lapping at my cunt. There is nothing I can do to him that will make him anything less, even when I say, "Lick my clit."

He does, circling it so that tense heat pushes under my skin, up through my abdomen to my fingers, down my thighs to my toes, which curl in my pumps. I'm close, my head lolling back as I push against his mouth. I let my head drop forward and open my eyes. The muscles of his back are rigid with excitement, and I can imagine the state of his cock, erotic ache verging on agony.

"Use your fingers," I demand. Cole works two fingers into my cunt and strokes in time with his tongue, but he isn't rough, doesn't rush. He coaxes me to the precipice, then over. Orgasm tears through me and my low cry, breathy and gratified, echoes in the room. He lightens his touch just enough to prolong the ebbing pleasure, sitting back only when I tug on his hair.

His hands once again lock behind his neck. I straighten and begin to unfasten the tiny, fabric-covered buttons holding my dress closed. His gaze roams hungry and desperate over my revealed skin while his cock throbs in time with his pulse. If I touched it, wrapped my hand around it, I'd feel no give at all, just rigid steel under sensitized skin.

It's an odd feeling to undress in front of a man knowing he has none of the typical male prerogative to touch what I expose to him. I shimmy out of the dress and unhook my bra, then stand with my

stomach mere inches from Cole's face to take off my garter belt and stockings. He moves only once, pressing a kiss into the damp skin just above my mound. The gesture, at once flirtatious, possessive, and a little bold, surprises me.

"That was very nice," I say as I use my index finger to trace his wet, swollen mouth, the mouth I've never kissed. Kissing him is a risk I'm not willing to take. "I want to come again."

Another shudder. "Yes, Miss Banks."

I lie back on the bed again and beckon him into position with one preemptory index finger. All lean, shifting muscle, he crawls over me, aligns his cock with my swollen pussy, and slides inside. I let my hands roam his back, my fingertips finding and exploring the welts lining his ass as he begins to thrust.

I wait a few strokes, then give languid little directives. "Slower," I say. "Your cock fills my pussy so nicely, Cole. I want to savor every stroke, feel you stretch me."

"Yes, Miss Banks."

His voice is low and strained, his entire body taut as he maintains the excruciating pace I demand while I whisper dirty, descriptive language into his ear and sink my nails into his reddened ass. Because I can, because he has asked me to torment him, I squirm under him, press my breasts to his chest, adjust his position until he's exactly where I want him. I give him no respite. Instead I make him fuck me slow and hot and strong until I'm lost in the sensations, lost in the sheer heat and power of his body at my command, until I'm lifting my hips with each stroke, trembling with need, my cunt slippery with my juices and our mingled sweat. His only concession to what this costs him is the slightly agonized tone of his groans as he labors under the spell of my pinching fingers, my wicked mouth, my hot, slick body, all working together to drive him crazy while he continues his unrelenting pace for my pleasure, my pleasure . . .

My pleasure. I implode around his cock, head back, throat straining, legs spread and my pelvis pressed to his. I take my pleasure in
the most biblical, old-fashioned sense of the phrase. Oh, yes, I take
it at his expense.

After the last ribbon of sweet, hot satisfaction flutters along my
nerves, I ease back onto the mattress and open my eyes. He's poised
above me, his gaze focused on my throat, his cock steel-hard inside
me, but his face is changing, as if the sweat trickling down his cheeks
and along his jaw etches fault lines into the mask he wears when
we're together.

I brace my hands on his chest. "That will be all, Cole."

A moment's hesitation. He inhales as if to speak, then he sits back
and allows me up.

"Yes, Miss Banks."

The quiet edge to the words gets my attention as I sit up and tuck
my legs under my bottom. He's kneeling, his big hands braced on
his thighs, his head bent. The edges of the fantasy begin to blur back
into reality. For the first time he looks directly at me, and the ferocity seething under the subservient mask glints in his eyes. In that
instant something I lock away in the most secret part of my soul
flares to life, then I slam shut the door his glance just opened.

But now I am in dangerous territory.

Now I am curious.

"Why do you do this?" I ask again.

He strips off the condom and leans forward to drop it in the trash
can. "Because it makes me hot," he growls as he sits back. "Why do
you do it?"

I have a ready answer to his challenge. "I'm five feet tall, Cole.
With me any man can play master. A man who can sublimate his
desires to my will and test the limits of his stamina and fortitude is
far more intriguing. And you didn't answer my question."

His hands flex against his thighs, and his gaze shifts to the

Manhattan skyline. "Because it's the purest adrenaline rush ever," he says in a low voice, as if he's admitting something. He is, but not to me. To himself.

I know he fears this as much as he needs it. Humans avoid what they fear. Cole squares up and stares pain down, and that unflinching courage makes *me* hot.

I look at the bike jacket, advertising a brand of speed bike, at his hard body, the set of his shoulders, remember the suits. "NYPD? FBI?" I ask, continuing the longest conversation we've ever had. He wouldn't be the first.

He flicks me a look through thick brown lashes. "Marine Corps."

That explained the stance, the willingness to push himself beyond endurance, but not the suits. "And now?"

"Trader for Cooper Bensonhurst," he said.

Trading on the stock exchange is fast-paced, stressful, and extraordinarily competitive. Every day is about the thrill of the kill. When traders bet well, they win big. A wrong bet means millions of dollars in losses.

"You're an adrenaline junkie," I say. "And I'm your current fix."

"You're tiny," he says distractedly. "You're . . . delicate. You strap me down, then you whip me and all I can do is endure the pain dished out by a hundred-pound woman dressed like she's walked off the *Mad Men* set, wearing pearls, fucking pearls. And then you make me fuck you!"

Of course I do. That's why he's here. That's why we're both here. We have unique needs, hard to meet. "You liked the pearls," I point out.

"They drove me insane," he growls. "You whipped the hell out of me, strapped me to the bed on my back, stripped to nothing but the pearls, and rode me like a cowgirl. Remember?"

"I remember." I came four times before I sent him on his way.

I still dream about it, and this sudden, personal conversation is making me light-headed. Details of the real Cole break against me like thunderclaps. In response, lightning flashes in my body, illuminating my needs, my fears.

"No control, no choices, no decisions. Just torment, all from a woman I could snap in two. The pain gets me so hot, so high, I float away. I feel the marks for a week." His voice is a low purr, and his erect cock pulses as he speaks.

Adrenaline junkies are always searching for a new high. I stop myself from folding my arms across my chest, instead looking around the room for my dress to avoid meeting his eyes. "What's the next rush?" I ask, keeping my voice light.

"This isn't the only thing that turns you on," he says as he shifts to the edge of the bed and stands.

His certainty halts me in the act of sorting out my dress. I have so many conflicting sexual urges it's sometimes difficult to breathe. I've long since given up trying to reconcile them, or find one man who can satisfy them. "Hardly," I say as I step into the full skirt and push my arms into the sleeve holes. "You?"

"Oh, hardly," he drawls.

The invitation is clear. My fingers steady on the buttons, I tilt my head and consider this proposition to transform our shadowy, intimate encounters into something ocean dark, ocean deep. "What do you have in mind?"

He laughs. It's deep and rough and fucking sexy as it tumbles into my ears and along my nerves. Then he nods toward the wrecked bed. "Find out."

That's a challenge, not an answer. Equally intriguing is the fact that Cole's sentence structure and cadence is becoming much less formal. It's faster. The words run together like whiskey pouring out of a bottle, the flickering heat making my cunt clench. Right before

my eyes he's transforming into someone completely unlike the man who waits for me on his knees. I'm absolutely, utterly transfixed.

I watch him dress. His clothes, removed within minutes, are immaculate while I look like I'm the one who was bound, whipped, and fucked. He pulls his jeans over the raw, reddened flesh of his ass and thighs, yanks the T-shirt over his head, and shrugs into the fitted motorcycle jacket I find sexy as sin.

But something breaks open inside me when he collects his belt from the floor. I watch him slide the dark leather through the loops in his jeans and fasten it with two quick movements.

Cole's seduced me as he dressed, and he knows it. He flicks me a grin and steps into his boots. "What's your name? Your real name."

I push my hair back from my face. Telling him this makes me the vulnerable one. Fear wars with curiosity as I speak. "Marin Bryant."

He flips the dead bolts and holds the door open for me. "Cole Fleming," he says, and holds out his hand.

After what we've just done it's absurd to shake his hand, but I do it anyway. I slip my hand into his. He wraps his long, strong fingers around mine, and smiles. He holds me in place for a heartbeat too long, then I tug free. He studies me for a moment, then nods slowly, as if to say *game on*. All gentleman now, he gestures into the hallway.

"After you, Marin."

With that I take a step into the unknown.

To find out what happens next with Cole and Marin,
flip to "Transformed" by Anne Calhoun in the Ecstasy *side.*

After doing time at Fortune 500 companies on both coasts, **Anne Calhoun** found herself living in a flyover state. The glamour of cube farm jobs in HR and IT had worn off, so she gave up meetings to take Joseph Campbell's advice and

follow her bliss: writing romance. Her first novel, *Liberating Lacey*, won the 2010 EPIC Award for Best Contemporary Erotic Romance. Her next release, *What She Needs*, was chosen by Smart Bitch Sarah for the Sizzling Book Club.

Anne lives in the Midwest with her husband, son, and a rescue dog named Kate. She holds a BA in English and History, and an MA in American Studies. Visit her website at annecalhoun.com.

THE SYBIL

JEAN JOHNSON

Ai-kan Fen Jul was not inclined to kneel before anyone. Warrior, mage, warlord, emperor, he had swept across half the continent in just five years. Some fought the encroachment of his armies. Others welcomed the order he brought, unifying dozens of petty, squabbling groups barely big enough to be called countries, never mind kingdoms. The emperor had defeated hundreds of would-be champions in personal combat, whether by sword or by spell, and his keen mind crafted strict but just laws, which he enforced for ranks both high and low. He bowed to no one.

No one, except the Sybil.

There were many women more beautiful than her in the world. Her face was plain, her eyes a muddy hazel, her waist-length hair an ordinary shade of brown. Her lips were thin, her nose hooked, her figure slim, somewhat short, and not as curvaceous as was fashionable.

Indeed, the Sybil could have vanished into any crowd, been overlooked for many reasons, save for the most important of all: The Sybil was a Seer, a divine mouthpiece of the Gods. Ai-kan, leader of the growing nation of Ai-ar, had been consulting her since the second year of his path for conquest, seeking her counsel after a rough series of setbacks.

Her tent was the only place where his bodyguards did not accom-

pany him. The only place where he did not wear his blades. And the only place where he did not use his spells, save at her command.

Here, in the heart of the Sybil's quarters, the only guards allowed were the *sybekoi*, warrior-women with shaved heads and kohl-painted eyes. The only weapons he ever touched were ones meant for discipline, not death . . . and the only spells used, aside from silencing runes he himself applied to the walls of her tent, were the chains of obedience she had gradually woven around him, body and mind.

"If I am to give you what you want," the Sybil had murmured to him at their very first meeting, *"you must first let me give you what you need. . . ."*

He needed. Ai-kan hadn't known just how much he truly needed what she gave him, but he did need it just as much as he needed her prophecies.

His boiled leather armor had been set aside for this visit to her tent. If he visited her while in armor, and he often did, he would get sound governing advice from her, for she was as sharp in her wit as any of his blades, and knew how to handle people. But he would not get a prophecy.

For this visit, he donned the brocaded linen robe she had given him after he had convinced her to leave her citadel and join him on his campaigns. Dyed in shades of blue and purple, it matched the purple-dyed sandals on his feet, his only other covering. Freshly bathed, his face shaved and his hair pulled back in a braid, he dismissed his guards and approached her tent. Whatever his men thought when he went to see her did not matter to Ai-kan. Whatever happened between him and the Sybil was strictly between the two of them.

The *sybekoi* guarding the entrance to her quarters came to attention when they spotted his approach. They also crossed their halberds in front of him, stout oak shafts supporting expensive iron blades.

Iron was rare and costly, and the process to craft it a closely guarded secret, but he had outfitted half of his army with short iron swords by now. Mainly because the *sybekoi* already possessed them, and had shown his men during his initial visit to her citadel that the new metal, while heavy, was far superior to the bronze blades most everyone else owned.

Stopping, he waited while one murmured through the tent wall, announcing his presence. A reply came back, and the halberds uncrossed. Ai-kan slipped between the oiled canvas folds of the entrance. Beyond the front tent of her private compound was nothing more than a receiving area. Rugs and furs covered the ground, scattered with cushions and low tables, gifts from those who had received her blessings and foresight as a Seer of the Gods.

More *sybekoi* served here, two women who may have been dressed in soft linen robes and jewelry, but whose muscles and bare heads warned all visitors that they were not the typical, soft, pampered girls normally picked to serve guests with refreshments. One glance at him and they went back to the game they were playing on one of the low tables. They knew that he knew his way to her inner quarters. Approaching without weapons as he did, they did not need to escort him into her presence.

The Sybil did not, she had reassured him early on, give prophecies in the same way to others as she did to him. Rather, they were tailored to a particular person's needs. The little grass courtyard beyond the first tent was often used for such moments with other visitors, if the front chamber did not suffice.

A statue of Talwah, Goddess of Compassion and Need, stood on a wheeled base surrounded by a pair of benches and various plants in pots, including a pair of small trees. Together, they formed a portable garden, a peaceful refuge from the rougher world of his war camp. They were a pain to transport, but Ai-kan valued the Sybil's presence more than the trouble of hauling bushes and benches from

place to place. Given that the Sybil sometimes gave foresight readings for his warriors as well for himself, they didn't complain too much about having to move her garden each time they settled in a new camp.

The garden was not his destination, however. Nor was the kitchen tent where the meals for the *sybekoi* and the Seer were prepared, nor the storage tents behind it, nor their barracks-tents, arrayed around the cloth-walled perimeter of her encampment. His goal was the Sybil's own tent at the heart of the compound. Black-walled and white-roofed, it was just as large as his own, and marked with the same symbols imbued with protective magic. He himself had marked them, from his growing library of mystical markings.

Magic needed to be studied. Regulated. Too many petty despots ruled their regions through fear and confusion; sometimes their magic worked as predicted, and sometimes it didn't. Ai-kan believed that magic, like civilization, had rules. It could be studied, crafted, replicated reliably, and used to better the world. Order was paramount, to him. Discipline. Control.

Two more of the *sybekoi* waited at the entrance to her tent. More were stationed around its perimeter, just as they were stationed around the walls of the compound. Perhaps it was selfish of him to keep most of her Seer abilities for himself, but she had not objected. The Sybil chose to believe that, by working with him, her influence would spread Talwah's Compassion to those who truly needed it. The day she had agreed to accompany him, Ai-kan had known the Gods were on his side. This continent would be unified, with peace imposed across the squabbling landscape and prosperity brought to all of its corners, rather than hoarded by a rare few rulers, or worse, spoiled by the rest.

One of the *sybekoi* drew the curtain of the doorway aside for him. The emperor of half the known world stepped inside. As the curtain

fell, the light glowing through the white oilcloth roof illuminated the naked figure of the Sybil lounging in a portable tub. Water trickled over her limbs, squeezed from a sea sponge brought all the way from the coast. The breath left his body the moment his eyes drank in this unguarded view of her.

Her hair, unbound from its usual plethora of braids, snaked over her damp breasts in wriggling dark-and-light brown lines. Unlike her warrior women, she did not shave her head, but like them, her eyes were outlined with dark kohl. The look she slanted him was one rich with desire . . . and control.

It was all he could to remember to turn and tie the curtain shut. To focus his inner strength, opening the channels of power in his mind, imbuing the runes painted on the tent to block out all sound. No one knew what the two of them did when he visited her like this. For the sake of his cause and the comfort of his army, no one dared know. It was the only spell he ever cast when coming to her like this.

Once the noises of her compound and the distant hum of the vast army surrounding them faded, he untied the shoulders of his robe and slipped his feet free of their sandals. He did not try to hide his erection when he turned around; the Sybil was not conventionally beautiful, but he did desire her. She had forbidden him to hide it whenever he came to her like this. No false pretenses, no faked reactions, just the honest truth of everything he felt in her presence.

Muscles flexing, he dropped to one knee, then the other. Lifting his arms, Ai-kan laced his hands behind his head and spread his knees, baring his upthrust shaft and the bollocks dangling below. It was a very submissive posture, self-bound and exposed like this. His erection was there simply because he wanted her, but the position he assumed so willingly was because he needed her.

She was his goddess, given flesh. The one woman with whom he was safe, no matter what she did to him. The only person who could

give him a glorious release from his overwhelming desire for control in his life.

His Mistress.

AWARE of his position, of his anticipation, Charlisse continued to bathe while he waited. Patience was one of the lessons she had taught him early in their relationship. She had also known he would come to her like this today. The day before yesterday, he had won a battle, and yesterday had been devoted to cleaning up the aftermath of that violence. Today, he was free to come to her. Or as free as any man burdened with so many responsibilities could be.

No one would interrupt them, however. Both her devoted guards and Ai-kan's own orders would stop anyone who tried. The *sybekoi* had been dismayed initially when she told them of her agreement to travel with the Emperor on his war campaigns. But as she had explained it to them, "I can do more for the world's future needs by guiding this one man's life than I could in a hundred years of receiving local petitions."

His life was hers, here in private. In public, she would do nothing to ruin his reputation for strength. Ai-kan was in command; even the Sybil, divine mouth of the gods, had left her secluded stronghold to join and support his cause. To all outsiders, she was one more tool in his quest to bring order to their continent. But here, he was hers to command.

Charlisse finished bathing. She could have made do like everyone else, bathing with a bowl of water and a scrap of cloth or in whatever stream might be convenient as they traveled, but the luxury of this large, carved wooden tub was both a declaration of her status to the rest of the camp and a subtle reminder to her host of who was really in charge. Not that she would dare try to lead this army herself, nor rule the mighty nation he was building, but it was vital that Ai-kan,

emperor of Ai-ar, knew down to his bones that all of his actions were accountable to someone else in his power-charged life.

That someone, by the will and grace of Talwah, was her. Mindful of his dark brown eyes on her body, devouring every scrap of skin she exposed, she uncurled herself from the tub. Water splashed and dripped, slowing to a trickle as it drained from her modest curves. He was a huge man, a full head taller than most men in his army, with great, scar-crossed muscles covering his frame. Compared to him, she looked like a slender reed at best, a delicate herb in danger of being crushed.

Looks were deceiving, however. Looks were about want, not need. What lay underneath was where the source of all needs began, and beneath her delicate skin lay a will as tough as iron. Staring down at him, she commanded Ai-kan with two quiet words: "Rinse me."

He hurried to do her bidding, muscles moving with the same quick economy he used on the battlefield. Uncurling his body, he lifted the tall silver ewer of warmed water waiting by the tub and carefully poured it over her. She enjoyed the feel of the liquid streaming over her flesh for a moment, then smoothed her hands over her hair and skin, rinsing off the lingering suds from the soap-leaf ointment she had used.

A soft sound escaped him, barely audible over the trickling water; the desire in his eyes, roaming down over her body, pleased her. Charlisse played with her breasts for a moment, then slid her hands down to her thighs, watching him watch her. Knowing the water would run out, she didn't linger, but turned so he could drizzle the last of it over her backside.

"Drying cloth."

He set the emptied ewer on the carpet-strewn ground and fetched a folded linen cloth from the table beyond it. Touching her gently, he mopped the droplets of water from her skin, then dried each foot as she stepped slowly out of the tub. A last careful wringing of the

water from her hair, and he set the damp fabric aside in favor of dropping to his knees, hands clasped once more behind his neck. Proud in his service to her, he lifted his chin a little, his dark gaze on her face, waiting for his next set of orders.

It came in three words.

"Ten-strand flogger."

He flinched subtly, but moved to do her bidding. Crawling to the chest by the portable bed frame—when Ai-kan was to be punished, he wasn't allowed to walk until it was over—he extracted the longish handle and longer strands of knotted leather. As he did so, she picked up the soft, clean robe waiting for her on her bed and stepped into it. Bringing it back, he offered it to her on his palms, waiting while she tied the shoulder straps in place.

Charlisse turned to face him. He snuck a glance up at her. She permitted it, though the slightest quirk of her brow sent his gaze darting down to the flogger in his hands. "Do you know why you are to be punished?"

He licked his lips. "No, Mistress. But you are just."

"I am," she agreed mildly. Reaching for the handle, she lifted the implement from his hands, letting the strands slide out of his fingers. "More importantly, my servants are an extension of me, and thus my servants are just. Correct?"

"Yes, Mistress. How have I failed you, Mistress?" he asked, his gaze now on the ground.

"Ten of your soldiers broke discipline on the evening of the battle." Her spies among his army had told her this. Laundry cleaners, camp followers, supply wagoners, and those among the locals her *sybekoi* contacted, all kept her apprised of whatever his men did. As did her goddess, since in this case, the culprits had been clever. "Three of them escaped justice."

Ai-kan tensed at her words. "I am sorry, Mistress. My men told me it was seven."

"It was ten." Strolling behind him, she hefted the flogger, gently swinging the strands back and forth, then hauled up and backhanded the straps across his ribs. He gasped. Thin pink lines bloomed in the wake of her blow. "Count."

"Thank you, Mistress, that was one!" he gasped, then repeated it as she struck again. "Thank you, Mistress, that was two!"

"Yes, you will thank me for this," Charlisse murmured tightly, striking him a third time, even harder. "What do you do with soldiers who rape civilians?"

"Thank you, Mistress, that was three! They are to be hunted down, castrated, and tied to a pole by the roadside for two days, sunrise to sundown!"

"I see seven unmanned bastards tied by the road!" she accused, flogging him again.

"Thank you, Mistress, that was four! My men did not tell me of the other three!"

"I know. They used magic to conceal their identities."

He hissed in a breath even before she swung a fifth time. The air exploded out of his lungs when she struck hard, welting him and not just blushing his skin. "Thank you, Mistress, that was five!"

The half-shout never left the tent, thankfully. What she had done to him initially in her fortress-like home could not have been replicated here without severely undermining his authority, save for his ability to muffle with a spell all sounds hitting the tent ceiling and walls. What little noise that might escape through the few, tiny gaps in the tent would not be heard by anyone but her *sybekoi*, and they would never tell another soul. Unlike his soldiers, they had the eyes of Talwah upon them, and of Talwah's Sybil . . . just as Ai-kan did.

"Discipline *will* be maintained," she warned him, pausing her strokes. "The Goddess has given me a glimpse of the ringleader's identity, of the three who escaped. Of the other two, one is Sergeant Praestor." She struck him hard, and waited while he gasped out the

count. "And one is Sergeant Tak-mah." Again, a pause for the count . . . and more. "Can you guess the identity of the mage-warrior who helped to disguise them on their rampage? I can see him now in my mind, by the blessing of Talwah . . . a vision roused by your need to be punished."

Panting from the seventh blow, Ai-kan blinked and licked his lips. "Praestor . . . and Tak-mah . . . are assigned to . . . to Captain Mage Chu-on. Are you saying . . . Chu-on did this?"

"I am. The vision in my mind, seeing what he did, is most unpleasant." Hauling back, she struck him again.

He cried out from the blow. "Sorry, Mistress! Thank you, Mistress, that was eight!" Breathing heavily, he clenched his fingers behind the nape of his neck. She gave him time to recover, and even enough time to ask, "Ah . . . are my Mistress and her Goddess sure of this? He, ah, wields great influence among the men."

"Talwah has granted me a vision . . . but if you need confirmation, there is a woman, a mage from among your lower ranks," Charlisse allowed, her attention turned inward for a moment. "This, I have also seen. She is a stone-shaper, a geomancer, and has been developing a way to purify and bless a certain kind of stone so that it can reveal a lie being told in its presence. Her name is Katmah. You will encourage her to develop these truth-telling stones, to refine her spells. This will take a turning of Brother Moon, maybe two . . . and when she has succeeded, you will confront Chu-on . . . and you will make an example of him that will never be forgotten by *any* mage-warrior in your ranks."

She swung hard and fast, two smacking blows that slashed loudly across his back.

"*Ah!* Thank you, Mistress, that was nine! Thank you, Mistress, that was ten!" Panting, trembling, Ai-kan clutched his hands together behind his back, awaiting another blow while the burning sting faded from his welted skin.

Hidden behind his back, Charlisse permitted herself a brief,

worried look. She stooped a little and studied the marks she had left. None looked like they had broken the skin. Not that he wasn't scarred; he bore several faded white lines and a few newer pinkish ones, all garnered from his life as a warrior. But she cared for him, a lot more than she felt free to admit at this particular moment. Straightening in silence, she gently swung the flogger around his shoulder, letting the strands patter across the front of his collarbone.

"This was your punishment for failing to instill discipline in your men. Next is your trade relations with the rafters of the River Morna, who ferry your army's supplies from the pacified lands in the east to the new conquests in the west. You have been concentrating too much of late on the forefront of the Empire. You must also be mindful of the needs of the lands you already control, and you, through your governing agents, have neglected their needs in particular.

"Put the flogger back . . . and bring me the candle."

Wordlessly, he complied. If anyone had told her as a young girl that one day she would be keeping track of the government needs of half the known world, she would have thought the predictor mad. But she did. It took time and preparation, a network of spies and informants, and the ability to see patterns as they developed across disparate situations; she couldn't rely just on whatever her Goddess granted her in a vision. It took vigilance and discipline to keep abreast of all these various things. But it was all necessary. Needed.

"Light it," she murmured when he had returned with the fat shaft of beeswax.

He frowned at the wick, settling once more on his knees. She could feel the pulse of his life-force gathering, thickening, heating. The twist of braided linen thread crackled to life, burning steadily. This use of his powers was permitted in her presence, at her direction. Pleased, she nodded and held out her hand. He placed the lit candle in her grasp and sat back, hands behind his neck, to await her discipline.

"Front or back, Mistress?" he asked after a while.

Attention on the pool of melting beeswax, Charlisse lifted her chin. "Front."

Sighing roughly, he shifted his hands to the small of his back and leaned on his heels, baring his belly at an angle. His shaft was still full, though not completely erect at the moment. It drooped a little even as she glanced his way.

"Do you object to my choice, my servant?" she asked him, arching a brow. The thick, honey-scented cylinder and its fat wick had accumulated a good-sized pool of wax by now.

"No, Mistress."

No doubt he was expecting to be rewarded for a successful battle. That was coming, of course. He really had done well; the battle had been cleanly fought as far as such things went, and it had been a decisive victory. Aside from the crimes committed by his captain and sergeants, no civilians had been harmed. It deserved rewarding. But first . . .

Tipping her hand, she drizzled the melted beeswax across his chest. Ai-kan grunted, breath hissing through his teeth. Slowly, carefully, Charlisse marked a symbol in hot wax. "This . . . is the rune-sign for Morna . . . Goddess of the Great River. Your men have been disrespectful of the river folk and their highest holy days."

He grunted again as a few stray drops hit his shaft, his stomach tensing and cracking some of the cooled lines of wax. To her never-ending amusement, his half-erect flesh stiffened. Scorch him with wax on his chest, he deflated. But torment his manhood, and it aroused him. She let it pass; he had earned this pleasure thanks to the recent victory.

"You will pass word down the line that the Ai-an nation will *respect* the gods and goddesses of the people who join our ranks. That includes their holy rituals and festival days." She scattered a few more drops up by his collarbone, making him flinch.

"But . . ."

Charlisse righted the candle, letting more wax pool. She didn't change the low volume of her voice—it wasn't necessary to shout when exercising her control—but she did sharpen her tone. "But, *what*?"

"Mistress, I do not understand," Ai-kan managed, panting to control his pain. "I know . . . I know you want them to keep their gods, but . . . shouldn't Talwah be worshipped over all? Her holy days should take precedence! I *don't* protest my punishment. I just . . . don't understand."

About to pour more beeswax on him, Charlisse relented. A puff of air blew out the wick. Acrid, honey-scented smoke curled up. Shifting away from him, she returned it to its cast-bronze stand, then came back. His dark brown eyes, framed by those long black lashes, flicked her face in a questioning look before returning to the carpet-strewn ground.

"I don't understand, either," she confessed quietly. "But Talwah sees the needs of the world in a degree of detail that not even I can comprehend. All we can do is comply . . . and She wishes Her sister goddess to be equally revered. As well as all others. You *will* comply?"

"Yes, Mistress, of course." His capitulation was not forced.

She nodded. "Then you have borne your punishment for today. You may remove the wax."

For a moment, he looked like he would question her, ask if this was all she intended to do. Instead, he sat up and began picking off the cooled wax. It clung to his skin in places, and everywhere it had touched, it had left a reddish mark. Charlisse busied herself by turning her chair from facing her writing table to facing into the rest of the tent. She adjusted the cushions just so, then returned to stand in front of Ai-kan, one foot extended, just as he finished scraping off the last curl of wax.

Without prompting, he prostrated himself, kissing the top of her

foot. Kissing her toes. Licking them. Charlisse shifted her left, planting her sole on top of his head. Lightly pressing his cheek into the
carpet, she asked, "Who rules the Ai-an nation?"

"I do, Mistress."

"And who rules you?"

"You do, Mistress," he swore.

Pleased, she untied the straps of her robe, letting it fall to the
ground. With his eyes on her, bright and hot with desire, Charlisse
retreated to her chair and seated herself. Like the plants and the
statue of Talwah in her portable garden, it was a luxury not normally
associated with a war camp. It rivaled the comforts of his traveling
throne, being broad-seated, ornately carved, and comfortably strewn
with brocaded linen cushions. Settling back, she lifted her legs one
at a time, hooking her knees over the armrests. His eyes widened as
he watched her, and she allowed herself a small smile.

"Worship me, Ai-kan."

Crawling forward, almost stalking on hands and knees, he moved
as graceful as a mountain cat. His lips saluted her left foot, then his
whole face nuzzled it. Nipping softly, he worked his way up the inside
of her calf, nuzzling and kissing and licking. A soft breath escaped
her as he crossed the sensitive flesh of her knee.

It morphed into a moan as he nibbled on her inner thigh, then
another sigh as he abandoned her left leg in favor of her right, once
again starting down by her toes. They knew each other so well; she
permitted him this tiny bit of control so that he could arouse her,
awakening the needs within her body, mind, and soul. Awakening
the connection between her and her Goddess, though he rarely asked
for such things lately. Formally, perhaps, but not in moments like
this.

Requested or not, the moment his breath feathered over her
nether curls, she could feel the Goddess of Need seeping into her

senses. Eyes closed, Charlisse rested her head on the back of her chair, giving herself up to the sweep of his tongue. And when his mouth latched on and suckled strongly, her inner sight opened wide. Words gasped out of her.

"Oh, Goddess—yes! I see . . . a mountain pass! . . . An army marching . . . too small to be yours . . . They . . . they march up into the hills! They . . . oh, gods, yessss . . . go to join the troops in Alescens, but . . . ohhhh, lick lick lick." She moaned, hands shifting to the back of his head. She gripped his hair, tugging in that way she knew he liked, rewarding him for his efforts. "Ah—yes! If you send diplomats to the people of Alescens . . . ohhhhh, *Goddess*!"

"Mmm?" he inquired when she panted instead of continuing.

Charlisse groaned, not quite there yet. The control, the power, the deep care she took when she oversaw his needs, all of it stimulated her as much as it did him, but she needed more. She felt his hands caress her thighs and moaned again. Her encouragement slipped his fingers up her belly, up to her breasts, where he tweaked her nipples.

In her shocked moment of freefall, a corner of her mind knew she would have to punish him later for such a liberty, but then she fell, soaring with a shout of pleasure. The little hint of pain was perfect.

"*Goddess!* Diplomacy . . . oh gods . . . will prevail! I see the armies joining to attack Alescens' neighbors to the . . . the south and west! Easier victories than if you marched north! Ohhh, Goddess! Claim the southwest, and the northwest will weaken!"

The vision ended, lost in the passion shuddering through her body, disrupting her mind. Ai-kan gentled his touches, stroking to soothe instead of incite. Panting, she subsided, slumping in the chair. It wasn't necessary for her to climax in order to have a vision, but where this one particular supplicant was concerned, her Goddess was quite generous in meeting Charlisse's own needs.

Face hot and damp with sweat, muscles tense with need, Ai-kan rested his forehead against her belly. "Have I pleased you, Mistress?"

A smile curved her lips. "Yes . . . Yes, you have. You may now address me by name . . . my Ai-kan."

"My Charlisse." Her name was a whisper of devotion. Of love. Shifting close, he scooped her up and gained his feet. He kissed her and carried her to the bed, where he laid her on the thick, feather-stuffed mattress. When he joined her, she looped her arms around his neck and her legs around his hips, welcoming him into her body.

"I saw something else, you know," she murmured, smiling up at him.

Delving slowly into her depths, Ai-kan gave her a puzzled look. "You did?"

"A child. Conceived at some point within the next turning of Sister Moon," she added as he stilled.

Ai-kan blinked. "An heir? Then we should be married. You cannot refuse me now."

Charlisse shook her head. She covered his lips with two of her fingers, silencing his protest. "We can wed if you like, but she will be *my* heir. Another Seer of the Gods. *Your* heir must be as I have told you. Selected from among the strongest, wisest, most capable mages of the land. Examine both the male and the female, but choose those who can craft and cast spells. Mages can be bound by their powers to serve the people . . . as you do so well, my Emperor."

"Your love," he corrected, moving again. Filling her in a slow rhythm, he tasted the corners of her mouth. "Let the rest of the world call me Emperor of Ai-an. First and foremost, I am your love . . . then your servant . . . and only last an emperor."

"Mm, yessss," she agreed, and nipped at his lips, tugging on his hair. Even in moments like this, where they were once again more or less equals, she still preferred to assert herself. Her tugs demanded

a faster pace than the slow lovemaking he had started in this, their bed. "Morrrre . . ."

Only to her did he bow and acquiesce, giving in to her every demand. The wooden frame creaked as he thrust harder, each stroke giving both of them greater pleasure. She permitted it because he had indeed pleased her.

This time.

CAGED

J.K. Coi

One

---✦---

"I didn't think you were going to come this week."

Nora touched her free hand to the stun gun at her waist, calibrated to her specific DNA pattern, and ignored the dark humor in that rumbled voice. She listened for the snick of the lock latching behind her before continuing forward. Only one small circle of fractured light shone to the floor from the bulb set near the back of the cell, behind a steel-grated fixture in the rock ceiling above. There was no furniture. The wolf didn't even warrant a cot for sleeping.

"You'd like that, wouldn't you?" she replied to the oppressive gloom at large.

A chuckle. The sound bouncing off the walls of the cavern, penetrating her clothing and gear until it felt as if he touched her overly sensitive skin. "What else would I do with my Tuesdays?"

She snorted. She didn't come every Tuesday, not often enough that he should have been expecting her. Some weeks she was able to resist, holding out until at least Wednesday or Thursday. And during the week of a full moon, she didn't come at all . . . at least she never had before. "How do you even know what day of the week it is in this place?"

He didn't respond right away. A few months ago she might have thought his refusal to answer her questions meant he was pouting over his lost freedom, but now she knew better. Pouting wasn't his style. Not when he could lie, manipulate, or simply tear things apart trying to get what he wanted.

Instinct told her he was on the move, circling, but damned if Nora could hear even the softest shuffle of his feet over the dirt floor.

No, the wolf didn't pout and he hadn't given in to the impossible reality of his incarceration, despite six inches of specially treated corundum lining the walls of his underground cell and the digitally monitored locks keeping him inside it these last six months. To him these were only puzzles to be solved, just as she was no doubt a piece he would try to play at the right moment. Nora recognized and accepted this because she had been using him too—if for a different purpose—and because she never forgot, not for a moment, what he was capable of.

"It quickly becomes second nature to keep track of the days and nights when so much turns on the phases of the moon," he finally said. His voice was now coming from behind her. The bastard had slipped past her in the dark.

Well, she was used to that. She was used to all the wolf's tricks now.

She found herself turning toward that voice. Despite the reasons why she shouldn't, why it was dangerous. Admitting that the danger was part of what drove her. "But if you can't see the moon, or feel its glow on your face . . ."

"Ha. If only that made any real difference in the grand scheme . . ." His words trailed off and she lost his position as the darkness swallowed him up again.

Angry, she made a fist at her side. The morose turn of his mood probably meant his meds had been increased, most likely in an attempt to keep him manageable during the full moon. If those useless doctors had drugged him so much his performance suffered, they were going to regret it, and she was doubly glad now that she'd decided to disable the cameras before entering the cell.

"Not to mention, the place lacks a certain feminine touch." The purposely cavalier tone set the fine hairs at the back of her neck on end.

He was directly in front of her now, but still moving.

"Although, every once in a while . . ." A single claw scraped a line down her back, not that she could feel it. It was just enough to pull at the fabric of her sweater, not enough to mar the Kevlar beneath. A caress really. "They bring me some take out."

Nora didn't react. She knew he would be gone in the time it took to spin around, and wouldn't waste her energy chasing shadows. Oh, yes. They had played this game before.

"Why *are* you here today of all days, Nora?" he continued. "The moon is full tomorrow, as I'm sure you know. Cutting things a little close don't you think?"

Her lip curled as he taunted her from the shadows. Blood pounded hard in her veins as she felt him draw near and then back again. Invisible and silent. Circling. Touching. Retreating.

"Cut the cheap talk, wolf," she snapped, feeling much like an animal herself. Caged. Agitated . . . And eager to draw blood. "I'm here for the same reason as always. Nothing more."

Are you so sure about that?

"Is that right?" Laughter. Cutting and cold as if he heard her own traitorous thoughts—which wasn't one of his abilities; she'd tested that already. No, he would never admit it, but the wolf hated her refusal to acknowledge his name as much as she despised his insistence on using hers. He did his best to turn her annoyance against her, always trying to find a way into her head, trying to make these confrontations more personal than they really were so that she would let down her guard for him to escape.

Yes, she knew very well how it worked with him, but Nora was no better. The wolf was just a means to an end, another way for her to become the best agent she could be. The only reason she had anything to do with him at all was to learn what she could about defeating his kind. Nothing more.

Liar.

"Then come get me, Agent Donnelly," he called. "The moon won't wait forever." His voice had deepened with the dangerous invitation. She realized with a disquieting mortification that she'd been straining to hear it again.

The familiar thrill rushed through her—the only thing she seemed to ever feel anymore. And despite herself . . . only here, only with him.

It had gotten stronger as the intensity of their sessions increased during the last few weeks. She took her life in her hands every time she locked herself in here. The cell might hold him. The drugs might distract him, and without direct access to the moon's compelling power his wolf might be marginally weaker. But he still topped her five feet eight by more than a foot. He still came with built-in weapons of razor-sharp teeth and pointed claws, the cunning viciousness of a wild animal, and the desperate determination of a caged one.

And she didn't care.

She told everyone she was doing this because it would be stupid not to take advantage of the opportunity to train with the only wolf that had been taken alive to date. She told herself it was necessary so she would be better able to handle herself against the horde when the time came, as they all knew it would.

But it was all lies.

Inside she knew the truth—and she could have lived with that no problem, except that . . . he knew it, too.

Two

---✦---

Ignoring the wolf's rough-voiced dare, Nora continued to wait. It killed her to stand still when she knew he circled just beyond her field of vision, but she had learned the hard way—the screaming in pain, bloody and broken way—never to rush headlong into danger, even now when the locks and the gun and the guards were all on her side and it seemed she was the one with the power.

She waited and scanned the confined space with all her senses, biting back the sharp taste of adrenaline, letting it make its way through her bloodstream to all her extremities. Nora's sight was limited in the dark without her goggles, but her hearing was far above average, and she had reflexes almost as fast as the wolf's thanks to the medical enhancements she'd paid for last year. Enhancements that had given her the speed and strength to put the smackdown on all manner of creatures just like . . .

Duck. She swung her leg out in a wide sweep. Missed.

But her elbow on the way back up didn't miss, and neither did the roundhouse that sent him stumbling two steps into the single circle of weak light. It was her first good look at his lean, dark body tonight, but her reaction was the same as every night—shortened breaths as exhilaration surged, a frisson of fear that skittered down her spine . . . and a dizzying rush of molten lust she was finding it harder and harder to ignore.

"Playtime's over, wolf." Her gaze dropped to the big clawed hand

he curled into a fist, the veins that bulged and wrapped all the way up his arm. She stifled the shiver of anticipation that started between her shoulder blades before it could show in her face.

"Or just beginning," he retaliated with a grin, flaunting teeth that could pierce her skin and tear out her throat in the blink of an eye if she wasn't careful. "Depending on how you plan to look at it."

A fierce glitter winked from those silver wolf's eyes as he dodged her offensive lunge forward and countered with a swing of that tight fist. The heavy blow connected solidly with the left side of her face, mashing her lips into her teeth and snapping her head back so quick and so hard she heard the vertebrae in her neck crack. *Better than any chiro visit.*

Mouth filling with the coppery tang of her own blood, Nora bit back the cry that got caught in her throat—not of pain, not entirely. She stuck out her tongue and prodded at the split in her lip until the sharp sensation subsided, and then she smiled, purposely stretching out the little pain.

Ah, fuck. Here we go.

Blocking his second pass with her forearm, Nora indeed let herself go, knowing she didn't have to hold back. For long moments the only sounds in the dim cavern were the meaty thuds and smacks of flesh meeting flesh, and harsh breathing from both of them as they whaled on each other without mercy.

Nora took a shot to the ribs.

Her fist met the solid surface of his abs.

Claws swiped across her navel, leaving gashes in her clothes and scraping through the protective sheathe covering her vest.

She kicked him in the kneecap and drew back for another go when he grabbed her ankle and pushed, sending her off balance and flat on her back in the dirt with a thud that knocked the air out of her in a harsh grunt.

He was on her before she could blink away the black globs hover-

ing over her vision. Nora bucked her hips and slugged him as hard as she could. She shoved his wide, heavy body off her chest with a shout and then arched her spine, pushing into an acrobatic spring back onto the balls of her feet.

They stood facing each other, both dressed in the same dark-colored military-issue fatigues. Nora's chest heaved with deep, ragged breaths that made a mockery of her pretense of control, especially when the wolf's knowing gaze narrowed. "It's not enough for you anymore, is it?"

She glared back at him, even as pulsing white-hot embarrassment mingled with the erratic beat of need in her belly.

"Be honest with yourself for once and admit the real reason you come here. The real reason for this weekly dance of ours."

"Don't bother talking, asshole." She spat a mouthful of saliva mixed with blood into the dirt at her feet. "You can't worm your way into my head, and you're not getting out of here no matter what you say or do."

His bark of laughter ended on a rough cough and he braced the flat of one hand high on his torso. Nora eyed the dusty, smudged boot print she'd made in the chest of his plain black T-shirt and smiled at the thought that she might have cracked a couple of his ribs, even while her own side ached and blood trickled down her arm from a nasty gash in the muscles of her biceps.

Before he could recover and lunge for her again, she beat him to the punch, literally, and then watched him fall to one knee, a satisfied sneer twisting her lips. She kneed him in the face, took a shaky step back. Even as the skin of her knuckles cracked and bled, the rest of her body sighed and begged for more, begged for a release she had never quite been able to reach before.

Nora knew how sick she was. She knew something had warped inside her when she'd lost her husband to the werewolves, and almost lost her own life as well. Because yeah, taking pleasure from kicking

the crap out of anyone—even the wolf—that was not fucking normal. It was the stuff of sociopaths . . . and it made her a very bad person.

But how much worse was it that she also needed to be hurt in return? That getting beat black and blue by this particular beast every week was the only thing that made her feel alive?

When he rushed her she sidestepped and kicked out, but they were too well-matched for this to be easy. He bounced back quickly, advancing on her again. The light in his eyes promised more. More of a challenge, more of the wolf . . . more pain.

Nora sucked in a sharp breath, trying once again to convince herself this was all about training.

She was strong, but the wolf had the added dynamic of the imminent full moon going for him and it was making a difference today. Nora felt the delicious power behind each hit he landed, as if he was closer to the beast and therefore less inclined to hold back—something she suspected he still did even though she'd ordered him repeatedly to cut that shit out.

"I'm already in your head, Nora," he said. Was he going to try double-teaming her by adding taunting mind games between every blow? "And it's a pretty fucked-up, dark place to be if you ask me—which is saying a lot, considering which one of us is supposed to be the monster."

"Nobody asked you," she snapped.

"Didn't you?"

A veil of red slid down over her vision as she kicked and clawed, fought to make him shut his damn mouth. But her pussy throbbed insistently, the wet heat distracting.

Anger and frustration were her undoing. Her coordination finally slipped.

He seemed to draw confidence and strength by watching her fumble, his retaliation taking on a brutal bite with harder blows and quicker moves that she was barely able to block.

"How far are you going to let this go, Nora?" He slammed an elbow into her gut and she gasped. "How much blood do you have to shed? How much does it have to hurt before you get to come?"

"Fuck you," she muttered, tongue thick inside her shredded mouth.

She took another shot to the face, the wave of pain spiking all the way to her pulsing, wet core. *Oh, hell yeah.*

He was right, damn him. She swallowed hard, feeling the heavy bruise that would color her cheek and eye black and blue tomorrow settling in nicely. He had her all figured out. Agent Nora Donnelly was *fucked up*. A sick freak who needed the pain and violence to feel . . . anything.

And she was using the wolf like her dealer, to get what she needed.

Three

Nora went for the wolf's throat but he spun her around and shoved her forward, slamming her face-first against the wall. The bridge of her nose scraped the stone. She turned her head to the side to sneer back at him.

"Do you think I want to do this?" he said into her ear, a ferocious growl that made her want to spit in his face and purr in response, both at the same time.

With his body plastered to her back, including the thick evidence of his serious erection, now she was the one to laugh. "Yeah, I do. In fact, I think you love this."

His fingers curled into the short strands of her hair, pulling until her neck was bared to him. "Maybe you're right," he admitted in a harsh whisper, ducking closer until his lips glanced across the bottom of her jaw. "And whose fault is that?"

Nora hissed, but her body stilled. No matter how much she hated him—what he'd become and what he'd done—the two of them were tied together. Always would be. Caught up in an ever-growing cycle of violence, anger, and pain, which only fed the raging fire of passion that had already been there from another lifetime. Nora had a sinking suspicion nothing would break it. This thing wasn't going to end between them until someone died.

And despite her predilection for pain and self-loathing these days . . .

. . . She vowed it wasn't going to be her.

He pressed her into the wall until she groaned, breasts smashed and aching beneath the layers of her clothing and gear. "Nora, Jesus. It doesn't have to be this way," he urged. "Can't we—"

"Don't. Fuck, don't you dare." Desperate to make him shut up, she shoved him, jabbing her elbow into his abdomen. This wasn't what she wanted. No amount of pain or pleasure was worth being forced to endure his sick pretense of concern. "You think I don't see through your pathetic attempt at—"

"So, then what?" His breath on her skin raised the fine hairs at the back of her neck. "You think you can keep coming here like this without consequence? Without it destroying the both of us?"

What did it matter? He was already a monster, and most of the time Nora wasn't any better.

She tried shrugging him off, but he wasn't moving, and then his tongue was on her skin, tracing a wet path down the column of her neck, from beneath her ear to just above her collarbone. *Goddamn.* Too gentle. Reminding her too much of the human lover who was gone forever. The man this wolf had killed just by being bitten into existence.

"Bite me," she muttered, tilting her head toward him at a deeper angle.

"What was that?" His hands tightened around her forearms. She felt the pinch of his claws and stifled a shudder as the sensation sent little shocks of pleasure straight to her already diamond-hard nipples.

"You heard me, wolf," she bit out. "Don't bother trying to hide the animal you really are behind some useless attempt at fake human sympathy. *Use. Your. Fucking. Teeth.*"

She felt the need gripping him, the gathering tension of the beast. "You've had the shot," he said. It wasn't a question. He knew very well she'd been inoculated against the poison racing through his system. It was the only reason they had agreed to start letting her

into his cell three months ago. In fact, Nora had been one of the first to receive it. She would have volunteered to be the guinea pig for the drug's trial if it meant getting into the field earlier, but that hadn't been necessary.

"Do it," she demanded.

Behind her, his hips bucked, the hard ridge of his cock beneath the denim of his pants an impressive presence against her ass. "Your elaborate game goes out the window then, Nora," he warned, his breaths coming as quickly as her own.

Oh, yeah, he was going to do it. Her pulse hammered fast and hard beneath her jaw, threatening to explode out the side of her neck.

"You think you've been living dangerously, Agent Donnelly? You haven't seen anything yet. Let me loose on you and there'll be no reining in later what you can't control. You'll get everything you've been asking for . . . and a shitload that you didn't."

Good. As long as he made it hurt. Hurt to drown out the nothingness she lived with every day. "Are you going to shoot your mouth off, or are you going to—"

"And they'll all know," he continued. "Everyone on the other side of that door is going to know what we've done in here. What you let me—not any better than an animal—do to you. What you *asked* for."

She didn't care. Nothing could touch her. Nothing but him. "Just. Do. It."

Despite her urgent demand, he remained motionless behind her as if he might actually be trying to pretend he had some human decency, that he was still a man and not a wolf . . . but she knew better than that. Nora had no more illusions left to her, not about him, not about herself.

She shifted slightly, but before she could turn he struck hard, his mouth hot on her skin, teeth sinking into the vulnerable flesh where her neck met her shoulder. Her mouth clamped shut as her body jerked involuntarily and a harsh gasp burst from her lips.

The burn was deep and immediate, better than she could have hoped.

"*Oh, fuck. Yes.*" Her desperate moan echoed in the cavern, but Nora was beyond embarrassment or denial. She planted both hands on the gritty wall, curling her fingers into the rock and pushing back into his equally hard body for a stronger connection, telling him without words that she wanted more.

Nora moaned again at the stinging drag of his teeth withdrawing from her shoulder, only to clench her jaw when he nipped the skin over the pulse pounding in her throat, and then again at her earlobe.

Not enough. She was the one growling now, struggling in an attempt to turn around and face him. When she did it was to be confronted with the one thing she hadn't planned on.

Tenderness. Shining from those silver wolf eyes.

Bastard.

She hit him hard, satisfied when his head snapped to the side. He swung back and the look on his face had been replaced by a wicked snarl that sent a shiver of anticipation through her.

He blocked her jabbing knee with his thigh but she was already moving on, going for that lying face with her nails. She scored a dark line of red across his cheek before he grabbed her wrist and yanked her forward. He dragged her off balance so she couldn't avoid the shot to her midsection, a more than appropriate retaliation for what she'd dealt him.

The breath whooshed out of her. She doubled over and would have fallen to her knees, but his fist buried itself in her hair again, pulling her back up until she cried out. Tears stung her eyes as she gazed into a snarling, wild-eyed face covered in blood, bruises, and streaks of dirt.

Nora knew she didn't look any better, probably worse in fact.

Dear God. What have we become?

Four

———◆———

Too much. All of it was suddenly too . . .

She slashed at his arm and kicked his shin. He let go of her hair.

A growl.

From him . . . or from her?

He might be a wolf, but Nora felt like the wild one, the one locked up in a cage of ice with only despair, anger, and hopelessness as her constant companions. For the first time in months she felt a glimmer of something brighter, and it didn't matter if it was born of agony, if it couldn't last. She needed to hold onto it for as long as possible.

She reached for him. Their mouths met in a furious explosion of pain and passion, but for once the passion was stronger, hotter.

They tore at each other's clothes. Nora's pullover was shredded in seconds and he moved on to the straps of her vest as she threw his dirty T-shirt to the ground. She felt a momentary twinge of self-preservation when the protection of her Kevlar was gone, but not enough to put a stop to the madness.

Especially when he was kissing her again, pulling her bottom lip between his sharp teeth, thrusting his tongue into her mouth when she gasped from the sweet sting.

Her bra was history, sliced apart and discarded without another thought by either of them. He cupped her breasts, pinched her nipples, and flicked them with his sharp claws until they were hard, aching points that could have cut glass.

Nora didn't even notice that he had guided the two of them back across the width of the cell until her shoulder blades hit the wall again with a thud that knocked a grunt from them both.

She helped him strip her boots and the rest of her clothes, but once naked, Nora couldn't be bothered waiting for him to take off his own. It was good enough that she got his belt unbuckled and his pants shoved low over his hips before digging her nails into his shoulders and climbing him like a fucking mountain.

"This is what you need," he rasped into her mouth, wrapping his arms around her and pushing inside of her in one strong glide.

Nora groaned, lifting her hips to meet him, tightening her legs around his waist. "Yes."

"Not the violence and the pain."

Her head thrashed back and forth. "Yes," she repeated, mindless to the pulsing of her pussy around the thick length stretching her, filling her. "Yes, I need it."

"No." He slid right out of her, his hard, wet cock throbbing between her thighs. "It's me," he insisted. "I'm what you need."

Her eyes flew open. He watched her, an expression of lust mingled with triumph. She shook her head.

"Yes." He marked his insistence with a savage thrust, making sure she felt the reality of every long, wide inch of his cock sliding into her again. And then again. "It's always going to be me for you." His voice had devolved to a guttural growl, thick with feeling. Nora tried to block it out, but her desperate body wouldn't let her. "It doesn't matter who we were, or what we've become. It always comes down to the two of us together in the dark."

With the slippery glide of his shaft and every word that speared her soul, Nora wound higher and tighter. Denial and rejection sat on the tip of her tongue, but she couldn't speak them. Pulling his head down, she kissed him.

"Nora, see the real me," he murmured against her lips. "I'm

the one fucking you, and I'll always be the one to make you come alive."

"Shut up," she moaned. "Please shut up."

"And do what?" He reached between them, twisting her nipple between his thumb and finger until she cried out and nipped at his chin.

"Do it, wolf," she whispered, arching to fill his hand with her breast, moving her hips to urge him faster. "Finish this." Part of her admitted she might be asking for something other than the oblivion of orgasm, but it was a small, weak part she would continue to smother for as long as she could.

Her spine scraped rock and her cuts and bruises burned as he fucked her, but she barely felt any of it anymore. As much as she hated to admit it, he was right that this wasn't about the pain. The only thing she felt now was him.

"Say my name." A harsh demand at her ear.

Surprised, she closed her eyes. "No."

"Say it. Give me that much after all that's happened."

She didn't want to. She didn't want to give him anything else when he'd already taken so much from her.

Insistent, he ground into her again and again until she was panting, her thigh muscles strained and her pussy coiled so tight she shouted for more, begged him for release. Looking up into his fiery expression, it wasn't the first time their gazes had clashed—wolf and woman—but it was the first time Nora let herself acknowledge the spark of humanity that lingered in the depths of his silver eyes.

Lifting a hand to his face, she hesitated before touching him. It would be the first time she'd willingly done so without the intention of hurting or using him.

"My name," he repeated.

The orgasm continued to build, spreading heat from her wet core through her whole body. Her fingers traced his brow and down his angular cheekbone to lips drawn back in a harsh groan. Was it plea-

sure he felt now, or had Nora's continued, violent rejection of what he was caused him as much pain as her fists and her boot?

Remaining silent, reveling in each of the wolf's quickening thrusts, she saw in his face the moment when he couldn't hold out any longer and she had won their stubborn stand-off, but Nora realized maybe she wasn't as cold inside as she'd thought. The word he waited to hear shot out of her with a fervent, honest cry.

"Marcus!"

His name. The name of her enemy, and of the man who had been her only love. Her husband, before being bitten by the wolf who had taken him over and ripped out her heart.

His hips jerked as he dropped his head into the cradle of her shoulder, biting down hard as he came inside her and set off her own orgasm. It crested again and again with pulsing colors and shattering lights to match the intensity of her explosion.

When she finally came down, Nora opened her eyes to find him staring at her, and reality rushed back in a potent wave of shame and disgust. Whether it was the moon itself or the ferocity of their fucking, his monthly transformation had begun. She could see it in the glow of his eyes, the curl of his lip. He was already bigger, hairier. The wolf was coming on strong. Fast.

"Let me go." She shoved him until he withdrew and let her legs fall from his waist. She cursed herself for being such a fool as she hurried to dress in what was left of her clothes, pulling on her pants and her boots, scrabbling for her vest and the long-forgotten stun gun that had been thrown into the shadows a few feet away. She drew it and trained the sight on his forehead. God, the tears were so close. She couldn't let him see . . .

She made a break for the exit without looking back, punching in her code with quick, hard jabs of the keys.

"Nora, wait." His voice was rougher, making it even clearer that she had committed a colossal, epic mistake. "Don't leave!"

The door slid open. He reached for her.

She jerked away, turning to walk out, ignoring the furious shouts echoing from the darkness at her back.

J.K. Coi is a multi-published, award-winning author of dark and sexy paranormal romance and urban fantasy. She lives in Ontario with her amazingly supportive husband and son, and their cat who is the undisputed ruler of the household. Please visit her at www.jkcoi.com, and if you're a real glutton for punishment, see what she's up to by following her on Twitter at www.twitter.com/jkcoi.

EACH STEP SUBLIME

BETTIE SHARPE

One

———◆———

"Pride must suffer pain," Grandmother says as she prepares me for my first trip to the surface. She says it as she lays a heavy kelp wreath across my shoulders, laces a girdle of abalone shells tight about my waist, and twists black sea-flowers into my silver hair. Three times she says it, and three times I nod. Pride keeps me silent, though I want to scream.

When Grandmother has made me as beautiful as she believes I can endure, my sisters sing to me. Theirs are the same sweet voices that call to sailors in the dark; that lure ships onto jagged rocks and unfriendly shores. Their song is the Song of the Sea. I know it as well as my own heartbeat. I love it as much as my next breath.

I kiss them each before I swim away, but once I've turned, I don't look back. I am too eager to see what lies above the waves—to behold the endless sky and finite land; to glimpse the realms of birds and men.

Up and up and up I swim, into the sunlight filtering down through the deep. Shadows flit across my skin like a school of fish passing overhead. It is a rain of debris. Barrels, casks, trunks, and men sink from the surface, falling slowly, casting darkness on all that lies below.

A form drifts past, trailing dark blood. Its warm hand brushes my cheek like a caress. I catch the body, stopping its descent. It is a

male of the human kind, with cloth coverings—*clothing*—upon his body and two gangly appendages in place of a tail.

I push at his clothing, curious to see what secrets it hides. Beneath, I feel muscle and bone—broad shoulders and hard ribs, just as he ought to have. And down below his abdomen just where his body splits in two, I feel the soft protrusion of a man's parts.

Except for his legs, he is so like a sea-person that I am almost sorry he will die. But death is not as close as I thought, for when I press the hard muscles of his belly, he coughs.

His eyes spring open. His out-flung hands tangle in my hair. His gaze is dark and dangerous as an animal's, but it shines with a spark of spirit I cannot deny. I seal my lips over his and breathe. He tastes of blood and salt, a not unpleasant flavor. Holding him thus, breathing for him, I swim to the surface.

The first thing I see when my head breaks the waves is not the sun or the sky, but the human's face, pained and streaked with blood. There is a menacing beauty to his features—that dark hair against pale skin; those full lips between a prominent nose and square chin.

Reluctantly, I turn my gaze to the world above the ocean. Here is all that I have heard described, but never understood. The sky is blue and endless as the infinite sea. The sunlight warms my skin, even as the air currents chill it. And far off on the horizon, a brown-green lump rises above the sea's majestic blue. It must be land.

I take the human to a quiet cove beneath a white palace with red pennants flying from its highest tower, and white stone stairs leading from the gardens straight into the sea. He climbs the stairs weakly, pausing to rest when he is but partway from the water. His hand stays tangled in my hair. Our eyes meet. "If you knew what I am," he says, "you'd have let me drown."

He pulls my face toward his. His lips are pain and pleasure. They move roughly over mine, spurring an excitement I can barely comprehend. It is foreign, yet so consuming that I don't push him away,

not even when he uses his tongue to caress mine within my mouth. Curious and pleased, I return his caresses.

He coughs against my lips, a burst of blood and breath. His hand loosens from my hair. His eyelids fall and his body goes limp. I cradle his head in my arms and lay it down gently. Though it should not matter to me, I long for him to live. I touch his cheek before swimming away, leaving him to the land.

Two

The human haunts me. I cannot fathom why, except that I liked the rough caresses of his lips and tongue. Since that day, I've found myself staring into empty water with my fingers pressed bruising-hard against my lips. Reliving his touch, remembering his taste.

When I can bear it no more, I swim to the stone stairway. It's night, and the moon is but a sliver. Any human who sees my pale head above the waves will think it only sea foam.

He stands on the stairs with the ocean lapping his boots. His dark hair is dry and tousled by the wind. His fists hang clenched at his sides, and on his face is a look of such harsh desire that I both fear and long to be its object.

"Come back." He speaks the words to the wind. Almost, I obey.

For all that he is human, he is like the sea—deep and dark and dangerous; unfathomable and unforgiving. And like the sea, I know that what he takes, he will keep. If I go to him, I will be as lost as a sunken ship upon the ocean floor, lost to the world that birthed me. Lost to everything I have ever known.

For the second time, I leave him to the land. But he will not leave me.

In my dreams, he says, "Come back," and I go. In my dreams, I am conquered. In my dreams I am free. I savor those dreams, and spend my waking hours reliving them. During the day I am distant and distracted. Come nightfall I am far too eager for sleep.

My family has begun to worry. "Perhaps she is ill," my eldest sister says as she huddles with my grandmother one afternoon in the gardens.

"I know of no ailment marked by such blank stares and breathy sighs," my grandmother replies. "She's cursed. We must employ the witch to free her from this spell."

The next day, they bring me to the mouth of the forest of grasping polypi. The polypi are vines like serpents with a hundred heads and a hundred arms. What the forest catches with its white, clutching hands, it holds forever. The sea-witch lives beyond it, in a house of bone.

I brought treasure with me, but the witch wants none of it. "I don't crave riches." Her aged voice is rough and brittle as dead coral. "I want something you hold dear."

"Anything I have. Only free me from this."

"I can't free you." Her voice sinks to a whisper, and her tail undulates like the polypi in their forest of death. "You've fallen in love. Magic cannot create love, nor counter it."

Her words sting like a sea nettle. "What am I to do?"

"You must go to him. I've a potion that will give you legs."

I fold my arms across my breasts. "At what cost?"

"Each step will feel like the point of a knife."

I shake my head.

She snakes her scaled arm about my shoulders. "Love must suffer pain, child."

"I thought that was pride."

"They have more in common than you'd think," she rasps. "Your answer?"

I cannot ponder the matter long, or else I must surely refuse. "Yes."

The witch's smile shows double rows of jagged teeth. "Now, about my fee . . ."

"My pain is your payment."

"Oh, no." Her smile widens. "Your pain is but a consequence of the potion—one I do not think you will mind nearly so much as you should. The price for my help is your voice. I'd like to have it for my own."

I imagine myself voiceless, never to speak or laugh or cry again. Never to sing ships onto rocky shores. "No."

"Come now, if you win his heart, you may have it back."

I hesitate.

"He'll find another girl who loves him as much as you."

Panic rises in me. I cannot stand the thought of longing for him while he lives happily with another. He must suffer as I do. I hold out my hand. "Give me the potion."

"Know this," the witch says. "If he returns your love, you win your voice, but if he breaks your heart, you will die. Your blood will turn to saltwater, your body to sea foam. All who ever loved you will forget your name."

"He will love me." I will make sure of it. "Give me the potion."

"Payment first."

I open my mouth to dispute her. She plucks out my tongue like an oyster from the half-shell. Pain sears me, scarring my senses wide open, sealing the moment in horror cold as a cage of ice. I watch, helpless, as she raises my struggling, severed tongue to her lips and swallows it whole.

Too late to stop her, I regain control of my body. I touch my mouth, expecting a hot flow of blood to match the pain of my missing flesh, and find my tongue right where I left it, warm, living, and now useless.

The witch speaks with my siren-sweet voice. "Drink this." She hands me a crystal vial.

The thick, bitter potion slithers down my throat as smoothly as

an eel into a crevice. It coils round the base of my spine, and sparks a fever that cleaves me in two.

"One last thing," she says as I writhe in pain. "Your prince is no prize. His own people believe him a monster. His past lovers declare him heartless."

Trapped, like the polypi's prey. What a fool I was to take the witch's bargain.

She bares her white teeth and pushes me from her home. "Go. Try to make the monster love you. It is your only hope."

Three

<hr/>

My first step from the sea is agony; the second, torture. The third step brings something like a revelation. It freezes the world in a crisp, crystalline shell of pain—a miniature eternity in which I notice the black night clouds limned with silver moonlight, the jewels of dew on each shadowed blade of grass. I taste the sea on the air and the sun beneath the horizon. Almost, it seems, the world's every mystery will be made clear to me, its every secret revealed. And then, I pass out.

He finds me at sunrise, fainted on his lovely stair. He is dark as the night past, clad in the colors of midnight. I am pale as the stone beneath me, wearing nothing but my silvery hair.

I stir when he touches me, my eyes burning with the morning light, my breath coming fast from the fever of pain. His touch is torture, cool and soothing. It contrasts so perfectly with the sensations that rendered me unconscious that it becomes, of itself, a new and different agony.

"Who are you?" He brushes my hair from my face. I exhale a silent sigh but do not answer. I have no voice, no name he could comprehend, and no way to reveal what brutal magic brought me to his side.

I meet his gaze with my heart in my eyes, everything about me soft and willing. Whatever words he meant to voice die on his lips

as they part, exhale. His pupils widen. His hand is hot against my wind-chilled skin.

"You need help. Clothes to cover you, medicine to heal you."

You, I say with my eyes. *You must cover me. You must heal me.*

"No." Regret and hunger war in his expression. "I warn you, I am no good for care or comfort. I would bring you only pain."

Then bring me pain.

Eyes haunted, he shakes his head. "You saved my life. You deserve better."

He moves to pull away from me. I catch his wrist. It's strong and thick; my fingers cannot close around it. *Please.*

"You will regret it," he says. "They always do."

He scoops me into his arms and ascends the stair in long, swift strides. He carries me through a scented garden of blood-red flowers with soft petals and vicious thorns. At last we come to the palace. A thousand glass windows reflect sea and sky. Within are rooms dressed in polished wood dark as black pearls, and jewel-toned fabrics softer than a seal's pelt.

He lays me on a padded bench and bellows for his servants. A woman comes, old and round, with silver hair darker than my own. Her lined face falls when she sees me. "So delicate, she is. Looks like a kiss might bruise her."

"Yes." His voice is hungry.

The servant's black eyes turn hard as volcanic glass. "The rumors were bad enough after the last one left. You know you cannot keep her."

He nods.

No! I force myself to my feet. Pain spirals up my body like a choking vine. With my next step, it blossoms into bloodred beauty, sweet as the flowers in his garden, hot as the pressure of his lips.

His breath catches. I meet his eyes and cannot look away. They

are so very dark, iris and pupil almost the same shade. His pupils widen as he watches me. I glimpse my reflection in his gaze; my pale body twined with the thorny vine of pain, kissed by the scarlet blooms of ecstasy.

In the corner of my vision, his servant drops her head, cheeks pink with shame at the sight of us. She clasps and unclasps her hands. "I'll prepare a room for her."

"Don't bother. She'll sleep in mine."

Four

—◆—

The servant leaves and my wits scatter like a surprised school of fish. Much as I crave my human's touch, the intensity of his attention frightens me.

He circles me. I clasp my hands to stop them from trembling.

His laughter seems as gentle as a mild tide lapping at a sunny shore, cold contrast to the cruel hunger of his smile. "Beware your wants, love, lest I satisfy them."

The witch called him a monster. Almost, I believe it. Yet I remember the rough press of his lips. The taste of salt and blood. The feel of his body tangled with mine.

"Come," he says. This time I obey, each step a joyous agony.

He touches my lips. "I was your first."

Yes. My eyes answer him, though I haven't a voice.

He trails his hand down my body to trace the seam of my sex. I shiver at this liberty, but do not deny him.

"I will be your first."

Yes.

Though I am yet an innocent, I've heard whispers of what transpires between the sexes. My sisters use words like "taken" and "ruined" when they speak of maids who let love lead them to a fall from grace. I've no illusion I can escape that fate. This man will take me. He will break me and remake me. A maid no more, I will become a most exquisite ruin.

I raise my face. He takes my mouth with his. Feeling floods me; his lips, his tongue, his hands. My heart hammers, as if in panic. My breaths come short and shallow. I am a sailor lost at sea, dependent on the fickle mercies of an element far greater than myself.

He touches me all over, making free with my body as though it exists only to please him. And yet, he pleases me, too. His hands seek out my secret spaces without shame or hesitation. Unerring, his fingers find my hidden pearl, toying and teasing until I scream, silent, at his touch.

Without warning, he slips his questing fingers into the channel of my sex. My muscles clench at his invasion, but he breaches me easily, hastened by the slick heat of my desire. Slowly, he spreads his fingers, testing me, stretching me.

"There will be pain." A slight smile plays across his lips.

Love must suffer pain. The memory of the witch's words stirs eager heat where I should feel the cold weight of fear. There must be some flaw in me, to make me crave his touch whether it brings pain or pleasure; to make me happily surrender what other maids hold sacrosanct until their wedding nights.

He puts his lips to mine again, pressing hard and delving deep. His hands toy with me, raising a tide of pleasure in my body that crests and drowns me between one breath and the next. I shudder in his arms, my new legs unwilling to support me. He catches me, holds me; his strength supports my soft and yielding form.

When the wild tide has ebbed, he sets me back upon my feet and frees his manhood from his clothes. It is not as it was that day in the ocean, soft and small enough to fit within my grasp. Now it is thick and heavy. When he places my hand on its heated length, my fingers cannot close around it. I try, though, squeezing gently, stroking lightly at the searing softness of his skin.

He trembles, much as I did when he caressed my pearl. It makes me bold to know I can control him thus. I stroke until his hand

encircles my slender wrist and twists it behind me. I offer the other, making myself his willing prisoner. He holds my arms pinned and walks me forward.

Each burning step wraps the world in glass, delicate and breakable. My senses become acute, aware, perfect in their perception, from the cool play of air across my skin to the harsh sound of his breaths as he bends me over the padded arm of the bench.

Roughly, he thrusts his hands between my trembling legs. He parts them and he enters me. There is pain as he promised, but it is no punishment. It is precious, sharp, and fleeting, never to be known again.

He moves, rhythmic, restless as the sea before a storm. Against me, within me. My body gives like a soft shore, shaping itself to his movement, welcoming each violent meeting, mourning each slow retreat. At last he crashes into me and spends himself. He clutches me tight, whispering praises in my ear.

Later, he carries me from that room. Each step takes me farther from the sea. He ascends a curving stair to a room with a wide, curtained bed. The pillows smell of him, of fresh water and human skin. I burrow into them, sighing at the softness.

He laughs. "Enjoy your pleasures, do you?"

I nod, shyly.

He catches my chin and forces my face to his. "It's too late for modesty, poppet. Not when you're naked in my bed. Not when your virgin's blood is drying on my cock."

I meet his eyes, trembling, wondering what he wants of me.

He holds my gaze for several long moments. "I belong to everyone—my family, my people, my country—but you belong to me." He grasps my shoulders hard. "Mine—every bit of you."

Shock must show in my expression, for he flashes his cold smile. "I told you, you should have let me drown."

I bow my head, but before I sink too deep in regret, servants come

and set a metal tub beside the fire and fill it with bucket after bucket of warm freshwater. When they have finished, my lover carries me to the tub and eases me into the sweet, steaming water. With the lightest hand, he washes the salt from my skin and his seed from my thighs.

So gentle is he that I begin to believe I imagined the ferocity of his voice, the absolute hunger in his eyes. But after he has dried me, he sets me on my feet and bids me walk to the bed and await him. It is six paces. Six steps of agony. He watches me take each one with an expression of such desire that I cannot doubt his predilection.

He bathes quickly and joins me on the bed. Had he not forbidden me the twin luxuries of modesty and shame, I would blush at the liberties I allow him. But since he bade me be bold as well as willing, I do not quail as he teaches me the harsher ways of love. He schools me with a regimen of bites and bruises, of binding ties and heavy hands.

I lose minutes, hours—*days*—to his whim and will, but I adore his every action. My love burns as hot as hatred. It sparks a hundred small rebellions meant to earn his ire. He repays them all with punishments divine.

I find a seductive freedom in surrender—a timeless now, immediate and eternal. It brings me pleasure, even when he does his best to bring me pain. I search each careful castigation for some sign of reciprocated love—a telling look, a careless word, or perhaps a declaration.

Of all my desires, this alone goes unfulfilled.

Five

"He isn't yours," the servant says as she sets up my breakfast tray. She smiles when my expression falters. "He's a prince. You cannot believe he would love such as you, common and dumb, washed up by the sea. He's promised to a princess, and must go to her soon."

I want to disbelieve, but soon enough the servants begin to close the unused rooms and pack his treasured possessions. The day before his ship is to sail, he comes to me with a bundle of clothes. Inside is a page's uniform. And a pair of golden scissors.

"I won't be without you." His voice is light and careless. "Don the uniform. Cut your hair."

I touch my hair, silvery as a fish's flank and long as I am tall. In the sea it floated around me as clouds float in the sky. It is not my only vanity, but it is chief among them. I want to shout denials at him, to curse this man for whom I've given up my home, my voice, and my proper form. I want to say he asks too much, but I will not refuse.

He seeks the limit of what I will endure. I've danced for him. I've bent and bruised and bled for him. But I will not break. I am too proud. I am too much in love.

He gathers up my hair from the floor and locks it in a box with some worn books and a battered sword. He runs his hand over my shorn head, and his gaze over my red livery.

"You look like a boy."

I cast my gaze down to hide my anger. He lifts my face and kisses me. It is a gentle kiss, the kind one might use to seduce an innocent. The kind a man might use to seduce a youth. He strips the uniform from my body, and takes me as men take one another. There should be no pleasure in this act for me, and yet I find it so. The heat of his hand tracing my spine, the mastery of his penetration.

It is not the first time he has taken me thus, but it will be the last. I cannot bear the thought of his marriage to another. It is the true limit of my endurance—the point at which I break instead of bend. I run my hand over my head, angry that I've given him everything and received so little in return.

I draw away from him when he tries to hold me afterward, only to obey when he orders me back into his arms. Yet acquiescence is not enough, for even when he has me close he whispers, "Come back," as I drift into sleep.

"COME back!" His cry wakes me from my troubled dreams the morning of his wedding. I open my eyes and find his focused on me with the dark intensity I loathe and adore. He doesn't look at me as a partner, but as a plaything. I'm not a woman; I am a warm body beneath him, a willing sheath for his randy cock.

I turn my head away, but he forces me to face him. "Look at me."

I hold his gaze as he touches me, as he takes me. As his clever hands wring pleasure from my ever-willing flesh.

"My poppet." He traces the length of my neck with his strong hand. "I'll think of you while I'm fucking my bride."

After he has gone, I stand before the tall mirror near his bed. *His.* How can I forget it when I am what he has made me—a legged thing that walks on land, soft skin marked with love bites, my hair shorn short as a boy's?

I strike the mirror with my fists. I cannot stop. Glass shatters, but

I don't feel the pain. Desperate and despairing, I grasp a shard of mirror and squeeze. Seawater bleeds from my cut flesh, hot and salty as my tears. Come dawn there will be nothing left of me save salt water and sea foam—my life wasted for the love of a man who would not love me back.

Six

I won't attend his wedding. I cannot watch him pledge himself to another and yet maintain the feeble thread of hope that keeps me alive. When evening falls, I walk to the sea to watch the waves break on the shore. Too late, I realize I am not used to such exertion. Except those times he bade me walk to him, he carried me in his arms. Even in my guise as a page, he gave me a fine horse to ride that I might accompany him wherever he went.

Immersion eases the pain of my aching feet. Waist-deep in the sea, siren-sweet voices call to me. My sisters rise, one after another, pale heads breaking the waves. Pale heads shorn as my own.

What have they done?

"We traded our hair to the witch for the means to free you," the eldest answers for them all.

The youngest raises her hand from the water to offer me a crooked dagger. "Take his life to save your own."

I take the dagger. If I cannot have him, I will at least have my sisters and the sea.

"Go," they sing. "It must be done before sunrise."

PAST midnight, I creep into my prince's chamber in the foreign palace. My bleeding feet leave a trail of salt water and sand upon the floor. His princess sleeps alone in her bridal bed, swathed in white

linen, her long hair unbound, her golden skin unmarred. I search the room for signs of him. Finding none, I leave soon after.

When I return to the ship, he is standing at the bow. He stares beyond the sea to where his white palace sits upon our distant shore. I touch his shoulder. He turns, his dark eyes lost and longing.

"I came for you and found you gone." He reaches for me. I shy away. "I dreamt last night of that first night, when you touched my cheek and left me on the stairs."

I shake my head, but he continues. "No matter how oft I say you're mine, I know you'll leave me for the sea."

I want to deny it, but all this time I have been waiting for love to run its course, to free me from its coils so I might return to the life I once knew. Even tonight, I did not refuse the knife when my sisters placed it in my hands.

I reach into my livery jacket and remove the crooked blade. He seems to grasp its purpose instantly, for he takes my hand and guides the dagger's point to rest above his heart. "If you mean to leave me, do it. I said I wouldn't be without you."

I gape.

"Little fool. Don't you know I love you?" He shakes his head. "No, how could you? I did not know it, myself, until I stood ready to marry that mawkish girl." He looks away from me. "Her eyes were wide as I approached the altar—frightened, truly frightened. And she'd a right to be—no girl wants to marry a monster."

Little fool, he called me. His princess is the true fool, to quail and quake at his approach. Never will she know such callousness; never will she know such care. He is a creature of contradictions, this monster. He is beautiful and menacing, and he is *mine*.

My heart, moments ago so close to breaking, heals and births itself anew. My fading flesh grows bright and warm again. I grasp the blade of the crooked dagger and scream with joy when hot red blood wells from the wound instead of water.

"What have you done?" He takes the weapon from my hand and throws it into the sea.

"I live." My voice feels rusty with misuse.

"Your voice . . . How?"

"The sea-witch said that if you loved me, I would win it back."

"And if I hadn't?"

I look away.

He gathers me to him and binds my wound with the fine white cloth that had been hanging loose about his neck. "You've no right to take such risks."

"I've every right." I brush his cheek with my bandaged hand.

"You love me." He whispers the words with reverence.

"Yes."

He turns toward his ship's quarters, left unlit on this, his wedding night. "Come."

I take his hand and walk with him into the darkness, each step sublime.

Bettie Sharpe is a Los Angeles native who enjoys romance novels, action movies, comic books, video games, and every other entertainment product her teachers said would rot her brain. She loves to write almost as much as she loves to read. For info on Bettie's backlist and upcoming titles, visit her website at www.bettiesharpe.com.

SAFEWORD

Delphine Dryden

I would have been fine if he had never made that joke about paddling. The whole thing could have stayed safely hypothetical, safely stowed in the subtext. Safe.

And it wasn't even the joke itself—off the cuff, wry, accompanied by that wicked quirk of his lips that never ceased to make me feel fluttery. No, it was the look in his eyes as he said it. That moment of distance, of resignation. Almost a wistful expression. It was the look a person gets when he talks about his first love, the one that got away.

I could feel how strained my face must have looked as I turned around, stopping us when we were still a block away from the office building. Another friendly lunch, another round of hinting at things we both assumed would never materialize. But on the way back, there came that one moment, and it changed us.

"Don't. Don't talk about paddling, okay?"

"What, Burke? Did I offend? You, really?"

"No, not really. But I can't be listening to you talk about stuff like . . . paddling."

I turned away and started walking again, feeling a furious blush rise. Disgusting. I wouldn't be at all surprised if my pupils were dilated, too. But I couldn't help it, because now the image of Nathan with a paddle was firmly implanted in my far too fertile imagination. Why had I said anything?

Fuck, fuck, fuck. FUCK.

"I'm confused."

He was at my elbow, shadowing me by half a step or so, although he could easily have outpaced me. It was his way of providing me with some space, perhaps. Or maybe he was just trying to give the crazy a little breathing room.

"Oh, that's probably for the best. Just forget it. Don't we both have work to do?"

Another ten steps would put me at the front door. My hand was already stretching out for the gleaming chrome handle when he stopped me, clasping my other arm just above the elbow. Lightly. He didn't need to exert pressure. He said, "Stop." I stopped on a dime.

If he had been the type of person I had often wished he were, that might have been a clue.

"Burke, what's the deal?"

I swallowed hard and turned around, looking somewhere past his shoulder, trying not to imagine that shoulder shirtless and flexing, drawing back for a carefully measured stroke. I was too late, however. But I knew Nathan, knew he was a nice, wholesome guy. A shameless flirt, yes, but a pure vanilla flirt. I liked that, and wanted to keep the sparkling promise of flirtation throughout my day, the subtle and none-too-subtle innuendos that could only continue as long as they were harmless and never, never taken too seriously.

"I just had a little moment, there. My secret, evil private life clashing with my respectable work life. Stuff was leaking over into the wrong compartment. It's all tucked back in now, nothing to worry about. Sorry."

He chuckled, and the tension began to seep away. "Okay. I still have no idea what you're talking about, but okay."

"It's just dumb."

He looked at me then, really looked at me, and I felt that all-too-familiar rolling thrum of unrequited lust assault my good sense.

When he smiled that same little cockeyed smirk again, I felt a pull toward his mouth like a magnet. That palpable. That elemental. He wasn't usually standing so close. When the breeze turned, I could just smell his cologne, and a hint of something that might be fabric softener.

"I doubt that. You don't do dumb, Burke."

That should have been the end of it. If it had been any day but Friday, I thought later, the whole thing would have blown over. Cooled off. He would have been distracted by something else before he had the chance to delve any further into the mystery.

As it was, I could feel his eyes on me throughout the afternoon. In the conference room, while we were both involved in taking a deposition. In the small law library our firm maintained, each of us working on our respective cases in a silence broken only by the steady tap of laptop keys. The tan and red spines of the law books on their neatly ranked shelves formed a tidy backdrop to the maelstrom of thoughts and images in my head. I was relieved when I came to a legitimate stopping place and left with only the smallest wave in Nathan's direction.

He watched me walk out the door. I knew, because at the last second I couldn't resist turning my head to check. And just before I bolted, files held protectively in front of my chest, I met his eyes and saw that wicked little smile again, and wondered what in hell I had unleashed on myself.

Whatever it was, pursuing it was out of the question. I couldn't, not with Nathan. I had known him for five years, since the beginning of law school. And these past two years as associates at the same firm, we had become friends. We had become each other's mainstays. I had spent many a weepy night wishing things could be different. But Nathan was straight, in every sense of the word. And I had long since come to terms with the fact of my own bent-ness. I liked who

I was. I liked the sex I had. But I was under no illusions that it was everyone's cup of tea. And I knew it wasn't Nathan's.

So I didn't really understand why I agreed to his suggestion that we grab a drink after work.

THIS is ridiculous. I shouldn't be here.

"So. You doing anything this weekend?" I didn't want to be the first to break the howling silence, but it was a small booth and I couldn't take the conversational void any longer.

"Nothing special. How about you?"

Reading bondage-themed smut novels, finishing the latest draft of a particularly tricky motion for filing next week, and hoping like hell I had extra batteries for my favorite vibrator so I wouldn't have to make a special trip to the store. Those were all on the agenda, but aside from the middle option, I thought my planned activities were probably best kept on the down low from Nathan.

"Me either," I said, nodding.

This can't possibly lead anywhere.

"So. Paddling, huh?"

"I beg your pardon?"

"Just trying to see if you were paying attention," he said with a wink. Something about the way he tugged a sip from his bottled beer suggested he wasn't as relaxed as he was trying to seem.

"You're not going to let this go, are you?"

"Are you going to tell me?"

Figuring it was now a hopeless case either way, I shrugged and took a fortifying sip of my wine. "What exactly did you want to know?"

"You like that kind of stuff?"

"If by 'stuff' you mean paddling, then yes, I like that kind of stuff. And flogging. And spanking, that's great, too. Not so big on caning,

although it isn't a hard limit. I haven't ever tried being bullwhipped. That seems a little too extreme, but you should never say never."

"Okay." He stared at his beer for a full ten seconds, an agonizing stretch of time, before taking another nervous sip. "Wow."

"Anything else?"

"Is there more?" He sounded equal parts horrified and enraptured by the prospect, and I couldn't help but laugh at the expression on his boyish face. Then he took another little sip of beer.

"Well. Let's see. Have I mentioned the thing about donkeys?"

It was worth it just for the classic spit-take. I cracked up, offering my napkin to help with the aftermath.

"Jesus, Burke!"

"Sorry. But you really should see the look on your face, it's priceless."

"Dammit. I just got this suit back from the cleaners yesterday."

"Well, that's what you get for keeping your jacket on when you go out drinking with me, fuddy-duddy."

He was already taking off the offending jacket, wiping at the damp patch on the cuff.

"Fuddy-duddy. I see how it is. So is that why you never went out with me? So much is starting to crystallize now."

I took a second to process that, trying to cover the pause with another laugh.

"I don't recall you ever asking me out," I said at last.

"I always got the impression I wasn't exactly your type."

"And now you know why you got that impression, I guess. Now that you know my type."

It hadn't been as painful as I thought, coming clean. Nathan didn't seem as put off as I had feared. Maybe the friendship was not doomed, after all.

Oh, but that little smirk when he looked at me, that secretive little gleam.

"So if you like to be paddled, does that mean you're a 'submissive'?"

My mouth went dry and I felt that same vertigo, that sense of my worlds colliding. Worlds I had spent years learning to keep separate from one another. "Um, yeah. I mean, I happen to be. Not everyone who likes all that is a sub, though. A submissive. Have you been spending too much time on the Internet again, Nathan?" Lord. What sites might he have run across?

"Either that or not nearly enough time. Why didn't you say anything before—never mind. Stupid question."

"And you don't normally do stupid."

"I feel pretty stupid not to have figured this out. If you want the truth, I never asked you out because I thought you were a lesbian. A really hot lesbian. But I mean, I thought that's why nobody ever saw you going out with guys. I just figured you were really, really discreet about it. But it always killed me."

"Oh." That hadn't ever occurred to me, that people might think that. I had thought that I was safe precisely because I was discreet. But apparently I should have been thinking in terms of acquiring a beard. "No, I'm more or less straight."

"More or less?"

What was it with guys and the girl-on-girl-action radar? "I'm straight. But you know, not everything about, um, what I do has to do with sex. Or not exactly. I like it best that way, but it doesn't have to involve actual intercourse. I mean, it could be a woman who was . . . Wow, I really wasn't expecting to have this conversation with you tonight. Or ever."

Why was I having this conversation with him, anyway? I didn't do this, didn't make a habit of satisfying the prurient curiosity of vanilla boys like Nathan. But here I remained. Because it was Nathan. Whose charm I had always had trouble resisting. And it was so very

charming, the way he was leaning in, managing to look innocent and roguish at the same time while asking me about the deep, dark side of me that he had never seen. With anybody else, I would have felt like the questions were about the deviance, the train wreck of humanity that person had suddenly perceived in me. But with Nathan, I just felt like he was eager to learn more about *me*.

"Show me."

"What?"

"Show me. Come home with me. Or take me home with you, because you're probably a little better equipped."

This couldn't be what it sounded like. I wasn't even sure I knew what it sounded like.

"What exactly are you asking me to do, Nathan?"

My hand was shaking a little even before his fingers curved over mine. Foolish, that the prospect of somebody taking my hand could make me so nervous. His hand was heavy, and a little cool from holding the beer. It looked and felt at least twice the size of mine.

"Ashley, why didn't you want to hear me talking about paddling?"

Oh, well, if he was going to use my first name this was an entirely new ball game. I couldn't remember the last time I had heard Nathan say my name. And it had never been in a dark booth in "our" bar, where he was holding my hand and asking me—telling me—to take him home with me. For paddling. And, I could only assume, sex.

"I try to keep all that separate from work. It's just easier that way. Compartmentalizing."

"I understand that. But am I just part of work?"

He was chiding. Gently, but enough. Whether or not he intended to be turning me on, that was the net effect. My panties were soaked; I was yearning. And all he had done thus far was hold my hand and scold me just the tiniest bit.

"No," I whispered. "You know you're not."

"Hey. Look at me."

I did. I shouldn't have. I felt like I might be damning him, pulling him into something that wasn't really meant for him. Asking him for something he might never be able to give.

"You've been holding out on me, Ashley," he continued in that same soft but stern tone. "We've both made some big assumptions. Turns out mine were mostly wrong. Maybe yours were, too. If you just thought I could never do stuff like that, maybe you were wrong. I really don't know. But I think I deserve a chance to try, at least."

I think a tiny part of me had always known it would have to come to this one day. I liked him too much to avoid it forever. He presented far too great a temptation, and I was feeling weak in the resisting-temptation muscles.

"Okay." I still wasn't sure what he was asking me for, and I suppose he could tell that.

"Why didn't you want to hear me talk about paddling? Why *me*?"

Oh. *That.*

I took a deep breath and let it out slowly, trying to let some of my dark anxiety loose along with it before I answered in the most direct way possible. In for a penny, in for a pound. "Because it turns me on too much to think of you doing that to me."

I was a trembling, overwrought wreck by the time Nathan had me naked in my bedroom. There had been a certain amount of kissing along the way there, but that hadn't exactly calmed me down. And now, here was Nathan in my apartment, looking very large, taking up a great deal of psychological space there. He had been there so many times, but he never seemed to fill up the rooms the way he did when he was naked and I was naked and there was needy flesh and

anticipation everywhere. He was a very good kisser, which didn't quite surprise me. But kissing only takes you so far.

If he had been a Dom, he would have told me what to do. That would have calmed me. As it was, I was a loose wire, zipping around and full of energy that I had no idea how to channel on my own. I wondered if he would consider tying me up, tying me down. Tethering me to something, anything. But I didn't have the nerve to spring any more complications on him just then.

"So how does this work?" he asked after his pants hit the ground. I had to take a second to gather my thoughts and tear my eyes away from the compelling sight of Nathan's cock—*Nathan's cock*—springing out from his body all ruddy and tense. Pointed at me, as if to make sure I knew I was the focus of his attention. It was a nice size, I noticed, and it wasn't even fully hard yet.

I shrugged, wondering how I could be so tongue-tied when I made a living speaking to intimidating people like judges and other trial lawyers and high-dollar corporate clients. "However you want it to work, I guess?"

Figure this out. Please just figure it out. Act out something you saw on the Internet, read in a book. Take the reins, somehow.

To my utter shock and delight, he did just that. Not perfectly, but well enough. More than well enough.

"Well okay then. C'mere." And sitting on the edge of my bed, he patted his legs suggestively. When I started to perch on his knee, he frowned and shook his head. "Not like that."

"Oh. You want me to . . . ?"

After an awkward few seconds I leaned over and slowly lowered my weight onto his lap, gasping as the coarse hairs on his thighs scratched at my hardening nipples. His erection prodded my ribs from beneath, while his arms reached over to tuck me closer.

"Yeah, like that." One of his big hands was pressed firmly between

my shoulder blades, the other at the small of my back. It was such a familiar feeling in so many ways. Except the only way that mattered was that this was Nathan, and I had dreamed of this, and it was the dream I had never been brave enough to hope would come true. And it was all happening very fast, somehow, despite being five years in the building.

"What is it you like about it?"

"Everything," I admitted, too fuzzy to make up a better answer. I could feel Nathan's chuckle before I heard it. Then I felt his hand sliding from my back to my ass, a stroke, and then a firm squeeze.

Then a spank, which I was not expecting. And hard. He hadn't held back.

"Be more specific."

If he had moved his long fingers just a few inches, he would have felt how wet I already was. He could be great at this if he wanted to be. My butt was warming under his palm, the pain dissipating into heat. If he had been a Dom, I wouldn't have answered the way I did.

"Start out a little softer," I said, feeling brave. "Then you can work up. That was a little too hard to start out."

Whack!

"Perfect," I muttered. "Your hand feels perfect."

"No paddle?" Oh, I could hear his smile. It made me nearly as wet as the growing heat that spread from my butt to my aching clit and pussy as he spanked me again.

"Not yet. Maybe later. Did your research cover sub space?"

"Yeah. I didn't really get it, though. I got the endorphin part. Oh, that's why the slow buildup, right?"

"Umm . . . right. Sorry. Not used to talking while I'm—*ah*!" That one was a little harder, but it was good now. I was ready for it.

"I really wish I had known about this during law school. I can't believe I thought you dug chicks. So much wasted time."

The next three smacks hit in rapid succession, light but steady on the same spot, leaving me breathless and squirming. I parted my legs a little, bracing one knee on the bed. "I would never have gone out with you in law school, silly frat boy."

"Frat boys know a thing or two about paddling," he pointed out. "Were you into this, even back then?"

I nodded, licking my lips. "You all thought I was studying on Saturday nights. It was my club night. Not a club any of you knew about. Oh, do that more, please!"

He had switched gears and started tapping in a firm, steady rhythm against the tender skin just where my rear end curved into my upper thighs. One side, then the other, the beat steady but the location changing unpredictably. I tried to widen my stance, angle myself so that he might give my pussy some much-needed contact. But whether by chance or design, he left that particular need unmet. When he finally stopped to scrape his fingers lightly over the marks I knew must be blooming on my ass, my hips tried to keep the delicious pace he had set. I ground against the edge of the bed and earned a single, sharper wallop for my trouble.

"None of that. I've read enough to know that much. I shouldn't let you come yet, right?"

He sounded so pleased with himself. It would have been adorable if I hadn't craved an orgasm so very much just then.

"That's one option," I said through gritted teeth. "There are others."

"Not yet," he insisted, patting my butt and then squeezing it again. His fingertips grazed against the wetness between my legs, and I groaned as he shifted his grip just enough to drag a finger over the outer folds of my cunt. I clenched at nothing, wanting his cock there already, willing to settle for a finger if that was all he would allow me. But for now he just played and teased, driving me even more

insane. "You were being safe all that time, right? Taking precautions and getting tested, all that?"

"You can't even believe how cautious." Not that my caution had helped much with the state of mild panic I periodically fell into, knowing how risky it was to frequent a kink club, even if I wasn't having actual sex with strangers. That had been a hard limit, one that meant I had precious little sex throughout law school. But some things were more important than that, and I'd been happy on the whole with my choices. I needed the other stuff more, to steady me.

"Is it just about the pain? Is that the deal?"

I shook my head. I was trying to stay lucid, but years of habit and training were starting to kick in. I could feel the rush of endorphins taking over, pushing me off the tiresome hamster wheel that was my usual mental state, nudging me into the fuzzy warmth of subspace.

"The pain is just a catalyst. It's a shortcut. It makes it easy."

"Makes what easy?" He slipped one finger inside me, and I groaned and pushed into his touch. "Oh, God, you feel so good. So fucking hot and tight. I've wanted you for so long, Burke."

That was news to me, although at the moment it barely even registered. His finger was long, thicker than mine, not quite enough but so close it almost didn't matter.

"Makes it easy not to think about anything else," I managed to choke out.

"Oh. You're thinking too much?"

"Always." He should know; he usually bore the brunt of it.

"What's the best thing? What gets your mind completely shut down?"

His fingers brushing against my clit were doing a fairly good job of that at the moment, but I didn't think he would settle for that answer. He would take nothing less than complete honesty, because that was his nature. I had no idea how I had managed to hide from him for as long as I had. I felt completely transparent, now, unable

to keep anything secret from him. He owned my soul, and he probably didn't even know it.

"Flogging," I finally said, licking my lips. They were dry, because I'd been panting with the effort not to come. "That's the best thing. Soft at first, elk hide or something. And then harder until it actually hurts. Makes me feel like all the bad stuff is just being beaten away until there's only me left. It makes me feel . . . clean." His fingers were moving with more purpose now, and he slid a second one inside me. The sting on my butt was fading now, leaving me sensitive but not remotely sated.

"Burke . . . Ashley. I don't want to hurt you."

"Then don't. You couldn't, Nate. I trust you." Did that make sense? I wasn't sure where my head was now, not sure at all.

"Can I have a safe word?"

I laughed loudly and pulled out of my fog just enough to turn my head and look up at him over my shoulder. His hair was mussed, dark brown strands falling over his forehead almost obscuring his pretty brown eyes. But I could see his need, his humor, his willingness to figure things out. It was almost like another point of contact, that look. It warmed parts of me that his clever fingers hadn't reached. What had I been thinking, to keep this at a distance?

He was already laughing at himself when I corrected him.

"The safe word is for me, Nathan."

"I know, I know. I meant—"

"I know what you meant." I tore my gaze away and rested my chin on my folded arms again. "Zombies. If I say zombies, you stop, okay?" I doubted it would ever come up. I would be pushing him as far as he was willing to go. I could only hope it would be far enough, because there was no way in hell I planned to go back to the way things had been. But maybe one day, if things went well, one day he would be the one pushing my limits.

"Zombies? That's gross."

"That's the idea," I reminded him. Then I reminded him of other things with a little wiggle and squeeze. His hand obligingly started to move again, and he curled his fingers to graze against the most tender spots he could find inside me. But then he removed it, prompting a whine of complaint from me that I wasn't proud of at all.

"Do you have a paddle?"

No, I did not. I had a very beautiful and much-beloved flogger, but I thought some training was probably in order before he attempted that, and I wasn't in a mood to stop for instruction.

"No, but I have something else you can use." I didn't need it, but I thought maybe he did. To show that he was able to take that step, that risk with me.

Standing up was a challenge, wobbly as my knees were. I shot Nate an equally wobbly smile and ventured into my bathroom to retrieve a certain hairbrush with a very wide, smooth back. I took just enough time to pull the hair out of it before I returned to the bed where he was still sitting. Legs apart now, elbows on his knees, looking strangely relaxed and at home in my bedroom. He took the brush from me and shook his head in disbelief.

"Seriously?"

"Oh, yeah."

"Okay. Climb up on the bed. On all fours. Let's do this!"

"I like your can-do attitude!"

I was already on the bed when he snickered and aimed a pat at my butt with the brush. "Smart-ass."

"You like my smart ass," I teased.

He tapped me again with the brush, not very hard at all. Just testing the thing. Figuring it out. "I like your ass, that's for sure. I think I could get used to smacking it around, too."

Whack!

He had leaned into that one, and he didn't stop at my yelp of dismay. Just laid down a tidy pattern of blows on both sides, working

from the meatiest part of my butt down to that magic zone just at the bottom crease, even landing an occasional lighter smack across my pussy. A pro couldn't have done a better job. Although I admit I was primed by that point. So ready for anything he might do that the last fleeting contact of the brush against my cunt almost made me come before I could get a handle on the process of resisting. Slow, steady breaths. The soft gray inside my pleasantly cloudy mind. The horribly delicious exposed feeling of being on all fours with my ass burning, waiting as I registered the soft crinkle of a foil condom packet being torn. Wanting only to be filled.

The tease of his sheathed cock rubbing against my clit was enough to make me whimper and spread my legs wider in an attempt to get closer. I probably looked like a bitch in heat, and the beauty of it all was, at that moment I didn't care what I looked like in the slightest. I just needed, and acted. And so did Nathan, finally pushing his meaty cock inside me and pulling my hips back hard until he was seated as deep as he could be. We both moaned, and then laughed at each other just a little. Laughed at ourselves. How easy we were, how ready we were. How stupid we had been to think we could avoid this when it was so obviously what we were made to do together.

He didn't hold back, didn't try to make it gentle. He was thick and hot and perfect inside me, and when he reached his hand under my hip to pet my throbbing clit I came almost immediately. It was hard, it was sweet, it went on longer than I thought possible. The ache in my ass melted away as pleasure zipped through me like a shock, building and cresting and then not quite going away before it started to build again. And it was Nathan, Nathan inside me, and the sound of his voice saying my name with wonder and delight brought me over again as he pumped harder still into the molten heat I had become under his touch.

When I climaxed the second time, he did too, cursing in the good way as his body shook in relief. Curses and my name, and then we

both laughed again because when we collapsed, flopping onto the bed like spent balloons, we landed on the upturned hairbrush first thing.

"With a real paddle, that wouldn't be such a problem," I pointed out, taking the brush from his hand and lobbing it over the edge of the bed. Then I relaxed on my back, next to Nathan on his. Holding hands, staring at the ceiling.

"Holy shit, Burke." He sounded awed, exhausted. But not remorseful.

"Holy shit yourself, Nate. Remind me why we never did this?"

His chuckle was a rich baritone rumble, a velvet shiver down my spine. "You were a hot lesbian and I was this guy without a clue, remember?"

"Oh, yeah."

A fairly companionable moment passed before Nathan spoke again. "You're my best friend and I didn't know this about you."

"Really? Your best friend? Wow."

"Why didn't you ever tell me?"

I thought about it. Now, of course, I thought of a dozen ways I might have told him. Now that I knew he would have accepted it. "I was afraid you'd freak out, I guess."

"I'm not freaked out," he said, and I waited for the "but" I could hear in the works. "But I have a lot of questions about how it all works."

I squeezed his fingers in mine, wondering at how comfortable that felt. How right and essential.

"Me, too," I said. "Me, too."

After earning two graduate degrees, practicing law awhile, and working for the public school system for more than ten years, **Delphine Dryden** ditched it all to start writing full time. She has published numerous contemporary erotic

romances, an erotic steampunk romance, and quite a few erotic short stories; she's currently hard at work on a mainstream steampunk romance series.

In addition to novel writing, Del blogs regularly about writing, BDSM/kink, and topics of general geekery at http://1800domhelp.blogspot.com and http://geekandkink.com.

Del and her family are all Texas natives, and reside in unapologetic suburban bliss near Houston.

STITCH AND BITCH

A.L. SIMONDS

Luisa was going to fall.

A split second before her skateboard caught a crack in the pavement and her balance shifted too far back, she saw it coming. The world tilted, the ground rose to meet her.

She smacked down on her side, hip and shoulder catching the worst of it, and slid a few inches down the asphalt ramp. The impact flashed across her vision and shook her nerves. She could have sworn she heard bells tolling.

She had to lie there, just for a couple seconds, in order to remember how to breathe.

When she struggled up—first onto her palms, then her knees, then to her feet—she rolled her shoulders and shook away the worst of the pain.

"Ow, dude," she said. "Ow."

As the pain cleared, she realized that she *did* hear church bells, over on the university campus, tolling six o'clock.

She had taken care to ask Charlie to watch the time for her, but, typical Charlie, he'd wandered away down to the hot dog truck and forgotten about her.

She'd been so absorbed doing a line—a sequence of tricks—that the seasons could have turned, barbarians invaded, and she wouldn't have noticed.

Now it was already six and there was no way she would not be late.

Cursing, she jumped to her feet, shaking off the reverberating pain of her fall, grabbed her bag from under the bleachers, and kicked off on her board.

She passed Charlie as she came out of the skate park and hit the sidewalk. He waved cheerfully at her and she had to swallow the urge to stop and give him a piece of her mind.

She'd just be later if she did that.

So she pushed faster, sailing off the curb into the street. Cars were hard to contend with when she was on her board, but they were big and easy to navigate around, unlike pedestrians, who were both slow and unpredictable. As she careened down quiet side streets, the low evening sun warmed her side and cheeks. She zigzagged through the lengthening shadows, breathing through the lingering ache of her fall, then turned a hard right onto Ossington Avenue.

She didn't have time to stop and change her shirt, let alone shower.

She caught a draft and zoomed forward.

"JUST like clockwork," Toni, her boss, said when Priya arrived at the shop. "You're a marvel, you know that?"

Priya grinned as she stowed her knapsack under the counter. "All in the planning."

Toni shook her head. "You take planning to a whole new level."

Priya allotted herself fifteen minutes on Tuesdays and Thursdays to walk from her seminar on campus to the yarn store, a window that was fairly generous, but not overly so. It was good to have the time to let the seminar sift and settle into her mind before she had to switch gears.

She was usually at least five minutes early. Today was no different.

"Quiet today," Toni said from the back, where she was eating a takeout dinner.

Priya looked around the store, all the vibrant colors and cozy furniture. "I'm sure it'll pick up."

Toni slurped up some sesame noodles. "And then we won't be able to get rid of them."

Tonight was Stitch and Bitch. A regular crowd always dropped in for gossip, advice, and crafting time away from families, jobs, and other responsibilities.

As the regulars arrived, Priya manned the counter to sell last-minute needles and splurge skeins of yarn. When she was not needed there, she tidied the shelves, returning stray balls to their rightful places, reorganizing laceweight and sockweight skeins, straightening and neatening the disarray from an ordinary business day.

"You don't pay her enough," one of the regular ladies told Toni when she emerged to join the group around the big table in the center of the shop. "Look at her work!"

Priya ducked her head and focused on finding the one ball of blue sock yarn missing its label. Toni did not actually pay her at all; Priya kept the books and helped out three nights a week in exchange for wholesale prices on yarn and the bachelor apartment over the shop.

She had been lucky to get that deal. When her fellowship at the university fell through, she had been forced to find a few part-time jobs just to cover tuition. A place to live had started to seem like an unattainable luxury. Although her apartment was little more than a creaky half-converted attic with questionable plumbing, she wasn't about to complain.

Finally, when Toni had nagged her enough and there truly was no more yarn to tidy or needles to inventory, Priya joined the group at the table. She pulled out her latest project, oatmeal-colored yarn flecked with green and blue, which she had unraveled from an

unwanted sweater. She had spent an entire weekend pulling the sweater apart, skeining up the yarn, then washing it and hanging it, weighted down with soup cans, to dry.

"Still doing the recycling?" Gillian asked. She was a relative new-comer to the group, and liked to wield her husband's corporate Amex card to buy the finest silk and cashmere weights. "Aren't you worried about"—her nose wrinkled slightly—"*pests?*"

Priya shook out the sock she was knitting up from the yarn and extracted the fifth needle from the center of the ball. "I didn't get the sweater out of the garbage or anything."

"Just *from* a piece of garbage!" Toni put in, and rubbed Priya's arm consolingly.

"My ex," Priya explained to Gillian, who was looking both puzzled and nauseated. "That's all she means. The yarn came from a sweater I made my ex."

Gillian tossed back her impeccably bobbed hair. "Well, wherever it came from, I don't see why you bother."

"I like it," Priya said, and pressed her lips together. She could have said more—recycling the yarn was therapy for her. Reclaiming what she had given to Amy, cleaning it up and making it into something new, all of that helped her not only move on, but to mark her move-ment, measure it as she grew further away.

After her breakup with Amy, she had instituted a long-term plan for herself: She gave up her ambition to become a theater director, she went back to school for a degree in elementary education, and she promised herself that any new relationship, if there ever were one, would be in harmony with her new goals. Simple, careful, and thoughtful were going to be her guiding lights.

Besides all of that, recycling the yarn was frugal. If she hadn't had knitting in her hands, she didn't know what she might do.

Gillian had turned her attention to someone else now, an older woman named Catherine, who was struggling with making a cable.

Priya sighed in relief, happy to have a chance to work a few rounds on her sock.

The sock would be knee-high, with a plain foot and leg in a trellis lace pattern. She loved the way knee socks looked on a woman's legs, at once rustic and sexy. The wool and lace interplayed delicately, the wool robust and reassuring, the lace subtle and coquettish, revealing small patches of skin like light dappling and splashing through the leaves of a tree on a bright summer afternoon. The combinations and contrasts were what captured her fancy: smooth skin and slightly scratchy wool, nudity and covering, the curve of a calf and strong line of a shin, maybe a nice leather high-heeled shoe over the snug sock.

As if her thoughts had made it happen, just then the bell on the shop door rang and Luisa crashed inside, a riot of color and wind and noise, skateboard in hand, corkscrew curls flowing around her face like a lion's mane. Her face was flushed, her smile wide and bright as she greeted everyone with high fives and quick hugs, pecks on the cheek, and squeezes of the hand.

Luisa had a way of entering a room as if she were donning it. The space shifted and molded itself around her, arranged itself so that she was always at the center. Priya knew that she was well liked here and did her best to be friendly and polite. But Luisa's warmth was of a different order. It was furnace-hot and pure, genuine and impossible to extinguish.

"How's it hanging, Gill?" Luisa asked as she dug in her ratty messenger bag for her yarn and other materials. "Having any luck with that crepe recipe?"

Even sour-Gillian smiled when Luisa collapsed into the chair next to her and knocked her elbow into Gillian's side. Gillian smoothed back her hair and sighed. "I'm working on it, but . . ."

"I took the worst digger just now," Luisa announced, tossing down a lumpy ball of yarn and her crochet hook. "Fell on my *ass* like some kind of newbie."

The ladies around the table tut-tutted in sympathy and asked for details, shared the names of their chiropractors, and offered advice about warm baths versus cold, compresses versus ibuprofen.

Priya set down her sock. "You probably want to wash up, right? Come with me."

Luisa tilted her head briefly, grinning at her, then scraped back her chair and bounded toward the little staff washroom behind the counter.

The washroom was barely wide enough for a sink and the commode. Somehow, Priya and Luisa squeezed into it.

Priya turned on the faucet. "You came right from the skate park?"

Luisa bit her lip and held up her shirt so Priya could press soapy, wet paper towels to her abraded hip and ribs.

"Pobrecita," Priya murmured. The first time she'd spoken Spanish, Luisa had staggered back and pretended to faint, as if Desi people didn't live all over the Antilles, including Trinidad, where Priya's parents were born.

There was no broken skin to speak of, just darkening bruises and the imprint of gravel overlaying the friction burn from Luisa's slide. Priya ran the water colder and swabbed it off again.

Luisa was looking down at her, lower lip gone white in her teeth, curls crowding her face.

"What?" Priya asked when she was finished.

Luisa smiled, slow and shy, and leaned back against the wall, foot up on the toilet lid. "Nothing."

"Liar."

Luisa tipped up her chin and reached for Priya, managing to graze her shoulder. Her shirt was still raked up to her armpits. The fabric was twisted across her breasts; one cup of her bra was held to the elastic band with a safety pin.

Priya plucked at the pin and cupped her palm around Luisa's

breast. She leaned in and rubbed her face in Luisa's hair. "Stinky, stinky."

Luisa breathed in sharply. "Nah," she said, her hand going around Priya's waist. "Just . . . alive."

Priya snorted with laughter and kissed Luisa quickly before pulling away. "We should get back out there."

"Don't wanna." Luisa curled two fingers into Priya's belt loops. "Do I have to?"

Priya kissed the tip of her chin, then bit down lightly. "Yes, you do. Be good."

"Fine," Luisa grumbled, and tugged down her shirt. "But you owe me."

Rolling her eyes, Priya slapped her lightly on the leg.

LUISA'S version of being good, however, was more than slightly naughty. Although she kept up several conversations for the rest of the evening, her eyes rarely left Priya. She told jokes, shouted with laughter, and all the while, tracked Priya's movements around the shop.

While the group became absorbed in helping Catherine untangle the mess, Priya helped a customer who had just wandered in. They selected a nice hank of gray wool and a set of large needles. Priya showed her how to cast on and start knitting a simple scarf. She knew Luisa was watching her. The attention, subtle but persistent as it was, warmed her skin. She became more conscious of her gestures, more careful with her words, as if she were performing, privately, for an audience of one.

When the newcomer was settled in, frowning over her needles, Priya started cashing out the register. Luisa interrupted her, waving a set of German stainless-steel needles, double-pointed, five in all, just two millimeters in gauge.

"You don't knit socks." Priya slid the package back to Luisa. The set was exactly the sort she longed to use, but she had never been able to justify the price. "These are hardcore."

"Hardcore," Luisa repeated. Before Priya could stop her, she had torn open the package and fanned the needles out, running her fingertip over their lethal-looking tips. She pressed the tips into the soft skin on the inside of her wrist. The points made tiny, perfect dents. "Sounds about right."

Priya swallowed hard.

Luisa saw her and grinned. "Ring 'em up."

"They're eighteen dollars."

Shrugging, Luisa tossed her a twenty. She only ever paid—when she did buy something, which wasn't all that often—with cash that came crumpled and damp from the depths of her pockets. Priya was not entirely certain where her money came from, or how regularly she was paid, if at all. This uncertainty was the only constant when it came to Luisa. She didn't seem to have a permanent address; rather, she crashed with various friends and acquaintances, an ever-changing and expanding population of skateboarders, musicians, self-appointed artists, and hangers-on.

Toni was excited that Luisa was taking up sock knitting. "It's addictive! Like chocolate," she declared. "Once you turn your first heel, you'll never go back!"

Luisa nodded amiably. "That's what I've heard, yes."

Another woman leaned in to confide, "My husband married me for my socks." She paused and waggled her eyebrows. "If you know what I mean."

Cocking her head, looking more than a little puzzled, Luisa just smiled. "That's something to consider, huh, Priya?"

"Sure it is," Priya said, not looking up from the register. Her chest felt tight, her face very hot.

The needles were still on the counter. They pointed like daggers at Priya, promising something irresistible.

LUISA met Priya at the crochet basics class last spring. Her sister was pregnant and wanted Luisa, probably to piss off their mom, to be the godmother. So she had set herself the task of learning how to make sweaters and booties and other tiny, cute things for the impending infant. After nearly strangling in cheap plastic yarn from the dollar store, she decided to take a class so she'd actually know what she was doing.

Priya taught the class with grace and good humor. She never lost her cool, not even when Luisa lost control of her crochet hook and sent it flying at Priya's face.

Afterward, pretty sure that she had felt a vibe between them, she asked Priya out for coffee.

Priya blinked, opened her bound planner, and said after a lengthy consultation, "How about next Wednesday at ten?"

Not only was that a long way off, it was really early in the morning, so far as Luisa was concerned. She twirled the crochet hook between her fingers and gave Priya her best flirtatious smile. "I was thinking more like right now?"

"No." Priya closed her planner and set it down on the table. "I have plans."

Luisa would come to learn that Priya *always* had plans; what's more, eventually, Luisa found that fascinating. Here was this beautiful girl, smart as a whip, working three jobs and going to graduate school part-time, and she barely let herself ever relax. Or, Luisa suspected, sleep.

But back then, Luisa figured she knew how to take a hint, and stepped away. "Okay, well. Maybe I'll see you around?"

She was nearly out the door when Priya grasped her wrist—she had very strong hands, probably because of all the knitting—and pulled her to a stop. "If you'd like, there's Stitch and Bitch the day after tomorrow. We could meet then."

Luisa had no idea what Stitch and Bitch was, but she liked the name right away. After adjusting to the sight of a roomful of suburban-looking moms and grandmas, she came to like the people a lot, too. She spent so much of her life skating and hanging with dudes that it was nice, almost restful, to kick back with females and work on cutesy baby accessories.

Her friends claimed she was going soft on them, but then they began to ask for toques and fingerless gloves.

Maybe she was soft, but if they'd ever met Priya, they would understand. She wasn't the type of lady you gave up on.

WHEN the last of the crowd had trailed out the door, Toni turned off the overhead lights and started locking up. Priya got out the push broom and swept, starting just in front of the washroom and working outward into the main area of the shop floor.

"I can do that," she told Toni, who was putting the chairs up on the table. "You should go home. You've had a long day."

Toni rubbed the back of her neck and didn't argue. After she had gone, Priya finished sweeping and ran the feather duster over the tallest shelves before she opened the washroom door.

Luisa stumbled out, blinking against the dark. "Dude, what took so long?"

Her impatience was equal parts charming and exasperating. Priya kissed her hard, like she'd been longing to do all night. Her mouth ached for it, and Luisa gurgled a little into the contact. Her hands ran restlessly up and down Priya's back, pulling Priya closer, holding her in place as she kissed her back.

The broom fell away as Priya backed Luisa up against the shelves, against the pillowy, welcoming warmth of balls of chunky merino yarn.

Priya cupped Luisa's neck with one hand while the other pushed under her shirt hem and curved around her bruised waist. Luisa hissed into the kiss, her teeth sudden and sharp on Priya's tongue, before she relaxed and pushed into the touch.

They moved well together; they had right from the start. Priya was a few inches taller, and Luisa seemed to like looking up at her, leaning back, opening up for her touches. In turn, Priya reveled in the chance to touch this girl, twist her arms up over her head and hold her there, teasing her breasts. It never took long before Lu wheezed and pleaded, face flushed dark as liver, eyes glittering, sweat spangling her collarbone, desperately twisting, trying to find more contact.

Priya's ex, Amy, didn't like being what she called "pushed around." It was both a political and emotional principle and point of honor for her that they were equal in all things, from their joint checking account to the number of orgasms they each had, as well as time spent on each one.

Luisa, however, did not seem to think of what they did as bullying. She gasped and grinned, whatever Priya did, pushing into her touch and asking for more. She could take a lot of teasing, nipples pinched and tugged, her mound and thighs lightly stroked and fondled until goose bumps broke out all over her body, until her breath caught in her throat and she grew so wet and desperate that she could be entered in a single slow thrust.

"Harder," Lu would say whenever Priya hesitated. And she did hesitate, especially in the early days, half-drunk on the sheer *fact* that it was okay to do this, half-nauseated by her own need to do more. "Please, harder. More."

That permission, phrased as a request, was precisely what Priya needed. Her acceptance, her eager need for this was astounding. Just

hearing the rattle of her breath and feeling her damp, flushed skin was enough to make Priya ache. She had to clamp down, clench, and release, ride her own need like something half-painful.

Tonight, as Luisa trembled before her, the traffic outside threw long, angular bright shadows across the ceiling, down the shelves of yarn, and illuminated her hands. Luisa's rosewood skin was blanched momentarily, then flushed again, darkness returning as Priya ran her teeth along the curve of her hip.

Luisa pushed her hand into Priya's hair, clutched her tight, and thrust up her hips. Priya outlined the jut of Luisa's pelvic bone with her tongue, then her teeth, before biting down and sucking hard. Luisa moaned.

She whimpered when Priya pulled away, but bit it off when Priya hushed her. When Priya returned from the counter, Luisa reached for her with blind, searching hands.

Priya stood out of reach until Luisa had quieted and stilled. Then, with the care of a master calligrapher, she drew the tip of one needle around Luisa's nipple, down the swell of her small breast, to the bite-mark. The sound Luisa made was nearly indescribable. It was greedy and choked, a moan and plea rutting together.

"Shhh," Priya said, not expecting Luisa to comply. She pinched the bite mark, then circled the needle over the tender skin.

Luisa banged her head against the shelf. She bit down on her lip, her chest heaving. Her knees started to buckle but she locked her stance.

Priya teased her for as long as she liked. She drew art nouveau swirls and curlicues, best suited to a Tiffany lamp, over Lu's warm, pliable skin. She strummed the stiletto point against one nipple, then the other, until they were both peaked painfully hard, the breast's skin puckered and goosepimpled.

She scratched runes and swept signatures across Luisa's taut skin, turned her around, and did the same across her lower back, down

the swell of her hips, until Luisa sank to her knees, a sob muffled against her arm.

She trembled and shook when Priya knelt behind her, a length of cotton yarn from the bargain bin in her hands. For a moment when Priya tugged at Luisa's arms, nothing happened, but then they rose over her head and Priya looped the yarn around Luisa's bony wrists, then eased her down onto the floor.

"Had enough?" she asked, straddling Luisa's thighs.

Luisa struggled to raise her head and meet Priya's eyes. The sharp curve of her smile was a dare and an acknowledgement. "Never."

The curls between her legs were slick to the touch. She shuddered, hard, and let out a wracking sigh when Priya slipped her hand through them and curled her thumb around the shaft of Luisa's clit.

"How about now?"

Luisa thrust up to meet the touch, canting her hips. Priya's index finger slid down between her inner lips to circle her hole. "More," Luisa said, the word half-gargled, "you're so *good*—"

Perhaps Priya should not have been so aroused by praise, but it felt so good, to no longer be bound by the "rules," to make someone, especially someone as hot, as *wild*, as Luisa feel this good. To be trusted like this was intoxicating. Two fingers inside her, she twisted and thrust. Luisa moaned in response, struggled to sit up, and reached for Priya. They kissed again, teeth clacking and tongues pulsing, as Lu fucked herself on Priya's hand, desperately asking for more, needing all of Priya to be in her, to answer and resolve the howling Priya had created. Two fingers, then three, then four, tightly wrapped on each other and crushed on all sides: they struggled to move, to reach ever deeper, as Luisa came, wet and cascading over Priya's wrist, down her arm.

Priya's body hurt all the way through, like her muscles were barbed wire wound around her bones. Luisa clung to her, wobbling, butting her face against Priya's throat. Priya let her head fall back as Luisa licked down her neck, sucked on the knobs of her clavicle, then

nibbled across the rise of her breasts. There was a moment, and then another, where Priya's pulse thundered between her legs, wrenched her nearly double. Luisa grinned and grazed Priya's mound, then her lips, with her knuckles.

Luisa pinched her clit between her index finger and thumb, and Priya snapped upright. Priya clenched and thrust against Luisa's palm, seeking sharp edges of calluses and rocky bumps of knuckle. She rubbed herself nearly raw, compelled by the need for release so deep it seemed to be squeezing her lungs and closing up her throat. Luisa bit her shoulder, mouthed the sharp pain, and bit again, pressing ever closer as Priya came. The waves and rattling throbs drowned out all the pent-up tension, soothed away the ache of desire, and she wanted nothing more than to open herself back up to Luisa's teeth and fists, and do it all over again.

Sex wasn't supposed to be like this. Shame hurt as much as any bite, and somehow, perversely, felt just as good. Priya gasped for air, riding the rippling aftershocks, and tried not to question herself.

She succeeded, but not for long.

WHEN Priya left the library around lunchtime, she had to stop abruptly when a skateboard flew across her path and tumbled off the curb. Only two days had passed since Stitch and Bitch; she was not due to see Luisa for another three or four days.

"Hey," Luisa said. Her voice was bright, feigning surprise. "Fancy meeting you here!"

Priya shifted her weight. "What're you doing here?"

Luisa shrugged. Her legs dangled against the low stone wall on which she sat, like a tramp riding a train. She looked out of place on campus, a little too dark, a little too wild and messy, amid the ivy-covered walls and quiet footpaths. As soon as she thought that, Priya cursed herself for it. By the same token, she too would be considered too dark.

She could not take out her own worries and discomfort on Lu. It wasn't fair.

"Sorry," Priya said, "I'm just . . . distracted."

"It's okay. I—" Luisa started. At the same time, Priya continued, "What *are* you doing here?"

They both stopped, then opened their mouths to speak again. Finally, waving off objections, Luisa mimed zipping shut her lips and motioned Priya to go on.

"Surprised to see you here, that's all," Priya said, and pushed her hair out of her eyes. "Is everything all right?"

Luisa slid off the wall and hopped from foot to foot. "Everything's great! I wanted to show you something."

Priya didn't like the sound of that. Luisa's enthusiasm was always contagious, but it was also immoderate, occasionally dangerous. Carefully, the words heavy in her mouth, she asked, "What did you want to show me?"

Bending at the waist, Luisa yanked up her shirt and pointed at her bare hip.

There, where the other night Priya had left a line of hickies and scratches, was a much more permanent mark. A dark-inked tattoo, shiny ink on swollen, painfully red skin, captured Priya's marks, made them indelible.

Luisa straightened up. "Isn't it awesome?"

"It's—" Priya didn't know what to say. She felt horrified and baffled all at the same time. "It's *permanent*."

"Yeah!" Luisa nodded rapidly, beaming a grin and crinkled eyes. She was so beautiful, if reckless. "Pretty much the whole point."

Gradually, the longer that Priya simply stood there, mouth open, frozen into silence and worry, Luisa's good mood dimmed. It wavered, then flickered, and finally, just winked out. She folded her arms across her chest. "What did I do now?"

She made it sound as if Priya were always taking her to task. That

wasn't the case. Maybe it was at times, but she was so heedless, so impulsive, that *someone* had to say something, haul her back from the brink.

"Nothing," Priya replied. "Do what you want."

"I wanted to do it for us," Luisa said. She wasn't looking up and she sounded sullen.

That was Priya's cue to make nice. She should apologize, she should reach out, cheer up Luisa.

She didn't exactly have the time, however, not with midterms rapidly approaching and her next shift at the grocery store starting all the way across town in less than half an hour. "For us?" she said. "What does that even mean?"

Luisa blinked up at her. There were sparkling tears on her lashes, and she looked heartbroken. Priya wasn't a monster; the sight made her chest feel like it had caved in.

"Us," Luisa said. Her voice rose to make it a question. "Us?"

Priya took in a breath, then another, reminding herself to keep the big picture in view. She really liked Lu; they connected on many levels, and the sex was fantastic, but she was nearly still a *kid*. Whatever age her ID said, she acted like a teenaged boy. She wasted her money on tattoos and six-packs of beer and punk concerts.

"There's no us," Priya said. It was the truth, wasn't it? "We just fool around."

For a long time, Luisa said nothing. She looked very small, round-shouldered, and slight, dwarfed by her glorious riot of hair and baggy T-shirt. "If that's what you think—"

She did not finish. Priya saw her swallow, watched the sharp line of her jaw as she turned away and dropped her skateboard to the sidewalk, and still, she could neither move nor speak.

AT the end of that week, Luisa went down to North Carolina to film lines for a video part for her sneaker sponsor. She stayed in Charlotte

when the shoot was over. Her tattoo scabbed over, then the scabs fell off. It itched all the time and she scratched it hard enough to make it scab again.

She wished that she skated the regular orientation. Then maybe she could fall and just scrape the damn thing off.

"Big talk," she could almost hear Charlie say.

He was right, of course. She didn't want to lose the *tattoo*. She didn't know what she wanted to lose.

PRIYA scored a B+ on one of her midterms, and an A- on her seminar short paper. She took over the group presentation, not quite trusting the others in her group to carry their weight. She picked up two extra shifts at the grocery store and maintained her regular schedule at the yarn shop.

Three Stitch and Bitches passed, and there was no sign of Luisa. Priya told herself that it was probably for the best. Luisa was so flighty and flaky that she made Amy—an actress and dancer, of all things— seem sensible and down to earth. She was the last sort of person that Priya needed in her life. She was charismatic, sure, and funny and sweet, but she was hardly going anywhere. Indeed, she seemed perfectly content to coast through life on her skateboard. Her life was much more organized, calm, and well ordered now that Luisa had disappeared. The calm reminded her of nothing so much as the lifting of a migraine or the effects of Novocain: the pain, or Luisa, might still be somewhere out there, but she could no longer feel a thing.

Ignorance was, it appeared, numbness. Not bliss. That fact was tolerable, but not exactly optimal.

LUISA returned to Toronto when the leaves were dead and gone. Black branches scoured the gray sky, and snow swirled in the air

without ever alighting. She skated indoors most of the time now, rising earlier in order to get the most out of the ramps before kids got off school.

The afternoon of the first snowstorm, when the city was abuzz with hype about expected snowfall, Charlie hipchecked her as they left the ramp and headed to the diner for lunch.

"Where's my toque, Venceremos? I'm going to die of frostbite and it'll all be your fault. I can't wait much longer."

It was a small comment, the first time any of the guys had mentioned her knitting and crocheting since she came back from North Carolina, but it stopped Luisa cold.

"You're right," she told him, and hung a sharp left to get to the subway station.

"I am?" Charlie stood on the corner, arms out, yelling after her. "What did I say?"

She didn't answer; she didn't need to.

The first thick, wet flakes were gathering thickly on the sidewalks when she left the subway station and dashed for the yarn shop. Half the businesses on this stretch had already closed early; the dusk was blue and gray, the color of old newspapers and older bruises. She slipped and stumbled in her worn canvas sneakers, trying to hurry, hoping she could catch Priya.

Priya was uptight and bossy and every other dark, angry thing Luisa had mentally called her over the past month. But she was also intense and melancholy and she kissed like an angel but made Luisa feel so good that only a devil could be responsible.

She had no idea what she was going to say. The likeliest scenario was that Priya would order her out of the shop, never to darken her doorstep again.

But she had to try. She was a woman who could practice the same tre flip for two weeks, all day, every day, all night too, and fall on her ass each and every time until, finally, she landed it. And then she

practiced it some more, kept at it, stubborn and bloody-minded, until the motion was as easy and familiar as walking up stairs. As knitting a scarf, as kissing a girl.

As she pushed open the shop door, a gust of frigid wind blew her inside. Luisa slipped in the puddle on the tiled floor and collapsed against the door.

Priya and Toni were standing at the counter, a pile of invoices between them.

Luisa untangled her long red scarf from around her neck and held it out as she walked up to the counter. The wool was soaked with her sweat and the snow; it was the first thing she had knit for herself, and there were holes where she had looped the yarn too many times, and knots where she'd lost stitches. She lay the sad, damp thing on the counter, arranging it into the approximate shape of a heart.

"It hurts without you," she told Priya, and did not look at Toni. She had to get this out. "I don't want it to hurt."

Priya's eyes were dark, her mouth pursed. She looked a little thin, hollow-cheeked, like her clothes were a size too big. "I'm sorry," she said. "I'm sorry I—"

"I want it to hurt *with* you," Luisa said, and wrapped the scarf around one of Priya's hands. "Does that make sense?"

Toni muffled a noise against her fist and left them alone.

Priya still hadn't said anything beyond "I'm sorry." Outside the big plate-glass window, the snow sleeted down.

"Don't be sorry," Luisa said, and tugged her hands until Priya leaned over the counter, their foreheads almost touching. "Just say yes."

"I made you some socks," Priya said at last. Her breath was warm on Luisa's cold cheeks, her lips very soft. She laughed a little, self-consciously, and Luisa kissed her.

"I'm sorry," she said a little later as she led Luisa up the narrow stairs to her apartment.

Laughing, Luisa slapped her ass. "Make it up to me. Make it hurt *really good.*"

A.L. Simonds came of age in Manhattan's East Village and now makes her considerably more sedate home in central Canada. An information professional, she spends her days wrangling electronic records, while her nights are devoted to dreaming about a punk rock revolution, yelling about pop culture, knitting too many socks, and writing speculative romances. She is currently at work on an original lesbian superhero tale.

BACHELORETTE PARTY

JESSICA CLARE

"What happens in Vegas, stays in Vegas," recited Haven, leaning across the seat and clinking her champagne glass against Ashley's. "Are you ready for a night of fun on the town?"

"Yes?" Ashley said in a dubious voice.

"That doesn't sound like a woman heading to her bachelorette party."

Ash clutched the glass even tighter and stared out the window of the limo. It was hard to mask the thoughtful look on her face. "It's just . . . weird. That's all."

"Last night of freedom?" Haven teased, grabbing the champagne bottle out of the bucket of ice that sat between them and pouring herself a refill. "I didn't take you for the type to have cold feet."

"I don't have cold feet," Ash protested, giving Haven a disapproving look from over her wire-rimmed glasses. "I love Josh very, very much. I can't wait to be his wife."

"Buuuut?" Haven added, tipping the champagne bottle and refilling Ashley's glass. "There's always a big fat 'but' in these kinds of conversations."

"No 'buts,'" Ashley insisted.

Haven snorted. "So you accomplished everything on your list, then? Color me impressed."

Ashley felt her face heat bright red. "I cannot believe you are bringing up that list now, of all times."

Haven only grinned.

The two of them had been friends since rooming together in college—an unlikely pair as Haven was the wild and carefree art student, and Ashley was the buttoned-up science major. But after Haven had been ditched by her boyfriend, the two of them had bonded over bottles of vodka and girlfriend solidarity. That night, both of them made a list of things to experience before settling down. Once the lists were complete, they'd exchanged papers and each girl kept tabs for the other. It had cemented their friendship.

For the rest of college and a few years after, they'd continued to get together and mark things off their lists. They'd seen the Louvre together, gone kayaking, climbed a mountain, and Haven had even run with the bulls in Spain one year. Over time, the lists had whittled down to almost nothing, and the two women had moved to different cities to pursue their careers.

Ash had almost forgotten about her list, and what insane, glaring item was left on it. How tacky of Haven to bring it up now, on the eve of such an occasion.

"It's the perfect time to discuss these things," Haven drawled. She reached into her pocket and pulled out a worn, many-times-folded piece of paper. "What a coincidence. I have the list right here!"

Ash gasped and reached over to snatch it, but Haven slid away, scooting down her seat.

"Not so fast," Haven said, pulling away. She held the list out of Ashley's reach. "We made a deal a long time ago that we'd complete our lists before settling down, remember?"

"We've completed everything reasonable," Ash protested, her face flushing with embarrassment. She resisted the urge to cross her arms protectively over her chest.

"Really? Because I think there's one thing that I don't have crossed off here. It's under the 'sex' category." Haven waved the list in Ashley's

direction. "Do you remember? Because I still haven't marked it off for you."

Oh, Ash remembered all right. She remembered that between slinging back their vodka shots, they'd scribbled out their list and divided everything into categories. When it came to "sex," Haven had immediately put down "threesome." Under her own list, Ashley had to be coaxed to answer, but when she finally did, she'd shyly written down "whipping." The thought of a man bending her over his knee, exposing her ass, and then whipping her bottom was intensely arousing for her. At the time, she and Haven had giggled about it, but it certainly didn't seem so funny now.

"It's taken care of," Ash bit out, blushing with a mixture of anger and embarrassment. Josh was a good man, and she loved having sex with him, but she had never—and would never—ask him to whip her. That would just make things weird between them. *Hey, baby, remember me? Your buttoned-up little wife? I'd really like it if you'd take a riding crop to my ass until I'm squirming under you.*

No, she couldn't see having that conversation with her fiancé. Even though wild Haven teased her about how boring and responsible she was, Ash liked who she was, and she wouldn't change anything about her solid relationship with Josh.

"It's not taken care of, because it's not crossed off. You would have told me. And it's too late to pull a stunt like that anyhow."

"Those lists don't matter, Haven," Ashley said in an irritated voice. "I love Josh. I would never do anything to mess up our relationship. Who cares if I haven't killed the final item on my list? I can live with it, so let it go."

To Ashley's surprise, Haven nodded and folded the list, tucking it in to her bra. "You're right. And hey, anyhow, the limo's almost here. Let's get your blindfold on for the party."

Haven had set up the elaborate bachelorette party for her, and

the blindfold was part of the surprise. Ash pulled her hair into a ponytail and obediently leaned in as Haven put the party blindfold over her face. She could hear her best friend's giggles as they got out of the limo, and Haven led her by the hand out of the street and into a building. A large building, judging by the echoes and murmurs of conversation around them.

"Did you rent a hotel room for the party?"

"Nothing but the best," Haven agreed, and Ash smiled.

Haven continued to lead her up the elevator and through the hotel, and when things seemed to get quieter, Ash knew they had turned down a hallway. She waited as she heard Haven fiddling with the room key card, then heard the click of the door opening. Ash braced herself, waiting for the outpouring of cheers from partygoers.

Silence. That was odd. Ash frowned and tilted her head, trying to see out from underneath the blindfold as Haven tugged her forward, grabbing both of her hands. "Are we here yet?"

"We're here," Haven said in an almost gleeful voice.

"I can't hear anyone," Ash admitted, still smiling. "Are they hiding?"

"Not exactly," Haven said, and then clicked something cool around Ash's wrist. Before Ash could react, Haven gently twisted her other arm behind her back, and linked the other cool object around her free wrist.

Handcuffs. Her hands were now tied behind her back.

Ash jerked at the cuffs, twisting her arms slightly. "Haven? What the hell?"

Someone reached over and lightly kissed her cheek. "You'll thank me for this later," Haven said in a cheerful voice, and then stepped away, a rush of cool air brushing against Ashley's skin. Moments passed, then the door to the room opened.

She's not leaving, Ash thought with panicked irritation, jerking at the cuffs again. "You are so dead, Haven. So. Very. Dead."

"She's all yours," Haven said to someone, and then laughed. "And

remember what I told you. Miss Prim and Proper here wants to be spanked."

"HAVEN!"

The door shut with a soft click.

Ash froze, then swung her head around. The blindfold was still on and she couldn't see anything. The room was silent, but who had Haven been speaking to?

She licked her dry lips. "Hello? Who's there?"

Footsteps moved across the room from her.

Ash turned toward the sound, forcing a small, nervous smile to her mouth. "I think there's been a misunderstanding here. A big one. I'm supposed to—"

A finger touched her mouth. "Shhhh."

The words dried in Ashley's throat. She could scent the man now, a familiar mixture of sandalwood and bergamot. It didn't stop the thrill rising through her body—the nervous mixture of excitement and fear that made her skin prickle.

"Who are you?" she demanded again, straining to see through the blindfold.

Her question was ignored. His finger slid from her lips and moved down her chin, down her throat, drawing a light, tickling line and stopping between her breasts.

Ash's breath caught in her throat when the finger paused. Would it move to the side? Touch her breasts? Or continue downward? She jerked away slightly, a reflexive action. She was embarrassed by her own thoughts—to think that she wanted this man to touch her! And that she wanted him to keep going, of all things.

Haven was so very *dead* when she got free of her handcuffs.

"Relax," the voice whispered, husky and close to her ear. "You've been quite a naughty girl, haven't you?"

She shivered and jerked again at the handcuffs. "I think there's been a bit of a misunderstanding here—" Ash said.

Her words were cut off when he laid his finger across her lips again, silencing her.

She spoke around his finger, determined to be heard. "I'd be happy to shut up if you'd just let me go so I can get out of here and back to my party."

There was a deep, rumbling laugh. "You're staying with me."

She felt a hand brush across her collarbone, to where her pale, lacy top exposed a small amount of skin. Again, Ash shivered. His hand skimmed along her collar and moved over her shoulder, then down her back. The touch was exceedingly personal, light but possessive at the same time, and she wanted to protest.

Except a deep, dark part of her secretly liked it.

The man's hand slowly wandered down to where her hands were cuffed behind her back and she stilled, breathless with anticipation, waiting to hear the click of the latch come undone.

But she didn't hear it. Instead, his hands went to the waistband of her swingy black skirt and wrenched it down. The charming side-button popped off the skirt and she heard it crack against the wall.

Ash gasped in shock, staggering slightly as the skirt slithered down her legs. It exposed her panties—modest, demure, and just a little bit lacy. Nothing racy. Not for her. No panty hose, either—Vegas was too hot for that sort of thing. Prickles moved up and down her skin. "Um, what are you doing?"

The fabric was caught around her legs, and she wobbled forward, trying to get away, only to have the man's arm lock around her waist. Next, he ripped at the collar of her pretty lace top, and it fell open, exposing her bra. His hand expertly went to the front of her bra and undid the clasp, and her breasts slid free of their confinement. She could smell his cologne again, could smell it even as he stood behind her, pressing his body against her own. The breath died in her throat when she felt the thick, prodding length of his erection against the

small of her back. When he pulled her forward a step, she dazedly followed.

His hand pressed down on her shoulders, at the base of her neck—a suggestion that she should lean forward. She did so, feeling unsure until her knees hit the edge of what felt like a bed.

"You've been a very bad girl, Ashley," he said, his voice a low growl. "Sneaking away from your fiancé and playing around with other men."

"No, I'm not! I didn't—"

When he continued to press her forward, she tumbled onto the mattress, her cheek planting into the covers. Awkwardly, she sprawled there, waiting.

He was right behind her. His hand sprawled possessively across the naked small of her back, and then moved. She felt him pull the skirt tight around her feet, then yanking it off her legs. With rough hands, he grabbed her hips and positioned her just the way he wanted—the side of her face pressed against the bedcovers, her knees locked together as he moved her. Her ass rose into the air, covered by nothing but a scrap of lacy white panties.

"Naughty," he said, giving her a warning slap directly on the seam of her sex.

Her body clenched. She felt the slickness between her legs, and her breathing became deep and slow with desire.

Ash realized what this was, now. Her fear gave way to need. Haven had Ashley's list, and had known that she would never ask Josh for rough, kinky sex. She'd never ask him for a long, hot session of spanking. It just wasn't in Ash to request that sort of thing from her sweet, caring fiancé. But Haven knew her dirtiest secret, and like a true friend, she was going to make it happen for Ashley, on her last night of freedom.

The thought was a heady one, and turned her on like nothing imaginable. He was going to spank her. *Hard*.

So when he ran a hand over her upraised rump, Ash sighed, even as her hips gave a slight roll. The anticipation was building inside her, making her nearly tremble with want.

His hands moved over her raised buttocks, skimming the flesh and trailing down her thighs, as if deciding what to do with her. Ash went absolutely still, not wanting to influence the decision. For some reason, it had to be his choice, and not through any persuasion of her own. She tensed slightly, even more when his hand rested on the curve of her buttock.

He gave it a light, stinging slap through the fabric of her panties.

Her sex clenched again, and she made a small noise of surprise, her body jerking. It wasn't a hard tap, just enough to make the skin sting with the impact. Her nipples tightened against the blankets and she gave a slight quiver, waiting for the next blow. It landed on her other buttock, as if he had to make sure both got the same amount of attention.

"Very naughty," he breathed over her. "Do you want to be punished?"

She squirmed slightly in response, the anticipation making her jumpy with need.

Warm hands rested on her upraised buttocks, and she gave a slight wiggle, waiting for the next slap against her flesh. To her surprise—and delight—the hands grasped her modest panties and tugged them slowly down her thighs, exposing her pale flesh to the air.

"We need a safe word," he said in a low, musing voice. "Any time you want me to stop, or if I'm hurting you, just say the word 'bachelorette.' Understand?"

Wordless, she nodded.

Again, the warm hand came down on the full of her buttock, this time a bit harder, the sting lasting a bit longer. A second hard swat on the same cheek caused her breath to intake sharply, the crisp pain

that much sharper this time. Her hips gave a slight roll of encouragement and she bit her lip to keep from moaning aloud. *Harder*, she wanted to say. *Go harder. Push me past the edge.*

But she couldn't bring herself to say it.

The hands caressed her ass, dancing lightly over the stinging flesh, before coming down in another hard smack. And another. She was totally wet now, her breath no longer soft and slow but quick and gasping. Each of the smacks seemed to be a little harder than the last, the sting with a bit more edge to it. He was careful to hit the full curve of her bottom, never too high. Just the right spot that would cause her flesh to jiggle in response, and that she'd feel the impact the most. It was incredibly erotic, made even more so by the fact that the other participant seemed to be taking his time—as if exploring her body and trying to determine what she liked the most. This went on for dozens of spanking slaps—some hard, some more gentle, some that stung for long minutes after the hit. Each one built her desire even more than the last.

"Are you enjoying this?" he would ask her.

She would give a small wiggle of distress as a response.

It would never satisfy him. He'd give her a slap on the behind, hard and stinging, until she answered. And each time, she'd have to answer with a small, breathless, "Yes!"

After a particularly bruising smack against the now-sensitive curve of her ass, she could bite her lip no longer. A long, moaning gasp escaped her and she rolled her hips, hard, desperately needing something more.

The man paused over her, his fingers rubbing at the sore spot on her skin. There was a long pause as his fingers continued to play with the curve of her ass, then he growled, "Did you like that?"

"Yes," she bit out after a moment, learning to respond to his commands. A blush suffused her cheeks. "I like it. I . . . like it harder, too." She bit her lip after that confession, suddenly shy for

demanding more. But if this was her night—her one last night of having her fantasy come to life, then shouldn't she ask? So she spoke again. "Harder . . . please."

The soft chuckle of his voice seemed to rasp all the way through her body, and her sex grew even more liquid with heat. If she could touch herself, she knew that her sex would be slick with need, but he hadn't touched her there. Not yet. He'd only spanked her. Odd how that was so thrilling and yet not enough at the same time.

The bed shifted suddenly, and he got up and walked away. Ashley frowned, turning her head toward the movement on the far side of the room. Was something wrong? Her throat went dry and the delightful throbbing centered around her hips seemed to ebb away.

Had she messed up? Because she wanted more? It didn't seem fair.

"If you want more, you'll have to tell me."

Ash swallowed hard. It went against everything in her, to ask him to give her more. Her cheeks burned with shame at the thought. What would Josh think if he knew her thoughts?

But . . . he wasn't touching her enough. The delicious spankings had stopped. His hand skimmed her flesh, but she needed more. She needed it hard, and rough—rougher than what he'd given her. And she was only going to get it if she asked.

So she wet her lips. Thought. Gave a little sigh, and then said, "I've dreamed about being spanked. For forever. I've always wanted it a little hard and rough, and just a little bit . . ." she hesitated. "A little bit rough."

"A little?" he asked in a husky voice.

She hesitated, then . . . What did it matter? So she added, "A *lot*. So rough that it . . . hurts . . . just a little."

He said nothing.

Her body tensed, waiting for his response with a mental cringe.

Would he find her weird because she was demanding that he hurt her? Or would he find it a turn-on? She froze in place, waiting.

But he gave a soft chuckle of acknowledgement, and she felt his hand glide over her ass again. "I think we can do that, since you asked so nicely."

Relieved and boneless once more, she relaxed as his open palm caressed the still-pleasant stinging curve of her ass.

A strange sound cut through the air—almost like a zipping noise—before she felt the impact of a small, thin, flexible whip crack across her buttocks. It wasn't hard, but the sudden jolting sting made her moan in surprise. Her words died in her throat.

He'd just . . . whipped her.

Oh, fuck *yes*. This time, she wasn't able to stop the moan rising in her throat.

He chuckled low in his throat at that. "You like that, don't you? Hard and just a little rough?"

She bit her lip, wriggling on the bed. The impact of the whip against her skin was much, much sharper than the crack of his hand against her flesh. And it was a total, complete turn-on. Her sex gave a deep throb and her entire body tensed in delighted anticipation.

"No answer?" he murmured low, his voice barely above a whisper. "That's very naughty of you. You know how we play." And he tapped it against her ass, waiting.

She shook her head against the covers.

"Tell me what you want. Now."

Her breath exploded out of her throat, and it took everything she had not to arch her back in a silent request for more. "I . . . Do it again. Please."

Crack! Again, it came down against her flesh. Oh, God, *yes*. She moaned at the sharp sensations that rocketed over her skin—a mixture of pain and pleasure. *Crack!* Down it came again, slightly higher,

slightly stronger. Each lash felt like it was leaving a long, throbbing trail on her skin.

It felt amazing.

Her sex clenched with each hit, and she began to shift against the mattress, back and forth. Her nipples had grown hard and they ached, the delicate chafe of the blankets against them increasing the pleasurable agony.

After several more slaps of the whip across her stinging buttocks, he began to rub the whip against her flesh before swatting her with it. It was a tease of anticipation, the smooth feeling of the flexible crop against her flesh, brushing against the curve of her buttock.

"Do you like that?"

"Yes," she whimpered against the covers.

"Ask me to spank you again. Tell me how naughty you've been."

"Very!" she blurted.

"Very . . . what?" He teased the loop of the crop against her throbbing skin.

She writhed on the bed, grazing her aching nipples on the bedding. Her sex clenched hard in anticipation of the next hit. "So naughty," she breathed, telling him what he wanted to hear to get the next crack of the whip against her skin. "Thinking dirty thoughts about being spanked hard . . ."

"And then what . . . ?"

She bit her lip for a moment, and then added, "And then fucked. Harder."

Ash was rewarded with the whip. It cracked hard against her ass, and she gave a squeal of delight at the hit. He was careful to aim it on the padding of her ass, and she began to anticipate that he would strike her . . . on her sex. Her knees moved apart a fraction with each successive crack of the whip until she was practically straddling the bed, her sex wide open and slick with need.

Would he hit her there? Would it hurt?

He rubbed the crop against the inside of her thighs thoughtfully. She moaned as the loop of the crop tickled the lips of her sex. He then skimmed the rod between her buttocks, rolling it slightly in the valley there. Ash whimpered.

"What do you need? Tell me," he asked her again. His other hand lightly grazed her buttock and gave it a light tap.

"More, please." She rolled her hips. "I ache . . ."

He shifted next to her on the bed, and she could almost feel the heat of him next to her. The whip tapped lightly against her hip, and his fingers skimmed along the lips of her sex. "Is it a good ache?" he asked, and she felt his breath against the small of her back, his knees brushing against her right one.

His fingers grazed over her flesh, then dipped in and brushed against her clit. At the same time, he gave her a light slap of the crop against her ass.

Her entire body shuddered and she gave a small cry. The sensations rocketing through her were overwhelming, but she wasn't quite at orgasm—not yet. It built inside of her, and she writhed on the bed, trying to maneuver his fingertips back to her clit again.

He listened to her silent request, his fingers dipping in and brushing against her clit, slick with need. Again, he raised the whip and it whistled through the air before cracking sharply, low across her ass, grazing the sensitive flesh of her sex.

She came. A cry broke forth from her lips and her entire body tensed with the force of her release as he brought the whip down lightly again, prolonging the sharp kiss of pain. Her body clenched hard and she rocked against his fingers.

But he removed them, and what could have been a long, languid orgasm was cut short. She gave a small cry of distress at that. It had been everything she'd ever wanted . . . just cut sadly short. Still, the languid feeling was moving through her body, and she sighed. It was almost perfect. Almost.

The man next to her shifted, and the bed adjusted as his weight came off it. She lay there boneless until he began pulling her to the edge of the bed. His hands pushed her hips down slightly, then grasped her thighs. His hands were rough as he tugged her backward, and his palms rested on her throbbing ass once more, palming the flesh and soothing it.

Then, he spread her legs wide and she felt the nudge of his cock butt against her sex, a split second before it slammed into her. "Like that?" he gritted. "Is that how you want to be fucked?"

The breath gasped out of her lungs. It hadn't hurt—she was too warm and wet for that—but it had been surprising, and the stretch of him seated deep inside her felt good. She rocked her hips back against him, encouraging another thrust.

Instead, he gave her a hard slap on the ass and ground against her, rolling her hips with the force of his own movement. "Tell me," he demanded. "Do you like that?" Again, he slapped her ass roughly.

"Yes!" she cried out. "Just like that!"

"How do you want it?"

"Hard," she moaned, her internal muscles clenched around him at having to describe it. "Hard and rough. Please. *Please.*"

He thrust again, and she was thrilled by the equally hard slap of his hand on her ass that reverberated through her body. The pattern continued—thrust, slap, thrust, slap—and she was helpless to do anything but raise her hips and encourage him with her cries of pleasure. Her buttocks stung from the onslaught, and every new crack of his hand just added to her heightened senses. One particularly crisp slap brought her close, and she writhed beneath him, rolling her hips and grinding them against his. "More," she breathed. "Harder."

"Sounds like sweet little Ashley likes it rough," he gritted out, and gave her another deep, digging thrust of his cock. "Like this?"

She felt him leaning over her, and then the whisk of the riding crop against her ass. Light at first, then hard. Then another hard thrust of his cock, his free hand digging into her hip.

"Harder," she demanded again, the orgasm close. Her toes curled in anticipation.

The crop slapped against her skin again, the sharp kiss of it sending her over the edge for a second time. Ash cried out her release, her body clenching wildly against his.

He was behind her, jerking against her hips and shouting his release a few seconds later. His hips rocked against hers for a moment more before he fell on top of her and rolled them both to the side on the bed.

Ashley panted, feeling boneless and wonderful. That had been the most spectacular pair of orgasms that she'd ever had. Ever. She could cheerfully lay there for the rest of her life.

He curled up behind her, his body pressed against her own, sharing warmth. One strong arm was locked around her waist in a possessive gesture that she liked quite a bit, and he smelled good. Sandalwood and bergamot. The scent of it made her utterly content. She could just melt into a puddle and sink away at this moment.

Well, except her arms hurt. The handcuffs were definitely starting to cut off her circulation. She twisted her arms once, and then sighed. "Josh, can you take these off me now?"

He stiffened against her, and then she felt the bed move and coolness rushed against her back. He'd been so warm against her. He returned a moment later, and she heard the click of the handcuffs before they fell to the bed. With a happy sigh, she sat up and took off the blindfold, and then rubbed her wrists.

Josh sat across from her, his short brown hair wildly rumpled. He rubbed his head and then grinned. "So how'd you know it was me?"

"I knew it was you as soon as I walked in the door," Ashley confessed. "I think the blindfold made me use my other senses a bit more. I was able to pick up the scent of your cologne." She smiled at him and cocked her head. "And you can't disguise your voice, even if you try to do that growling thing low in your throat."

"Huh," said her fiancé, and then rolled back into bed and wrapped his arms around her again. "I suppose it's good that you knew it was me the whole time."

Ashley rolled her eyes at the miffed sound in his voice. "Do you think I would have let just anyone spank me like that?"

"I don't know," he said, grinning. "Is it on your list?"

"Ha-ha. Very funny."

Josh leaned over and gave her a kiss, and she leaned into his embrace. "Next time you want to try something kinky in the bedroom, why not just tell me?"

A hot blush covered her face, and Ash looked away. "It's not exactly something that comes up in conversation."

"Why not?"

She squirmed a little. "It's just something I feel weird asking about. It's not exactly a normal thing you can say to your fiancé. I feel weird about it. I never would have asked if Haven hadn't gotten that crazy idea in her head."

Josh leaned in and kissed her nose. "Haven is a genius."

Still a little put out at her friend's meddling, she gave a mock frown. "As soon as she turns her back, I'm going to find her two strapping hot men and a pair of handcuffs for her so she can finish *her* list."

"She'd probably like that," Josh said. "But I can't thank her enough for coming up with this crazy idea." He rubbed her deliciously sore bottom and grinned. "If you'd have never made that list, we would have lost out on hundreds of crazy nights of sex."

Lifting an eyebrow, Ashley regarded her fiancé. "Hundreds?"

He gave a solemn nod. "Through sickness and health, for richer, for poorer, and for lots and lots of future naughty spankings."

She laughed.

Jessica Clare is the pen name of the artist formerly known as Jill Myles. She feels totally like Prince when she mentions that, too. Jessica Clare's first steamy contemporary for Berkley Heat, *The Girl's Guide to (Man)Hunting*, will be out in May 2012. You can visit her website at www.jessica-clare .com.

WICKED WEDDING NIGHT

MARGARET ROWE

One

HALLAM ABBEY, KENT
NOVEMBER 1815

"Why?"

His new wife gazed up at him with barely contained terror. That would make the next hour so much easier, he supposed. A modicum of suffering on her part would prolong his pleasure. He wasn't proud of the fact, but there it was. Since his time in a French prison as a guest of Emperor Napoleon, Viscount Lucien Ransford had had a problem pretending to be a bland, bloodless aristocrat. He'd had the decency beaten right out of him. Repeatedly.

His limits to vice? He had none now that he could recall.

"Why not?" Someone should have warned her before she so foolishly trapped him into marriage. "Did you not just hours ago promise to obey me?"

"But this is . . . You are . . ." She paused, her sea-blue eyes awash in virginal tears. At least he assumed she was a virgin—her trap had been too clumsily set to hope she had any skill in the bedroom. She tried to shake a plump ankle, but his skill held her quite fast. "I don't believe this is *normal*."

Lucien gave a hollow laugh. "There is nothing about us that is *normal*, Maida." He tightened the silken cord at her throat, draping the ends between her breasts. The thought of leading her around on all fours made his cock stir. "We've known each other three days,

the last two of which have been spent preparing for the benighted wedding. It took you precisely one day to wander into my bedroom uninvited and crawl into my bed. Sleepwalking, you said. When you woke up, your screams were quite affecting. And effective. The entire house party was witness to your so-called mistake."

"It *was* a mistake!" she cried, struggling again at the bonds that tied her to the bedstead. "I've walked in my sleep since I was a child."

"Then someone should have tied you to your bed long before this." He stepped back to admire his handiwork. His bride was sheet-white where she was untouched by dark curls and shadow, an entrancing chiaroscuro. She might be a stranger, but she was an attractive one. Once he broke her to him, she would do.

For a time.

Lucien couldn't think too far ahead. His captors had robbed him of that, too.

"P-Please don't do whatever it is you're thinking."

He leaned over her. "And what do you think that is, my dear?"

"I don't know, but you're scaring me. I shall do my duty to you without these—these restraints."

Duty. An empty word. Duty to King, duty to country. He'd had enough of that.

"It is your duty to submit to me in any way I choose. Surely your mother told you that between her bouts of gloating." Maida Clement's mother, a viciously ambitious harpy, was more than pleased to see her daughter rise above her station, no matter how the feat had been accomplished.

It would serve her right not to consummate this farce of a marriage. It wasn't as if he had any interest in continuing the Ransford line. He could not imagine himself as a father. What could he teach a son? How to tie an untieable knot? How to wield a whip to greatest effect? How to bear endless beatings without breaking an oath?

A wave of despair threatened to plunge him further into darkness, but he picked up his glass instead and drained it.

The day had been interminable. The grim ceremony was held in the abbey's empty chapel—Lucien had refused entry to anyone but his hosts and his bride's smug parents. A falsely cheerful wedding breakfast, with toast after toast to the health he would never have, had gone on for hours as the food in front of him curled and curdled. A torrential downpour, even now spattering against the black bedroom windows, had prevented him from leaving his cousin's estate after the festivities. He was doomed to spend his wedding night with the house party revelers and his own threadbare conscience.

The guests had not expected a scandal and resultant wedding and had not ceased giving him advice, ribald or otherwise. The ride to Town and Doctors Commons to obtain the special license had not been far enough to escape their meddling, thought it had given him a respite from the smirks and whispers for a few hours.

His cousin Harry had thought it the greatest joke that Lucien had been caught in such a compromising position—Lucien, who had led Harry far afield before his wife reformed him.

"Your wings have been clipped for good, Luc. My wife says there's nothing more satisfying than restoring a rake's virtue, although little Maida has her work cut out for her, I expect."

At present, little Maida looked incapable of doing anything more than blubbering into the bedsheets. And she was not so little. In stature, yes—the top of her dark head barely came up to the middle of his chest, but her breasts were luscious, ruby-tipped globes. All of her was a fleshy paradise, really—gentle rolls of marble skin gleaming in the candlelight. Lucien had stripped her of her plain white night rail a while back, pleased to see her skin blush with embarrassment as her nipples puckered. She had been still as death until he pulled the cords from his dressing gown pockets, and then she'd come to rather surprising life attempting to alter her fate.

Served her right. *Sleepwalking.* The oldest trick in the book, worthy of the plot of some gothic romance written by a singularly idea-challenged author. A pity she had not fainted at his feet in the conservatory instead—he would have stepped over her and moved on through the pots of forced amaryllis.

But now she was his *wife*. A woman he knew precious little about, save her mother was a grasping harridan, her father a cipher, and she herself had spectacularly lovely tits.

Lucien knew how the story would end. But until then, he'd make best use of this night and all the ones to follow.

Two

Maida Clement would have risen from the bed and throttled her mother if she were not so neatly bound in place. The viscount—she refused to think of the fiend as her *husband*—was perfectly correct to think he'd been tricked into marriage. She had been desperate enough to agree to her mama's scheme three days ago, never dreaming how this night would turn into a nightmare.

Lucien Ransford was every young girl's dream—golden, gray-eyed, gorgeous. A war hero to boot. But she was no young girl, which was one of the reasons she had taken a deep breath, loosened her night rail ribbons, and walked into his room.

Maida knew he'd be sleeping, virtually unconscious. According to Vivienne, her husband's cousin took a draught nightly to ward off unpleasant reminders of the war. He kept a lamp burning, too, which had been helpful in their discovery once she'd started shrieking.

Maida was thoroughly ashamed of herself, and now she was about to pay for her folly. How foolish to think she could finally escape from her miserable home life into a marriage based on deceit. But she was six and twenty. Her one relatively dedicated suitor had the misfortune to be killed at Salamanca four years ago. None of her mama's conventional schemes to replace him had worked, and Maida was exhausted from trying them.

If she'd had different parents, she would have been content to

climb on the shelf with her books and gather society's dust, but Mama made that impossible. There was no escape from her mother's vituperative tongue and endless machinations except for death or marriage, and surely marriage was preferable. How hard could it be to find oneself married to the beautiful Viscount Ransford?

Hard, apparently. Maida closed her eyes, blocking out the sight of Lucien Ransford's tented dressing gown. Unquestionably he desired her in this shocking state—splayed before him, split open, tethered tight, every inch of her exposed.

Her mama constantly snatched the tea cakes from her hand, and had once locked her in her room for a month with tea and gruel only in an attempt to turn her into a sought-after sylph. Well, Maida wasn't willowy or fashionable. She was short, plump, her dull brown hair frizzed in damp weather, and she read books. Maida wasn't the romantic sort. She had known from the time she was small there was no romance in her future. Major Everett's death had proven that—though he was not the romantic sort either, just a widower looking for a stepmother to his son. The little boy had been sweet, and, apart from a few chaste kisses, Maida had been hazy as to what would transpire on her wedding night.

Somehow she'd imagined the major would lift the hem of her nightgown and breach her useless maidenhead in a dignified way, not truss her like one of Cook's Christmas geese. It seemed her desperation would only become more profound every minute she spent with Viscount Lucien Ransford.

And yet.

For good or ill, she had his full, undivided attention. No man had ever looked at her this way, as if she were a feast and he a starving man.

"I'll scream."

His lips twisted. "You do that well, loud enough to wake the living dead such as myself. But Harry's wife has placed us in the abbey's

unused wing for privacy. I doubt anyone would hear. Or care. A man may do as he pleases with his wife."

Maida knew this was true. One did not reach her advanced age without hearing some of the horrors of the marriage bed. Her own mother had told her to lie still and submit to whatever depravity Ransford asked of her, but Maida had never expected the golden viscount to be quite so depraved.

"I won't enjoy this," she finally ground out.

Ransford lifted a gilt eyebrow. "Does that matter to me? I'm afraid not."

"You are abominable!"

"Yes. I am. And now you are stuck with me. You didn't anticipate the consequences of your actions, Maida. I never planned to marry, to spare a good woman the indignities that seem to be so necessary to me. But you are not a good woman."

She felt her cheeks grow warm. "How dare you? I am so!"

"Come now. You lied and schemed to get into this bed. Admit it."

Maida swallowed. The devil was right.

"Ah. No argument, I see. Perhaps we can deal together once you know what I require."

"I don't care about pleasing you! We can have the marriage annulled. I'll go back home"—the words burned her but she continued—"and we can pretend this never happened."

"As if I'd let you go now that I've seen you. And *you* have seen what I'm capable of."

He shook his head, a loose lock of fair hair casting a shadow on his temple. "No, as I said, we're stuck with each other." He untied his robe and pulled the belt from its loops. "I don't care to be judged by you, Maida. Perhaps if you're blinded—"

She gasped, but he merely chuckled. "Such a literal girl. I'm going to cover your eyes. I rather like the idea of you guessing what comes next."

In a trice her eyes were wrapped beneath midnight blue brocade. The last she saw was a slice of his burnished body—nicked and scarred—between the open folds of his robe.

What had happened to him? Something dreadful. Something that had destroyed more than the smoothness of his skin.

Maida fought back her mounting panic. She was helpless—there was nothing she could do *but* scream, but she didn't dare to. What if someone actually came to her rescue and discovered her in such a vulnerable position? Ransford could simply say it was all a game. He was a viscount. She was nothing more than the daughter of a country squire.

And a lying adventuress who was getting much more of an adventure than she had bargained for.

Ha. She was a viscountess now, although no previous foray into the ton had prepared her for this particular aspect of her rise to the Upper Ten Thousand.

Her mother had told her not to move, but she had no choice about it. Nervous, she licked her lips and listened hard, sorry that the wrapping covered her ears as well as her eyes. She sensed Ransford moving about the room, although he may as well have been a cat, so quiet was he. At last she heard the squeak of a trunk's hinges, and then the thud as the lid dropped.

"Wh-What are you doing?"

She felt him cup her cheek, his hand quite cold. "Disciplining you. I'll have no more deceit, Maida. You've played me for a fool just the once. Never again. You may hate me tonight, but you will learn not to cross me."

"I didn't know who you were," she whispered.

He sighed. "No, you did not. I imagine you had your reasons to trap me. Tell me, are you pregnant with another man's child?"

Her mouth fell open. "No, of course not!" She may have been foolish, but she had some honor, not that he'd ever believe her.

"Good. That will make things easier for me. But not for you."

She heard the air split and felt the first lash on her thighs. Maida stifled her urge to scream—she deserved his wrath. She had indeed been very bad—and doomed them both. Licks of pain darted across her skin. In truth, it was not so bad she couldn't bear it. He struck her twice more, with less force each time, then tossed the crop to the floor.

The room was silent save for Ransford's rasping breaths. She herself was speechless with shock and something else—something ink dark that bloomed at the pit of her stomach. Maida wished she could see his face—was he triumphant? Repelled? She waited for his next move.

And then flinched as his fingers traced the welts. Flinched again as she felt his weight on the mattress. His lips replaced his fingers, his warm tongue sweeping across her left thigh. A wave of gooseflesh spread across her chest, tightening her nipples. She opened her mouth to protest but was struck dumb by where his tongue went next.

This certainly was not normal, was it? Lucien Ransford was between her thighs, parting her private seam, licking her. Nibbling, really. How—How unsanitary. Maida dug her heels into the bed in an attempt to buck him away, and would have been successful had he not chosen just that moment to encapsulate a morsel of her flesh in his mouth. His wicked tongue swirled unceasingly and a long finger slipped inside her, the two appendages working in tandem until she could truly not bear the sensation a minute longer.

This was worse torture than the binding. Something odd was happening—a sharp, sweet longing overtook her reason and she groaned aloud. Ransford's—Lucien's—intensity increased at her response and he suckled more thoroughly, another finger spreading her passage open.

She was shamefully wet below and hot everywhere despite the

damp chill of the room. Hot inside and out, her skin slicking as Lucien tormented her. This was lust, pure and simple, transcending sense and transforming her in a way she could not understand. Words spun just out of reach, but "stop" was nowhere to be found.

Maida lay in her dark world as the stranger who was her husband pressed his mouth to her center and splintered her apart.

Three

———※———

The lying little witch tasted sweet and clean. Some maid had prepared her for tonight with an herb-filled bath, and Lucien's nose, buried in Maida's mink brown curls, detected rosemary and lavender. He felt her pulse around his tongue and smiled inwardly.

He'd said he didn't care if she enjoyed herself this night, which was not entirely true. There were still some vestiges of gentlemanly behavior in him—not many, to be sure. No gentleman tied up his lady wife without her permission, and Maida Clement had made it clear from the scratches on his forearms she had been opposed to his methods.

But not right now. She sighed and cried and moved as much as she was able. Her completion burst forth on his tongue and his cock jerked in response.

He disengaged reluctantly and gazed at the pink stripes on her legs, nearly the color of her inner folds. He was a wretch to abuse her no matter what she had done to him, but he was forced to. There was no stimulation for him without complete mastery—he'd come home and tried to be good, but he was useless. When he discovered the cords and the cane solved his little problem, he had found satisfaction for the first time in years.

But he'd not meant to marry. Ever. And what he was to do with Maida Clement for the rest of his life, short as it would be, he had no idea.

No point to looking into the future. Lucien need only concern himself with the next fifteen minutes or so. Possibly much less, much to his shame. He needed relief. Release. Respite from the dreams that would surely come into the night. He'd have to leave his bride—after untying her, of course—and seek another bed somewhere in this vast unoccupied wing. Lucien didn't care if he choked and died on dust—he did not want a witness to what might happen when his night terrors came.

But now—what to do? Her mouth, her cunt, or her pretty white bum? He glanced up at her rosy lips, still open in dazed surprise. Was that her first orgasm? She was rather old for such innocence, but perhaps she was not experienced, even by her own hand.

"You said you would not enjoy it, my dear," he drawled.

Her mouth snapped shut. A bright coal popped from the fire to the carpet, and Lucien left her bedside to sweep it back into the hearth, repositioning the screen. They could have burned the abbey down if they'd been truly engaged with each other, but Lucien never lost his wariness now.

When he turned, she had arranged her face so there was no trace of the earlier bliss.

"Are we done?" she asked in a bored tone.

"My, but you are a selfish chit. I'm afraid I'm an adherent of the proverb 'All work and no play makes Jack a dull boy.' I'm ready to play. We have yet to relieve you of your virginity. If you have it."

"Of course I do, you horrible man. And I'd like to keep it, if it's all the same to you."

Lucien experienced a surprising sting. "You'll not be getting your annulment. I'm fully capable." But perhaps an alternate route would suffice—there would be no possibility of a little Ransford.

"Will you untie me now?"

No, it couldn't be done. He preferred his partners helpless. Perhaps he should reconsider gagging her, but he rather thought to kiss

those scornful lips at some point. But the blindfold—he wanted to see her eyes, see if she looked at him with any appreciation. He'd given her pleasure, no matter what she said.

She was a liar. A conniving wench who was now Lady Ransford, for his sins. But the eyes—they were windows to the soul, were they not?

He bent and fumbled with the knot, disarranging her dark curly hair, and tugged away the fabric. Maida glared at him, faint creases from the blindfold high on her flushed cheeks.

She sniffed in indignation. "I suppose you expect me to thank you."

"For what? The restoration of your sight or your orgasm?"

Her brows knit. "My what?"

Oh, dear Lord. Either she was a very good actress, or she was more ignorant than he imagined.

"*Le petit mort.* All those delicious waves within. You came apart for me. Don't deny it." He tasted her come on his tongue even now, and acknowledged to himself he was aching to fuck her despite her trickery. His reaction to her bound body was more than he had hoped for—she was exquisite in the firelight.

And his to do with what he wished. His *wife.*

"Oh." She blinked, her long eyelashes bent from their temporary prison. "I didn't know what happened to me at the end. Is that a usual occurrence?"

He smiled at the foolishness of this conversation. "If one is lucky."

"Did you tie me to make sure I stayed still for it?"

His smile vanished. "No. I tied you because it suits me. It *excites* me."

Her storm-sea eyes dropped to his cock, which poked out rudely from the gap in his robe.

"Oh," she repeated. Her pink tongue darted out as she gave a nervous lick to her lips.

That settled it.

"You will do to me what I did to you."

"I beg your pardon?"

"You will service me with your mouth."

"I—I have never—I can't—"

"Yes, you can. I'll teach you. I'll even untie you, more or less."

Lucien enjoyed the blatant shock on his wife's face. Perhaps he was being an even bigger fool than he had been three nights ago, when he slept through her assault to his bachelorhood. She had teeth, after all, quite pretty ones, small, white, and even. But his need was great and he was anxious to take himself away as soon as possible. A moment in her mouth would be more effective than if he chose to rut in her.

He untwisted the rope at the carved headboard and freed her arms, keeping the bonds around her wrists. She rubbed her hands before her, working plump fingers into the palms. "Will you not remove these bracelets, my lord?"

"Not yet. Sit up."

Maida struggled, her long hair falling down her back in a torrent of deep chocolate. She swayed a bit and he put an arm around her. "Normally, I'd prefer to have you on your knees, but I think this will do." Her legs were still wide and immobile, her cunt glistening, and he was aroused beyond measure.

Lucien shucked the robe, kneeled on the bed, placing a hand on her neck. "Bend and suck me."

She raised her eyes to his face. She really was a little bit of a thing, lovely with her cloud of dark hair and fresh skin.

"Will I still be a virgin?"

"Yes. I won't fuck you in the traditional way until we get to know each other a bit better." That was a sufficient sop to his dishonest bride.

"I am sorry, you know." His cock tingled with each warm expelled breath from every word spoken. "I had no idea—"

He gripped the back of her neck with more force. "That you married a monster?"

She shook her head. "I don't think you are a monster."

"Never tell me you like being bound and beaten."

She flushed, a wave of color washing down her chest. "It wasn't— It's not— It's not so bad."

Lucien lifted her chin. Her eyes were clear, no trace of tears or the stormy anger he'd seen earlier. His heart skipped.

"I want to explain. You've met my mother. You've seen what she's like."

He had indeed. A few minutes in Mrs. Clement's presence and he'd thought about poisoning her tea. Lucien could not imagine living with the woman on a day-to-day basis. Maybe Maida was justified in thinking that he was a better alternative.

But he wasn't.

"If you were looking to escape, I'm afraid you've gone from the frying pan into the fire."

"P-Perhaps I have. But I was very unhappy at home, so unhappy that I did a terrible, deceitful thing when I came into your room. I thought we could just have a convenient marriage, like everyone else. Be polite strangers. But you've been unhappy, too."

An understatement if there ever was one. "You have no idea."

"No, I don't," she said in a small voice. "You could tell me."

"True confessions? No time for them, Maida. If you haven't noticed, I'm randy as Pan."

Her lips turned up and her bound hands cupped his stones. "Oh, I noticed. You are rather noticeable, my lord. Quite beautiful."

It was Lucien's turn to color. "What kind of virgin are you?"

She stared into his eyes, a look of bemusement on her face. "A wicked one, I believe. I don't know much, Lucien. But you could show me."

He could. He suddenly found he wanted to rather badly. "I thought you had no interest in pleasing me."

"I misspoke."

His hands came to her throat and he tugged at the silk cord, tightening it. "I won't be kind. I can't be. I've tried."

She nodded, swallowing beneath the splice of roping. "Do your worst."

What kind of a game was she playing? If she was truly agreeable to his stark needs, his life might change and he wouldn't have to put a gun to his head in the near future. The thought of her plush white arse striped from the crop stiffened him into near-searing pain.

"Open your mouth and take me in."

It was over in seconds. The sweet heat of her untried mouth was his undoing. His hands tangled into her curls as she consumed him, offering no objection to the emission of his seed. Her dark lashes had fluttered a bit at first but she didn't pause, and for that alone he knew he had to keep her.

Ridiculous. She had tricked him—had ruined his life.

Or would she be the making of it?

Four

— ◆ —

Extraordinary. Impossible. She, plain Maida Clement—well, Maida Ransford now—had power over this beautiful, tortured man. She wouldn't fool herself to think she'd make him love her—that would be quite outside the boundaries of her capability—but he seemed inordinately attracted to her.

As long as she was tied and helpless.

And what was the harm in that? It actually gave her a frisson of desire to be at his mercy. Her submission was a relief from constantly trying to think and plan and outwit. She need do nothing but receive.

And in receiving, she gave him something—a sort of peace permeated him now. The lines on his face and the tension from his body had eased. Lucien had collapsed onto the bed and taken her with him, and she was now nestled in his arms, her bound hands still forbidden to stroke him as he stroked her.

But he had not kissed her yet, and Maida very much wanted him to.

He thought he was a monster. Oh, no, he was not that—he might be peculiar, but his peculiarity did not trouble her. She could bear his discipline, because she knew somehow he would never go too far. At heart—even if he didn't think he had one—Lucien Ransford was a hero.

She'd heard of his exploits. His imprisonment. Someday she

might get him to talk about it, but tonight she wanted not words, but action.

She cleared her throat, still tasting his essence. "I've changed my mind."

"No annulment. We've gone too far," he mumbled into the top of her head.

"But not far enough. Will you . . . fuck me, Lucien?"

He laughed, the first honest laugh she'd heard from him since this wretched house party began. "You overestimate me, my dear. Give me half an hour and you just may get your wish."

Half an hour seemed an eon. Her wet passage clenched as she imagined his shaft replacing his tongue.

"Kiss me then."

He arched a dark gold brow. "Why?"

"Because . . . you should."

"There are many things I should do. Convince me." He flopped back onto the bed and she twisted toward him, her heavy breasts brushing against his side. She wished she could crawl atop him, but her legs were unfortunately still tethered.

She sighed. "I've never been properly kissed."

"There's nothing proper about me, Maida."

"Oh, do stop demonizing yourself! You are hardly the spawn of Satan. You are just . . . a bit unconventional."

Another laugh—delicious, rumbling. His gray eyes gleamed silver. "You are a constant surprise. I believe I should be happy you invaded my bedchamber."

"I said I was sorry for that, but in a way, I'm not. This is . . . You are . . . I quite like it all."

"Do you?" he asked softly.

"I do." The second time she had spoken those two words today, and she meant them this time. Lucien Ransford did something to her insides that was inexplicably wicked.

And welcome. Maida felt alive—like a *woman*—for the first time in her life.

He toyed with the cording at her throat, wrapping the ends around his long fingers. "This is not a game to me, you know. I have a need to . . . to control. To punish."

She did know. There was a darkness in him that was almost palpable, despite his golden good looks. He suffered, and this marriage would never be easy. Would not be what a well-brought-up young woman expected or possibly even deserved.

But she didn't care right now, only knew that she wanted his mouth on hers, dominating, demanding her surrender. He had it, even at a distance.

"Kiss me, Lucien."

And then he did, a kiss at first so sweet and feather light that she couldn't credit it. But it was not long before he withdrew and pulled her arms back over her head, lashing her to the bed. His large hands weighed her breasts and pressed her nipples almost painfully between his fingers. She ached as he suckled and nipped, working his way back up to her throat, surrounding the corded necklace with savage kisses. She would bear his marks with pride—he needed her, needed *this*, and she would make sure he got what he needed.

And God help her, she needed it, too.

When he entered her, she was more than ready. The brief moment of difficulty was secondary to her satisfaction that he was seated within her, *hers*. Their eyes locked as he strained above her, pushing himself ever deeper with each thrust. Her bare skin sang in response as he crushed her beneath him to kiss her everywhere again—her eyelids, her temple, her nose. He captured her lips, conquering her cry as he poured himself into her, flooding her, *fucking* her.

When it was over, they lay heart to heart as the November wind howled and rain rattled the ancient windowpanes. Their wedding night was nearly over. Whatever their future held, Maida would

never regret tonight. If this was punishment, she planned to be very bad again as soon as possible.

Lucien rolled away, and to Maida's dismay, left the bed to rummage in his trunk again. She wondered what he'd find this time.

Oh dear. A knife.

But he merely cut the cords that bound her.

"Thank you." She was too lazy with lust to see if her limbs still worked, so she lay in the bed, hoping for her husband's return to it. He paused over her, his face shadowed.

"I'll leave you now."

Maida scrambled up and clasped his hand. "Oh, no! Please don't go."

A muscle twitched in his jaw. "I must. I don't sleep well."

"Then we needn't sleep. We can talk. And do other things." She really couldn't wait to do those other things, she thought ruefully.

She watched him struggle with the thought of staying. The tension had returned to his lean, battered body. Despite the web of scars, he was magnificent. Maida longed to kiss them, just as he'd done to her.

"All right."

And it *would* be all right. Somehow they would make this marriage that began so badly work, one word, one knot, one kiss at a time.

Margaret Rowe is a former teacher, library clerk, and mother of four who woke up in the middle of the night and felt absolutely compelled to create the perfect man and use as many adverbs as possible doing so. A transplanted New Yorker, she lives with her not-quite-perfect husband in Maine, where the cold winters are ideal for staying inside and writing hot historical romances. For more information, please visit www.margaretrowe.net.

SHAMELESS

Edie Harris

PHILADELPHIA, 1859

The corset helped.

Her lover, James Pierpont, lounged carelessly next to her in the second-level opera box, his attention firmly fixed on the soprano floating across the stage. "*La traviata*," he had declared before the curtain rose, "is a good lesson for you, Caro. Pay attention." He then proceeded to ignore her.

So the corset, forcing her posture to mimic attentiveness, helped.

Though Caro's understanding of Italian was limited, she understood the opera's general story: A courtesan falls in love, is forced to leave her lover, and subsequently dies.

Lucky woman.

Once a week, she attended the opera on James's arm. It didn't matter if they'd seen the production before; on Saturday evenings, like clockwork, his carriage would roll up to her modest townhouse, whisking them both to Broad Street for a night of music.

In theory, these public outings should have been romantic. The golden glow from the gas-lit chandelier, plush red velvet everywhere she looked, and the obscenely wealthy man responsible for her silk gown and glittering diamond earrings at her side—combined, these elements should have set her heart all aflutter.

Her stomach roiled with shame.

Caro's mother, the estimable Mrs. Davis, had died ten months earlier, secure in the knowledge that her affianced daughter would march down the aisle and become a respectable young matron. But as soon as Mrs. Davis found her final resting place, Caro smothered her grief in the arms of her fiancé. Out of wedlock. And without the estimable Mrs. Davis looking out for her only kin, Caro remained decidedly out of wedlock.

She'd never become Mrs. Pierpont; instead, she was Mr. Pierpont's mistress.

Now, pressing a hand to quell her aching abdomen, Caro watched the first act come to a close, the soprano now center stage, her face alive in the footlights with her arms outstretched. From James's box, Caro could see into the far wing, where the stagehands waited to draw the curtains. As her gaze delved the dark corner, a tall figure seemed to materialize in the shadows, leaning against the ivory column marking the edge of the proscenium.

He simply stood there, a faceless entity on a stage that must be blisteringly hot. The soprano bustled past him, but he didn't move. The conductor brought the orchestra to a halt, and he still didn't move. Applause pulsed against her eardrums, but he gave no sign of noticing it. She sensed James stand and exit the box, but she remained seated, her wrist aching as she fanned herself with a delicate contraption of stiff lace and polished bone that matched her dress perfectly.

Caught. She felt trapped as she stared at the shadowed man. She would turn away. She *would.* Any second now.

Finally, when the tightly laced corset no longer seemed like such a blessing, he stepped forward. Probably no more than an inch or two, but suddenly the chandelier's crystallized light illuminated his features.

It also illuminated the fact that his gaze was locked on her.

Unable to help herself, Caro leaned forward, dropping her fan to rest both hands against the polished railing. He wore simple cloth-

ing, simpler than most stagehands: dark wool trousers, a thin cotton undershirt rolled up to his elbows, heavy boots, and loose suspenders. His lack of attire highlighted his broad shoulders and thick musculature, very unlike James's, she thought. Her lover was considered quite handsome, with his slender build and strikingly dark coloring.

This man, however, had close-cropped blond hair and dark eyes. His face would never be thought of as handsome, but the defined angles and broad planes worked together to create a craggy sort of appeal. That appeal, coupled with his undeniable masculinity, called to her body in a way James never had.

What does that mean?

Her trance broke when a firm hand settled on her shoulder. She looked up at her former fiancé, unable to muster her customary smile. Blue eyes gazed down into hers, their gleam growing colder with each passing moment. Lean fingers tightened until she felt his nails dig into the exposed flesh at her collarbone.

Stifling a wince, she turned back to glance at the blond man.

He was gone.

"After the performance, I'll be heading backstage." A weighted pause filled the opera box. "To pay my respects to Miss Lorenzo," he murmured, naming the soprano.

Caro didn't react. She'd known it would happen, from the moment he had mentioned his aversion to marriage nine months ago. That he'd mentioned this after spilling himself inside her didn't seem to bother him. In that instant, Caro hated him—more, she'd hated herself.

"What would you like me to do?" she asked softly, eyes trained on the dark corner where she'd first seen the blond man.

"Take the carriage, go home." The words rang with damning finality.

They didn't speak again. Not during the second act, nor the second intermission, and certainly not when Miss Lorenzo died in the

arms of the long-haired tenor playing her true love. When James jumped to his feet at the close of the curtain, clapping madly, all Caro could think was, *Lucky woman.*

She remained in the box long after James left, wondering if the unhappiness churning in her gut had more to do with anger at being thrown over or worry over the future of her situation. Her options were so limited: find another "protector"—how she sneered at the word!—or leave Philadelphia. No matter her respectable upbringing, society now knew her to be a fallen woman.

She wished she could lay the blame entirely at James's feet, but she had been the one to ask him to make love to her the afternoon of her mother's funeral. She was the architect of her reputation's demise; James merely played opposite her, much like Miss Lorenzo's tenor.

Sitting here wasn't doing her any favors, so she stood, collecting her fan from the floor, holding her breath as her corset compressed her ribs to the point of pain. Every one of her senses felt drenched in a dull lethargy as she glanced once more at the shadowed wing that housed the curtain pulls.

And there he was, leaning against a Corinthian-style column as he stared into the box.

Caro froze.

Everything in his posture screamed of capable confidence; in her current state, his poise pulled her as surely as if he'd tied a rope around her waist and tugged. Some unidentifiable sensation simmered beneath her stays as she steadily met his gaze from fifty feet away.

A minute tilt of his head indicated the darkened corner at his back, and he lifted a brow in question. He wanted her to . . . to meet him backstage? Caro stopped breathing.

The small quirk of a smile stretching his lips decided her. Before she could think better of it, she smoothed a hand over the bell

of her skirts and swept out of James Pierpont's opera box for the last time.

She must have stayed in the concert hall longer than she'd realized, because the second-floor lobby stood empty. The heels of her evening slippers clacked loudly as she hurried across the varnished wooden floorboards. A small door at the lobby's rear led down a curving stair, and though she didn't know where she was going, her body drew her unerringly toward the stage.

One heavy-paneled door stood between her and the wings. Patting a hand over her nerve-riddled stomach, she pushed it open.

After all, I have nothing left to lose.

A few stagehands loitered among the brightly painted set pieces, but she didn't see the blond man anywhere. Not sparing a moment for self-doubt or recriminations, she wandered along the back wall, amongst the pulleys and chairs and barely avoiding a rack of sparkling costumes that appeared out of thin air in front of her. Small boys with arms overloaded rushed past her as if she were invisible.

Caro rather thought she liked being invisible.

By the time she made her way into the left wing, after nearly knocking her head on a wall-mounted ladder, Caro was convinced the blond man had left, that she'd misread his nod and his smile and the way he watched her. Flipping open her fan, she basked in the cool air wafting over her face as she studied the vast, almost-abandoned stage to her left.

"What's your name?"

She whirled around, snapping the fan closed and brandishing it in front of her, saber-like.

The blond man laughed, a rusty sound that heated her recently cooled skin as quickly as if she'd been doused in flames. "Easy. Didn't mean to startle you." His voice carried the hint of a foreign accent.

"I wasn't startled," she muttered, lowering her makeshift weapon. "I thought you'd left." Her tone was accusatory.

"I wouldn't leave." He crossed his thick forearms over his wide chest, and her gaze strayed to the muscles delineated there. "What's your name?" he asked again.

"Caroline Davis."

A single gas lamp lit their corner, the ropes of the curtain's pulley system throwing line after line of shadow across the man's face. They stood behind a black half-curtain, shielded from view on three sides but open to the main stage. In the low lighting, she could see his eyes were a deep, clear brown, the color of rich liquor in a cut-crystal tumbler.

"Thomas Vaughn," he murmured in that husky voice of his. He couldn't be a singer, not with those smoky vocal chords.

How did one go about this, the impetuous assignation? Caro felt herself coloring the longer they stared silently at each other. She had made a mistake. She should go, *now*, and—

"I saw the man you were with."

"What?"

"The man with you, during the show. I saw him come backstage."

Her blush consumed her. "Ah. Yes. He, uh, wanted to see Miss Lorenzo."

"And left you alone?" His tone conveyed his disapproval.

One of the good things about assignations with complete strangers, Caro decided, was that she could ignore polite constraints and be perfectly honest. "We've ended our liaison. As of tonight."

He leaned back against the taut ropes. "He's a fool, then."

"No more a fool than I." She shrugged, the short sleeves of her gown falling off her shoulders at the careless movement. His eyes immediately flitted to her newly revealed skin. Suddenly, she wanted to remove the dress in its entirety, simply to see what he'd do. "Are you one of the hands?"

He shook his head. "No. The choreographer."

She felt her eyes go wide. "You're a dancer?"

A quiet bark of laughter greeted her incredulous question. "I choreograph the fight scenes. I'm the company's combat master."

Which meant he would leave when the troupe moved on. *Perfect ... Wasn't it?*

He uncrossed his arms, reaching out to trace the curve of her collarbone. "I saw him hurt you." Every pass of his roughened fingertip over her skin made her shiver.

"So?" She didn't care what he'd seen, didn't care what he thought. She just wanted the anger still heating her blood to go away. And she desperately wanted a reprieve from having to make a decision about her future, if only for a short while.

"Is that why you're here? Because you enjoy being hurt?"

"What? No!" His question perplexed her, made her wary.

His shrug caused the suspenders to dig tightly into his brawny shoulders. "Some women like rougher men."

"Is that what you are?" James had never been violent with her. Only quick. "A rough man?" Saying the words had a singularly interesting effect on her body: wetness dampened the apex of her thighs and her mouth went dry. She licked her lips.

His finger dipped to edge of her neckline, skating across the plumped tops of her breasts. Hooking that finger into the top of her bodice, he pulled, yanking her two fumbling steps forward until a scant inch separated his chest from hers. "Yes."

"Yes, what?" she breathed, having lost her train of thought at his nearness. Heat pulsed off him, causing sweat to bead at her temples. Her body had never reacted this strongly, this sexually, to anyone before, and it both thrilled and terrified her.

Vaughn leaned in until his lips hovered next to her ear. "Yes, I'm a rough man," he whispered, his nearness making her nipples bead within the tight confines of her undergarments. "And you're an angry woman."

His tongue darted out to trace the shell of her ear, and a strangled

sound escaped her, though her emotions from the evening were still too tumultuous to make room for something so impractical as embarrassment. "I *am* angry," she whispered back, as honest as before.

His mouth, open and blistering, skimmed over her jaw until their lips met. It wasn't a kiss so much as one gentle brush after another, mouth against mouth. His tongue wet her lower lip, then caught it between his teeth. The nip made her gasp, and he slanted his mouth over hers, delving in and tasting her.

She met him stroke for stroke, open and oh, so willing to let him kiss her until she forgot James and the shame she feared would haunt her eternally. Though they touched nowhere other than their mouths and where his calloused finger rested between her breasts, she felt him imprinted on every pore as he took her tongue in a daring dance that left them both panting.

Perhaps the man is a choreographer, after all.

Abruptly, he pulled back, lips swollen from their assault on hers.

"Hit me," he commanded, husky.

She blinked, certain she'd misheard him.

He wrapped his wrists around the curtain pulls, effectively trapping himself in the thick cord of two ropes. With arms splayed above his head, he widened his stance and eyed her with an arrogant gleam. "I said, hit me."

His gaze and tone rankled. "No," she snapped, stepping back. "I don't know what it is you think I want, or what it is *you* want, but I won't hit you."

"Your lover threw you over tonight. For a woman who won't even be in Philadelphia past next week." Each word felt like a slap, and she bit the inside of her lip to avoid flinching as he continued in a quietly mocking voice. "He left you in your box to go to her, while you were still in the building. He's probably fucking her right now."

The fan snapped in her hand. "I don't care."

"If we're quiet enough, I'd wager we'd hear her cries."

Her fingers flexed, and she realized she *wanted* to hit him. Hit Vaughn, this complete stranger who made her ache, both physically and emotionally.

Yes, she would hit him, if only to stop his goading, to wipe that smug look off his compelling face. *This isn't you*, her conscience whispered.

Caro ignored her conscience.

Letting the broken fan clatter to the floor, she balled her right hand into a fist and drove it into his stomach. His hard, unyielding stomach.

Pain immediately shot up her forearm, and she hissed, shaking her hand in an effort to hurry the sharp discomfort away. Taking a second to glance up at him, she noted the way his chest rose and fell, as if he couldn't quite catch his breath. She glared at him. "Happy?"

He shook his head, not releasing his grip on the ropes. "You can hurt me without hurting yourself. Curl your fingers in, and wrap your thumb . . . Yes, just like that." He sounded eager.

She was surprised to find herself following his directions, but more intrigued by the way he stood before her, like a top wound too tight. *He truly wants me to hit him.* It didn't seem fair, though, that he should receive pain with her feeling nothing.

"Keep your wrist firm or you'll break your fingers."

All right, so she didn't want *that*, but still. "Why won't you let me hurt?"

"Because it doesn't get you hot." He paused. "Or does it?"

Why not be honest? "Right now . . . I like my anger. It makes me tingle, feel alive." And if she stayed angry, she could drown the shame dogging her every step.

His eyelids drooped until long lashes cast shadows across his high cheekbones. After darting out the tip of his tongue to re-wet his bottom lip, he murmured, "Every time a woman hits me, I get that tingle. I feel alive. And hard."

She risked a quick glance at his groin; her thighs clenched when she saw the way his erection pushed greedily against the rough wool of his trousers. "So." The word was breathy, too breathy, and she cleared her throat before continuing, "You want me to hit you?"

He nodded, his brown eyes never leaving her face.

"Where? In the stomach?" To test him, and herself, she let her fisted knuckles gently brush his hard abdomen. When he sucked in a breath but remained silent, she moved her hand upward. "Or maybe the shoulder?"

The muscles beneath her fingers tightened.

"No? How about . . ." Slowly, so slowly, she trailed her fist down the taut length of his torso, over one jutting hipbone, until she could press firmly against his upper thigh. "Here?"

Every part of him trembled, but he didn't say a word.

Power, sensual and heady and absolutely exhilarating, coursed through her. Unable to keep a grin off her lips, she smiled at him and moved her fist up and in, placing it on the sensitive tendon below his groin. She kneaded his inner thigh with the backs of her fingers, and he gasped.

What a delicious sound. "Now?"

"Y—" He broke off with a groan when she punched him. She imagined the way shocks of pain would zing up and down his leg to curdle in his gut. She imagined the vulnerability of his bruised thigh and how, maybe, if she held her wrist firm, she could deliver a hard enough hit to leave him dangling in the curtain pull.

And because the thought made her angry, she jammed her fist against the spot again.

She heard him grit his teeth, heard the moan caught in the back of his mouth. His legs wobbled, and she watched his hands grip the cords over his head. Muscles strained against the slim sleeves of his cotton undershirt as he fought to keep his knees from buckling.

Still, anger simmered in her chest, making her breathing choppy

and uneven. "Did you like that?" she asked, unable to strike the bitterness from her tone.

"Y-Yes," he mumbled. His eyes had closed the moment she'd hit him. Now, those warm whiskey-brown irises focused on her, flitting from her breasts to her lips to finally settle on her eyes. "Did you?"

No! she wanted to shout. No, she didn't enjoy acting like an animal. Or like a man, for that matter. She didn't appreciate the fact that she'd felt relief the moment she planted her fist in his leg—a relief from the impotent anger pounding her down tonight.

No! she wanted to shout, because in the second she'd caused him pain, she felt her own lift and a lightness-of-being flash through her very core.

But damned if she'd allow Thomas Vaughn, an opera company's combat master from God knows where, to turn her into a liar.

"Yes. Yes, I liked it."

"Did you—" He broke off when his voice cracked. "Did you hurt yourself?"

She flexed her fingers, breaking their gaze to eye her wrist. "No." A burst of pride flooded her, warmed her.

"You can hit me again. You can hit me anytime you'd like."

Scowling, she lightly punched his shoulder. "I don't like that I enjoyed hitting you." Again, for a split second, she felt powerful and weightless as her fist connected with his body. He grunted in appreciation, catching his bottom lip between strong, straight teeth.

"But when you hit me, you stop being angry." He took a step forward until his arms stretched back to where he still gripped the ropes. Her heart stuttered at his nearness. "Do it again. Do it until you're not angry anymore."

Caro didn't stop to think—she simply let her hands deliver glancing blows into his torso. Every time she hit him, he moaned; every time he moaned, she grew wetter. With each punch, she inched closer, until her breasts were mashed against his chest and her fists

simply pressed into his sides. She gasped as his hips thrust forward into her skirts.

Light-headedness swept over her, enhancing the soaring emancipation she felt with each press of her body against his. "I c-can't breathe," she stuttered out, flattening her palms to run them over his heaving chest. Her fingers traced the grooves of each muscle, his body delighting her even through his clothing.

His hands slithered down the ropes. "Turn around." Deft fingers slid the buttons of her gown from their holes and dug into the lacing of her corset. She yanked her arms from the sleeves of her gown as he tugged loose her stays, then tossed the stiff garment aside when it drooped forward.

She spun to face him, trying not to trip in the massive pool of silk at her feet. His hands dove for her waist, and her crinoline soon joined the skirts it once shaped on the floor. Toughened fingers rid her of the delicate chemisette and pantaloons, until she stood before him in nothing but stockings, garters, and low-heeled evening slippers.

A burst of air chilled her overheated skin, and she shivered.

"Caroline," he murmured, blatant appreciation coloring his voice.

"Caro," she corrected with a mumble. She refused to acknowledge the disadvantage at which he had her, clothed modesty to stark nudity. "I—"

But she didn't have the chance to say anything more, because his mouth covered hers. Every hint of gentleness was gone as he crushed her to him. She reveled at the steely strength of his arms as they banded around her, one hand cupping the back of her head, the other sliding sinuously down her spine until he reached her buttocks. His fingers delved the cleft until he found her slick entrance. Without warning, he shoved two fingers into her tight channel.

She writhed.

"Caro," he groaned against her mouth. "You're so wet."

His fingers thrust in and out, twining together inside her with each decisive jerk of his wrist. Her sex throbbed around him; she'd never been so close to orgasm with so little effort from her partner. "Mr. Vaughn . . . Thomas . . ." She didn't know what to call him.

"Vaughn."

Their teeth scraped as he tried to get a deeper taste of her mouth, but she tore her lips from his, leaving him gasping in protest. She needed her tongue on his skin, needed a taste of his body as he repeatedly invaded hers.

His only exposed skin was at his throat, so she sank her teeth into the tendon connecting his neck and shoulder. She bit *hard*, and he groaned, holding her head in place as she laved the sting of her bite with soothing strokes of her tongue. He tasted of salt and sweat; she shuddered with want, feeling herself grow even wetter.

Vaughn sensed her excitement and withdrew his fingers from her dripping sex. Using the hand at her nape, he pulled her back to meet his eyes. Slowly, deliberately, he sucked his glistening fingers into his mouth. She watched him erotically lick his skin clean until she knew her legs wouldn't hold her upright much longer.

She yanked his fingers from his mouth and drew them into her own, letting the musky sweetness still lingering on them heighten her arousal. She used one hand to fumble at the waist of his trousers, wanting to see him. Taste him. Impale herself upon him.

"I've got it," he grunted, brushing her hand away and pulling his fingers from between her lips with an audible popping sound. Most of his actions were hidden in the shadows cast by the solitary sconce, but soon enough his erection slapped against her belly, heavy and burning hot against her soft skin.

Kneeling in the lake of silk currently crushed beneath their feet, she gripped him hard in one hand, admiring the length and thickness of him. "Beautiful," she whispered as she brought the head to her lips.

"You like my cock?" One hand tangled in her loosened coiffure, tightening in the tangled mass to hold her in place; his other hand circled the base of his shaft.

"Mmm." She licked him, and here was the saltier tang she'd so desired. Swirling her tongue around the throbbing head, she moaned hungrily. Unable to even contemplate seducing him slowly at this point, she immediately bobbed forward to swallow as much of his length as possible.

"Caro. Fuck, love, that's the way." He rocked his hips until the head of his cock touched her throat. "Take it all."

She did. Concentrating on opening to him, she coaxed him in with warm, rhythmic contractions of her throat muscles. Her clit ached to be touched, so she snaked a hand through the curls between her thighs to rub the swollen nub. Whimpers escaped her as she sucked at him, marveling at how this act, with this *man*, could turn her body completely liquid.

His hand clenched in her hair, causing her to accidentally scrape his silky shaft with her teeth. He gave a yell, his only warning before hot seed shot down her throat. She drew her lips to the head of his cock, suckling hard as spurt after spurt landed on her tongue, filling her mouth with his come.

Before he could go completely soft, he dragged her from her knees, hooking his big hands beneath her arms and hauling her against him until they were nose to nose. She worked to swallow the remnants of his seed still lacing her tongue, but he kissed her open-mouthed, demanding entry. His tongue lapped at hers, certainly tasting himself there as she arched her body into his. God, she needed release, and she needed it *now*.

Recognizing the insistent call of her body, he flipped their positions until it was *her* back against the system of curtain pulls. "Hold tight."

As he cupped her buttocks in both hands, keeping her aloft, she twisted the rope around her wrists as she'd seen him do earlier. The cording abraded her skin, and perhaps Caro understood what Vaughn meant about pain, at least a little bit—the sting did nothing to cool her passion; if anything, her pain was like the oil necessary to turn a bonfire into an inferno.

The head of his cock, stiff again, teased her entrance. "Vaughn!" She'd never been reduced to this level of uninhibited wanting, never thought it possible.

"Tell me, Caro, are you angry now?"

"N-No." And she wasn't. Even the shame wasn't there: just that precious, freeing power she'd tasted while hitting him.

One sure thrust of his hips had him inside her, filled and stretched. She cried out, squeezing his hips between her thighs as he pounded into her sex. "Such a sweet cunt, Caro," he ground out, closing his lips over the nipple of one bouncing breast.

The sound of flesh slapping against wet flesh echoed in the confines of the corner, the curtains doing nothing to dampen the easily recognizable noises. Not that Caro cared whether anyone heard—all that mattered was keeping Vaughn deep inside her, because nothing, *nothing*, had ever felt this good.

"A little rough?" he groaned, his tongue stroking her sensitive areola as he spoke. His fingers gripped her hips so fiercely she knew she'd bear bruises in the morning.

She could do nothing but nod her assent, feeling her body coil in preparation for orgasm. He bit her nipple, those strong teeth of his coming down hard and sending a shock of pain straight through her belly to explode in her clitoris.

Caro came on a keening wail, trembling, clutching the ropes with all her strength as she clenched around Vaughn. Three more thrusts, and he'd followed her over the blissful precipice. In the midst of her

ecstasy, she acknowledged the tenuous connection between them, that this stranger made her believe herself whole. The feel of his second orgasm hitting the walls of her womb sent fireworks of sensation coursing over her skin in the most delightful aftershock of her life.

When nothing but their harsh breathing filled her ears, Caro released the curtain pulls to link her arms behind his neck, allowing him to lower her to the ground. The slide down his still-clothed muscular body made her tingle, her sex contracting though his cock no longer filled her.

For a quiet minute, she simply stood in the circle of his arms, her forehead pressed against his heaving chest. His heartbeat thudded steadily, if a little quickly, and she knew her own matched it. "Thank you." His undershirt muffled her voice.

"For?"

Honesty, she reminded herself. "I don't always like who I am, but this, with you . . . It made me forget." A rush of tenderness had her nuzzling his chest.

Shockingly, his arms tightened around her, turning their embrace from intimate to genuinely affectionate. "Before I became the fight choreographer here, I was a bruiser, for entertainment and for hire. The man who gave me this job found me in a pub after a fight and said something I'll never forget." He paused, his heart slowing beneath her cheek as she contemplated snuggling deeper into his hold. "'Man can endure pain, but shame? Shame will break him.'"

With a sigh, Caro extricated herself from the warmth of his strong arms. "Wise words."

He shrugged. "It's the truth. If you're ashamed, Caro, you'll break."

"Is that what I did tonight? Break?"

"No," he murmured, his gaze warm as it met hers. "You endured."

As she stood there, breathing in the scents of their passion, she searched her soul for shame . . . and found none.

Endure? "Yes." She smiled up at him. "Yes, I did."

Edie Harris studied English and Creative Writing at the University of Iowa. She is a professionally produced play-wright, a private voice instructor, and an avid reader/tweeter/blogger. Living and working in the Midwest, she is a member of Romance Writers of America. Stop by her website, www.edieharris.com.

TAKEN

Rebecca Lange

Myriam had not felt a man's hands on her since her husband died. Not from hostility but lack of interest and interesting opportunity. Even after she moved in with her brother and his wife, the glancing, respectful touches and groomed reserve of her nephews left her barely able to remember the last time she felt the weight of a man's body pressed against her. She chose not to count the randy attempts several of the older men in the village had made—a few well-placed gropes and some not so coincidental body brushes—because she had not really been tempted to anything more since Tobias's death.

Until now. Until this man with his bronze skin gleaming in the firelight and black eyes glowing with an almost demonic brightness. It was perverse, even cruel, this wanting to reach out and touch his long, thick hair. Would it be coarse, like a horse's tail, or smooth, like her own dark locks? Would his muscles feel as hard as they looked? She let herself imagine, just for a moment, reaching out to touch the skin of his thigh visible between breechcloth and leggings, the sinews there that helped him to move so quietly and gracefully. She knew his skin would taste salty, from the way the fire drew its moisture to the surface, and as her tongue reflexively ventured out past her own lips, he lifted his head, sensing, somehow, where her thoughts were at that moment. It was another one of those cues that he was different, strange even, in ways that both drew in her curiosity in and frightened away her sense.

Something was going to happen; she could feel it gather in her throat like a cough, a thickening of the air around her, and a terrible, terrible waiting.

Hiro knew that if he did not act now, he would not have another chance. The past days had not seemed to reassure her, and he knew her anxiety was about to surface again. She was not like most of her people. Her skin, while much lighter than his, was not that sickly pale of an unhealthy woman, but a light golden color, a perfect complement to her dark hair and eyes that changed color depending on the light—sometimes brown, sometimes gray, and, when she seemed to go away in her mind, blue like the sky right before a thunderstorm. Not small-boned or breasted, she would bear children well, and the way she tossed back the long, heavy shanks of her hair, long-ago loosed from its fastenings, told him she was experienced with a man. He knew she wanted him. At least, she wanted his body. And he had wanted her, all of her, the moment he laid eyes on her in the settlement.

Few words might have passed between them over the past five days, but their bodies, finally, were in complete harmony. Not the melancholy wanting of the flute's song, but rather the darker, more complex rhythm of the war drum—the steady percussion of blood seeking its destiny in either life or death. Tonight it was going to be life.

With the echo of that drum propelling from his squat on the ground, Hiro started to draw around the fire toward her. The fineness of her skin, the slenderness of her wrists, the trembling beneath her skin all beat in his blood and his cock, and as her tumultuous gaze moved across his own rough, sweaty skin, he knew himself captivated. If the touching was as powerful as the looking, he could finally be certain of his choice to take her as his wife. And then she could finally feel safe, as well, her own blood bound to his, her security better assured with him than her own people.

As Myriam watched him rise, the long tail of ebon hair scraping over his broad, bare shoulders and back, she did not know whether it was fear or desire that trembled under her skin. For a moment he just stood and looked at her, acknowledging her shaking with a small sigh and the hesitancy of a difficult decision. A glance away, a look back, straight into her face, his gaze so piercing she stopped shaking as if on command. Witchcraft. He must be a powerful magician among these people.

And yet, when he moved again and brought himself down next to her, almost touching her leg with his own thigh, he seemed very much a man. A tall, muscled, almost graceful man, smelling of peat and smoke and sweat, and the peppery combination shocked her nose, which did not, strangely, object to the combination. It had been so very long since she had been interested in the smell of a man, so long since her body acknowledged its own desire for those sensations. Fear must have heightened her senses; that was the only explanation. That, and the witchcraft, of course. Still, when he was sliding down next to her, she wanted so badly to reach up to his solemn face, to find out if his lips were as soft as her bewitched body knew they would be.

Which is when she remembered her bound hands. A hysterical bubble of sound pushed past the terror clogging her throat as she raised her bloody, chafed wrists, first up to her face, so she could witness her own self-treachery, and then over her head like a club, awareness of what was about to happen pushing her desires in an entirely different direction.

HIRO felt badly about her skin, hated the look of her bloody wrists and the hopefully temporary need to keep her bound, but she had no idea why she was here—that the clan had brought her to him to replace his wife, lost in last winter's raid. Until she trusted that they were not going to hurt her, that, in fact, she would live a much better,

freer life among his people, that she would be the strong, beautiful mother of his children, he had no easy way of making her understand and accept that . . . yet.

But if he did not act now, she was going to try something desperate, and then he would likely end up hurting her even more in trying to retrieve her and hold her safe from things far more dangerous than she could presently imagine. She had no idea how dangerous her little settlement had become, how his enemies were only a day behind his hunting party. Should they have taken her and her people, she would be nothing more than a war prize, a pawn played between greedy nations. If he could not persuade her of that with words, he would find another way to subdue her. He knew several places on the body that would induce her to sleep if touched just the right way. He didn't want to harm her any more than she had already been hurt, but there was such a tension in his body, an aggressive need to do something to stop her from looking at him with so much confused fear and desire, he did not know how long he could hold himself back if she tried to fight him.

MYRIAM recognized the look in his eyes and knew she should fight to the death before this man, this *savage*, had even one moment of dominion over her body. What kind of man could inflict himself like that on a woman, could feed off her vulnerability and fear, and make her an empty vessel for his unholy lust? Now it was clear why he had been so patient with her over the past few days, why even the women refused to subdue her beyond binding her and keeping her restricted to one of the strangely long houses in the camp. She should have known their current isolation was calculated so that this man could have his way with her. How dare they try to wear her down with such false kindness. No, no, no, this was not going to happen to her, even if she did not survive the escape.

When she saw his hand reach out toward her leg, she understood that she had only a second to make up her mind about where to strike. She may not have shoes, but she still had feet, and there were plenty of soft places on a man's body where she could make him hurt long enough to scramble out of range.

Hiro knew, the moment his cock began pulsing in awareness of her proximity, that she was going to try something foolish, and that he could not let her succeed. But he was still a second too late when her foot shot out from under her skirt, straight into his groin. Boom! The pulsing quickened to a warning beat, the pain shooting into his back and legs, the automatic curl of his body the only thing that kept her from being able to pull away from him. Instead he ungracefully fell on top of her, her bound arms swinging in front of her and her hair whipping around her face while she thrashed.

Down, down, down he pushed her into the pallet, using the weight of his body and the heaviness of the pain she laid on him to hold her down, if not still, at least subdued by his almost dead weight.

Even as Hiro lay heaving on top of her, Myriam knew she had lost her chance. The shock of his body all along hers seized up every muscle, but she could neither stretch out nor curl up to get relief. Her breath came in shallow, panting bursts, her breasts crushed against his naked chest, the stiff whalebone of her stays offering no protection from the heat of his body, let alone whatever retribution he intended. So when he brought his hand up to her cheek, she anticipated the blow by closing her eyes and imagining her skin an iron mask.

At first there was nothing, and Myriam squeezed her eyes more tightly closed, hoping it was all a bad dream. Maybe she had been drugged by the gamey stew they gave her for supper. That might account for the horrible thoughts she had been having earlier about her captor's body. Then came the lightest touch on her face, and the shock of his fingers gently grazing her cheek was far worse than any

blow. The soft gentleness of his touch shot an excruciating pain into her chest and shaking through her whole body. Oh, God, it was real, after all.

Across her startled mouth his fingertips moved, charting the distance with such care she could only hiccup on the taste and the smell of him. Hiro knew he had shocked her, and he moved quickly in that second before she could strike again to keep her distracted and hopefully draw her attention to other needs her body had.

MYRIAM could not prevent the tears from coming, nor could she stop them, as her bound hands were trapped on her belly, which was shuddering uncontrollably against her captor's bare abdomen. They forced her to open her eyes, which made everything more frustratingly real. She could feel her body surrendering, and she had no idea how to fight it. The mix of fear and desire in her body set her teeth to chattering, the snap, snap, snapping of her jaw only a mild annoyance compared to the torture of this man's soft attentions to her face.

His eyes were not so dark as she first thought, although the desire that flared through those umber irises was surely the devil's fire. For the first time in five days she was grateful she could not move her arms, because she knew they would betray her without qualm, so overwhelming was the need to feel the soft tickle of his dark lashes against her searching fingers. His lips were moist too, and surprisingly pink, matching the color that gathered across his arched cheekbones. Oh, God, what was happening to her—what was this terrible game he was playing with her?

Before she could close her eyes against her body's obvious desire, Hiro slowly crossed the seam of her lips with the tip of his own tongue, the rough surface catching on her dry mouth until he could slip underneath to the wetter, slicker inside of her upper lip.

Every thought Hiro could muster was focused on her delicious,

terrified mouth, and as he pressed into the rest of her body he knew, somewhere behind all the lust and urgency, that he was hurting her, her smaller body and uncomfortably bound arms given no quarter beneath his torso and legs. He could feel his cock grinding into her belly as he opened her mouth with his, felt her squirming as much as she could, but he would not question himself now, knowing he could not go back without becoming her forever enemy. The only thing he would allow himself to be conscious of was the way her skin was heating beneath his hand and the reluctant curiosity of her own lips and tongue.

She wasn't reciprocating, exactly, but she wasn't resisting, either. A shy response, uncertain and afraid, and the power he felt as he worked to calm her threatened his self-control. A part of him, and he knew exactly which one, wanted to push up her skirt, push past the second skirt she wore underneath that one, and thrust into her before she could refuse him. It had been so long since he felt this close to a woman, so long since the softness of a woman's body tempted him this way, he could barely even understand what was happening with them.

As the tears began to twist down Myriam's cheeks, she didn't know if they were hers or his. Had her arms been free she knew she would have slapped him and pushed him off her, kicking whatever she could reach before she fled. Whatever lay outside this strange place, it had to be better than what this man was doing to her, the cruel seduction of his mouth on her neck, her collarbones, even the shell of her ear. It had been so long since anyone paid attention to her body like this, and even as her mind shouted *No, No, No, No, No*. The agony of this pleasure he was forcing on her kept her mouth shut against the sound of her own voice. Please, she silently begged, just get it over with and let me go. Slap me, push me, force me— anything but this. Anything but this.

Hiro murmured to her in a language she could not understand,

words that sounded like the rush of water on his tongue, words that had no meaning beyond the terrifying knowledge that she was lost to this heartless man who would take her away from her home, keep her bound and imprisoned for days, and then force himself on her so gently, so carefully. For the first time, as she looked up into his face, she saw everything she knew but had not recognized: the depth of his dusky eyes, the dominant hook of his nose, the lush, sensitive lips, the perfectly congruent planes of his face. Her eyes burned with the beauty of his face, and as his burnished hand brushed across her now exposed chest, she was startled into speech. "Your name . . . What is your name?"

Instead of answering—what made her think he could ever understand her—he kissed around her breasts, drawing down her shift and stays, pushing away the sleeves and their ties, inhaling deeply the musk of her body, breathing out lightly on the pink tips, watching them plump for his mouth, feeling them stiffen under the light attentions of his tongue. He heard her say something, but what he could not think, answering instead with more pressure on her nipples, a slight pinch with his lips and a drag of his teeth across the sensitive skin there. That he could see her skin pale and then redden under his possessive fingertips made him squeeze harder, and when she cried out breathlessly, he did not look to see if it was in pleasure or pain, just dug his fingers in again, needing to keep her from thinking she should—or could—stop this.

Myriam had no idea how to stop anything. Already she was throbbing deep inside, the pain in her arms and now in her breasts, the only thing keeping her from fainting dead away. Every prick, every sharp scratch across her skin reminded her she was awake and alive, and even as she hated feeling this, she could not wait for the next touch, could not think beyond the myriad sensations pummeling her body and her mind. When she felt him lift his body away,

she actually spasmed like a drowning person trying to breathe, terrified he was going to end the torment. Her relief at his hands on her skirt, pushing it and her petticoats up toward her hips, had her throwing her head back with a groan.

Thank the spirits, Hiro thought, that she wasn't going to refuse him this. Already he was so hard he ached, and as he pushed her skirts up to get to her softest flesh, he promised himself that next time he would take his time and savor more of her body. But once he put his hands on her thighs, her muscles contracted and her legs jumped, revealing her to his gaze. Her dark hair and golden skin captivated him here, as well, and as he reached out to touch her, ever so lightly, she jumped again, throwing her head back and pushing out her chest.

His mouth watered at the sight of her breasts thrusting high, but his cock knew its purpose better than the rest of him, and it wanted immediate entrance to her softest, tightest, wettest place. His blood beat in time to her desire: I want, I want, I want. His fingers trembled as he drew them down each side of her pink lips, and he watched her open to him, plumping with her own moisture, inviting him in. Not yet, his mind whispered, not ready, it said, but his cock convinced him it was time and as what was left of his mind emptied, he bent between her knees and filled her in one thrust: I want, I want, I want.

Everything had been so astonishing, and when he forged into her, she felt his thrust everywhere. Her thighs contracted around her hips, and the sharp pain reminded her of what she was doing . . . and of what she was letting him do. That it felt so good only confused her, and as her body turned in to his over and over and over, as she felt her mind trying to make sense of the pleasure, her panic grew. Before he could draw out just a little, she brought her bound hands up to pound against his chest and pushed her hips up to unseat him. Instead, she met him on the down thrust and their pelvic bones met

in that perfect way, burning through any final resistance her body might have offered. Still, as the unearthly thrill unraveled inside her, she could hear herself crying and pleading with him to stop. But he was beyond seeing or hearing anything except the throbbing rush of his own release, blistering hot and perfect.

NOT witchcraft after all, just brute force. And she could not even turn away to hide the shame of her own powerlessness. It was bad enough that he had forced himself on her like that, but so much worse that she had wanted exactly that. Only once it happened it was too much, too overwhelming, too soon. Oh, God, why was this happening to her? Whatever test this was she had utterly failed, so perhaps this was her punishment for being so wicked. Is that why the pleasure was so intense? She was still throbbing in the most intimate way, her skin tingling at the surface, her mind circling around the same confused sense of shame and disappointment. She felt utterly defeated.

HIRO knew that something had gone terribly wrong, but his body was reluctant to surrender the bone-deep pleasures her body had just given him. If she was only fighting him now, thrashing her arms and legs and pushing him away with the same force she had before. If he was being honest with himself, the chances were good that he still would not let her leave, but anything would be better than the choked sobbing he heard beneath him. Her face was turned away from his, and even after what had just happened between them—because of that, perhaps—he felt shy of intruding on her despair. But still it bothered him that she sounded so diminished, that perhaps he had just taken all her strength and determination instead of filling her with his. At what point had things changed? He still did not

understand exactly what happened, but he knew that she was hurting and that somehow he had caused it.

MYRIAM finally just let herself drift. Her mind was still cloudy, her body was still twitching with its own wakening awareness, and she felt, rather than heard, a rhythmic chanting above her. She had no idea how many minutes had passed before she opened her eyes to find his serious face so close to hers, his lips reciting the strangest sounds, a soothing, melodic repetition, accompanied by the lightest touch to her forehead, cheeks, nose, lips, and chin. With what seemed like reverence he kept up his chanting and touching, lulling her into the depths of his intent gaze, feeling the weight of his words even though she could not understand them. Perhaps it was another kind of spell, but for the first time in five days, she did not care what happened to her, did not even try to resist the mesmerizing litany that stole through her tired, sated body like a prayer.

In his own language Hiro told her over and over again how beautiful she was, how essential: resplendent like the red-leafed maple, full of strength and courage like the bear, sweet like the stalks of tender young corn, beautiful and mysterious like the night sky. He knew she could not understand the words, but he hoped to revive her with the sounds of his language, which were so much more pleasing than the harsh syllables of her own. And indeed, as he spoke to her, sang to her, really, she seemed to come back to herself, staring up at him with a new attentiveness, which he breathed into himself through the scent of her desire, which began again to stir between them.

Even more slowly this time, he moved toward her mouth, singing his song of praise, sharing its secrets with her, lips to lips, tongue to tongue. Gradually she opened to him, first on a small sigh, and then with a bit more interest, her eyes not leaving his while her small

tongue searched the secrets of his mouth. But he continued to sing to her, if not with his mouth, with the rest of his body. Hands moving reverently over her shoulders and between her breasts, soothing and reassuring, drawing languid patterns on her warm skin. Her own arms were still bound, and he ached to release them, but he was afraid that if he drew attention to her current state it would recall her to resistance and this moment would be lost forever. But the new eagerness of her mouth and her legs, both unabashedly reaching for him, told him all he needed to know about her willingness and desire. While her feet rasped up the sides of his legs, the tickle against his hair and skin there almost unbearably pleasurable, her mouth grasped his with increasing urgency, the wetness of their kisses noisy against the background of the steady fire and their beating hearts.

And then, in a moment he knew would decide everything, he rolled over onto his back, drawing her with him, and sitting up with her before her confusion broke the spell of their coupling. With experience he hoped she didn't stop to question, he kept up the frantic kisses and arranged her legs and bottom, her skirts around and across them, his leggings giving her a small respite from the shock of his own bare lap. That she seemed to know what to do shouldn't have surprised him, but he hid it anyway by dropping his head back and letting her take him over.

And take him over she did. Myriam no longer cared if she was bewitched or damned or anything else she would have to pay for later. Right now she had no idea how she had managed without a man's intimate touch for so long, but she was angry and desirous to take from this man what she had previously denied herself. Fumbling a bit with her voluminous skirts and bound hands, she reached underneath and took hold of the most intimate part of the stranger beneath her, wondering at how easy it was to touch him, how hungry she suddenly felt for the power he was offering her.

Without looking down she joined her hands at the base of his shaft, startled by the softness of the hair there, so much softer than her experience had led her to expect. Only now she noticed that this man was mostly smooth, with only a bit of hair around his flat nipples and a small mapping beneath his belly button. The lush lock of straight midnight black hair on his head suggested something much different than his body revealed, and she wondered if he removed his body hair somehow, or if he was naturally smooth like this. She liked it, though, so much that she wanted more.

Moving awkwardly backward, she could not make him understand at first what she wanted; only when she started to tug at his leggings did he untie the lacings above his knees and strip them off while she kneeled above his legs, watching the muscles flex and ripple across his abdomen. There was no doubt that he was incredibly made, a temptation and a sin to be sure, but one she could—and would—no longer resist. His smooth thighs felt wonderfully warm and firm beneath her own, and as she moved her hands back to his shaft, she moaned at the way his clenching muscles inadvertently massaged her own intimate flesh.

Still, she was in control this time, and as she wrapped her fingers around the part of him that had so maddened her before, she looked right into his dark eyes, seeking a connection she was not yet ready to acknowledge could exist. She knew he wanted to touch her back, but her rough touch insisted that he keep his hands on the pallet, his arms shaking with the effort to let her set the pace. Good, she thought, see how you like being powerless. And as he had done to her, she took him into herself in one smooth motion, bringing her hands up at the same time and securing them around his neck. With the shock of her aggression clearly visible on his face, Hiro barely noticed when she wrapped her hands around his scalp lock, as he was so enraptured by the feeling of his cock inside her. But when she began to pull in rhythm to the short strokes she had set, he was torn

between the bright pleasure and the sharp pain of their rough coupling.

It took everything in him not to reach up into her hair, swinging loose now across her luscious breasts, tripping across her small pink nipples. When she shoved his face into her chest, though, he opened his mouth over whatever soft, musky flesh he could reach as she pushed herself up and down, subtly changing her strokes to catch the best angle, grunting and moaning as she moved. One minute Hiro was afraid he would suffocate, the next he was sure his neck was going to snap under the frantic pressure of her hands clasped in his hair. But none of it mattered as long as she kept moving over his cock, her abundant wetness keeping the slide easy and fast, his only concern now that she would finish him before getting her own pleasure back.

When Myriam felt his fingers between her legs, searching through her wet folds, she wanted to slap his hands away. She wanted to push him down, tie him up, make him do exactly as she wished. The command was almost out of her mouth when started to feel that tingling, and then the rush that made her seize and clench in on herself, that electric pulse racing through her body, flashing in and out through every pore.

This time, the pleasure reached so deeply into her that she had no awareness beyond moving away and lowering herself to the pallet. Hiro was already attuned to the patterns of her breathing, so he knew she was asleep, but his own languor kept him still beside her. In a few moments he would rise and retrieve his knife, cutting the bindings on her wrists while she was still asleep, and then he would wait until she awoke and understood that she was free to go. First he would explain to her—in her language, much as he hated to use it—what she could expect among his people and what she would likely encounter if she tried to return to her settlement. He did not know what the chances were that she would stay with him, but he

knew it must be her choice, and that already, he could not bear the thought of losing her to the savagery of her own people's wars.

With a prayer to the spirits to look over both of them, he rose and moved away, while she slept on, beautiful, strong, and, for now, at least, safe.

Rebecca Lange writes in several different venues, not having been trained to do anything more practical. She doesn't have any heroes, but she still has a few ideals left. Rebecca doesn't sew or knit or craft, but she does pour a mean glass of wine, wishing only that she had more leisure time to enjoy it.

WETWIRE

Sunny Moraine

I was free-drifting the night Kim neuroburned me. I wasn't looking for him, floating through seas of data without an angle or an object, so when he fingered me it was a surprise. I didn't jump—you can't really jump with no body to do the jumping—but I felt all my awareness jerk, and then I was arcing out toward him, skimming over the surface of him like a gull over a wave. I was glad to see him. And he always knew just how to touch me.

Tia, baby, he breathed into my netspace, words firing through me like synapse sparks, *you need to disengage.* He was always teasing me about that, about how much time I spent jacked in. Like he had any room to talk. He got me hooked in the first place, back in the final months of our senior year in high school, one night at a party, music too loud and too much bad shit in the air and in our bloodstream. He backed me up against a wall, stuck a thigh in between my legs, and ground up, lips against my ear: *Let's jet. I got something back at my place, blow your fucking mind.* And half an hour later I was lying on his narrow bed, looking up at his ceiling, cracked and plastered with posters of bands I never heard of. I remember thinking hazily that they might be all that was holding up the roof. He wasn't rich. But he got money for the console somehow, unless he stole it, and right then and there he jacked me in and fucked me while I watched the cracks in the ceiling widen and turn into oceanic

trenches, seething with heat, boiling magma towers, clustering hungry life. I came, a steam vent exploded into raw binary. I watched it all happen from a strange, removed distance, floating through everything in my little submersible. Stranger in a strange fucking land.

You never forget your first time.

That was years ago. Years, a boyfriend, two girlfriends, three semesters of college, which ended in dismal failure, two cities, a string of shit jobs. After the third one, it occurred to me that I might be financing a habit. But at the end of my first year of college, back when I was still on the downward slide, I found him in there, floating in the datastream, and it was just like old times.

Kimber. Hey. He was tweaking me, tickling my nerves. He was the only one I ever let do that, because it was dangerous: wrong person gets in, tweaks you, you go into cardiac arrest and they find you a few weeks later when they'd probably just as soon not, with how you're smelling. But I trust Kim. Kim is safe.

Well. "Safe" might be relative. But I do trust him.

Let's meet, he said, slipping feelers deeper into me. I gasped because he was already getting me close, and because he'd never said that before. We hadn't met, not since that last time after graduation. I didn't know where he was. I didn't go looking; he gave me every indication that he didn't want me to; that our little net-trysts were all he cared to have from me. I get the inclination to not be found. It's possible that I'm hiding, too; after all, one girl I know is head of cybersecurity at Apple, another guy went on to Harvard, and here I am in a messy twelve-by-twenty studio with wires in my goddamn head.

But he wanted to meet. I tried to fight the orgasm back. Somewhere a million miles away, my fingers froze halfway to my cunt. I needed to process. *What?*

You heard me. He slid lower, circling around me like a snake—

then I felt the expanding pressure between my legs and I realized what he was doing. *Oh, you bastard.* I felt him laugh. I suddenly had a body—just a construct, but that was what made it so malleable. Net-clit and real clit, they were both wired to the same part of the brain. And he was in there, building on it, tricking my senses even further than the console was already tricking them. Growing me a dick. One of those failed attempts at a girlfriend—I don't even remember which one anymore—used to like to do this with me, and I made the mistake of telling Kim about it. At first he did it just to tease me. Then I guess he got to liking it, because he got better at it, more detail and subtler sensation. I felt it throbbing gently, twitching into the construct of his hand as he stroked me.

Now he was just being difficult. I twisted in his grasp, irritated as much as I was turned on. *Asshole, cut it out. I want to talk about this.*

Nothing to talk about. I want to meet. Kohl Cafe, downtown, 10. I'll buy you a latte. His construct-hand was moving faster, jerking me with swift, expert precision. His control always was unreal. *Feels good, right? I got something that can make this look like a tickle. Trust me.*

And I did. I tried to tell him fine, okay, but I was already coming, thrusting up into his construct, neurons convulsing and splayed out all over the place in a way that would have been embarrassing if either of us cared.

See you. And just like that he was gone, and I couldn't hang around there anymore. I snapped back into myself, naked and slumped down in my chair with my hand between my legs, still buzzing that post-orgasmic hum. I looked at the console, a little black box sitting under the TV, wire leads snaking across the floor to me. I pulled them loose, sat up, stretched. Everything was gray, the light coming in the windows thin and listless. I went to the window, pinched the shades, looked out at the sprawl. *What the hell?* I tasted

myself on my fingers, still warm and salty-sweet. Yeah, I was going
to meet him. He knew it. *Dammit.* And I always did steer clear of
class reunions.

THE consoles were new, then. I guess they still are. It was strange
tech when it first hit the markets, and it never got any less strange.
They had been saying that something like it was coming for a while,
but when it appeared, it was a thing looking for a reason, a little black
box called into being for no immediately obvious purpose. Some
people insisted that it was going to be revolutionary, finally removing the meat-wall between people and their machines. No more
screens, no more hands and fingers; even touch-sensitive displays
were going to look outdated. You'd go into the net, be part of it,
control it with will alone.

But it was ahead of its time. There was no viable translation language, no way to turn all that data into something a person could
fit into the coherent framework of their own experience. By now
there are a few sites out there optimized for it, and even then, on the
day I stepped out onto the rainy streets, my breathmask tight around
my face, there were a few places to go if you knew where to look for
them: dataspaces where you could emerge into a world that actually
worked along rules you could recognize. You could understand it,
move parts of it around.

Here's what they didn't realize: there were too many of us who
didn't want that. We were the first ones in the pool, sinking in
the data-seas, surfing on waves of raw binary, slammed against the
shores of our own perception and then straight back out for more.
We loved it. It was like being there at the beginning of the universe,
an explosion of unformed potentiality, the point of cosmic orgasm.
I tossed out my name after I dropped out of college, and I called
myself Tiamat because I floated in the watery chaos of that world

like it was home. Once Kim gave me a taste I never wanted to come back. We were out there, Kim and me and all the rest of the net-jetsam, drifting through a paradise of incompatible coding, where anything could be and was and would be forever.

I know about things like this. I took some classes in college on the history and sociology of tech. There have always been cases where something arrives and no one is ready for it, and it takes a few years or even a few decades for the rest of the world to figure out how to make it fit. What they didn't teach us about was ourselves, about people who make their own space in that lag time. What they didn't teach us was where we go when the time runs out.

I didn't bother with an umbrella. Most of my clothing was water-proof by then anyway—a necessary expense for anyone living in the lower-middle latitudes where eight months out of twelve is soaked with rain. I had moved for a job and then stayed after the job disap-peared. Living so many hours a day on the net, it doesn't matter as much where your meat sits.

I pulled the slicker closer around me and headed down the street toward the metro, people passing, faceless jostling here and there. On the steps of the metro, I tilted my head back and let the rain beat onto my breathmask. I thought about crashing waves of code, rhyth-mic and beautiful, hitting my brain like good sex. How do you define addiction? Whenever you're not doing it, you're thinking about doing it. That might work as well as anything.

I was twenty-three, then. I was too skinny, and my hair was get-ting too long, and my hips, my tits, my cunt, the arch of my back . . . they were getting abstract. They were coming unfocused. They were getting as hazy as the neon through the rain.

The Kohl Cafe was packed with people. I pulled off my breath-mask. Sweat, the smell of coffee and burned sugar and wet dog, lazy,

half-lidded eyes. Candles everywhere, tangles of Christmas lights. Screens showing nothing but fuzz and snow. Would I know Kim when I saw him? It had been years, and free-drifting had a way of changing you, burning you down to your essentials. But I knew his touch, and when it hit the small of my back I turned and there he was.

He hadn't changed all that much after all. He was basically as I remembered him, except, like me, he was skinnier. Dark eyes, hair at once cropped and too shaggy, high cheekbones, thin mouth that always seemed a centimeter away from a smirk. He carefully touched my cheek, my lips, like a ritual greeting, but I knew what he was really doing. Dogs sniff each other. Free-drifters, we tell by touch. We know someone by the wiring of their nervous system, the pattern of firing synapses. Stimulus, response. I let go a delicate shiver and that hint-smirk became a full-on smile.

"Hi, Tia."

"Hi, Kim." I nudged the bridge of his forehead with my nose. "How about that latte?"

So we talked. I don't know how long. Kim leaned closer to me, and I could smell him over everything else, that familiar scent of chewing gum and metal. Hot metal. Lines of solder like crystallized cocaine. He was excited, talking fast, but I was finding it hard to focus. There wasn't any catching up; he didn't seem even slightly interested in either of our lives before the present and everything that could stretch forward from that. "I got something," he said. "New tech. I think it could make the whole free-drift experience something. . . ." He grinned. His teeth looked silver in the uneven light, chrome-plated tombstones. "Something really special."

I asked how. He shrugged. He was being mysterious, trying to get me prying at him. Sometimes I found that endearing, and sometimes it really fucking pissed me off. I finished the latte, looked around at the faces lit by strobes, a series of still images, flashes of frozen conversing mouths.

"So why tell me, Kimber?"

He answered me by touching me again. One finger on the point of my chin and sliding down between my collarbones, just to where my skin dipped between my tits. It stopped there, hovering, so that with every breath his fingertip stroked the fine hairs on my skin into gentle erection.

Then he pressed. Sudden, hard. His fingernail jabbed into my flesh, and I yelped and swatted away his hand, staring at him with more shock than I wanted to ever show anyone. You never want to let people know they can surprise you. They'll keep trying to.

"That's why," he said, leaning forward with his chin on his hands. "Did it hurt?"

"*Yeah*, it hurt, you asshole. This is bullshit, I'm outta here." I was turning to push myself out of the chair, hand on my breathmask, but he caught my arm with more strength in his grip than any weak meat free-drifter ought to have had.

"Tia, I want to test it out on you. Trust me, I think you'll like it. And you respond better than anyone else I know."

"Bullshit," I said again, but I wasn't leaving. "Ask Aggie. Jack. You know a lot of people."

"I know a lot of burnouts." His hand was sliding up under the sleeve of my slicker, fingers moving like little nibbling fish. I was thinking about the bodies surging around us, about how when you were packed in this close, fucking was just a short step sideways. Meat could be so slippery like that. "People with their nerves fried six ways to Sunday. You're fresh, Tia. You're sharp. You always have been. You know that."

He was turning on the charm. He knew where the ego was; he could find it like crackers sniffed out holes in hash algorithms. I was proud of the fact that I had been drifting so long without burning out. Now he wanted it. He wanted to use me for something. Some people hate that, being used. But how else to do you know what you're worth?

So I didn't push away his hand and I didn't walk out. And I said yes.

PEOPLE talk about time being cyclical, but I don't think most of them really know what that means, how absolutely fucking weird it is to feel like your whole life is doubling back on itself, and you wonder what the last decade or so was all for, if it was just going to get you right back here again. There were things about this that were different, of course; we weren't in high school anymore, we weren't lit up with drugs and booze and the simple glow that comes with just being a horny teenager. But he pulled me up the grimy steps of his building, hulking in darkness spattered with halogen and neon, backed me into a corner of the entryway, and stuck that knee between my thighs, lips against my ear, and I thought about all those years ago. *Let's jet. I got something back at my place, blow your fucking mind.*

And now I was here, and that night was why.

He didn't say anything, just nipped at my earlobe and laughed when I shoved him away. Up the stairs, three flights and down a short, dim hallway. He keyed open the door and waved me inside. It was a messy, single-room deal like mine, a tiny bathroom off to one end, futon piled with clothes and junk, old kitchenette, and those posters again, plastered over the cracks on the ceiling and on the walls. At one end of the room was a workstation, a long desk and slim towers that hummed like purring cats, monitors, touchpads, parts, hardware. A workstation like I dreamed about sometimes, but didn't expect to ever be able to afford.

He was grinning at me as I pulled off my breathmask and slicker, clearly pleased, proud of what he had. I wondered how many people he showed it to like this. Unusual setup for a free-drifter, I was thinking . . . unusual focus on the visual, when all we really need for

that are our little black consoles. I arched an eyebrow and he must have seen the question on my face.

"I have a job," he said. "I run code for one of the investment firms downtown. I designed the GUI for their entire system and I do updates for it. But that's just to pay the bills."

I nodded. But I was looking around for his console, and he must have seen that too, because he moved past me, reached down to a shelf by his workstation, and fished it out. I looked at it and felt the familiar hungry ache of the consummate junkie, that deep-down need to be out of the meat and drifting.

"In my spare time," he said, "I work with this."

I looked at him like he was maybe a little stupid. "I know," I said, and he shook his head and laughed.

"No, not like that. I mean, I *work* with it. It's been around for how long now? And the military uses it, and some of the bigger firms. But the rest of us, the plebes, we're just fucking around with it. We use it for maybe a tiny percentage of what it can really do." He carried it over to a low table in front of the futon and set it down, untangling the leads and jacks. I watched him as he unfolded a little black netbook and brought up a program, tapped something on the keyboard, and turned to me.

"Come here."

He hadn't ever talked to me like that before. I wasn't sure how I felt about it. I don't much like being told what to do—it's part of why college didn't work all that well, part of why I never managed to hold down a job for any length of time—but the way he said it . . . it was low, soft, coaxing as much as it was commanding. I felt my body carrying me forward. Rebellious meat. But not rebelling, not now—at least, not against him.

I sat down next to him on the futon and he turned to me. He reached up and pushed my hair aside from the jacks, gentle in a way that made me want to cringe back from him. It wasn't that I was

scared or that it hurt, but no one had touched me like that in . . . Fuck, years maybe.

He seemed to be examining me, leaning close to look at the tiny metal holes in my temples, and I smelled him again, the scent of solder. I was opening my mouth to say something else, to inhale him—and he touched the jacks.

No one touches the jacks. The doctor touched them when he installed them, and I touch them to wire myself into the console, and besides that, no one does. I've heard of tech fetishists who like to touch, but to me it's a means to an end, like the rest of the meat, so when he touched me like *that,* circling each jack with delicate fingers, I didn't know how to process it. I jerked, some indefinable sensation shooting down my spine to lodge itself like shrapnel in my cunt, hot and liquid. He smiled at me and pulled his hand back.

"See? You respond so well. You're ideal."

"Kim." I was trying to get my breath back. I wanted to fuck. I wanted to shove him over and claw his cock into me. I hadn't wanted it like this in . . . about as long as it had been since someone touched me with that kind of delicacy. "What the *fuck*?"

"The jacks are hardwired into your nervous system," he said, leaning over the netbook again. "They have to be, to give you the kind of input you need to drift."

"I *know* that, Kimber, Jesus."

"So they're designed for input and output, both concurrently. But the input is passive. It's just feeding you information you can process. So I started thinking, you have hard-line access to the entire nervous system through those things. You can feed in data . . . but you can also go in and fuck with it. Change the wiring."

"Kim . . ." Now I was nervous. What this sounded like . . . It sounded like a one-way ticket to total neuroburnout. "Look, I don't think . . ."

"You can trust me," he said again, and he looked at me with those eyes that always had a way of making me give in. "It works, and it's safe . . . and you have to fucking feel it. It's not like anything else."

He knew how to hook me. Tell me something is new, tell me it'll blow my fucking mind, and I won't be able to say no. Free-drifting, you live out there on the edges of things, right in the liminal; you make a home there. Then you don't want anything else. You always chase the new shit.

What the fuck. I said yes.

He grinned at me, reached down for the leads, leaned up close again, and kissed me. It was hard, no delicacy now, and his teeth bit down on my bottom lip. I gasped, jerked, but it wasn't exactly pain, because just at that moment he touched one of the jacks, and what I felt . . . Was I coming? I'm still not sure. It was sharp, like a whip-crack in my spine, and I cried out, heat and stickiness bursting between my legs.

And he jacked me.

I must have blacked out. When I opened my eyes he was there, leaning over the netbook again. I looked around, confused, reached up to feel the leads snaking their way to my skull.

I wasn't drifting. I wasn't out there in the data-sea. I took a breath. "Kim, what's going on?"

"I'm not giving you any AV input," he said. "You are getting input, though. It's just a different kind." He reached over to his side and picked up something that I couldn't see, got up suddenly, and moved around behind me. He leaned down, touched my face, took one of my wrists in his hand.

"Just making this a little more interesting," he said, finding my second wrist. And then I saw a flash of red. A scarf, and then it was

around my wrists, tying them back behind my head, against the back of the futon. I tugged; I felt a pull against one of the frame's crossbars. I stared up at him. He laughed and touched my face again, gently.

"You can tell me to stop anytime," he said. "If you really don't like it. And I swear, I will."

At first there was nothing. I watched him go back to the netbook again, and I squirmed a little, experimentally, but as he tapped on the keyboard I caught myself starting to doubt this whole "input" thing, starting to wonder if this was all just some kind of kinky prank.

Then he hit a key and my fucking brain started buzzing.

It was a low hum at first, but it ramped up until it was a purring between my temples. My vision doubled; I shook my head, trying to clear it, and then he was crouching over me. I licked my lips, tried to gather myself enough to speak, and he touched me again, light, running the tips of his fingers up the insides of my bent arms. It was like the raking of little needles over my skin. I jerked and he laughed.

"Kim, tell me what the fuck—" His fingers moved back down, quick, and he pinched my nipple through my shirt. No gentle teasing, just one hard pinch. It should have made me yell, and it just about did—but it didn't hurt. It was like someone pressing a slick finger down on my clit, flicking it so fucking perfectly, all pleasure. I dropped my head back and whimpered.

"I rewired your peripheral nervous system," he murmured, lips against my ear as his fingers kept twisting, pulling my skin out of shape. "Pain is some of the most intense shit you can feel, right? Pleasure is harder, more subtle . . . So I figure, if I switch which makes you feel what . . ." He gave my nipple one more hard twist and released me. I let out a whine of disappointment, but it cut off when his hand smacked hard against the side of my face.

Tears flooded my eyes. He'd avoided the jacks, but I could feel my cheek burning . . . and it was hard to describe what else. It was

all the pain I would feel from a slap like that, but *flipped*. Sweetened. It was lingering, a warm honey-glow spreading down my neck, all through me. I gasped, twisted a little, but I wasn't trying to get away.

"You like that?" He flicked his tongue against my ear, and it was like he'd dug his fingernail into the lobe. I tried to get words out—what I would have said, then, I have no idea—and they didn't come. Should it have been scary, what he'd done to me? Maybe. I hadn't known exactly what was coming. But I hadn't really asked. Because I'd wanted something new, I'd wanted to be surprised . . . and here we were, and I wanted . . . Fuck, I wanted him to hurt me.

I turned my head and I kissed him, and it felt like burning, like the rasp of sandpaper over my lips without the friction, like standing too close to a fire. And even the pain wasn't pain like I was used to. It was pain with a sweet edge, pain with a memory of a time when it hadn't been pain at all. I kissed him hard, stroking my tongue along the top of his, and when he bit me again I arched up against him and made a loose, hot sound.

I hadn't enjoyed being meat like this in a while. I hadn't loved my own skin, what it could give me.

Kim pulled away from me suddenly, and I looked up at him and he looked down. His expression was hard to read, but under that hot metal scent I could smell sex; I could smell the memory of the pre-come at the head of his dick, the way his sweat always smelled when we were done, collapsed together in a tangle of human hardware.

I lifted my hips in an unspoken request, and he yanked my pants down. He didn't bother with my boots, barely bothered with unbut-toning my fly, and his nails raked against me all the way, so hard I wondered if he was drawing blood . . . and fuck, it felt so good. My cunt was wet, getting wetter, my thighs sticky and the air cooling them when he slapped them apart, slapped them red and angry, and every time his hand hit me it was like the most amazing, most per-fect set of fingers in me. He slapped his way up my legs, and when

he got to my cunt, gave it one sharp smack and shoved his fingers in, I came so hard I screamed. I came so hard I *hurt*, and that part was good, too.

My arms were stiff, but I didn't care. I was tired, stretched out, and strained and pushed to a place I'd never been before, but I didn't want to leave. I lifted my hips again and I grinned at him, and he grinned back, hands already working at his fly.

"Thought you'd like it," he said, pushing his pants down his hips, his dick bobbing free and glistening in the low light, the netbook's screen, the neon through the windows. He reached down to the table and somehow he got the condom on without ever taking his eyes off me. And that look . . . it was like that sweet slap to the face. I'd forgotten what it was like, being wanted like that. In the flesh. The flesh part of the wanting.

It hurt when he thrust into me, until he did it again, harder. I keened and kicked my heels against the small of his back, and the whole futon rattled as he slammed into me, one hand gripping my tit under my shirt, fingers digging into my flesh. Now something stranger was happening: now it was getting blurry, the pain and the pleasure harder to differentiate, like a photo negative bleeding its lines. His hands were all over me, squeezing, scratching; he closed his hand on my neck so hard at one point, I knew there would be bruises. He bit down on the skin where my neck met my shoulder. He could have done a lot more—could have ripped at me, torn me, done real damage . . . and I know I would have loved it.

"Harder," I gasped, and he laughed and fucked me harder, the muscles in his arms trembling as his hips pistoned. He was lunging into me, so hard I thought maybe I was bruising down there too, but the harder he did it the better it felt, and I bit down on my own lip and just about saw sparks, tasted a light bloody tang, the scarf rubbing my wrists raw. I wanted to touch my clit—but it wouldn't have

worked the same way, I somehow knew. I bared my teeth, hissed at him like an angry snake.

"Pinch me,"

"What?" He lifted his head, sweat rolling down his face, his eyes wide and glazed. I bucked against him, meat on meat.

"Fucking *pinch* me. My nipple, you asshole. Pinch it hard."

He pinched both. Twisted, nails in my flesh. It was hard and sharp and so, so sweet, just like I needed, and it was a lightning bolt straight down into my cunt, every synapse firing and firing. I arched my back and screamed again, gushing around him, and he swallowed the scream down with his teeth raking against my lips, sucking at my tongue. We were free-drifting, lost in the sea that was my own fucked-up nerves, a mess of data that he had turned into the best kind of chaos. I floated, and it blew my fucking mind.

LATER, when he had untied me and pulled off the leads, and we were lying there just like old times, I noticed that it felt good when he touched me. So it was reversible, then, and at some point, after he had left me lying there in a daze, he reversed what he'd done. I expected to feel relieved, and then he made me come the normal way, his fingers slick with his spit and my juices . . . but it wasn't the same. And he knew it.

So he blew my mind, and he showed me something new. He delivered. But I didn't expect him to deliver on what he actually gave me. I've spent years trying to get out of the meat, but he used the console, the instrument of my goddamn coded liberation, and he slammed me right back into it, the whole slippery mess. And he made me like it again. Made me see it new.

I still free-drift. And I like that, too. And I see him in there, and he knows just how to touch me. But sometimes, when the data-sea

gets stagnant and the chaos all starts to look the same, I come see him, and he touches me in a whole different way.

There are more sites now that can handle what the console does. The world is catching up to us. The lag time is running out. But that's okay, I think. Because when what I have stops getting it done, I'll still have Kimber, and he won't let the meat get old on me anytime soon.

Sunny Moraine is a carbon-based humanoid creature of average height. To date, she has published numerous pieces of fiction of varying lengths in various places, including *Shimmer, Icarus,* and *Strange Horizons.* When she was younger, she would dress up as her family's pastor, but now she writes stories about ghosts and space and ghosts in space, as well as stories that would make her pastor blush horribly (you've come a long way, baby). She lives with her husband in the suburbs of Washington, DC, where she writes sociological analyses of violent events and dreams of mountains and Mars. Online she can be found at sunny moraine.com, among other places.

ABOUT THE EDITOR

Jane Litte is a blogger, a reader, and now a collector of stories. *Agony/Ecstasy* is a collection of very steamy stories that explore the twin concepts of pain and pleasure. These stories represent fresh new voices in erotica and erotic romance, exploring the interiors of the bedroom and the mind.

Readers can learn more about Jane and her love of books at Dear Author, a website devoted to discovering good books, or they can send her an e-mail at jane@jdearauthor.com. Follow her on twitter, @jane_l, to let her know what you thought of the selection of shorts. She is always looking for feedback and recommendations for other readers.